BARBARIC JUSTICE

BARBARIC JUSTICE

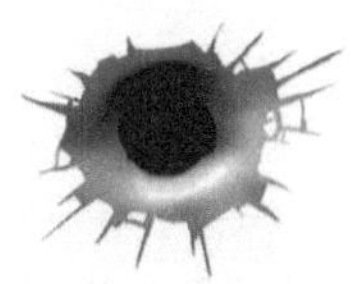

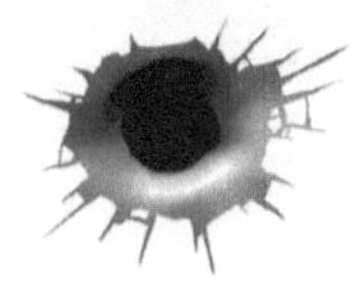

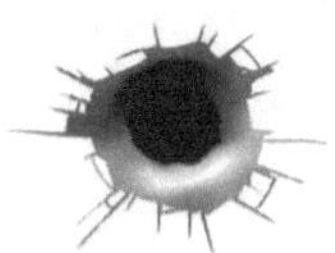

DAVID COPPAGE

CITIOFBOOKS, INC.
3736 Eubank NE Suite A1
Albuquerque, NM 87111-3579
www.citiofbooks.com
Hotline: 1 (877) 389-2759
Fax: 1 (505) 930-7244

Ordering Information:
Quantity sales. Special discounts are available on quantity purchases by corporations, associations, and others. For details, contact the publisher at the address above.

Printed in the United States of America.

ISBN-13:Softcover979-8-89391-727-7
            eBook979-8-89391-728-4

Library of Congress Control Number: 2025911428

TABLE OF CONTENTS

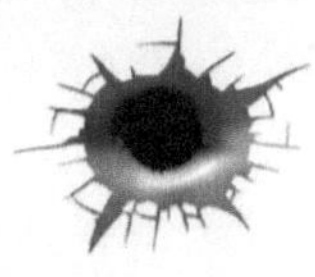

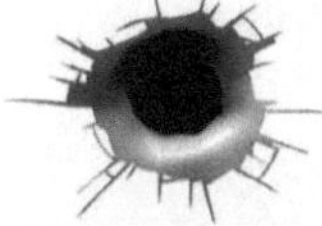

DEDICATION

To my beautiful wife Melissa, and our two awesome children,
Casey and Kyle.

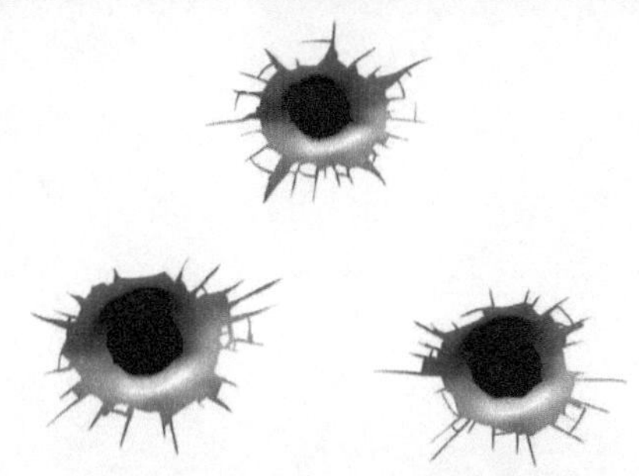

ACKNOWLEDGMENTS

Special thanks to my dear friends John Shirley and Mike Rich, who, along with my wife Melissa, did a phenomenal job of reading my rough draft and giving me well-needed feedback. Thanks to you all.

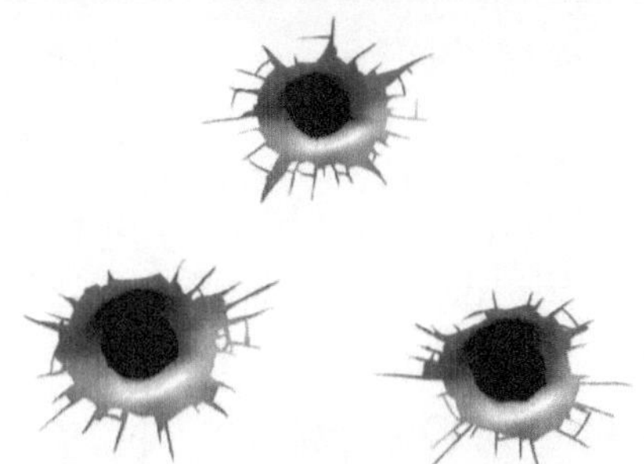

PROLOGUE

For more than two centuries, the mantra *liberty and justice for all* has been part of the fabric of the United States of America. Schoolchildren used to recite it every morning as they stood in front of the flag and pledged allegiance to their country. In one form or another, the words have been etched into stone on buildings and monuments across the land.

But today, they are only words harkening back to bygone days. Too many in political and financial positions of power and influence have abandoned the notion that liberty and freedom are what make the U.S.A. the greatest force for good in the history of civilization.

Politicians continually refuse to work on behalf of the citizens who elected them to office. They seem more attentive to the needs of the special interests funding their campaigns and ignoring the rights of everyday people.

Laws are passed limiting owners' control over their land and water because an environmental group is distressed over the *rights* of a snail darter. The *rights* of individuals to use public restrooms are now a matter of choice. Children being exposed to predators can no longer be an issue and addressing some parental concerns will label you a bigot.

Too many of our leaders turn a blind eye to the rampant crime flourishing on our streets, while making excuses for the guilty. Instead of punishing criminals and terrorists, we are told we must understand *why they do what they do.* Few are willing to acknowledge the real evil existing in our world. Evil that must be confronted and destroyed, even if it means using methods some deem *barbaric.* Political correctness has run amok and left-wing politicians, in concert with a biased and liberal media, will stop at nothing to silence anyone who might dissent with their ideology.

We stand at the edge of a chasm dividing the country with few willing to do what is necessary to arrest the downward spiral of civilization into oblivion. Paralyzed by the fear of being criticized, too many who decry the leftward tilt we are forced to endure will not stand up and be counted. For justice and liberty to prevail, the culprits must be punished. More specifically, they must be destroyed, and half measures will not suffice.

A small group of patriots, men who bravely served their country in uniform, have taken it upon themselves to right some of the wrongs inflicted on society by those unwilling to acknowledge the inherent rights of Americans guaranteed by the U.S. Constitution. Assuming the role of judge, jury and executioner… a secret cabal stops at nothing to exact revenge on the nation's enemies… including the utilization of legal murder… to restore our great nation to its rightful position of world prominence.

To them, *barbaric justice* is indeed justified.

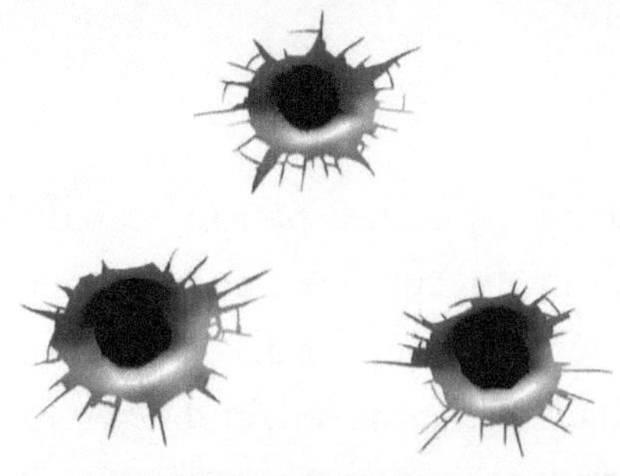

CHAPTER ONE

A bevy of commuters packed themselves into the D.C. Metro beginning their way home after a long workday in our nation's Capital. Pulling into the DuPont Circle Metro station, one passenger, an elderly gentleman with a slow and measured gait, exited and began walking west towards 21st Street, NW.

With temperatures in D.C. hovering in the low 90s, his dress is out of character for the weather. An oversized dark hoodie masked the ball cap pulled low on his brow to hide his face. Large sunglasses, a fake mustache and beard completed his outfit.

Turning south on 21st Street, he walked until he stood in front of the *21st Street Bijou Movie Theater*. The marquee announced the day's attraction: *"American Taboo"*. The glaring *XXX* designation both preceded and followed the film's title. Yet another generic adult film ultimately showing innocuous couples ending up in each other's bed sans all clothing. The elderly gentleman bought his ticket and went inside.

He had been coming to the theater on a regular basis for the past two years. Making his way inside the dimly lit room, he found his *regular* seat situated on the far side of the room against the wall and sat down to await the start of the film. With only fifty or so other moviegoers present, he was able to sit by himself. Shortly after taking his seat the lights faded as the screen began showing the opening credits.

As the movie played, another patron seated further back quietly made his way to the row directly behind the man in the hoodie. He also wore a baseball cap pulled low on his face, dark jeans and a dark t-shirt. The clothing labels had been removed, and he wore no jewelry, not even a watch. His pockets were empty except for one item: a small cyanide pill carried in his left breast pocket. He also had an eight-inch-long piece of a metal bicycle spoke taped to the inside of his shirt.

He slipped into the seat directly behind the elderly man without being noticed. Sliding down in his seat he looked around to see if anyone had noticed him changing seats. *Checking his six* (a commonly used term in military parlance denoting looking at one's *six o'clock*) had become a habit he practiced daily, multiple times a day. It had been ingrained in him during his Special Forces training and reinforced during his multiple tours of duty in the Iraq war. Although now a civilian, it is a habit he will never break.

Assured no one in the theater had an interest in anything other than the movie screen, he removed the metal spoke from inside his shirt. Staying low so his head movement would not bring undue attention, he reached forward with the sharpened end of the spoke and thrust it into the base of the skull of the man in front of him. It easily slipped through the cotton hoodie and encountered little resistance as it penetrated the man's cranial vault. Death came swiftly.

The assassin (known as Orcus by a small and select group of colleagues) quietly dropped the spoke on the floor and rose from his seat, making his way to the exit. As he walked away, he did so with a pronounced limp due to an injury received during his last tour of duty in Iraq. While on patrol outside the Iraqi city of Tikrit, the military Humvee he and his buddies were riding in inadvertently rolled over an IED (Improvised Explosive Device) that exploded and blew a hole in the bottom of the vehicle. The force of the blast blew off part of his left leg below the knee. Following surgery and several weeks of recovery, he was fitted with a prosthetic device and discharged from service.

Minutes after leaving the movie theater, the assassin reached the banks of Rock Creek, a tributary to D.C.'s Potomac River, and retrieved a plastic bag he had previously buried. From inside he pulled out a *burner* cell phone (a pre-paid phone untraceable to the owner) and typed out a text message that read: *liberty prevails–NSOL, Orcus.*

After pressing the *send* button, Orcus dropped the phone down an overflow grate located beside Rock Creek and left. He walked a half mile to the Woodley Park Metro station and boarded a northbound train on Metro's Red Line. Two stops later, he got off at the Van Ness station and got into his car. Forty-five minutes later he pulled into his driveway in Woodbridge, Virginia, about 30 miles south of D.C.

Back at the theater, movie credits were rolling as patrons began filing out. A custodian with a broom and dustpan made his way down the aisles to clean up and ready the theater for the next show. He noticed a man in a hooded sweatshirt slumped down in the seat. Assuming he had fallen asleep during the show, the custodian stepped into the row behind him and nudged his shoulder.

"Hey buddy, get up. The movie's over."

When the guy didn't move, he nudged a little harder.

"Hey, did you hear me? You gotta go, the next movie is about to start," but there was no response.

The custodian then noticed blood seeping through the back of the man's hoodie. He dropped his broom and dustpan and ran to find his manager.

"I think there's a dead guy in there. Somebody needs to call the cops," he said to his boss.

The manager ran inside to confirm what his worker had said. He too tried shaking the man to see if he was asleep or if it was as serious as his employee had suggested. Unable to rouse the man, the manager also noticed bloodstains on the hoodie. He closed the theater and dialed 911.

"I'm calling from the *21ˢᵗ Street Bijou*. We need the cops. There's a dead guy inside," he shouted into his phone.

The 911 dispatcher confirmed the address of the theater and upon learning the manager had placed the call, said a police unit would be in route and suggested he immediately close the theater and remove the patrons.

"Already done that," the manager replied. "Tell them to hurry," he added. "This won't be good for business."

A Metro D.C. patrol unit responded to the theater to render assistance to the team of D.C. detectives, already in route.

Detective Sergeant Jimmy O'Rourke, a grisly 28-year veteran of the Metropolitan D.C. Police Department, would be the detective in charge of the investigation. A large man, he stood six feet four inches tall and weighed about two hundred and forty pounds. A former defensive end on Woody Hayes' Ohio State University football powerhouse, O'Rourke was once projected to be a third or fourth round draft pick by the NFL. Unfortunately, he blew out his knee in his final collegiate game, a 45-21 loss to Alabama in the Sugar Bowl. After three different surgeries failed to completely repair his damaged knee, he gave up any dreams of playing pro football and decided to pursue a career as a cop.

Although he still maintained the same playing weight he had in college, his 33-inch waist and nine percent body fat proportion had long ago disappeared. No doubt due in large part to his love of Guinness Stout and Philly cheese steak sandwiches. The same intensity which he had brought to the football field was equally present in his work as a street cop. Detective O'Rourke is the last guy you would ever want to challenge in a street fight, and the first guy you wanted to have your back if things got physical, not uncommon on the streets of our nation's capital.

Jimmy, long past retirement eligibility, had been giving serious thought to hanging it up and moving to the small farmhouse he and his wife had bought years earlier in Front Royal, Virginia. Seeing more than his fair share of dead bodies, abused children and rape victims, his sensibilities had been sufficiently numbed by now and the idea of retiring seemed more attractive. He had become all too familiar with what cops all over the country see on a day-to-day basis. Namely, those sides of humanity most people only see on T.V. or in the newspapers and it had most certainly taken a toll on his psyche. His partner this evening was a young detective named Charlie Bass, recently elevated from the rank of D.C. patrolman. Sergeant O'Rourke had taken Charlie under his wing, providing him with the mentoring all new detectives need.

"Let's go Charlie. We got a hot one," Jimmy said to his young charge. "Dead body in the *Bijou* on 21ˢᵗ. Let's hope this doesn't turn into an all-nighter."

Detective O'Rourke knew all too well not to predict anything. He had been on enough dead body calls to know this could be anything from a simple heart attack to a murder that may never be solved. Hopefully it will fall somewhere in between.

"Never assume anything," he had told Charlie at least a hundred times, "until all the facts are in."

Working homicides is a big part of a detective's job in Washington, D.C. Sergeant O'Rourke had worked more than his share and could barely tolerate the eighteen-hour days some of those cases required. His wife could tolerate them even less.

Maybe, he thought. *This one won't be too bad.*

He couldn't have been more wrong.

Jimmy and Charlie pulled up to the *Bijou* a few minutes after the patrol unit had arrived. About twenty-five moviegoers were waiting outside to purchase a ticket for the next show, unaware of what had transpired inside. Jimmy approached one of the patrolmen.

"Do me a favor," Jimmy said to the officer, "let's see if we can get these people to go home. I don't care what you tell them. Make something up if you want. Tell them there's a city code violation or something and the theater will be temporarily closed," he told the officer. "Anything to get them the hell out of here."

"You got it Sarge," the officer responded.

Jimmy went inside to find the manager and noticed a guy hovering by the ticket office door. Standing about 5'5" and weighing no more than 125 pounds, the man wore a paisley jacket with velvet lapels. His face was excessively wrinkled, and he had greenish teeth.

This must be the manager, Jimmy thought as he approached the man.

"I'm assuming you're the manager," Jimmy said as he introduced himself and extended his hand to Mr. Green Teeth.

"I am," the man replied as he shook Jimmy's hand, "Frank Lloyd's the name."

"Great, nice to meet you Mr. Lloyd," Jimmy said. "Can you tell me what happened?"

"Not much to tell," the manager began. "After our last show ended my custodian went in to sweep the place up and found this old guy still sitting in his seat. He thought he had fallen asleep, so he tapped him on the shoulder to wake him up. When the guy didn't move, he noticed some blood on the back of the guy's sweatshirt and ran out here to find me. I went inside to check it out for myself and called you guys right away."

By this time, Charlie and one of the patrolmen were inside the theater standing in front of the body. A crime scene photographer had also arrived and began taking photos of the deceased man. Jimmy asked the manager to wait in his office and excused himself to join his partner inside.

"Hey Jimmy, check this guy out," said Charlie as Jimmy approached. "The hoodie, the dark glasses and hat. I don't think he wanted anybody to recognize him."

"Try not to disturb the body but see if you can slide his glasses off so the photographer can get a picture of his face," Jimmy responded.

Charlie carefully reached in and grabbed the frames of the decedent's glasses. As he began sliding them off his face, a portion of the dead man's beard began to move as well.

"Look at that," said Charlie. "This guy is wearing a fake beard and mustache."

"Pull the beard off, too," said Jimmy.

With the lights up and the glasses and fake facial hair now removed, they could clearly see his face.

"Oh shit," whispered Jimmy.

He turned to the patrolman and the crime scene photographer and told them to leave him and his partner alone.

"Go outside and make sure everyone is out of the lobby," Jimmy ordered. "Once you've cleared the theater, secure the door and don't let anyone else in. Nobody comes through the door, and I mean nobody."

The patrolman and the photographer quickly did as they were told and left the two detectives alone.

As the door closed behind them, Charlie turned to Jimmy with a look of bewilderment on his face.

"What's that about? You look like you've seen a ghost," said Charlie.

"I wish it was a ghost," replied Jimmy. "Don't make any plans on going home tonight, this just got really complicated."

"What are you talking about?" asked Charlie. "Do you know who that is?"

"Do you not recognize him?" Jimmy asked.

"No, just some old guy," replied Charlie. "Why, should I know who it is?" he asked.

"Yeah," said Jimmy. "It's none other than Hayden Byers."

Charlie looked up at Jimmy with a surprised look on his face.

"Do you mean Hayden Byers, the Supreme Court Justice?"

"That's exactly who I mean," Jimmy said.

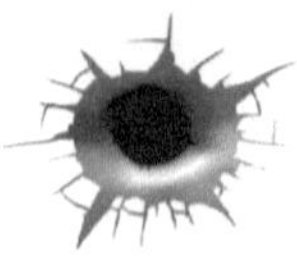

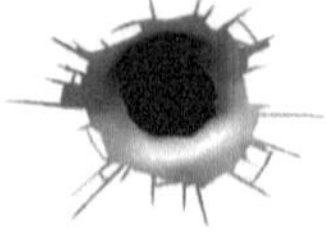

Chapter Two

Seated around the table in the back of the Capital Grille restaurant in downtown, D.C., a small group of powerful men met. Two of the men, Tom and Elias Kirkbride, were brothers who had taken their father's fertilizer supply company and spent thirty years growing it into a multi-national conglomerate with more than 100,000 people on its payroll. Their combined net worth is over twenty billion dollars. Also in attendance were three high-powered K-street lobbyists with a client list of movers and shakers equally influential and, more importantly, equally wealthy as the two Kirkbride brothers. The men all had one thing in common: they were sick and tired of witnessing the systematic destruction of their beloved country, courtesy of the Rob Ferrell administration.

President Rob Ferrell, halfway through his second term in office, seemed to be relishing his lame-duck status. His far-left liberal appointments to the federal judiciary, his unlawful use of executive orders and his general disdain for the U.S. Constitution were some of the points of contention among this group. The time had come, they felt, to do something to take their country back from the grasp of the communist loving, weak-kneed socialists who had hijacked the Democrat party and were now running the country.

President Ferrell had run roughshod over the Republican Party for the better part of his entire administration, never showing the least bit of desire to work with them. Even after the Republicans wrested control of both houses of Congress following the most recent mid-term elections, President Ferrell's attitude did not change. In response to his party losing complete control of congress, he upped his rhetoric and continued to paint the Republican Party as a bunch of homophobic racists bent on destroying the middle class and attempting to line the pockets of their rich friends. It didn't matter to him and other Democrats the very policies of the Ferrell administration were most responsible for the economic malaise engulfing the country.

Equally irrelevant was the fact median wages in the country for all groups (especially minorities) were down substantially since he had assumed office. President Ferrell thought himself a populist and tried to convince as many people as he could he had their best interests in mind. Actually, he and his party wanted to create as many dependents as possible to ensure they would continue electing Democrats. Creating a permanent underclass, convinced they couldn't make it through the day without some kind of handout from the government, had become the goal of modern-day Democrats. President Rob Ferrell adamantly asserted such a handout would only come from him and the Democrats.

The table also included another important man. The special guest at this luncheon, Brian Smith, currently served as the senior Senator from the State of New Jersey. Senator Smith served as chairman of the Senate Judiciary Committee as well as the Senate Appropriations Committee, both enormously powerful positions in the U.S. government. Tom and Elias Kirkbride, as well as the lobbyists at lunch, were trying their best to recruit Senator Smith to make a run for the Republican nomination for President.

Years earlier Brian Smith left his home in Jackson, New Jersey, and volunteered to fight *The Cong* during the Viet Nam war. When his first tour ended, he volunteered for another. When that one ended, he volunteered yet again. It's who he was. As long as another mission or another battle needed to be waged, he wanted to be in the middle of it. And nothing more exemplified this character and spirit than what took place in the tiny village of Khe Sanh, in the northwestern province of Quang Tri in South Viet Nam.

Brian's unit had hunkered down outside of Khe Sanh preparing for an assault to the north the following morning. The Battle of Khe Sanh had been raging for weeks and had turned into one of the bloodiest encounters of the Viet Nam War. With their unit's water supply running low, Staff Sergeant Smith loaded several empty water containers in the back of a *Deuce-and-a-half* (a nickname given to the two-and-a-half-ton Army cargo truck indispensable to the war effort in Viet Nam) in search of more water. He planned to drive a mile and half from his unit's campsite and replenish their water supply from the Dakrong River. When he returned two hours later with a fresh supply of water, he found his unit overrun by Viet Cong forces. Seeing his fellow soldiers trapped on the side of a hill and surrounded by the enemy, Sergeant Smith watched his unit be relentlessly pounded by small-arms fire. Taking action, he retrieved one of the M2 Browning .50 caliber machine guns concealed in the woods on the southern perimeter of their camp.

Moving to an elevated position and taking cover behind a large boulder, Sergeant Smith began firing down on the enemy forces assaulting his unit. As soon as the enemy became aware of where the shots originated, they began firing back on Sergeant Smith's position. As bullets from the return fire ricocheted around him, Smith continued firing, killing as many of the enemy as he could. When his ammo began running low, he radioed for air support and vectored the U.S. planes to drop bombs on his own position. As air units began raining down missiles, Sergeant Smith crawled underneath the rock he had been using for cover in hopes of staying alive, all the while continuing to fire at the enemy.

The gunfire Smith laid down, coupled with his call for air support, caused a break in the enemy's line and provided his unit with an avenue of escape. His fellow soldiers were able to make their retreat with minimal casualties. Sergeant Smith's brave actions saved the lives of every man in his unit. In a White House ceremony ten months later, he received the Congressional Medal of Honor from the President for his bravery.

After completing his tour of duty, Brian returned to the peace and tranquility of his New Jersey home. Still possessed with a burning desire to serve his country as a private citizen, Smith decided to make a run for Congress. Declaring himself a Republican, he announced his intentions of running for the congressional house seat in New Jersey's 4th Congressional District that included his hometown of Jackson. His status as a local hometown war hero helped him easily defeat the two-term incumbent Democrat. Following the completion of his second term in the U.S. House of Representatives, he ran for and won election to the U.S. Senate where he currently serves. He is considered by many to be one of the most rock-ribbed conservatives presently serving in congress. His support group seated around him at the Capital Grille had hopes of getting him promoted to Commander-in-Chief.

No one at the table yet knew about the dead body at the *Bijou* theater, but all would find out in due time. Since the role of the Senate Judiciary Committee would be to hold hearings on potential Supreme Court nominees, Senator Smith's influence would soon drastically change.

"Let's be clear, Senator Smith," said Tom Kirkbride. "We are just the beginning of the level of support you can expect to receive. There are a lot of people who feel as we do. You would make a fine candidate and a formidable foe for the Democrat's nominee, more than likely the sitting Vice President. So, let's be clear about something up front ... funding this campaign will not be a problem."

"The question we have," chimed in Elias Kirkbride, "is whether you have the fire in your belly to make this run. If you do, we are confident there will be a ground swell of support behind you. We've made some initial inquiries and believe it will be no problem putting together a list of significant donors wanting to get behind your campaign. As a matter of fact, several are already lined up and ready to go. I'm sure you feel as we do; the Democrats must be defeated in next year's Presidential election. We can't afford another four-year term by these guys."

Super PACs (Political Action Committees) have become a major force in the financing of political campaigns. The 2010 Supreme Court decision known as *Citizens United vs. The Federal Election Commission* opened the floodgates of unlimited money able to be donated to political campaigns. Under *Citizens United*, campaign donations, even if from anonymous donors, can be donated into a Super PAC instead of directly to a particular candidate. The men at the table courting Senator Smith were experts at utilizing the new way to financially influence the outcome of national elections.

"If you tell us you're interested, we've got people on the ground in Iowa and New Hampshire ready to go," said Tom Kirkbride. "We can help put your team together and get the super PACs formed. Once accomplished, we'll start calling our friends and have them open their wallets. It's going to take a lot of money to mount a viable campaign and the sooner we get started the better. But first, we need to know if you're interested."

Senator Smith sat quietly throughout the luncheon, listening intently to the cajoling and coaxing being heaped upon him. Slowly leaning forward to grab a glass of ice water, he took a long sip before clearing his throat and looking the other men squarely in their eyes.

"I'm certainly flattered by your confidence in me, gentlemen. You can tell your friends I am definitely interested."

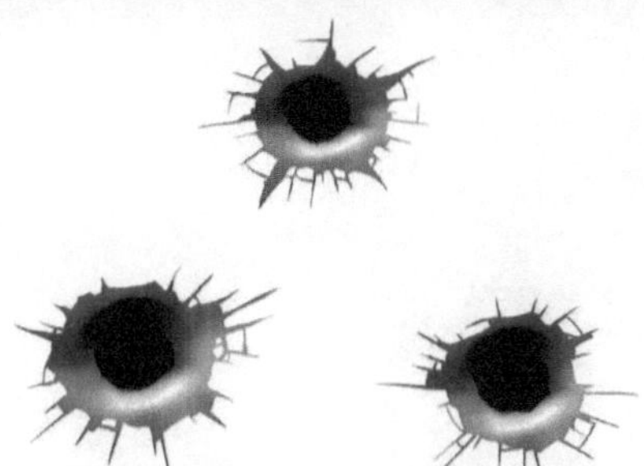

CHAPTER THREE

A man known as Jupiter to a unique and select few of fellow patriots reached into his pocket and retrieved his phone, which had begun vibrating indicating an incoming text. The men under his charge knew he wanted confirmation whenever a mission he sent them on had concluded. He had been anxiously anticipating this particular message.

Although short, the text carried great meaning to Jupiter. It read: *liberty prevails-NSOL, Orcus.*

Good! Jupiter thought, *we're on our way to making things right.*

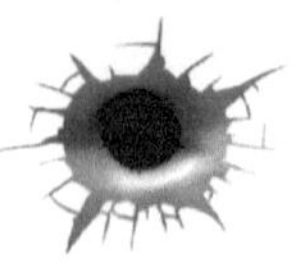
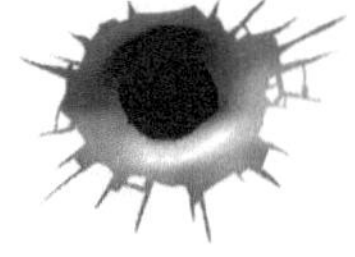
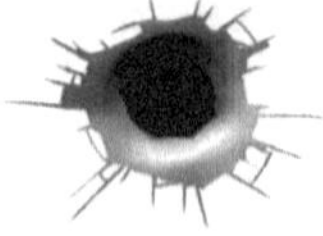

CHAPTER FOUR

Jim Roberts, currently serving as the Presidential Chief of Staff, had been President Ferrell's law professor at Columbia University in New York where they developed a close friendship. An exceptionally brilliant man, Mr. Roberts had a professorial appearance. In other words, he was basically a nerd. Skinny as a rail, he wore his glasses perched on the tip of his nose and nobody could ever remember seeing him in a suit properly pressed.

Mr. Roberts had been an ardent supporter of his one-time pupil's political career and shared his boss's liberal ideology. Blindly loyal to the President he now served; Roberts enjoyed a well-deserved reputation of being vicious towards anyone not exhibiting his same degree of loyalty to the President. Every minute of every day he spent protecting the legacy and reputation of his former student, which is precisely why the phone call he received so alarmed him.

"Mr. Roberts," said the caller. "I've got some bad news."

The caller was the current head of the United States Marshals Service. Among their many duties, it is the responsibility of U.S. Marshals to provide protection to federal judges. More importantly, they are responsible for the safety of Supreme Court justices.

"What is it?" asked Roberts.

"It's Justice Byers," came the response. "He's dead."

"What? What the hell happened?" asked Roberts.

"This is all preliminary at this stage. But he's apparently been murdered. I've been in touch with the FBI and they're sending an agent over to meet with the D.C. detective working the case."

"You're kidding me," exclaimed Roberts. "How did this happen and when? What happened to his protection detail? Were they with him?"

"It happened a few hours ago. I spoke with the team leader of his protection detail right before I called you. Apparently, Justice Byers dismissed his detail after he got home earlier in the evening, telling them he wanted to do some work in his home office and then go to bed. The Marshal on duty saw no reason to hang around after that. To be perfectly honest with you Jim, Justice Byers often ditched his protection detail. Looks as if he paid the price for it this time."

"What do we know about the murder?" asked Roberts.

"We're trying to get it all worked out. We'll know more in a few hours, but there's something else you need to know."

"Oh shit," replied Roberts. "What else?"

"It's about where they found his body.".

"Yeah? What about it?" asked the Chief of Staff.

The Chief Marshal continued. "His body was found in a triple-x movie theater in northwest D.C. Also, he was wearing a fake beard and mustache with a hoodie pulled over his head when they discovered his body. He obviously tried to disguise himself."

"Good God," said Roberts. "Who else knows about this?"

"Just us, the D.C. detective and pretty soon the FBI."

"Thanks. Let's keep this under wrap as long as we can," said Roberts. "I want to be notified as soon as you know anything else. In the meantime, I'll give the FBI Director a call and see if he can keep this quiet. Justice Byers was President Ferrell's appointment and this won't look good."

As soon as Roberts hung up the phone, he placed a call to the White House.

"Mr. President, it's Jim," Roberts said. "Sorry to be calling at such a late hour but this couldn't wait."

"What is it, Jim?" asked President Ferrell.

"Mr. President," he continued, "I got a call from the Chief of the Marshals Service. Justice Byers has been found dead. Looks like it could be murder."

"Dear God," exclaimed the President. "What the hell happened?"

Roberts filled in the President with everything he knew, including where his body had been discovered. Roberts assured the President he would reach out to the FBI Director and encourage him to keep the whole thing quiet, at least for now.

"Make it happen," said the President. "I don't need the shit storm this will cause if it gets out. And for God's sake, Jim, keep me posted."

"Will do Mr. President," replied Roberts before hanging up his phone.

The body of Justice Byers was quietly transported to the D.C. morgue. FBI agent Rich Michaels, assigned to work the investigation alongside the D.C. Homicide squad, had been instructed to meet with D.C. Detective Sergeant Jimmy O'Rourke, who escorted the body to the morgue.

Agent Michaels, the most experienced and savvy criminal investigator in the Washington, D.C. FBI field office (WFO), had been with the Bureau for twenty years, assigned to the D.C. office for the past ten. He began his career as a police officer for the Hollywood, Florida police department after graduating from Florida State University, where he had been an All-American on the university golf team. After a brief run at becoming a professional golfer, he developed a bad case of the *yips* and couldn't sink a five-foot putt to save his life. He knew right then trying to make a living on the PGA Tour would never happen. He quickly traded in his 5-iron for a Glock 9mm pistol and became a cop.

After working the streets of South Florida for five years, he applied to the FBI for a position as a Special Agent. After scoring extremely high on the entrance exam, Michaels accepted a position with the Bureau and reported for duty at the FBI training academy in Quantico, Virginia. Finishing first in his class of thirty recruits, he received his first duty assignment to the Atlanta Field Office, where he primarily worked kidnapping cases, bank robberies and financial fraud investigations.

What made him a bit of a legend within the ranks of the Bureau came as the result of a case he broke, which had baffled law enforcement for years.

A Russian mafia group had been smuggling women into the U.S. for years, forcing them to work in the prostitution industry in Metro Atlanta. A dozen of these women had gone missing over a three-year period, but Atlanta police did little about it due to their lack of information about the foreign women. Few involved in the prostitution trade were willing to talk to cops. That's when Special Agent Michaels got involved. Every day for three months Agent Michaels spent hours perusing the streets of Atlanta, watching streetwalkers ply their trade, copying down the tag numbers of *Johns* and talking to as many people in the industry who would listen to him.

One particular *John* who caught Michaels' attention turned out to be a former factory worker from the Ford Motor plant in College Park, Georgia. Agent Michaels had seen the guy several times meeting with different prostitutes and decided to follow him home one night to a dilapidated farmhouse in Sharpsburg, Georgia, thirty miles southwest of Atlanta. The following day, after seeing his suspect leave the house, Michaels asked the Coweta County Sheriff's office for support, who responded by sending a deputy sheriff with a cadaver dog to assist. As the deputy and Agent Michaels approached the farmhouse, the dog began to *alert* when they got close to the house and began scratching at the ground beneath the front porch steps. While the deputy stayed behind, Agent Michaels rushed to the U.S. Attorney's office and got a search warrant for the home. Upon returning with warrant in hand, Agent Michaels and the deputy proceeded to kick in the front door and were met with the unmistakable stench of decaying flesh. The deputy began puking up the biscuits and sausage gravy he had consumed for breakfast.

Twelve bodies, some completely decayed, were ultimately discovered buried in shallow graves in the dirt-floor basement. An All-Points Bulletin on the suspect's tag number and vehicle description went out over police airwaves. In less than an hour, Coweta County deputies found the suspect pumping gas into his pickup truck a few miles from his home. Following his arrest, the suspect was tried and convicted for murder and sentenced to the electric chair. After ten years in Atlanta, Special Agent Michaels transferred to the WFO.

***

The sensitivity surrounding the murder of Justice Byers makes it the most important criminal investigation Agent Michaels will ever work.

"This must be thorough," the FBI Director told Michaels. "Nothing can be left to chance. We have to do this right, and we have to get to the bottom of it. The President is counting on us."

The body of Justice Byers lay on a large metal table inside the morgue when Agent Michaels walked in the door. D.C. Detectives Jimmy O'Rourke and Charlie Bass were already there along with the D.C. Medical Examiner (M.E.).

"Special Agent Rich Michaels, FBI," he said extending his hand to the detectives. "Tell me what we've got so far."

"Right now, not much," said Jimmy O'Rourke, "just this," as he held up a plastic bag containing a small metal rod. "Looks like an ordinary bicycle spoke with the end filed to a point. We found it on the floor directly under Justice Byers' seat. Seems our esteemed Supreme Court justice had been a regular at the *Bijou*. At least that's what the manager is telling us."

"I spoke to our Director on the way over here and he expressed to me, in no uncertain terms, we need to keep a lid on this for as long as we can," said Michaels. "The White House is concerned if the details of his murder get out, namely where we found his body, it will cause tremendous embarrassment to the President. I have to say I completely agree with him."

"Obviously, we can't keep his death a secret forever," Agent Michaels continued, "but let's see if we can keep most of the details out of the press. At least for the time being, that is."

"Understood," responded Detective Sergeant O'Rourke.

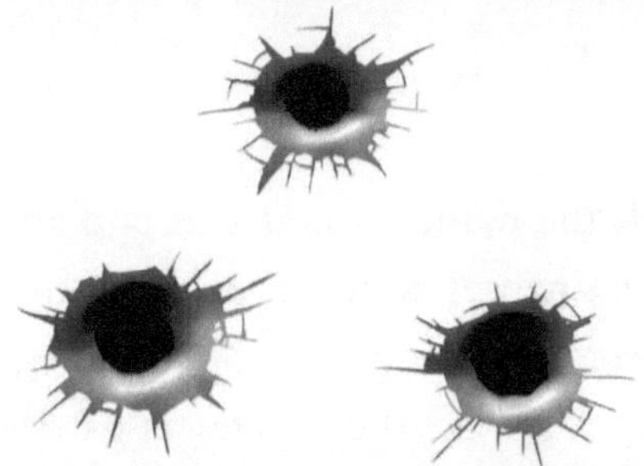

CHAPTER FIVE

A block from the Foggy Bottom Metro stop near Georgetown, a quiet suburb of D.C. where many Washington *elites* call home, sat a three-story townhouse on a quiet tree-lined street. A basement door in the rear of the home provided access to a small group who had gathered for a secret meeting. The five men in attendance had painstakingly taken circuitous routes to avoid any possibility of being followed. No one attending this meeting would want his presence known.

A man known to the group as Orcus arrived first. After parking at the Huntington Metro stop, he boarded the Yellow line bound for the city and rode the train as far as the L'Enfant Plaza Metro station where he exited. A few blocks later he re-boarded the train, taking the Blue line directly to Foggy Bottom.

Apollo arrived next. After boarding the Red line at Union Station, he rode as far as McPherson Square where he exited the Metro, walked to the Farragut West station, only to get back on the train and take the Blue line to Foggy Bottom.

Neptune and Janus were the final two to arrive taking similar precautions as the others.

The Foggy Bottom townhouse belonged to a man known as Jupiter and the undisputed leader of the group. Jupiter had given each of his colleagues their code names. A passionate enthusiast of Roman mythology, the code names Jupiter assigned were the names of various

Roman gods. He felt the names added a certain air of panache. All had previously agreed real names were never to be uttered when they got together for these secret meetings, which were beginning to take place with more frequency. Viewing themselves as patriots, the five men had formed the group to discuss what they could do to get their country back on the right track.

An essential element they shared was their belief that the lurch to the left the country had taken since the rise to power of the current version of the Democrat Party must be arrested. In their collective view, the current man in the White House and others in powerful positions both inside and outside of government had taken the country down a path of destruction. Holding those individuals in utter contempt, the group felt the country had become a culture no longer valuing innocent life; where policies promoted by those in power encouraged dependency on government; where the U.S. Constitution was being systematically shredded; and where political elitists embraced policies more consistent with governments like Castro's Cuba or Chavez' Venezuela.

Jupiter and the others were ex-military. Although now in his early sixties, Jupiter kept in tiptop physical shape and ran two or three marathons a year. His biggest vice was his penchant for expensive red wine. Apollo, a few years younger than Jupiter, was not nearly as refined. Residing on a small horse farm in Leesburg, Virginia, Apollo chewed three packs of Redman chewing tobacco a day and felt most comfortable in worn out jeans and cowboy boots. His only workouts consisted of shoveling horseshit around his barn.

Orcus, several years younger than Jupiter and Apollo, regularly worked out at his local gym near his home in Woodbridge to keep in top physical form, despite his obvious disability. He had a penchant for removing his prosthetic leg and rubbing his stump against Janus, who would get completely grossed out by the ordeal. The exercise usually got the biggest laugh from the men whenever these meetings convened.

Neptune and Janus were basically overgrown kids. Much younger than the others, they were off the chart when it came to physical conditioning. Gym rats to be sure, they were solid rocks of granite with exquisitely chiseled frames. Both in their late twenties, they often hit the local bars and did not suffer from a lack of female attention. *Bird-dogging the ladies,* as Janus described it, was like shooting fish in a barrel for them.

Four of the men served together for a time, most recently during the Iraq War. Apollo's real name is Major Bill Allen. Major Allen served as executive officer of 1st Battalion, 5th Special Forces (SF) Group, based out of Fort Campbell, Kentucky. Having grown up in a military family, he never had any intention of doing anything other than serving a long military career. As a young officer, he had participated in the U.S. invasion of the tiny island of Grenada, a military mission ordered by then President Reagan to overthrow the recently installed communist regime. Like the rest of the group, Major Allen hated communists.

He retired when it became apparent civilian leadership of the military no longer wanted to oppose regimes he felt were antithetical to American values. American values, that is, as he defined them. He was convinced the rules of engagement the military operated under throughout the wars in Iraq and Afghanistan did not allow American forces to achieve victory. After seeing how the current administration had abandoned turf he and his fellow soldiers had bled and died to secure, he knew the time had come to get out. Major Allen had been involved in the battle to secure the Iraqi city of Fallujah and watched several of his men die in the skirmish. Watching the Ferrell administration tuck tail and run, ceding Fallujah and other areas to groups such as Al Qaida and ISIS, he could stomach military life no more. He now wanted to make things right.

Jupiter and Apollo were long-time friends and spent many hours discussing how bad the country had gotten under the leadership of the current Democrat Party. Equally disgusted at how many Americans were buying into the far-left ideology embraced by the Democrat party, they felt too many people were being influenced by prominent voices of liberalism, hell-bent on destroying the tenets that made America the greatest and freest nation in the history of the world. In their view, if something weren't done to stop the leftward tilt toward socialism, the country they fought and bled for would be lost forever. And they were not about to sit idly by and watch it happen. It had been Jupiter's idea to form a group of like-minded individuals who were willing to take whatever steps necessary, no matter how drastic, to do something about the cancer which had metastasized in the U.S. and continued to grow at an alarming rate. Major Bill Allen agreed with everything Jupiter espoused. And he, for one, did not believe in half measures. If they were going to attack the festering problem, he felt it would have to be done in the most extreme manner possible. On this point, the two former warriors were in total agreement.

Apollo and Jupiter knew they would need to recruit at least three or four more patriots sympathetic to their cause and whose dedication and trust would be as unwavering as their own. Apollo knew where to begin his search for these men. Ultimately, the three men he recruited to join the mission had served under his command during the war and were now civilians. Knowing them to be diehard patriots with an intransigent sense of loyalty, Apollo trusted each of them implicitly.

"Can you set up a meeting with them?" Jupiter asked Apollo.

"That's easy enough," Apollo replied. "They all live in this area. We get together often for beers and I can tell you their sentiments towards what is happening to our country are very much in line with ours. I'm confident I can convince them to join our cause."

"Let's bring them in," Jupiter said, "and see if they're willing to get their hands dirty. We need to know from the outset how strong their resolve is and how far they are willing to go to further our mission."

"Don't worry about their resolve," Apollo replied. "I served with these men in battle, and I can tell you unequivocally being timid and reticent are characteristics they do not possess."

"Outstanding," said Jupiter. "That's precisely who we need if we're going to make a difference in our efforts."

Apollo reached out to his three friends individually and told them about the project, whose mission would be to right some of the wrongs inflicted on their country. Appealing to their sense of patriotism and duty were the buttons Apollo knew to push if he were to convince his former soldiers to join the cause. Knowing how much they hated the left-wing anarchists running the country, Apollo felt confident they would take whatever actions were needed to stop them. In this regard, he was correct. They all agreed if they were willing to go fight and kill the enemy on foreign soil, then why not here as well? After all, the cause for liberty and freedom often requires taking drastic actions against those in opposition, no matter who they are or where they exist. And this battle, they felt, would be no different than the battle they waged in defense of liberty and freedom when they wore the uniform.

Orcus, Neptune and Janus told their former commander he could count on them once again. Wanting to get back into the fight and again be relevant, each man wanted to do his part in restoring to America the principles and ideals which made it the greatest force for good in the history of the planet. Even if it meant taking actions others would consider barbaric.

Orcus' real name is Master Sergeant Steve Lick. A former sniper with the 5th SF Group, Sergeant Lick had over a hundred kills to his name. Born and raised in West Palm Beach, Florida, Steve attended Stetson University where he had received a football scholarship to play middle linebacker. After watching the carnage left behind by the 9/11 hijackers, he withdrew from Stetson, gave up his scholarship and joined the military. Instead of decapitating running backs and receivers coming over the middle, he wanted to kill terrorists.

Sergeant Hal Masters, Neptune, and Sergeant David Kyle, Janus, were also soldiers serving in Iraq with the 5th SF Group. While fighting side-by-side as U.S. military forces were engaged in the battle to take Fallujah, their platoon sergeant led an assault on a large warehouse that needed to be secured. Masters and Kyle were the first through the door, laying down suppression fire all the way in. As the rest of their platoon followed, a barrage of bullets began to rain down from an elevated platform inside the warehouse. From positions of cover, Sergeants Masters and Kyle returned fire killing ten enemy fighters hiding behind boxes. Five of their buddies were killed during the assault.

Both men were awarded the Bronze Star for their actions. Eventually, they too became disenchanted with the civilian leadership of the Armed Forces when months later the Pentagon, under orders from the White House, began a systematic pullback from Iraq. They felt the Ferrell administration had dishonored the memory and sacrifice of so many of their fellow patriots by ceding back to the enemy the ground for which they had fought and died. For this reason, they left the Army when their enlistment periods ended.

"Welcome back men," Jupiter said to the others as they began to gather around his basement bar. "Good to see all of you here again. Grab a glass. I just opened this bottle of Chianti. We have much to celebrate tonight."

This marked the fifth time this group had convened. They knew each other's real names, of course, but would never use them at these meetings. Collectively, the group identified themselves as *The New Sons of Liberty* (or *NSOL*). Jupiter had taken this name from an underground group of colonists known as the *Sons of Liberty* formed prior to the Revolutionary War. Back then, the *Sons of Liberty* worked to defy the British Crown and oppose efforts to impose new laws and taxes on colonists as a way of funding the British King's desire of building up his military. *No taxation without representation* became their rallying cry. The original *Sons of* Liberty used a method of punishment known as *tar and feather* to humiliate government leaders and others with whom they disagreed. The current-day version of the *NSOL* would use more drastic measures to accomplish its goals.

"We are on our way gentlemen," continued Jupiter. "Orcus has carried out his mission flawlessly. In a short period of time the limp dicks running this country, as well as other communist-loving pricks trying to destroy the American way of life, will understand they are now in a battle. And it's a battle, gentlemen, I don't think they'll have the guts to engage in."

"Well done, Orcus," chimed in Apollo. "Let's all raise our glasses and toast our friend."

"Here, here," added Neptune and Janus.

"Let's have a seat, men," said Jupiter. "We need to do a post-mission debrief before moving on to new business. Orcus, the floor is yours."

Orcus rose and moved to the front of the room to address his colleagues.

"It went pretty much as planned," he began. "That prick Byers was certainly one demented piece of shit, I can tell you that. Having to sit through the first fifteen minutes of the God-awful movie proved to be the worst part of the mission," he said as the others laughed. "The several weeks of surveillance I did on him paid off. He seemed to be a regular at the *Bijou* so it wasn't hard to figure out where to find him. I got in and out in only a few minutes. No problems whatsoever. I'm not sure anyone even noticed me get up and walk out. As for now, we'll probably want to keep an eye on the press to see what is reported. I have a feeling they're going to want to keep this as quiet as they can for as long as they can."

"You can bet your ass on that," added Apollo as he spit what must have looked like a half pint of tobacco juice into a foam cup before standing to take the floor. "Our dick-head leader is sure to be embarrassed when the public finds out he put a pervert on the Supreme Court. Believe me, we're all better off not having that pile of human debris making important decisions anymore which affects us all. Good riddance I say. Now as far as new business is concerned, Jupiter and I have been discussing something we would like to bring to the group. I'll turn the floor over to him and let him catch all of you up to speed."

"Thank you, Apollo," said Jupiter as he rose to address the *Sons*. "As all of you know, our esteemed President has been systematically undermining the U.S. Constitution and doing everything within his power to erode our God-given rights. Since he lost control of Congress, he has been trying to accomplish his goals through unlawful and unconstitutional executive actions," he continued. "Unfortunately, there are too many spineless Republicans out there who are either too scared or too timid to do anything about it, so it falls on us to take action."

"One of the President's strongest and most influential allies is a group we are all familiar with," he went on. "The Secular Progressive Alliance, run by that bitch CeCe Diamond and funded primarily by Chris Dyess, another anti-American bastard. I initially suggested to Apollo we needed to discuss which one of these fine human specimens we should consider for our next mission. Specifically, which one would make a better target for our purposes? Our esteemed colleague here pointed out if we want to have maximum impact, we should consider doing them both. I must admit perhaps I wasn't thinking big enough. He has convinced me both would make worthy targets."

The other *Sons* all nodded in agreement.

"Let's discuss Ms. Diamond first," Jupiter continued. "In case you haven't been watching the news lately, they are getting ready to hold a rally in support of a cop-killer in California. It's bad enough they are funding the rise in the number of abortions in this country and backing politicians who want to take away our second amendment rights, now they seem committed to evoking sympathy for a scumbag illegal alien who murdered two cops. It's time these bastards realize they are not going to continue to get away with this shit. It's high time someone put them in their places, and that someone is going to be us."

Apollo stood and looked at one of his former soldiers.

"Janus," he said as all eyes turned to look at the former Special Forces warrior. "We think the Diamond job is perfect for you."

"You can count on me, sir," responded Janus. "I will not let you down."

"Alright then," said Jupiter. "Let's go over the plan. We have one week to implementation. Mr. Dyess is not as time-sensitive and frankly, I think he'll be a lot easier target. Let's go over the details on Diamond and then we'll discuss Dyess. We'll meet back here in ten days to debrief."

The *New Sons of Liberty* spent the next three hours discussing logistics, scheduling and any potential contingencies possibly impacting the Diamond mission. As far as the hit on Chris Dyess, the group agreed Apollo would handle the job solo.

"Meeting adjourned," declared Jupiter after their session had concluded.

Each of the *New Sons of Liberty* exited the townhouse as they had entered. One at a time, they slipped out the back door and made their way to the Metro. Once aboard the train they each made several stops, getting off and back on, until each reached their respective homes.

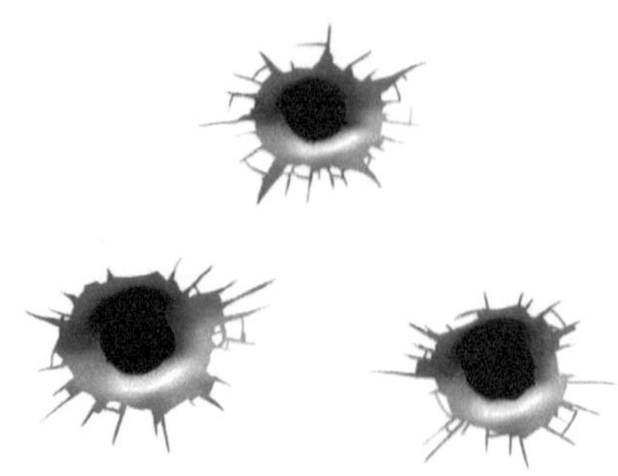

CHAPTER SIX

The White House press corps began filing into the East Room of the White House. The White House Press Secretary had quietly leaked to a few friendly reporters Supreme Court Justice Hayden Byers had met an untimely death and the President wanted to speak to the country about it. No other details were given.

Justice Byers, known to be one of the more far-left justices to ever sit on the Supreme Court, had recently authored the majority opinion in *U.S. vs. Merciful Angel Ministries* (M.A.M). The case pitted the U.S. government against a small not-for-profit organization providing counseling and other services to women, most of who were victims of domestic abuse. M.A.M. also ministered to pregnant women seeking counsel before undergoing an abortion. A devoutly religious and faith-based group, M.A.M. counselors prayed with and for the women they counseled and used Bible passages to encourage those to whom they ministered. The group also offered adoption services to those contemplating an abortion as an alternative to ending their pregnancy. This, of course, angered many on the Left who wanted abortion services to be as easily accessible to pregnant women as an oil change for their cars. And they wanted it all paid for by the government.

The Supreme Court's ruling on *U.S. vs. M.A.M.* hinged on whether the Merciful Angel Ministries had a constitutional right to refuse to provide contraceptive and abortion procedure services in their organization's employee health plan. The group claimed any mandate requiring them to provide such services violated their constitutional right to religious liberty. Contending such a right did not apply in those circumstances, the government claimed any group, regardless of their religious affiliation, had an obligation to abide by the National Healthcare Act guaranteeing those services to women. A strong proponent of the abortion industry, Justice Byers did not like religious conservatives and made no attempt to conceal his bigotry.

"Much to the chagrin of some religious zealots," began Justice Byers' majority opinion in the case, "there is no constitutional right of organizations to deny to its employees that which Congress has deemed appropriate, and which this Court has previously ruled just. The constitutional rights of the defendants in this case to worship in a manner of their choosing is intact and is not impeded by their obligation to follow settled law."

This opinion by Justice Byers solidified his status as an enemy of the Political Right and inextricably endeared him to the Progressive Left.

Justice Byers' legal career had begun almost forty years earlier as an attorney for the American Civil Liberties Union (ACLU). Having built his reputation as a staunch defender of various left-wing causes, Byers at one time sat on the board of The Tides Foundation. A group who over the years had given hundreds of millions of dollars to anti-free enterprise groups, gun control advocates, anti-private property groups, abortion rights groups, anti-military groups, the Black Panthers and other organizations most conservatives feel are seeking to destroy America's constitutional basis.

Before joining the board at The Tides Foundation, Justice Byers had been a member of the National Lawyers Guild (N.L.G.), which at one time worked as the legal arm of the U.S. Communist Party. Over the years the N.L.G. provided free legal support for people arrested for domestic terrorism, spying on the U.S. and the killing of police officers. While attending law school, Justice Byers once roomed with William Kunstler, one of the most anti-American, radically left-wing lawyers who ever lived.

When former FBI Director J. Edgar Hoover once referred to the Black Panther Party as *the greatest threat to the internal security of America,"* Justice Byers stepped in to ardently defend the group, making numerous claims about the FBI and other law enforcement agencies doing nothing more than harassing innocent people and denying them their constitutional rights. Every opportunity made available to Justice Byers to go on national television and trash the police, he did so with vigor.

Shortly before his nomination to the Supreme Court by President Ferrell, Justice Byers had become active with radical environmental groups, such as Greenpeace and the Earth Liberation Front. Although never proven, many believed Justice Byers participated in a meeting of fellow radicals who planned and carried out the bombing of a large timber plant in California. A bombing that resulted in the deaths of eleven innocent workers.

When President Ferrell nominated Hayden Byers to the Supreme Court during the first year of his first term, conservatives throughout the country were loud and clear in their dissent. The Republicans in the Senate, however, could do nothing to derail his elevation to the highest court in the land. With control of both houses of Congress and a super majority in the Senate, Democrats prohibited the Republicans from filibustering the Byers nomination, confirming him on a party-line vote. Not a single Republican Senator voted in favor of the nomination.

"I won and you lost," said President Ferrell at the time, when many on the Political Right expressed outrage at the Byers confirmation. "And elections have consequences."

The President basically stuck up his middle finger to the Republicans. With Democrat majorities in both houses of Congress at the time, the President knew his pick to the Court would go through and nothing his political opposition could do would stop it. At Byers' confirmation hearing, Republicans were able to bring to light the dubious past of the nominee, but to no avail as his confirmation sailed through aided by a political party who no longer seemed to care about decency and justice. The Democrats seemed only to care about beating Republicans and disrupting their conservative agenda.

President Ferrell now stood behind the podium in the East Room of the White House to inform the American people of the passing of Justice Byers.

"Ladies and gentlemen," began President Ferrell. "I received word late last night Supreme Court Justice Hayden Byers has passed away. The circumstances surrounding the cause of death are under investigation by the FBI and have not yet been determined. I have instructed the FBI Director to conduct a thorough investigation and get back to me with his findings. Until then, I will not comment any further on Justice Byers' death because I do not want my comments to have an adverse impact on their investigation. I will simply close by saying Justice Byers' death is a national tragedy. A titan in the legal community, he worked tirelessly every day of his life to protect the rights of average, everyday citizens."

"Mr. President," shouted a member of the press. "Can you tell us if he died of natural causes or is there some kind of foul play present?"

"I've said all I will say at this time," the President responded. "Until the FBI investigation is completed it would be inappropriate to comment further."

Another reporter asked, "Mr. President, will you consider naming a replacement for Justice Byers, and if so, can you tell us when you think the nomination will be made?"

"I will consult with the Attorney General and begin compiling a list of possible replacements," responded President Ferrell. "I would expect the process to be completed in a few months."

Senator Smith sat in his office in the Russell Senate building watching the President's press conference. "My ass, you will," Smith said out loud.

Knowing the following year would be an election year, Senator Smith would make the case to his Senate colleagues to thwart any attempt by this President to get another radical leftist on the bench right before leaving office. As chairman of the Senate Judiciary Committee,

Senator Smith would have great influence on whether any Presidential nomination would be confirmed. With the Republicans now in the majority, he had confidence in being able to make the case the next President should be the one to replace Justice Byers, not this one. Of course, the next President he referred to happened to be himself.

***

D.C. reporter Casey Dean sat in her office at the Washington Chronicle watching the President's press conference. A twenty-year veteran with the Chronicle, Ms. Dean currently covers the Supreme Court. After graduating from the University of Maryland School of Journalism, Ms. Dean began her career with the Chronicle initially assigned to the Metro Desk, primarily covering local crime stories. Known by her colleagues as a hard-nosed reporter, she built a reputation as someone not easily intimidated by the powerful people inside of the D.C. government on which she often reported.

A glaring example of this occurred seven years earlier when Ms. Dean worked on a story about possible corruption within the D.C. police department. One of her sources in the department tipped her off about a concerted effort by high-ranking officials to suppress drug trafficking statistics in order to give the appearance the drug problem in D.C. was under control. According to her source, the police major in charge of the department's patrol division had instructed his officers to *clean up* the area of the city most frequented by tourists. The major's plan to accomplish this involved his officers encouraging the local street dealers to move their operations to the seedier parts of town in northeast D.C., letting them know if they limited their drug dealing to those specific parts of the city, the police would give them leeway and not crack down on their activities.

This strategy accomplished the desired results. Drug dealers were no longer accosting tourists and other *decent* people in the friendlier parts of the city. The overall drug arrests went down, giving the appearance the police were getting the District's drug problem under control. The fact that low income, mostly minority neighborhoods were being ravaged by the scourge of illegal drugs did not seem to bother the leaders of the D.C. police force.

When Ms. Dean prepared to break the explosive story, she visited D.C. police headquarters to get comments and reactions from police hierarchy about her article. The D.C. police chief reacted by calling the managing editor of the Chronicle and demanding the story be spiked. Furthermore, a police captain suggested to Ms. Dean if she went ahead and ran the story, she might find it extremely difficult to find any cop in the city who would lift a finger to help her should she ever need police assistance. This overt threat to her safety only hardened her resolve. The story ran as planned and eventually led to the resignations of five high-ranking officers.

As Ms. Dean listened to the White House Press Conference about the death of Supreme Court Justice Byers, she got on the phone and started working her police sources. One source told her the case had been assigned to D.C. Detective Jimmy O'Rourke, a friend she has known for many years, and that the FBI had taken over the investigation.

She grabbed her cell phone and hit Jimmy's number on her *speed dial.* "Jimmy, this is Casey, can we talk about the Byers investigation?"

"Well, that didn't take long," Jimmy responded. "There's not much I can tell you right now, Casey. Anyways, the FBI has taken it over. It's their baby now and I'm along for the ride to provide whatever assistance I can."

"Well," Casey continued, "I listened to the press conference and it sure sounded to me like there's something about Justice Byers' death our leader wants to keep quiet."

"Casey, you know I can't say anything else right now," said Jimmy. "I'm on my way out the door, I'll talk to you later."

"I'll hold you to that," responded Ms. Dean.

✳✳✳

Agent Michaels, along with detectives O'Rourke and Bass, were on their way to the home of Justice Byers, a townhouse on Canal Drive along the banks of the Potomac River where the justice had lived alone. Losing his wife to cancer ten years earlier, Justice Byers had never remarried. His two grown children had families of their own and lived in other parts of the country. With a search warrant in hand, the investigators were hoping a search of his home would give them a clue as to why he had been murdered.

After searching for over an hour and finding nothing of note, Jimmy O'Rourke discovered a small daily planner in a desk drawer in Byers' home office. Jimmy thumbed through each page. For the most part, the entries were inconsequential, dealing primarily with things like his upcoming court schedule or speeches to various civic groups. Jimmy also noticed Byers had written several scathing comments about some of his more conservative fellow justices. When Detective O'Rourke got to the time period within a month of the murder, he found an entry written by Justice Byers that piqued his interest. The entry read, *second day in a row ... man with a limp ... not sure if he's following me or not?*

Thumbing through the next few pages, he looked for related entries and found nothing of significance until ten days before the murder. *Came home tonight and thought I saw the guy with the limp again. Not sure if him or not but seemed to be following me.*

That was it. No more mention of the mysterious man and nothing more of interest up to the time of his passing. Detective O'Rourke showed the book to his partner, Charlie Bass, and then to Agent Michaels, who took possession of it and added it to his case file on Justice Byers. The investigators continued their search for another two hours but found nothing more of relevance. After concluding their search, they departed and left for home.

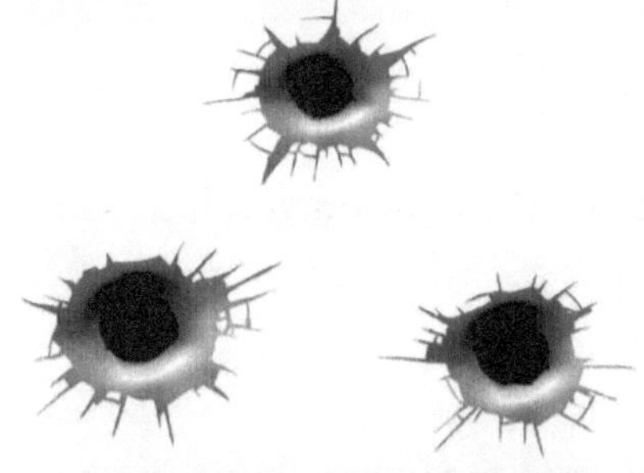

CHAPTER SEVEN

The Secular Progressive Alliance (S.P.A.) had originally been founded in 2002 to oppose the U.S. war in Iraq. Its membership list grew to over 100,000, consisting of atheists and agnostics and other far-left zealots. Since its inception, the S.P.A. has branched out to include the promotion of liberal causes such as abortion rights, gay marriage and social and income inequality... to name a few.

For years, a leftist billionaire named Chris Dyess has provided the organization with the bulk of the funding necessary to stay in business. A longtime supporter of liberal causes, Mr. Dyess also contributed heavily to the candidacies of several left-wing Democrats including the current President. The President of the S.P.A. and its most outspoken proponent is a woman named CeCe Diamond, a long-time disciple of Saul Alinsky, a man who had attained cult-hero status within the liberal community.

Mr. Alinsky, a communist-loving radical from the 60s, started out as a community organizer and believed in the necessity of uniting low-income communities of the *have-nots* in society, empowering them to gain social, political, legal and economic equality. Their purpose: challenge the status quo by rising up and opposing those in government taking advantage of otherwise helpless citizens. According to Alinsky, powerful people in government did little more than line their own greedy pockets off the backs of those less fortunate. Shortly before his death, he penned *Rules for Radicals: A Pragmatic Primer for Realistic*

Radicals. Alinsky, and by extension his followers, believed anyone in power to be a potential foe who needed to be defeated... precisely why CeCe Diamond viewed him as a hero.

A famous quote of Alinsky's, etched into a plaque on her office wall, illustrated her devotion to the liberal icon. The quote read: *Lest we forget at least an over-the-shoulder acknowledgement to the very first radical: from all our legends, mythology, and history and who is to know where mythology leaves off and history begins—or which is which, the first radical known to man who rebelled against the establishment and did it so effectively that he at least won his own kingdom—Lucifer.*

Ms. Diamond had mastered the art of Alinsky's strategy of always creating an enemy her group of followers could rally behind in opposition. She had an abiding hatred of Christians, and more specifically, conservative Republicans in government who espoused Christian values. The S.P.A. has been a major contributor to Planned Parenthood, the primary provider of abortion services in the U.S. for the past few decades. With Ms. Diamond at the helm, the S.P.A. led many rallies designed to disrupt pro-life demonstrations whenever and wherever they took place and have given millions of dollars each year to fund political campaigns. Not coincidentally, all the campaign contributions went to support the election of Democrats. Not above twisting the arms of Democrats in Congress to promote legislation near and dear to her heart, Ms. Diamond stood in strong support of laws designed to curb the rights of Americans to religious liberty, as well as their right to keep and bear arms.

San Francisco's Golden Gate Park, located in one of America's bastions of liberalism, provided the perfect setting for a gathering of S.P.A. devotees who had come together to rally in support of a convicted cop-killer set to be executed for his crime. Ten years earlier the scum they had all come to lionize murdered two California Highway Patrolmen while they ate their lunch at a local diner. The officers met at *Joe's Eats*, a small deli off the Southern Embarcadero Freeway in San Francisco, to have lunch together and catch up on each other's day.

After sitting down in a booth near the front window of the restaurant, they placed their order with their waitress. A few minutes later, Juan Ramirez, an illegal immigrant who had been arrested multiple times before, calmly walked up behind them as they sat in their booth and opened fire with a Smith & Wesson 9mm semi-automatic handgun. After unloading his 10-round magazine in both patrolmen, shooting each in the head several times, Ramirez calmly walked out of the diner and drove away.

One of the officers and his wife, married less than seven months, were expecting their first child. The other, married seventeen years, had four kids aged nine to fourteen. The only reason Ramirez had been there that fateful day was because he had taken advantage of San Francisco's status as a sanctuary city. Although previously convicted of felony assault and other misdemeanors, Ramirez had served only two years in jail before being released for good behavior.

Instead of turning Ramirez over to Immigration and Customs Enforcement agents for deportation, San Francisco officials decided it would be better to ignore federal immigration laws and let him back into the general population of San Francisco. This total disregard for the safety and well-being of its law-abiding citizens by San Francisco officials led directly to the deaths of these two public servants. Twenty minutes after the murders, police arrested Ramirez inside a local bus station five miles away as he stood in line to purchase a ticket to Phoenix. Subsequently tried, convicted and sentenced to the electric chair, Ramirez had exhausted all his appeals and his ten-year wait on death row had come to a close. The date of his execution was imminent.

The S.P.A. rally in Golden Gate Park had been less about the impending execution of Ramirez and more about the group's general disdain for law enforcement and the government's practice of executing human garbage like him. A golden opportunity for CeCe Diamond and her minions to complain about the existence of guns in the U.S., the rally provided a platform for these nut-jobs to excoriate those who believe in the fundamental right provided to Americans by the Second Amendment. She absurdly contended the officers would still be alive if only stricter gun laws had been in place at the time of the murders. Her reasoning, although misguided, indicated how demented liberal thought could be at times. She felt if tougher gun laws had been on the books, poor old Ramirez would never have done the shooting in the first place because the restrictive gun laws would have prohibited him from possessing the gun he used in the killings. Taking their theory one step further, one could logically conclude Mr. Ramirez is actually a victim in this shooting.

Nonsensical crap like this is exactly what stirred the ire of reasonable, decent Americans and made CeCe Diamond a highly sought-after target of the *New Sons of Liberty*. As the rally at Golden State Park got underway, several local Democrat politicians took the stage prior to Ms. Diamond's address, attempting to make themselves relevant and defend their policy of maintaining San Francisco as a sanctuary city. After blathering on about how valuable hardworking immigrants were to the vitality of their great city, each politician took time to chastise the rest of America (and specifically Republicans) for referring to people like Ramirez as *illegals*. Instead, they preferred to describe Ramirez and others like him as simply being *undocumented Americans*. After the elected officials had finished, a few other radicals took to the stage, ranting on about how the U.S. had become nothing more than a police state. When Ms. Diamond finally strolled up to the microphone, the crowd had been worked up to an expected frenzy.

A full mile south of Golden Gate Park, a man dressed as a construction worker wearing a hardhat and donning an orange vest emblazoned with the words *City of San Francisco*, climbed the five flights leading to the roof of a building adjacent to the Sunset Reservoir. Former Special Forces Sergeant David Kyle, known to his friends as Janus, carried with him a backpack and large plastic tarp as he ascended the stairs leading to the roof. Once a sniper in his former SF unit, Janus did not have nearly as many kills as his mentor and colleague, Steve Lick, known as Orcus. No slouch when it came to handling a high-powered sniper rifle, he proved his efficiency at hitting an intended target from as far away as 2,000 meters during the Iraq war on several different occasions. His shot this day would be a mere 1,500 meters.

He thought, *I've done this many times before. Piece of cake!*

When Janus got to the roof, he took a blanket out of the backpack and laid it over the top of a large air conditioning unit at the northwest corner of the roof. He then unrolled a six-foot-length plastic tarp. From inside the tarp, he removed a Cheyenne Tactical Intervention .408 caliber high-powered rifle; anything but normal construction equipment. Similar to the sniper rifle he had used in the service of his country, when fired, the CheyTac .408 rifle would send its 305-grain brass projectile down its 29-inch barrel and out the muzzle at a speed of 3,500 feet per second toward the intended target. Removing two rimless bottleneck cartridges from his pocket, Janus loaded his weapon and proceeded to stretch out across the blanket lying on top of the air-conditioner. With the air almost completely still, he knew adjusting his aim to compensate for wind would be minimal.

From his vantage point he could see the large crowd of people gathered at Golden Gate Park. Looking through the scope on top of his rifle, he could make out various faces on stage, including his target whose face he had studied in preparation for this mission. Still seated on stage behind some guy addressing the crowd, CeCe Diamond waited for her turn to speak as Janus continued eyeing her through his scope.

Come on, Janus thought. *I wish this idiot would shut up and sit down.*

A minute later Ms. Diamond rose from her chair and approached the podium.

Estimating Ms. Diamond's speech would probably last several minutes; Janus took his time in acquiring the perfect *sight picture* of his target.

"Ladies and gentlemen," began Ms. Diamond. "Thank you all for coming out on this glorious day."

Janus released the safety on his rifle and gently placed his right index finger on the trigger as he began taking slow, measured breaths.

"And thank you to the great men and women who run the San Francisco City Council," continued Ms. Diamond. "It is because of your strong leadership and other Democrats like you, we will one day be able to overcome the forces of hate and division so prevalent in today's Republican Party."

Janus gradually began applying more pressure to the trigger while making sure the crosshairs of his scope rested perfectly on the upper torso of Ms. Diamond's body.

CeCe Diamond now hit her stride. Obviously in her element, she continued throwing red meat to her crowd of admirers by maligning what she deemed to be the extreme elements of the political Right. Who cares if they were all lies? Not this crowd. They ate it up.

"And furthermore," she went on, "let's not lose sight of the fact our colleague Mr. Ramirez sits rotting in jail because of a corrupt and oppressive government. We can never grow tired of this fight because fight we must, until the forces of evil have been forever vanquished."

The crowd had been worked into a feverish rage. Like most crowds of left-wing anarchists and agitators, they were long on passion and short on truth. Cheering for a man who had gunned down two law enforcement officers in cold blood, they exhibited contempt for a society now holding such a man accountable for his deeds. They couldn't care less about the carnage left behind by the two murders, like the wives who lost their husbands or the five children who would grow up without a father. If they were inclined to show contempt it should have been for their local leftist government responsible for Ramirez being on the street in the first place. Not this crowd, however. They viewed Ramirez as one of them.

Ms. Diamond paused for a moment to savor the mood as she reached for a bottle of water. Taking a long sip, she allowed for the anticipation of her next words to build. Words, however, that would never come. In a split second, everyone there would know Ms. CeCe Diamond had taken her last breath on earth.

When the hammer struck the firing pin, the round exploded causing a slight recoil into Janus' right shoulder. Needing to reacquire another sight picture in case the first shot missed its mark, he quickly aimed in again preparing for a second shot, knowing he would have no more than a second to fire if needed. It would not be needed. Janus' last sight of Ms. Diamond looking through his scope would be of her falling straight back and out of sight behind the podium. The bullet, which had struck her below her left breast, passed entirely through her body and left an exit wound in her back the size of a large man's fist. CeCe Diamond died before hitting the stage platform. Quickly rolling the rifle back inside the tarp, Janus repacked his backpack, put his hardhat on his head and calmly walked downstairs and onto the street.

Like Orcus before him, he had no identification on his person and carried only a single cyanide pill he had sworn to swallow if captured by law enforcement. The pill would not be needed today.

The scene on stage in Golden Gate Park became one of total chaos. Two city councilmen, standing a few feet from CeCe Diamond when she spoke, were covered with blood splatters and small chunks of Ms. Diamond's internal organs. The crowd could do nothing but stare at the stage in stunned silence. Her close friends and supporters on stage knew at once calling for medical attention would be pointless. The unmistakable tinge of death could clearly be seen on Ms. Diamond's face. No doubt this group of people, who moments before were decrying the mere existence of the police, would soon be imploring them to do their job and find the killer.

Janus walked five blocks south away from the Sunset Reservoir to an older model pickup truck parked in front of the McCoppin Park tennis courts. After placing the rolled-up tarp behind the seat, he got in the truck and simply drove away. Pulling onto Santiago Street he opened the glove box and retrieved a *burner* cell phone. After punching in the numbers to the phone of his leader, Janus typed out the text message he knew Jupiter would be expecting. The message read: *liberty prevails—NSOL, Janus*. After pressing the *send* button, he drove further south and tossed the phone out his window into Lake Merced.

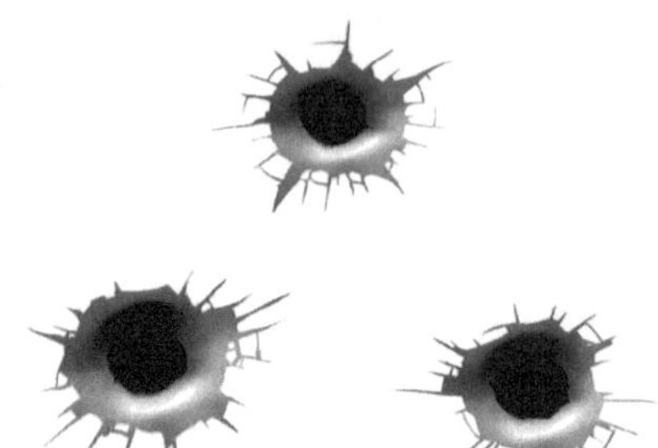

Chapter Eight

It had been several weeks since Senator Smith's lunch meeting at the Capital Grille with his new group of political backers. After deciding to enter the race for the Republican nomination, he had quietly begun putting together a campaign staff to be headed by his campaign chief Amy Killen. Ms. Killen, a long-time veteran of Republican politics, had run the campaigns of Republican candidates six times previously, notching five victories. Her one loss, Maryland's gubernatorial race four years earlier, was nothing to be ashamed of, especially considering how difficult it is for any Republican to win a state-wide race in heavily Democrat-leaning Maryland. Her candidate for governor made the election closer than most political pundits predicted thanks to an exceptionally run campaign by Ms. Killen. Two days before the election, polling eighteen points behind his Democrat contender, her candidate closed the gap considerably by the time actual votes were cast. Ms. Killen's candidate lost by only four points, a decent showing by any measure for a Republican in a blue state like Maryland.

Of her five victorious campaigns, two were for the U.S. House of Representatives and three were for the U.S. Senate, one of which turned out to be most responsible for building her reputation within Republican political circles. Having taken over the campaign of a young, little known U.S. House member in Illinois running for U.S. Senate against an entrenched Democrat incumbent, Ms. Killen discovered the Democrat Senator had been carrying on a three-year affair with one of his young staffers. Knowing she would eventually use the information against the Senator, Ms. Killen decided to hold back on making his affair public until she politically strategized the time would be right. During the incumbent Senator's campaign for reelection, he went to great lengths to portray himself as a good family man who the people of Illinois would be proud to have representing them in the halls of Congress. Attempting to show the voters of Illinois his deep devotion to his lovely wife and their three teenaged children, he ran several ads during his campaign which included his family and the tag line: *A Senator you can be proud of.*

That's when Ms. Killen struck. She leaked the story of the affair to the press, making sure the reporters knew the identity of the *other woman.* The cheating Senator denied the reports, of course, and accused his Republican challenger of dirty politics. Characterizing the media reports of the alleged affair as total lies and dirty politics, the female staffer in question made a statement to the press about how much she respected both the Senator and his wife. Much to the chagrin of the Senator, however, Ms. Killen had an ace in the hole and she waited for the right time to play it. She had in her possession a series of photographs of the Senator and the female staffer kissing in the lobby of a hotel in Champaign, as well as photos showing the two love birds waiting for a hotel elevator, presumably to go upstairs to a private room.

Devastatingly incriminating in their nature, the photos were *anonymously* released to the press and created the desired effect on the Senator's candidacy sought by Ms. Killen. The damning photos had been given to Ms. Killen by one of the Senator's former staffers who had been fired for trying to use his boss's influence to have some D.C. traffic tickets fixed for a friend. Having held the pictures for over a year, the scorned staffer had been waiting for a moment such as this to use them. After the pictures went public, the young woman broke down in tears when accosted by a reporter from *The National Enquirer* and subsequently admitted to the affair. The scandal eventually sunk the Senator's prospect for reelection as the voters turned on him and booted him out of office.

It would now be the job of Amy Killen to get her new boss elected President of the United States.

***

Senator Brian Smith stood on stage before a crowd of five hundred plus congregated in front of the V.F.W. (Veterans of Foreign Wars) Lodge in his hometown of Jackson, New Jersey. After letting it be known to a small group of reporters he would be entering the race for the White House, Senator Smith approached the microphone to make his official announcement he would indeed be a candidate for President of the United States.

"Ladies and gentlemen," he began. "For the last seven years our democracy and our way of life have come under assault by the current administration. Our economy is in shambles and the median income in this country has gone down while our taxes have gone up."

The crowd cheered.

"We're not creating high-paying jobs anymore," Senator Smith continued. "It has gotten more and more difficult for hardworking Americans to find decent employment. This has not been an accident. President Ferrell and his administration have repeatedly pursued policies which have proven detrimental to our nation and it must not be allowed to continue."

The roar became much louder as T.V. news cameras began scanning the crowd of supporters.

"President Ferrell told us after his election he would work every day of his administration to try and bring us together as a nation," the Senator continued. "Instead, he has driven us farther and farther apart. We have never been more divided as a nation since the Civil War and it is shameful."

The crowd of supporters, now clearly energized, cheered loudly while waving signs passed out by campaign staffers reading, *Smith for President.*

Now beaming, Senator Smith raised his hands to the crowd in an effort to quiet them so his every word could be heard.

"I had the honor of serving this great nation in uniform during one of the darkest chapters in our country's history, that being the Viet Nam War," he continued. "And for the past twenty-two years I have had the privilege of serving the people of New Jersey in the United States Senate. It is now time for me to answer the call yet again. It is for this reason I am announcing today my candidacy for the Republican nomination to be your next President."

As the crowd of supporters erupted in joyous applause, yelling and screaming as loud as they could, the setting of the Senator's announcement did not go unnoticed by the reporters covering the event. With the backdrop of the V.F.W. Lodge, the on-air reporters for CNN and Fox News could not avoid talking about the Senator's status as a genuine war hero, including the fact he had won the Congressional Medal of Honor for his bravery when in uniform. With a reputation as someone who dearly loves the military and whose ardent support of veterans throughout his political career has become legendary, his campaign, the reporters opined, would no doubt be formidable.

"The election is a little over a year away and we've got lots of work to do," Senator Smith continued. "God bless all of you for coming out today and God bless this great nation of ours. Thank you very much and now it's on to Iowa!"

Senator Smith walked off the stage and waded into his crowd of supporters, shaking hands and signing autographs. It had been quite a while since he had actively campaigned for office. His popularity in the state of New Jersey allowed him to win his two previous senatorial races with only token opposition. Hardly needing to leave Washington and hit the campaign trail for those two elections, Senator Smith won those contests with over 70% of the vote. Running for the presidency would be the most difficult undertaking of his political life and he knew it. Up for the challenge before him, Senator Smith truly felt his country needed him now more than ever.

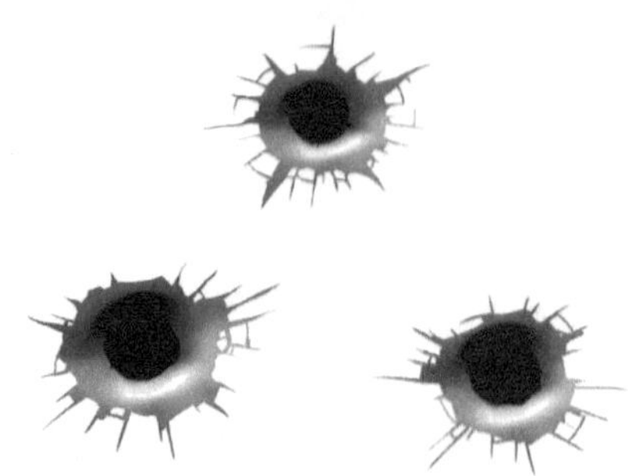

CHAPTER NINE

At about the same time Janus flew out to the west coast to take care of his business in San Francisco, Apollo made the four-hour drive up I-95 from Washington, D.C. to New York City and the Manhattan Plaza Health Club on West 43rd Street, his intended destination. Chris Dyess had been a member of the club for several years and made regular visits whenever in town.

Frequently the subject of articles in the New York City tabloids, Mr. Dyess thoroughly enjoyed the attention his daily activities received. Especially fond of people knowing how much he liked to work out, Mr. Dyess took great pride in maintaining such good shape for a man of his age. Once the subject of a cover story by Men's Health magazine, Mr. Dyess had been lauded by the publication for the workout regimen he regularly put himself through and extolled him for being in better shape than most men half his age. The twice-divorced billionaire, the article pointed out, could frequently be found in the company of women more than thirty years younger. His vast wealth, of course, probably had more to do with that than his figure.

Apollo arrived at the health club a few minutes past noon and stopped by the front desk to purchase a one-day trial membership. After telling the health club employee he had recently moved to the area and wanted to find a local gym, Apollo convinced the young man behind the desk The Manhattan Plaza Health Club topped his list of possible clubs to join. After a perfunctory welcome, the employee gave Apollo a quick tour of the facilities. After finishing the tour, Apollo received a towel and locker assignment and quickly dressed for his workout.

Working up a good sweat as he passed the three-mile mark on his treadmill, Apollo looked through the large glass wall in front of him to the juice bar below. There he spotted his target. Mr. Dyess had finished lifting weights and stopped at the juice bar counter for refreshment. After taking a few swigs from his drink, he wiped the remaining sweat from his brow and made his way to the locker room. A few minutes later, Apollo stepped down from his treadmill and walked into the locker room as well.

Chris Dyess set his drink down on the bench beside his locker and began undressing for his shower. Apollo, standing in front of his locker no more than ten feet away, reached into his gym bag and retrieved a small plastic squirt bottle containing what appeared to be water. But instead of water, it contained the equivalent of six doses of a drug called adenosine.

Adenosine is a drug prescribed by doctors to treat a condition known as supraventricular tachycardia, or ST. Essentially, ST is found in someone suffering from an accelerated heart rate. When injected in the proper dosage, adenosine will reduce the flow of blood to the heart, allowing the patient's rapid heart rate to subside and return to normal. If, however, adenosine is taken at too high a dosage, the drug will cause the heart to stop, giving all outward appearances of a full cardiac arrest.

Apollo casually walked behind the bench where Dyess stood as he reached into his locker for fresh clothes. Without anyone noticing, Apollo quickly reached down and squirted the bottle's contents into Dyess' juice bottle. Returning to his locker, Apollo retrieved his clothing and dressed. As he began to leave, Apollo looked back and watched as Dyess finished the contents of his juice bottle, and then quickly left the gym.

Chris Dyess would soon depart the locker room as well. Except in his case, it would be on a stretcher brought in by the New York City E.M.T.s responding to an apparent heart attack in the men's locker room at the Manhattan Plaza Health Club. The news reports of Mr. Dyess' death later in the day would simply state after one of his usual brisk workouts, he collapsed and died in the locker room from an apparent heart attack.

Everyone viewing the report of his death on the New York nightly newscast, or reading about it in the papers, made the obvious assumption his death occurred due to his advanced age and the fact his heart could not handle the strenuous workout he was famous for. There would be no need for an autopsy as the cause of death on the medical examiner's death certificate indicated the subject died of a heart attack due to excessive exercise. No one would ever know the *heart attack* had been caused by the introduction of adenosine in his juice bottle by one of the *New Sons of Liberty*.

After driving away from the Manhattan Plaza Health Club, Apollo pulled onto the ramp for I-95 South, taking him away from New York City and back to D.C. As he drove, he removed the *burner* phone from his glove box and typed a text message he knew Jupiter anxiously awaited: *liberty prevails–NSOL, Apollo.*

Smiling as he drove away, Apollo pressed the *send* button on his phone, content in knowing another successful mission had been carried out in the pursuit of liberty.

***

Every evening news program led with the story of what happened at the Golden Gate Park in San Francisco. Chris Dyess' death received a mention, but no in-depth coverage. The connection between Chris Dyess and CeCe Diamond's Secular Progressive Alliance did not get mentioned. Her death had been referred to as an assassination with initial reports intimating the killing might possibly be linked to a White Supremacy group upset over the positions of support taken by the S.P.A. for a cop killer, and against the police. No one had remotely theorized the killing of CeCe Diamond had any connection with the death of Supreme Court Justice Hayden Byers, and certainly no connection with the death several hours earlier of Chris Dyess. And for now, the *New Sons of Liberty* could not have been more pleased.

At the daily White House press briefing the following morning, President Ferrell's press secretary was asked if the President would be making any comments about the assassination of the head of the S.P.A., Ms. Diamond.

"The President is obviously troubled by the events of yesterday," commented the press secretary. "He wishes to express his condolences to the family and friends of Ms. Diamond. I would like to add the President has instructed the FBI to lend whatever assistance law enforcement officials in San Francisco may need to help them solve this crime. Currently, however, it appears to be a local law enforcement matter."

The last statement brought a smile to the faces of five particular men.

The press secretary looked around at the room of reporters and pointed to Casey Dean seated in the front row with her hand raised.

"Yes Casey, go ahead," he said.

Casey rose from her chair and began her question.

"Can you tell us anything more about the investigation into the death of Justice Byers?" she asked.

"As you know, Casey, the FBI is still investigating and it would be inappropriate for me to make any comment regarding the case. When the FBI has concluded their investigation, I will be happy to comment, but not before."

Not yet ready to sit down, Casey continued. "Can you tell us anything about whether or not the President is prepared to make a nomination to replace Justice Byers?"

"That is also something currently being discussed at the White House and when the President is comfortable with naming a successor he will do so," responded the press secretary.

"But sir," continued Ms. Dean, "the Republican Senate Majority Leader said just this week that he believes it would be in the best interest of the country to have the next President pick Justice Byers' successor. Can you comment on that?"

Slightly agitated, the press secretary replied, "Ms. Dean, it is the responsibility of the sitting U.S. President to fill vacancies on the federal bench, whenever and wherever such vacancies exist. The President will do his duty. I will add, however, it seems a bit interesting the Republican majority leader of the Senate would take this position in light of the fact his Judiciary Committee chairman just happened to announce he is running for President. Now I don't want to sound cynical, but I do think it seems to be a strange coincidence. Next question, please."

Not to be lost on the press secretary or most of the liberal press (especially all the anchors on CNN), the Republicans in the Senate most certainly were preparing to thwart any effort by President Ferrell to name another liberal judge to sit on the Supreme Court. Never mind the Democrats had taken the same position in the past under a Republican administration. The Senate Republican leader and his caucus had decided to not openly oppose the President making the nomination, which he had a right to do. They were, however, going to be united in opposing the nominee's confirmation after going through the motions of holding a *fair and impartial* hearing when the new nominee appeared before the Senate Judiciary Committee.

For several years, and without regard for which political party held the White House, the naming of Presidential appointees to fill Supreme Court vacancies had become politicized. This would be no exception. The Republicans knew they held all the cards regarding Senate confirmation for Presidential appointments and they were not about to roll over and cede such power to President Ferrell and the Democrats.

The Republicans would be quick to remind the administration the U.S. Constitution calls for the President to appoint and for the Senate to *advise and consent* on all nominations to the federal bench. They would also point out *advise and consent* does not mean rubber-stamping a President's nomination and simply voting to confirm whoever received a nomination. Although no Republican would say so publicly, *the fix was definitely in.* There would be no way the Republican-controlled Senate would confirm any nomination by President Ferrell to the Supreme

Court. Period! Their only hurdle would be how to accomplish it in a manner appearing fair and nonpartisan.

Casey Dean left the press conference with more questions than she had going in. She felt the President's press secretary held something back about the death of Justice Byers and she needed to find out what it was. After dialing the number to the D.C. Medical Examiner's office, Casey spoke to an assistant handling phone duty and identified herself as a reporter for the Washington Chronicle. Telling the assistant she wanted to write a follow up story on the death of Supreme Court Justice Byers, Ms. Dean asked if she could come by for a copy of the death certificate.

"I'm sorry but it's not ready to be released at this time," she was told.

"When do you expect it to be released?"

"Actually, I have no idea," came the reply. "Look, this is not your run-of-the-mill homicide, with him being such an important person and all, so you're going to have to be patient. The Medical Examiner is the only one authorized to release the death certificate and he's not ready to do it yet."

"Did you say homicide?" Casey asked with a slight level of incredulity in her voice.

Ms. Dean only heard silence, followed by a *click* and the familiar dial tone.

Casey hung up her phone and called one of her contacts at D.C. police headquarters, a desk sergeant on duty that morning. After telling him she was working on something he might be able to help her with, Casey invited her contact to lunch. Not wanting to pass up a free meal, the police sergeant quickly accepted her invitation.

"Sergeant," began Ms. Dean as their waitress delivered a plate of sushi and crab cake appetizers to their table, "I've been trying to do a story on the death of Justice Byers but can't seem to get anywhere. Everybody who knows anything keeps telling me they can't comment because the case is still being investigated. Do you know what's going on?"

"To tell you the truth, Casey," responded the D.C. police desk sergeant as he soaked a piece of California roll in a bowl of soy sauce, "everything I know I get from Fox News. I probably know less about this case than you do."

He couldn't have been more accurate.

Not to be deterred, Casey continued digging to see what, if anything, she could get from the sergeant.

"Would it be possible for you to get me a copy of the printout from dispatch for all the calls received the night Justice Byers died? I don't need to see the names of anyone identified in the printout so feel free to redact those. I'm interested in looking at where patrol units were sent the night he died."

"No problem," responded the Sergeant. "But don't forget, you didn't get it from me."

"Of course, sergeant," said Casey. "Just like always."

The initial report on the death of Justice Byers made public did not indicate any specific time, only that his death occurred in the *evening hours* of the night in question. She sat at her desk and began pouring over the report she received from her police contact, paying particular attention to dispatch calls made to patrol units between the hours of 6 p.m. on the night Byers died, and 6 a.m. the following morning. With well over a hundred calls falling within this time frame, Casey wanted to first eliminate the calls she knew had nothing to do with Byers. Knowing the police codes backwards and forward, she began crossing off the calls where patrol units responded to things such as traffic accidents, burglar alarms, etc. One of the calls even mentioned the sighting of a UFO. After this initial culling of the dispatch call list, she could cross off about half the calls from the night in question but would have to do some leg work on the remaining fifty or so.

Pulling out a city map from her desk drawer, Casey proceeded to mark the location of each of the remaining calls in question. For the rest of the day and most of the next, she went to each location to see if she could learn anything new.

As she pulled up in front of the *21ˢᵗ Street Bijou*, she noticed the marquee on the front of the building, indicating the theater showed only XXX-rated movies. Looking at the dispatch report provided to her by her police contact, Casey noticed the patrol unit which had responded to the movie house on the night of Justice Byers' death, had been sent there to meet with detectives and provide assistance. The report provided no other information.

Normally it would not be unusual for cops to respond to a place like this for some kind of disturbance, she thought. *But this wasn't a disturbance call. They were called here to assist the detectives. But what were the detectives here to investigate?*

Her mind continued to race.

It makes sense, she surmised. *If Byers died here, it's no wonder nobody wants to say anything about it. It would be too embarrassing for the President.*

She went back to her office and called her friend, D.C. Detective Jimmy O'Rourke.

"Jimmy, it's Casey," she spoke softly into her phone. "How's it going?"

"Working my butt off as usual," he responded. "It's getting harder and harder to come in anymore. My wife keeps coming up with all these plans for our place in Front Royal. Now she wants me to build a greenhouse. Says she wants to start growing tropical plants or some shit."

Casey laughed. "I never knew you had a green thumb," she said. "I can picture you playing in the dirt with your little spade and watering can."

"Yeah, me too," Jimmy added sarcastically. "If I can make it to the end of the year, I'm definitely thinking about pulling the plug."

"You certainly deserve it, Jimmy. More so than most, I would say."

"I know you didn't call me to check up on my welfare." Jimmy asked, "What's up?"

"Actually, you're right. Although you know your welfare's always on my mind," Casey said with a laugh. "But ... I do have a serious question."

"What is it?" asked Jimmy.

"It's about Byers," replied Casey.

"What about him?" Jimmy asked.

"How long had he been going to the *21ˢᵗ Street Bijou?*" Casey asked without hesitation, hoping the question would catch him off guard.

"How the hell did you figure that out?" replied Jimmy. "Never mind," he interjected before Casey could answer, "something tells me I don't want to know."

"You're not my only source," she said with a smile, "even though you are my favorite."

"Yeah, right," he answered. "You know I can't give you anything, Casey. Anyways, the FBI has taken lead on this case. A guy named Rich Michaels is running the investigation. He's a good guy from what I've seen so far. Seems to be a pretty good agent, too."

"Can you at least tell me if he died from natural causes or not?" she asked Jimmy. "Something tells me he didn't. It's the way they're trying to keep a lid on this. Maybe I'm being my normal paranoid self, but it seems to me there's more to this than simply trying to avoid the embarrassment of people finding out about the secret nocturnal habits of the President's glorious Supreme Court appointee."

"I couldn't care less about their embarrassment," said Jimmy. "And as far as his death being by natural causes or not? It most certainly was ... if you consider having someone drive an eight-inch metal spoke through the back of your skull to be natural."

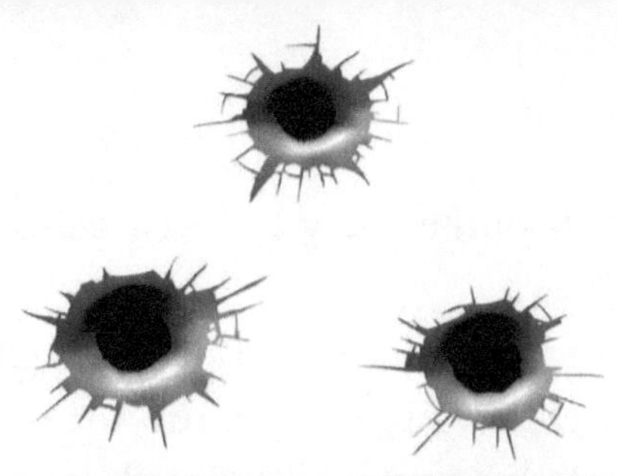

Chapter Ten

President Rob Ferrell made no secret of the fact he wanted his Vice President, Eric Hogue, to succeed him as the next leader of the free world. President Ferrell went through the motions of appearing to be neutral in the Democrat nominating process, but everyone knew where his loyalties lay. V.P. Hogue had token opposition in the upcoming Democrat primary and President Ferrell did not want to appear to be picking sides this early in the process. No one doubted V.P. Hogue would run in the general election as the nominee of the Democrat Party.

Rob Ferrell had picked Eric Hogue to be his running mate when Ferrell beat the other contenders for the Democrat nomination seven years earlier. At the time, Hogue had been Governor of Virginia and carrying that swing state would be pivotal to Ferrell's chances of winning the Presidency. Governor Hogue proved to be a tireless campaigner and successfully delivered the Commonwealth and its Electoral College votes in the Presidential election. Mr. Hogue had also been considered a hero to the Left in the country. As Virginia Governor, in order to placate his pro-abortion constituents, he vetoed a parental consent bill passed by the Virginia legislature, which pertained to young women under the age of eighteen obtaining abortions. A strong opponent of gun rights and the N.R.A., Mr. Hogue also vetoed several bills expanding the rights of gun owners, including one allowing gun owners with carry permits to be armed on college campuses. He once publicly declared the N.R.A.

posed more of a threat to the safety and well-being of Americans than Al Qaida.

After more than seven years as President Ferrell's right-hand man, V.P. Hogue announced his intention to run for the office in hopes of succeeding his boss. Stating he would essentially be running for President Ferrell's third term, he listed all the things a Hogue administration would fix. He talked about the tepid economic growth, the loss of jobs, the declining middle class and the high rate of black unemployment and how his policy initiatives were going to make all those things better. Of course, he failed to point out all the problems he listed had only gotten worse over the past seven years since he and his boss, President Ferrell, had been in office. V.P. Hogue also knew the liberal media would never challenge him on those points.

"Since you claim to be running for what will essentially be a third Ferrell term," a hypothetical political reporter might ask, *"why is there a need to fix all of these problems you say you're going to fix?"*

As long as Hogue stayed away from Fox News reporters or anyone else who still had journalistic standards, he knew such a question would never be asked. His strategy would be one embedded in the Democrat playbook for all political campaigns: promise more government programs and handouts, and demonize the opposition as being racist, homophobic Neanderthals who want to take away women's rights, keep black Americans from voting and kill the elderly. Pretty simple, really. Unfortunately for the country, the strategy had worked repeatedly in the past and he wasn't about to try and rewrite a winning playbook.

The primary season on the Republican side had been well under way. Besides Senator Brian Smith, there were seven other announced candidates vying for the Republican nomination. A steel magnate along with sitting members of Congress and a couple Republican governors rounded out the field of eight contending for the nomination.

Every four years as the election season rolls around, Iowa gets a lot of early attention from the slate of candidates who fancy themselves to be the next leader of the free world. The reason Iowa is important in primaries is because it's the first time in the election process voters have a say in whom they prefer for the nomination of their respective parties. Polls are important to some degree, but the actual vote cast by caucus voters in the first contest in Iowa is considerably more important. Since Iowa gets to go first every four years, candidates who do well can provide their campaign with the all-important *Mo*– that is to say, momentum.

It had been several months since Senator Smith's announcement speech in his hometown of Jackson, New Jersey, and he had concentrated most of his campaigning in Iowa and New Hampshire. So as not to give the appearance of neglecting his day job, he made several trips back and forth to Washington to deal with matters of the Senate. No problem, he surmised, in skipping Senate votes for things such as deciding on whom to name a post office or government building after. But if important issues were to be debated on, he made sure to be there. National polls leading up to the Iowa contest had Senator Smith and Indiana Governor Joel Alan neck-in-neck at the top. The other six candidates were polling well behind and would need a strong showing in Iowa if their campaigns had any chance of continuing. Senator Smith had been barnstorming the state, holding town hall meetings and pressing the flesh with as many Iowans as possible. His town hall meetings provided him with the best opportunity to meet voters and lay out his agenda should he win the nomination.

Ms. Killen had been conducting focus groups for the past several weeks and poll-testing different campaign ideas to see which ones best connected with Iowa voters. The economy and jobs topped the list, followed by national security, illegal immigration and out-of-control spending by the federal government. Social issues, which in the past had rated high on Republican voters' lists, were almost non-existent in this election cycle. The election this time around would be won or lost based on whether a particular candidate could convince voters he would reverse the destructive course the country had been put on by the ultra-liberal administration of Rob Ferrell. Senator Smith undoubtedly believed he would be the one best positioned for this task. Based on polling information, Senator Smith and Amy Killen crafted their campaign strategy to address the issues most appealing to the voters of Iowa, as well as Republicans across the country.

At a town hall meeting in Ames, Iowa, ten days before the Iowa Caucus, a voter asked Senator Smith a question.

"Senator Smith," the voter began, "the National Healthcare Act President Ferrell signed into law is killing jobs and making healthcare too expensive. How will you address this problem if you are elected President?"

"Thank you for the question," Senator Smith replied. "When President Ferrell had both the Senate and House in Democrat control, he rammed down the throats of the American people a healthcare law which, as you rightly point out, has crippled our economy. The law passed without a single Republican vote. I know, because I did everything I could to stop it, including joining other Republicans in attempting to filibuster the legislation. We didn't have enough votes in the Senate to sustain a filibuster and derail this piece of garbage. So, unfortunately, the legislation passed."

"Since then," he went on, "the American people have voted to return control of Congress to our party. The voters sent a clear, plain and simple message. They want us to do something about the direction the Democrats and President Ferrell have taken our country. I can tell you right now, if elected, one of the first acts of my administration will be to repeal the National Healthcare Act and replace it with something more affordable. I want to give Americans more choice in their healthcare options and do it in such a way they will pay lower premiums, which have been rising not falling, as the President promised when he championed his healthcare act. Our nation has suffered under the President and it must change. The numbers don't lie. Vice President Hogue must not be allowed to win the presidency in November because if he does, we will continue to get more of the same policies we are getting now, causing additional harm to our country. This campaign is going to be about giving the American people a better option about what direction our country is going to take in the future. Vice President

Hogue represents the status quo and will not change the direction this country is now on. I will."

Another voter stood and asked the senator about his views on national security and what a Smith administration would look like with regards to protecting the U.S. from the threat of terrorists. The question is known in political circles as a fastball down the center of the plate.

"As most of you know I wore the uniform in service of my country over four decades ago during the Viet Nam war. Now I know many of you may be too young to remember Viet Nam, but I'm sure most of you know Viet Nam is not a fondly remembered chapter in our nation's history. The reason it is a dark chapter is not because of anything done by those of us who served there. The problem revolved around the civilian leadership in Washington, not allowing fighting soldiers like me to win the war. The actions they took were done purely for political reasons. And now we are seeing the same thing repeated by this President."

"President Ferrell," Smith continued, "and to some degree the administration before him, has prosecuted the war against Islamic terrorists as incompetently as anything I have ever seen. We are less safe today than at any time in our nation's history since WWII. Look at the President's actions and his rhetoric. He coddles the terrorists, makes deals with our enemies and won't identify who it is who's trying to kill us. Has anybody ever heard our President utter the phrase *Islamic terrorist?* No, you haven't and neither have I. And to make matters worse, our one true ally in the Middle East is Israel and he treats them with more disdain than he does our enemies."

By this point he had the crowd eating out of his hand. The Senator didn't need to talk about his own personal heroism during his time in the military. There were enough media outlets covering this town hall event who would remind their viewers about his actions during the Viet Nam war, which won him the Congressional Medal of Honor. A simple portrayal of strength is exactly what he needed to project. The time had come in our nation's history, he believed, when Americans were looking for strong leadership. A stark contrast to what the country had been getting for the past seven years.

"One thing I will not do," continued Senator Smith, "is tie the hands of our soldiers behind their backs like the current administration has done. President Ferrell has decimated the morale of our men and women in uniform and has gutted the Pentagon in favor of his far-left welfare programs. This will end when I am in the White House. The war against radical Islam is real and when I become Commander-in-Chief I will give the Generals one clear order: *Go win*. And mark my words ladies and gentlemen. After we achieve victory, your sons and daughters who will have won the victory will come home and receive the thanks of a grateful nation."

The crowd erupted in applause. Senator Smith knew he hit the fastball out of the park. Ms. Killen and a few other staff members stood behind the crowd with huge smiles on their faces. Amy Killen's strategy for her candidate had been simple up to this point: be positive, be patriotic, and stay away from the negative stuff, at least for now. Ms. Killen knew Senator Smith's main challenger would be Governor Alan, who enjoyed the backing of evangelicals, who make up a large portion of the Iowa Republican electorate. Because Iowa sat in the heart of America's Midwest, as did Governor Alan's state of Indiana, both Ms. Killen and Senator Smith had no illusions about winning Iowa. They did, however, know how important it would be for them to attain a strong second place finish, setting them up for the primaries to follow. The voters of New Hampshire and South Carolina were the real targets of this town hall address. Those upcoming contests would more than likely determine what two or possibly three Republican candidates would still be around to battle it out for the nomination.

The days leading up to the Iowa Caucus vote saw Iowans bombarded with political ads. Most of the candidates, not named Smith or Alan were doing anything and everything they could to improve their chances and make the race more competitive by incessantly hitting the two front runners with negative ads. Their strategy of trying to drive down the poll numbers of the two leading contenders was the only chance they had in making their campaigns more competitive.

The first Republican debate, hosted by the Fox News Channel, took place three days before the Iowa Caucus. Before questioning began, each candidate had a minute to make an opening statement. They each took time to tell everyone how he, and not any of the other seven, would be more successful at putting the country back on the right track. They also spoke about their support for policies they felt would be most effective in stopping the leftward tilt caused by the liberal Ferrell administration.

Because Senator Smith and Governor Alan were leading in the polls, most of the attacks by the other candidates during the debate were aimed at them. Senator Smith received criticism for being a political elitist because of his many years serving in Washington, while Governor Alan received criticism for being the two-term governor of a state losing jobs and currently running a budget deficit. Governor Alan quickly pointed out that net job creation had actually gone up under his administration since first elected to lead his state. As far as the recent budget deficit and the slowing of his state's economy were concerned, he reminded voters those things were due to President Ferrell's healthcare law which forced employers to lay off workers so they wouldn't be saddled with the high cost of providing mandatory health insurance for their employees.

"This is precisely why," said Governor Alan, "this terrible healthcare law must be repealed. I have a plan to get rid of this law and replace it with less expensive healthcare coverage that will provide Americans with more options. They will be able to shop for plans across state lines and the competition between the different healthcare providers will cause prices to drop, not go up like we are seeing now under the administration's disastrous healthcare mandates."

This got the second loudest cheer of the night. The loudest would come later when the candidates addressed the issue of national security. Governor Alan successfully portrayed the Ferrell administration of being out of touch with hardworking Americans and of wanting to make as many citizens as possible dependent on government welfare programs.

"The Ferrell-Hogue administration," Governor Alan said, "is doing their best to turn us into a socialist society where too many of our citizens are dependent on government programs. They must not be allowed to succeed. An Alan administration will bring fiscal sanity back to Washington by ending the era of excessive regulations which have stifled the entrepreneurial spirit of this country and put more people in the unemployment line."

"Senator Smith," began the question of one of the moderators, "this election has taken on new meaning with many Republican voters because of the recent passing of Supreme Court Justice Hayden Byers. Not counting the Byers vacancy, the next President may appoint as many as three new justices to the Supreme Court considering the ages of the current justices on the bench. You currently serve in the Senate as chairman of the Senate Judiciary Committee, whose responsibility it is to hold confirmation hearings on the President's judicial appointments. While the President has indicated he will nominate a replacement for Justice Byers, many Republicans in the Senate believe the next President should name his replacement. Here's my question: Should the President make such a nomination now, or do you believe the nomination should be made by his successor?"

This question came as no surprise to Senator Smith, acutely aware voters might be cynical of his views on this issue because the Senate Judiciary Committee which he chairs, has the power to deny the President his nomination. In addition, some voters might be skeptical of his view on this topic since he would be the one making the appointment should he be so fortunate as to win the election in November. Both Ms. Killen and Senator Smith had discussed this before the debate and agreed the Senator needed to give the appearance of being non-partisan. At the same time, he needed to let Republican primary voters know he would not allow another far left liberal to get through his committee, causing the Court to continue its tilt to the left. He felt ready for the question.

"The U.S. Constitution directs the President to make appointments to the Supreme Court," Senator Smith began his answer, "and gives a role to the Senate as well. The constitutional role of our body is to *advise and consent* on Presidential nominations. This does not, however, mean the Senate is obligated to confirm such nominations. As a matter of fact, there is no obligation on the part of the Senate to even hold hearings on the President's prospective nominee. Speaking personally, I have no problem with the President making his nomination and I certainly have no problem with holding hearings for whoever his nominee might be. But rest assured, the Senate will not give him a blank check and confirm his nominee simply because he made it. I take my role as Judiciary Committee chairman quite seriously. Our committee will act as we always have since I became committee chairman. We will properly vet and give due consideration to any nomination brought before us and we will be open and transparent in our proceedings, which is exactly what the American people demand."

Senator Smith could not, however, say what he really thought about the issue. Having discussed the matter privately with the Republican Senate Majority Leader, the two Republican Senators were of one mind. Namely, there would be no chance of anyone nominated to replace Justice Byers being confirmed by his committee, no matter who was nominated. The two men also agreed because of Senator Smith's candidacy for President, he would have to appear to be acting above board whenever the issue came up during the campaign, as they both knew it would.

The most animated portion of the debate occurred when the moderators turned the attention to national security. All the candidates agreed the Ferrell administration had totally botched their responsibilities when it came to keeping Americans safe.

It is shameful, some said, to see so many of our vets not receiving competent medical attention in a timely fashion, despite the fact they are deserving of nothing less. Unfortunately for Senator Smith's competition, only he had worn the uniform in service to his country, and he was not about to let this fact go unnoticed.

"Having served in the military," began Senator Smith, "I am keenly aware of how bad war can be. We've all heard the stories of how poorly the soldiers were treated when they came home from Viet Nam. It may have been an unpopular war, but those who served did so because they were called by their country to serve and ordered by their Commander-in-Chief to go and fight. I can't tell you how many times I have been asked over the past several years if I regretted my time in Viet Nam. My answer has always been the same: *Hell no!*"

"The reason my fellow soldiers and I went and fought in Viet Nam is so our children wouldn't have to when they got older. Our warriors today fight for the same reason. They are willing to make the ultimate sacrifice if necessary so today's children won't have to fight when they become adults. The problem we are seeing today is the same one I saw when I wore the uniform. We have a Commander-in-Chief who is not serious about defeating the enemy. President Ferrell refuses to bomb the enemy because he's afraid the explosions over there might send harmful gasses into the air and harm the ozone! He's more concerned about limiting what he perceives as damage to the earth's precious eco-system than he is about destroying an enemy who has vowed to kill us."

"And Vice President Hogue is no better," the Senator continued. "They both have declared climate change is a greater threat to our national security than Islamic terrorism. This level of incompetence is staggering. They refuse to acknowledge we are at war with radical Islam. I make this solemn promise to the American citizens: When I become Commander-in-Chief of our military, I will untie the hands of our men and women in uniform and unleash the might of our military force and completely destroy the radical terrorists who have pledged their lives to our destruction. I couldn't care less about what religion they want to practice, but when their religious beliefs call for our annihilation, then it's time for us to act and wipe them off the face of the earth, which is exactly what I am going to do as President."

The live audience present for the debate erupted in thunderous applause, despite the debate moderators' suggestion at the outset not to display reactions to individual candidate's remarks. They simply couldn't help themselves. Senator Smith's remarks were exactly what Republican voters had been longing to hear, which were in stark contrast to the mollycoddling being done by the Ferrell administration towards the threat of global terrorism. Following the debate, the political pundits doing commentary agreed Governor Alan and Senator Smith had the best night, with a slight edge to the Senator. The momentum was definitely on their side and most prognosticators predicted the Iowa contest would be a close battle between the two.

The Iowa polls leading up to the debate and one poll taken after the debate proved to be accurate. Governor Alan carried most of the evangelical vote in Iowa and won the caucus 35% to 32% over Senator Smith, who did better amongst voters who considered national security to be their top issue. The *also-rans* divided up the remaining vote, but the overall results were clear: it would be a two-man race to the end.

The Democrat side of the Iowa Caucus was another story entirely, as V.P. Hogue had only token opposition. Everyone knew Hogue would be the presumptive nominee of the Democrat Party, but the party elites felt it necessary to go through the exercise of pretending a legitimate race existed on their side. They felt it important to portray to voters whoever got the Democrat nod for President would have to work and earn it. Utter nonsense, of course, as only Vice President Hogue had a shot at the Democrat nomination and everyone knew it.

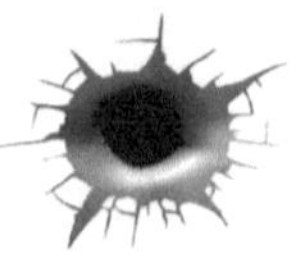
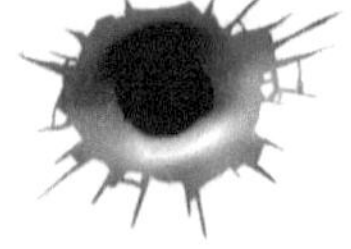
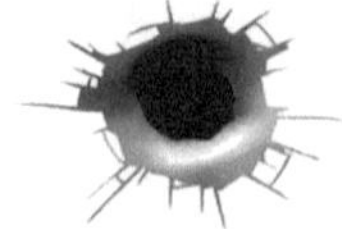

Chapter Eleven

In bold letters above the fold of the front page of the Washington Chronicle read the day's headline: *Byers Murdered, Body Found in Porno Theater.*

Casey Dean had broken the thing wide open. Quoting anonymous sources close to the investigation, her story revealed Justice Byers had been murdered inside the *21st Street Bijou* movie theater, known to show only XXX-rated movies. After her conversation with Detective O'Rourke about the investigation, Casey went back to the theater and spoke with the manager and several other employees. While somewhat reluctant to speak to a reporter about the dead body found inside his theater, the manager surprisingly knew almost nothing about the murder, telling Ms. Dean he had always assumed some old guy just died of a heart attack.

"Did you not see any signs of foul play?" she asked him.

"I remember seeing a little blood on the seat behind his head, but I figured he hit his head or something when he passed out," the manager answered. "I had no idea the guy had been murdered."

"Do you know the name of the victim?" Casey asked.

"No. No idea," he replied.

"Hayden Byers," she said. "Does that name ring a bell?"

"Never heard of him," the manager responded.

She thanked the manager and the other employees for their time and left. Before running her story, Ms. Dean asked for official comments from the D.C. police and the FBI. She got a bunch of *no comments* in response.

President Ferrell's press secretary would not have the luxury of that response at his daily presser. Knowing he would be hounded about the article in the Chronicle, he nonetheless faced reporters at his daily press briefing shortly after the publication of the article.

"The article in this morning's Washington Chronicle," began the first question, "indicates Justice Byers was murdered. Is the article accurate, and if so, why are we just now learning of this?"

"First of all, as I have said many times in the past, this case is under investigation by the FBI. If the FBI wants to comment on the status of their investigation then I'm going to leave it up to them."

"I'm not asking you to comment on their investigation," the reporter continued. "I'm asking whether or not Justice Byers was murdered as this morning's article alleges."

"I think it's safe to say Justice Byers did not die of natural causes. The FBI now considers this to be a murder investigation but until they reach a conclusion, I don't feel comfortable stating emphatically here today a murder occurred. I don't know what the investigation will inevitably uncover."

Rising from his chair in the back of room, another reporter asked the press secretary a follow up question.

"Is it true the police found Justice Byers' body inside a triple-X rated movie theater?" he asked.

"Yes," responded the press secretary. "That part of the story is true."

"When did the President hear of Justice Byers' death and had he been told where they found his body?" came another question.

"He received a call the night of Justice Byers' passing and yes, he was told where his body had been found," came the response.

For obvious reasons, the one word any administration would never want to be associated with is the word *cover-up*. The next reporter dropped it and the press secretary reacted as one would expect.

"Did the administration try to cover up some of the details surrounding the death of Justice Byers for political reasons? Were they afraid of being embarrassed if the details came out about Justice Byers' whereabouts at the time of his death?"

"That's a ridiculous question," sniped the press secretary. "Look, there is no cover-up here. The FBI Director felt the less information made public, the better chance his investigators had in solving the case. The President agreed with his assessment. And let me add, Justice Byers has a family. I think it's safe to say the President thought about them when he decided to heed the FBI Director's advice and keep some of the details out of the press."

The same reporter continued.

"The article quotes an anonymous source close to the investigation," he said. "The information from this source indicates Justice Byers had been stabbed in the back of the head. Can you verify if this part of the story is also true?"

"That is something for the FBI to verify, not me."

The press secretary turned and left the podium with several other reporters shouting additional questions as he left the room. Shortly after the press conference concluded, the FBI Director confirmed the nature of Justice Byers' death by stating he had, in fact, died as the result of a stab wound to the back of his head.

"The FBI will use all of its resources to identify the person or persons who committed this heinous act and bring the perpetrators to justice."

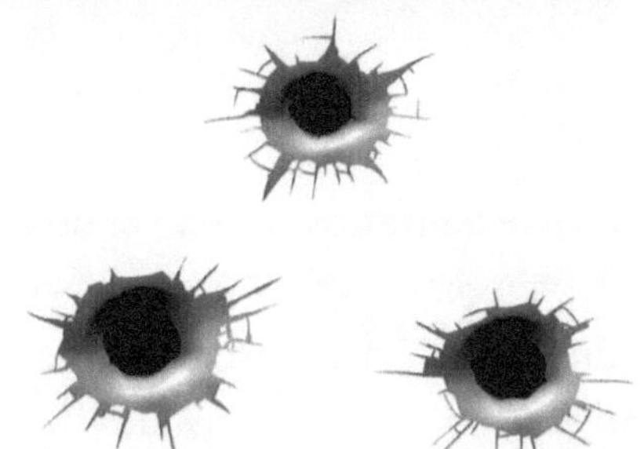

CHAPTER TWELVE

Walking off the 18th green at Lee's Hill Golf Club in Fredericksburg, Virginia, FBI Agent Michaels heard his cell phone ring inside his golf bag. Seeing the name of Detective Jimmy O'Rourke, he assumed he called with an update on the Byers investigation.

"Rich," Jimmy said, "I'm at the medical examiner's office. The autopsy report is back. Can you meet me here?"

"I'm finishing up a round of golf down here in Fredericksburg," Rich replied. "Give me a couple minutes to clean up and I'll be on my way. Shouldn't be more than an hour or so."

"Take your time," replied Jimmy. "I'm not going anywhere. What'd you shoot, by the way?"

"Seventy-five!" Rich replied. "And that's with a double bogey on the last hole."

"Holy crap! You gotta take me out and give me a few pointers," Jimmy responded. "I'm not sure I could shoot that on the front nine. I'm thinking seriously about pulling the plug at the end of the year and I'm going to need a hobby to keep me occupied. I don't think my wife is keen on the idea of me being around the house all the time."

"Understood," replied Rich with a laugh. "Maybe we can get out early next week. I'm walking in the locker room right now so let me go and I'll see you in a few."

"Sounds good," said Jimmy as he hung up his phone.

Rich Michaels took a few minutes to shower off in the clubhouse and got in his car for the drive north to the M.E.'s office in downtown D.C. About forty-five minutes later he walked into the Medical Examiner's office where he found Jimmy seated alongside the M.E. He dropped a bag of Chick-fil-A sandwiches down in front of Jimmy before taking a seat.

"Help yourselves," he said pointing to the bag. "Best chicken sandwiches on the planet."

"What, no waffle fries?" said Jimmy as he peeked inside the bag and removed one of the sandwiches.

"No offense Jimmy, but you might want to stay away from waffle fries," Rich said with a sly grin as Jimmy and the M.E. laughed. "So, what do we have?"

The case file, filled with several photographs and various reports the medical examiner had written, sat open on the table in front of Jimmy. He slid it over in Rich's direction so he could take a closer look. The first picture on top of the file showed the back of Justice Byers' head with the skin of his scalp peeled around the front of his skull, revealing a puncture wound at the base of his skull.

"I'll let the M.E. tell you what he's told me about this photo," said Jimmy. "Go ahead, sir," he said to the medical examiner.

The M.E. leaned over and pointed to the photo in Rich's hand.

"As you can plainly see," he began as he pointed to a spot on the photo showing the entry wound, "penetration of the skull occurred here, right below the occipital lobe. Once the metal spoke entered that portion of the cranial cavity, it completely passed through the occipital lobe, all the way through the temporal lobe and partially into the frontal lobe. This other photograph shows the destruction of brain tissue by the entry of the foreign object into his brain, with more damage occurring upon removal of the object."

"Do we know exactly what the metal rod is?" asked Agent Michaels.

"It appears to be an ordinary bicycle spoke," replied the medical examiner. "A normal spoke would be about fifteen or sixteen inches long. This one had been snipped in half to about eight inches in length.

As you can see, one end has been sharpened, presumably to make it easier to penetrate the bone."

"I don't suppose there would be any way to trace something as common as a bicycle spoke, is there?" Rich asked.

"Not likely," responded Jimmy.

"What about prints?" asked Rich as he held up the plastic bag containing the metal spoke for a closer look. "Any chance our killer left any?"

"Not a chance," replied Jimmy. "Probably wore gloves."

"How about DNA?" came yet another question from the ever-inquisitive FBI agent.

"Good question," replied Jimmy. "Obviously the killer had to get right up next to the victim, so one would think there would be some minor transfer of DNA by the killer. Unfortunately, we couldn't find any. The blood and brain matter from Justice Byers were the only DNA on the metal spoke. My guess is besides wearing gloves; our killer probably wore a long-sleeved shirt or jacket as well. We swabbed every square inch of Byers' seat, the seat behind him and three or four others, looking for anything the killer may have left behind. If he were the least bit nervous about committing the murder, you'd think he would have left behind a hint of perspiration or something. Unfortunately, he didn't. No trace of anything."

"I think we can rule out this being a random killing," commented Agent Michaels. "The judge still had his wallet in his pocket and an expensive watch on his wrist, so it's safe to assume robbery wasn't the motive. This shows every sign of being a professional hit. This guy obviously knew what he was doing."

"All right," continued Agent Michaels, "so the guy had to be sitting directly behind the victim when he stabbed him through the back of the head. Assuming our killer had to wait to see where the victim would sit, I'm guessing he came in and sat down after the movie started and after the judge had taken his seat."

"I think that's probably correct," said Detective O'Rourke.

"So, once he's seated," continued Rich as he scooted forward on the edge of his seat, attempting to mimic the movements of the killer, "he takes out the metal spoke, leans forward a little bit and drives it into the victim's skull. But nobody saw or heard anything, right?"

"That's right," replied Jimmy. "With all the moaning and groaning going on in the movie, I'm not sure anyone would have heard anything anyways."

Agent Michaels and the M.E. laughed.

"Were you able to determine the exact time of death?" Rich asked the medical examiner.

"We can never be precisely accurate on the exact time," replied the M.E. "At least not to the minute. But more than likely, looking at the nature of the wound, I would say death occurred within moments of the attack, somewhere around midnight. Because of the small size of the entrance wound, there isn't much blood evidence to process. As you can see in this other photo, the bleeding that did occur caused a small blood stain to the back of his sweatshirt here," added the M.E. as he pointed to another photo showing the back of the victim's hoodie.

"The injury to the brain most probably caused immediate incapacitation followed by the blood loss," continued the M.E. "Once unconscious, the damage to his brain would have basically caused the rest of his body to shut down. His heart quit beating and he quietly died in his seat."

"If we can agree this wasn't a random killing," Agent Michaels said, "then why the judge?"

Rich looked at Jimmy and said, "let's check the D.C. police database and see if Byers' name comes up anywhere. Has he been the victim of a crime before this, or has he ever filed a police report in the past?"

"Way ahead of you, partner," replied Jimmy. "No records of him in our database. As a matter of fact, there is no record of any police unit ever responding to a call at his house. Ever."

"Tell you what," said Rich. "I'll head back to the office and start putting together a file on his background. Perhaps he made a ruling since being on the Supreme Court that pissed somebody off. Enough to want him knocked off. That's probably as good a place as any to start."

"Agreed," replied Jimmy.

Agent Michaels thanked the medical examiner for his work and put the file on Byers in his briefcase and left for his office.

"I'll give you a call if I turn anything up," Rich said to Jimmy as they parted ways in the parking lot. "In the meantime, get your clubs out of storage and wipe the spider webs off. Hopefully we'll be able to hit the links next week. But forget asking for strokes, something tells me you're trying to sandbag me."

Jimmy smiled as he got into his car.

"By the way," Jimmy said to Rich, "here's the number to someone I know who has been covering the Supreme Court for several years. I'm not sure if she can help you or not, but she knows more about the Court than anyone I know. She's a reporter for the Washington Chronicle and can probably help you with background stuff on Byers. Her name is Casey Dean."

"Thanks," replied Rich. "I'll definitely give her a call."

Back at his office, Agent Michaels began researching everything in Justice Byers' past he could find. Spending about an hour on the phone with Ms. Dean, Rich picked her brain about Supreme Court decisions handed down since Byers' confirmation to the Court. Casey thoroughly impressed Rich with her depth of knowledge of how the Supreme Court functioned and how decisions were reached. He knew a little bit about some of the Supreme Court decisions Byers had been involved with, but Casey gave him insight into the justice's thinking and how some of those decisions were reached.

"Take a look at his past," Casey told Rich. "When you read some of his opinions on cases the Court has ruled on since he's been a sitting justice, it sounds like he lost his mind. Then, when you look back thirty years or so at his radical past before becoming a Supreme Court justice, his decisions start to make a little more sense."

"You're looking for suspects?" Casey asked Rich. "People who might want this guy dead? Well, let's see now. How about ultra conservative

Republicans, religious zealots, gun lovers, right-to-lifers, blue dog Democrats, white supremacists, Catholic nuns. It's a pretty long list. Radical leftists, so-called progressive Democrats and communist sympathizers all loved the guy. Other than them, everybody else pretty much hated him."

"So, my suspect list starts at about ten million?" asked Rich. "Is that what you're telling me?"

"I'd say more like twenty," Casey replied.

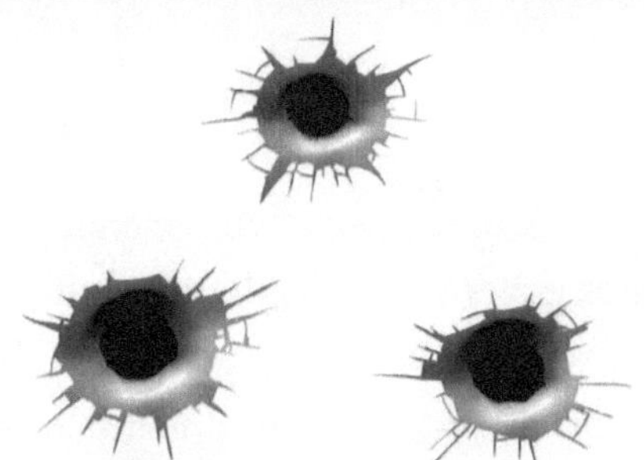

Chapter Thirteen

The New Sons of Liberty sat around the dinner table in Jupiter's basement enjoying an impressive spread of steak, lobster and Maryland crab cakes. After opening a case of fine wine, shipped in from the Tuscan wine region in Italy, Jupiter filled the glasses of his fellow patriots from a 2005 bottle of Chateau Rauzan Segla, one of his favorites.

"Let us raise our glasses," he began, "and give a toast to Janus and Apollo for the work they did to help further our cause."

"Here, here," said everyone at the table in unison, as they brought their glasses together above the center of the table.

"We have struck another mighty blow against the forces of evil attempting to strip us all of our God-given rights," Jupiter said, "not to mention the liberties guaranteed to us by the U.S. Constitution. Two more pieces of human garbage that worked tirelessly to weaken our country have been eliminated. We should all be proud of the job done by our worthy colleagues."

Everyone around the table smiled and began slapping their hands on the table in front of them in recognition of the successful missions carried out in San Francisco and New York by Janus and Apollo respectively.

Setting down his glass of wine and shoving a wad of chewing tobacco into his mouth, Apollo rose to address the group.

"Right now," began Apollo, "we have the element of surprise on our side. Our incompetent government leaders and the rest of their commie friends have no idea what's happening to them. They haven't figured out yet their way of life is under assault and for now this works to our advantage. Sooner or later, however, it will become apparent to them war has been declared on their leftist agenda."

"I'm fine with that," said Neptune in response. "I want them to know what's going on. In fact, I want the entire nation to know these radicals are no longer going to be able to continue destroying our country with impunity. All of us at this table have fought to preserve the freedoms we have and I'll be damned if we're going to sit idly by and watch a bunch of communist sympathizers turn our great country into a bastion of socialist liberals."

"Amen to that," responded Janus.

Everyone else nodded his head in agreement.

Walking over to his basement bar to retrieve a file folder, Jupiter returned and opened the file in front of them.

"Time to discuss new business," he said. "I want us to consider a new target. And as always, we must be unanimous in approving this so I want to present this for your consideration."

"Who is it?" asked Orcus.

"Senator Edmund Riley," replied Jupiter.

"The Democrat leader in the Senate?" asked Neptune.

"The same," replied Jupiter. "Let's look at some facts".

Jupiter proceeded to inform the group about how radically to the left this United States Senator had become. Now in his early sixties, Senator Riley currently served as the senior Senator from California and had been in the U.S. Senate for over thirty years. His first election for the Senate took place during the George H.W. Bush administration, at a time when California began lurching further leftward. Although Ronald Reagan had won California in the 1980 and 1984 elections, the state had become much more liberal and considered nearly impossible for any Republican to carry in a statewide election.

Senate Democrats elected Edmund Riley, one of President's Ferrell's closest allies in Congress, Senate Majority Leader two years before Rob Ferrell's election to his first term. Throughout the Ferrell presidency, Senator Riley had basically carried the water for President Ferrell. During the first two years of President Ferrell's first term, the Democrats controlled both houses of Congress and enjoyed a filibuster-proof majority in the Senate. When President Ferrell proposed his massive government takeover of the nation's healthcare system, Senator Riley strong-armed fellow Democrat senators into supporting the legislation, resulting in a new healthcare law essentially shoved down the throats of the American people. The legislation passed without getting a single vote of support from the Republicans.

The first mid-term elections during President Ferrell's initial term in office saw control of the House of Representatives change hands in favor of the Republican Party. Senator Riley, however, continued to serve as Senate Majority Leader following the election, as Democrats were able to hold onto power in the Senate. With the House of Representatives in the hands of Republicans, dozens of pieces of legislation passed the House and were subsequently sent to the Senate for consideration. In almost every case President Ferrell opposed the legislation passed by the Republican-controlled House. Instead of moving the legislation to the Senate floor for consideration, Senator Riley shelved it, refusing to allow the bills to be considered. Presumably, the Senator did this so President Ferrell would never be forced to veto a bill most Americans might support.

Edmund Riley had begun his political career as the Mayor of Fresno, California. Before the term had become well known in political lexicon, he strongly advocated in favor of Fresno's status as a sanctuary city. He felt then (and more strongly now) illegal Mexican immigrants should not be forced out of the country by deportation because of all the services they provided to U.S. employers, especially those businesses in the California agriculture industry. Furthermore, like most other Democrats, he believed if these illegal immigrants were ever afforded the ability to vote in U.S. elections, they would most certainly vote for their side.

Senator Riley grew up in a middle-class household in Madera, California, a small town north of Fresno. After graduating from Cal-Berkeley (a well-known citadel of liberalism), he moved to Fresno where he ran for and won a seat on the city council. After serving two terms as a city councilman, Riley was elected Mayor. During his second mayoral term, he decided to run for the U.S. Senate when one of the sitting Senators announced his retirement. Enjoying extremely high popularity as Mayor and a well-deserved reputation as a liberal stalwart, Riley easily won election to represent California in the U.S. Senate. Despite a mayoral salary of only $60,000 a year and a U.S. senate salary of $175,000 a year, Senator Riley had somehow been able to amass a personal net worth of close to ten million dollars. No doubt this had a lot to do with his ability as the Senate Majority Leader to steer billions of dollars in government programs to his state and, more specifically, to his many friends in the California agriculture industry. Political conservatives truly detested Edmund Riley.

"Gentlemen," said Jupiter as he looked around the room at each man individually, "you know how I feel about this piece of crap, but this is not my decision alone. We must all be of one mind. Your thoughts?"

Apollo rose first to chime in, seeming a bit more reserved than the others.

"Look," he began. "I have no argument with you this guy is a genuine piece of shit. God knows if we were in the business of taking out every asshole we came across we'd end up running out of bullets. But this group is about changing the dynamics of this country. Our job, as I see it, is to let the bastards who are bent on destroying the liberties we have enjoyed for the past two centuries, know they have encountered a movement, a force if you will, that's going to destroy them if they continue. This guy is certainly a first-rate piece of garbage, but essentially, he's just another politician. For God's sake, he could be voted out of office and would go back to being another nobody."

"Are you sure he's just another politician?" asked Janus as he rose to give his perspective. "As the majority leader in the Senate, he used his power to advance every left-wing program put forward by this worthless President of ours. He stood on the Senate floor at the beginning of Ferrell's presidency and said his purpose in life is to work with President Ferrell in fundamentally transforming America."

"But you're making my point, Janus," Apollo replied. "He's not the majority leader any longer. The Republicans control the Senate now. Riley is powerless to do anything. If this bastard still ran the senate, then I think I would agree to put him at the top of our list for consideration."

"But with all due respect, Apollo," interjected Neptune. "I think there is one thing you are overlooking."

"What's that?" asked Apollo in response.

"The message," said Neptune. "Part of what we are doing is sending a message. I'll cede your point right now Senator Riley is not in the powerful position he once occupied. And you're right; theoretically, he could be voted out of office in the next election. But you could also say, theoretically, the Senate could go back to the Democrats and if that happened he would go right back to being in charge, doing all the same shit as before."

"But regardless of that," Neptune continued, "my point is the matter of sending a message. I want anybody, irrespective of position or political affiliation, to know what happened to Riley can happen to them as well if they try going down the same road."

"So, it's more than retribution against Senator Riley," replied Apollo. "You see this as a way of discouraging someone else from taking the same actions as he did."

"Exactly," replied Neptune.

"Not bad," Orcus said to Neptune. "I wasn't sure myself which way to lean, but I have to hand it to you, that's a pretty good argument."

"I see your point as well," Apollo conceded. "My reticence may have been a bit premature. I'm willing to side with the majority on this one."

"Jupiter," Apollo said addressing the leader of this group directly, "if you feel strongly about this one then I am on board. Count me as a yes."

"I most certainly do," replied Jupiter.

The vote was unanimous. Senator Edmund Riley would be the next target of the *New Sons of Liberty*, sentenced to death by the collective will of this group of patriots for the commission of crimes against the liberty and freedoms they so reverently held.

"Mark my words, gentlemen," said Jupiter. "This one will not be easy. He has security around him everywhere he goes, especially in the Capitol building. There's going to be U.S. Marshals, Capitol Police, a bunch of staff assistants. We can't be sloppy on this one. I don't want there to be any collateral damage."

"Don't worry, sir," said Neptune. "There won't be".

"Alright," said Jupiter to the group. "Now that we've settled on him, let's move on to the next item. Apollo, why don't you fill us in on what you've been working on."

After spitting out a mouthful of brown juice into a paper cup, Apollo rose to once again address the *Sons*. He removed an 8x10 photo from a manila envelope and passed it around the table.

"Who's this schmuck-looking douche bag?" Neptune asked with a laugh.

"I'll get to him in a minute," Apollo replied with a sly smile. "As I'm sure you all know, there's an election happening next November we all should be concerned about. If the Democrats hold on to the White House, what we've been witnessing for the past several years under our current bastard-in-chief is going to get worse. And believe me, the Democrats are going to do everything they can, fair and unfair, to hang onto power. Now, Jupiter and I are old enough to remember what happened in 1960 when Kennedy stole the election from Nixon. So, let me give you youngsters a quick history lesson."

Apollo spent the next ten minutes recounting to the group the history, or at least the version of history many Democrat detractors believe, of how Kennedy won the presidency by *stealing* the election from Richard Nixon. During the 1960 election, so goes the popularized theory, Texas Senator Lyndon Johnson, Kennedy's V.P. running mate, used his powerful Texas political machine to ensure Kennedy carried the state of Texas by outright fraud in the election process. Many believe to this day surrogates working for the Kennedy-Johnson ticket manipulated the vote tallies in Texas by including the names of people casting votes for Kennedy who were either dead or simply did not exist. Likewise, in the state of Illinois, the powerful Democrat mayor of Chicago, Richard Daley, supposedly used his influence to accomplish the same, helping to deny Nixon a victory in that state as well. Although never proven, if true, the flipping of those two states in favor of the Kennedy-Johnson ticket most assuredly changed the outcome of the election. Despite the controversy and the allegations of *vote fixing*, Nixon refused to contest the election results; saying at the time it would tear the nation apart.

"And that brings us to this guy," Apollo said while holding up the photograph of the man destined to be another target of the *New Sons of Liberty*.

"Who is he," asked Janus, "and how does he fit into our plans?"

"His name is Fred Stein. He's a community organizer in Cincinnati," replied Apollo.

"A community organizer?" Neptune asked with some level of skepticism in his voice. "What possible danger does this guy pose to our cause?"

Orcus and Janus also looked somewhat puzzled at Apollo as he continued to address the *Sons*.

"I know at first blush it doesn't seem this guy would make a worthy target of ours. But let me assure you he is indeed worthy of our attention. First off, let me remind you how important it will be to deny that piece of shit Hogue a victory in Ohio in the general election. They know if they can pull off a win there, the election will most certainly go to them since no Republican has ever won the presidency without winning Ohio. Stein is a darling of the political left and is close friends with both Ferrell and Hogue. He's spent more nights sleeping in the Lincoln bedroom than anybody else over the past year. Jupiter and I have no doubt they are using Mr. Stein to exert his influence over the voting districts in and around Cincinnati to rig the election in their favor. Stein has been one of the leading advocates against voter ID laws and we all know why. He wants as many people currently residing in Cincinnati cemeteries to cast their vote for the Democrat nominee. We can't allow it to happen. What happened to Nixon in 1960 is not going to happen again this year if we can help it."

"We all know how important the upcoming election is going to be," chimed in Janus. "How do you want us to handle Stein?"

"I'm glad you asked, Janus," interjected Jupiter. "This one is going to be yours. We want you to head to Cincy in a few weeks and start doing recon on Stein. His office is on St. James Avenue near Eden Park. You can pick him up there and see where he goes. Get back to Apollo with your ideas on the best way to take him out and we'll go from there."

"You got it boss," replied Janus. "Now if you guys don't mind, I've got a date tonight with a delicious little co-ed from George Mason. Apparently, those weeny college boys don't do it for her. I'm going to give her a chance to see what it's like to be with a real man. I think she likes these big guns," he added, flexing his enormous biceps for the rest of his colleagues.

"Hopefully she likes little dicks as well," added Neptune as everyone else laughed.

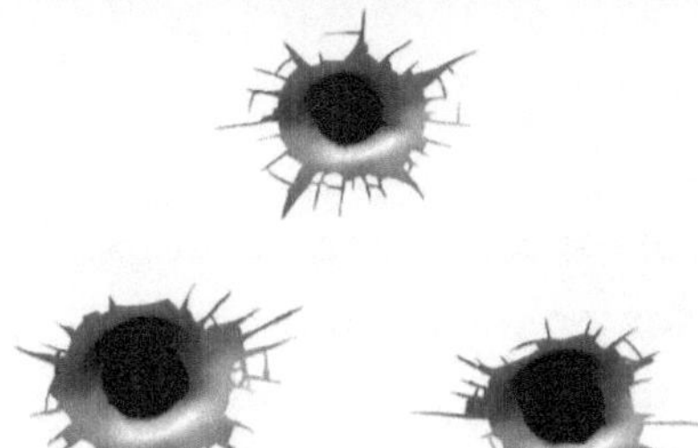

Chapter Fourteen

Indiana Governor Alan clearly had the momentum coming out of Iowa. His victory there propelled him to the top of the national polls, slightly ahead of Senator Smith and way out in front of the others. With campaign donations drying up, the other contenders were not long for this race.

Money has been called the *Mother's Milk* of politics because no candidate has a chance of being relevant without it. The steel magnate, Mark Wooddall, had plenty of his own money to spend so his campaign was much less dependent on donations.

Senator Smith had a huge lead in the New Hampshire polls, partly because he hailed from another northeastern state–New Jersey. His performance at the Republican debate and his strong second place finish in Iowa established him as the front-runner. Governor Alan would be the only thing standing between him and the nomination.

Wooddall was from Pennsylvania and felt the strength of his campaign would be in the primary states that made up what is known as the Rust Belt. A region of the country once considered an industrial powerhouse, the Rust Belt includes the states of New York, Pennsylvania, Michigan, Ohio, West Virginia, Illinois, Indiana and Wisconsin. Wooddall had been hammering Governor Alan and Senator Smith with ads depicting them as part of the political establishment who were nothing more than tools of the political elite. Portraying himself as a genuine outsider, Wooddall tried to convince primary voters he would not be beholden to the special interests and lobbyists who have been controlling Washington politicians like puppets.

It's the politicians who have gotten this country into the mess we're in, read one of his ads. *If you want the mess to continue, then elect another politician. If you want somebody to go to Washington and clean up the mess then you need to elect me. I'm not a Washington politician and I won't go there and become one.*

After nearly eight years of an administration that looked at everything through a political lens, Wooddall felt the country, and more specifically Republican primary voters, wanted someone to represent them who was not part of the political class. He certainly had a point. Wooddall had no political experience but had managed a strong third place standing in the national polls. His biggest problem would be how to convince voters he had the intelligence and skills necessary to govern effectively. While many voters certainly despised the political class in Washington, many others were wary of turning the reins of government over to someone with no political experience.

Wooddall had another political problem and the Alan and Smith campaigns were beginning to hit him on it in their political ads. Namely, Wooddall's previously held position of supporting U.S. tariffs on imported steel several years earlier. As the President and CEO of American Steel, Inc., Wooddall had once testified before a congressional subcommittee on the merits of the U.S. imposing crippling tariffs on imported steel. At the time, the steel industry in America had begun hemorrhaging jobs and profits due to cheap steel being dumped into the U.S. from China, Japan, Europe and a few South American countries. As a steel executive, Wooddall's support of the tariffs showed he cared less about the American consumer and more about protecting his company's bottom line.

When the administration at the time approved the imposition of the steel tariffs Wooddall backed, competition from foreign steel producers went away, having an immediate effect on the bottom line of American Steel, as well as Wooddall's personal pocketbook. His company increased its profitability almost overnight because the steel coming in from other countries became too expensive to import due to the high U.S. tariffs. Although the tariffs may have had a positive impact on Wooddall's company, it proved detrimental to the country, causing unintended consequences now troubling the Wooddall campaign.

The protection of the U.S. steel industry through the imposition of steel tariffs had perverse effects in this way: it reduced production of steel in the U.S., increased costs to users, and increased unemployment in associated industries. Furthermore, the tariffs ignited an international controversy as well. As a response to the action by the U.S., the European Union announced if the U.S. tariffs were not immediately rescinded, they would impose retaliatory tariffs on U.S. goods coming into Europe. They specifically targeted goods like oranges from Florida and cars from Michigan, a strategy designed to hurt the economy of those two political swing states. The Alan and Smith campaigns attacked Wooddall on this issue by accusing him of being against free trade and for supporting policies that caused significant job loss and rising prices for American consumers, neither of which were considered conservative ideals.

Wooddall would not be deterred. Aggressively campaigning in New Hampshire with several rallies and town hall meetings, Wooddall pounded home the theme of him being the only outsider running. While this may have appealed to some New Hampshire Republicans, as well as primary voters throughout the country, Wooddall knew he had no chance of winning New Hampshire. He merely sought a respectable finish, which would establish him as a viable contender. Conventional political wisdom held there would only be three tickets out of New Hampshire and he wanted to be one of them. With a winnowed field of only three candidates, he felt his outsider status would give him a real shot at the nomination. He was wrong.

The results of the New Hampshire vote were exactly what Senator Smith's campaign had been praying for. He won decisively with Governor Alan coming in a distant second and Mark Wooddall a distant third. "Thank you, New Hampshire," shouted Senator Smith to his adoring crowd gathered in the ballroom of the Manchester Marriott Hotel. "We came to New Hampshire with one goal in mind: to be victorious. All the volunteers, the knocking on doors, the thousands of phone calls, have resulted not just in a win, but in a resounding victory!"

The sounds of boisterous applause and cheers began to reverberate all around the room. Supporters began waving *Smith for President* signs while chants of USA! USA! echoed throughout.

"Iowa picks corn," continued Senator Smith, alluding to the Iowa caucus results where his main contender Governor Alan won, "but New Hampshire picks candidates!"

More cheers and more applause.

"As this campaign continues and gets ready to move south," Smith continued, "we will continue to tell the truth about what President Ferrell and his administration are doing to the American way of life. The Ferrell-Hogue philosophy of governance has been one of higher taxes and more regulations, which have dealt a devastating blow to our nation's economy. They have launched an all-out assault on our religious liberties and are doing everything in their power to take away our second amendment rights. This will not stand!"

The cheers and applause reached a crescendo. All the cable news channels were carrying his victory speech live and all agreed on the importance of Senator Smith's astounding margin of victory. Exit polls, they reported, showed late deciders breaking for Smith. Although favored in the polls going into the election, he did better than the polls indicated. With his campaign now surging, many of the pundits doing post-election coverage on T.V. acknowledged the Senator looked poised for the nomination.

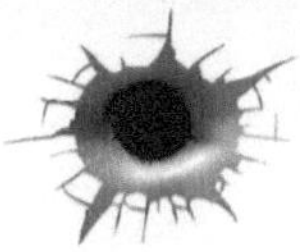

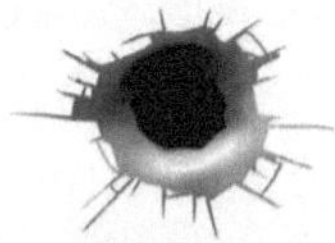

CHAPTER FIFTEEN

Rich Michaels sat at his desk in the FBI's Washington Field Office on 4th Street, NW, when Jimmy O'Rourke walked in the door. Jimmy removed two foam containers from a bag and placed them on Rich's desk.

"What'd you bring me?" Agent Michaels smiled.

"Take out from The Old Ebbitt Grill," answered Jimmy. "Jumbo lump crab cakes. I figured you wouldn't have taken the time to go get lunch."

"You figured right. Thanks, they smell good. Pull up a chair."

Rich had the Byers case file opened on his desk, looking over the autopsy report and photos, while thumbing through the daily planner they had retrieved from Byers' home.

"I've been going over his planner again," said Rich, "and I think I have an idea which might be worth pursuing."

"Go on," said Jimmy. "This investigation could definitely use some new ideas."

Agent Michaels opened a desk drawer and pulled out a map of D.C. and spread it out in front of Jimmy.

"Now, the Byers murdered occurred here at the *21st Street Bijou Theater*," Rich said as he pointed to a spot on the map where the theater is located. "His car sat in his garage at his house, so let's assume he got there on the night in question by taking the Metro."

"Sounds reasonable so far," added Jimmy. "Go on."

"Now," said Rich as he continued to concentrate his gaze on the map before them, "the DuPont Circle Metro stop is the closest one to the theater. It's right here," he said pointing to its location on the map. "And the *Bijou* is right here (pointing to another spot). Assuming he took the Metro to the theater on the night he died, he probably got out at the DuPont Circle stop and then walked the three blocks or so to the theater."

"I'm with you," said Jimmy. "Go on."

"Now, in his little book here," Rich continued, tapping his finger on the daily planner found in Justice Byers' home, "he thought someone had been following him on at least two different occasions. Both of his entries, I might add, were within days of the murder."

"Yeah," said Jimmy. "He thought he might have been followed by some guy with a limp."

"Exactly," replied Rich. "Now we agree the killer was no amateur. And according to the manager, Byers came to the *Bijou* frequently. I think it's safe to assume our killer knew that as well. That being the case, he either followed Byers to the theater or went there on his own and waited for him to show up. In either case, it's possible we've got a video of our killer at one of the Metro stations near the theater."

"You mean on the video surveillance cameras inside each of the Metro stations?" asked Jimmy.

"Yes," replied Rich. "Do you know anything about their taping system?"

"As a matter of fact, I do," Jimmy responded. "I worked a murder case last year which happened inside the Union Station Metro stop. Let me clarify that. It started out as an accidental death investigation. Some guy fell onto the tracks as a train pulled into the station. A couple hundred people were standing around when it happened and everybody I talked to said the guy lost his balance and accidentally fell onto the track when the train pulled in. It became a murder investigation after I got hold of the video feed. The tape clearly showed the guy being pushed from behind two seconds before the train arrived. No accident to be sure."

"How long do they hang onto those tapes?" Rich asked.

"The video feed for every station gets transferred onto a DVD every night after midnight," responded Jimmy. "They're stored at the corporate office over on 5th street. I think they keep them about a year or so before destroying them."

Agent Michaels again looked down at the Metro map on his desk.

"Okay," he began. "Let's start with tapes from the DuPont Circle station and the Metro stations closest to it. There's Farragut North, Woodley Park, Cleveland Park and Van Ness on the Red Line. Then we have Columbia Heights on the Green Line and Farragut West and Foggy Bottom on the Blue. That's as good a place as any to start. It should keep me busy for a while."

"Do me a favor," Rich said to Jimmy. "Give them a call over at the Metro headquarters and tell them I'm going to need two days' worth of tapes for each of those Metro stations leading up to the day of Byers' murder. In the meantime, I'll head over to our Regional Counsel's office and pick up an administrative subpoena for the tapes. Tell them I'll be there within the hour."

"You got it," replied Jimmy.

Rich Michaels, back at his desk two hours later with a box of DVDs, popped the first one into his laptop and settled back in his chair for what he knew would be a long night. This part of the job a lot of other agents would not be willing to do. The idea of sitting at one's desk for hours looking for a sliver of a clue on a computer screen does not appeal to most investigators. Not Rich Michaels, however, which is one reason he enjoyed the reputation of being so good at his job. Considering this anything but wasted effort, he would spend whatever time necessary to find something, anything, to help him break this case. Knowing he wouldn't make it home until after midnight, if at all, Agent Michaels called his wife and told her not to wait up.

Seven hours had passed when Agent Michaels polished off his second pot of coffee. A crumpled bag from the DGS Delicatessen on Connecticut Avenue lay on the floor beside his chair, with crumbs from his roast beef hoagie scattered across the top of his desk. He had already pulled up the tape from DuPont Circle and identified Justice Byers getting off the train and making his way to the exit. Playing and replaying the tape several times, he could not spot anyone else in the crowd appearing to have a limp. Now looking at the tape from the Woodley Park station, he noticed the time stamp on the video feed indicated the recording had taken place approximately one hour before the start time of the movie Byers had attended. As he glared at his computer screen, Agent Michaels noticed a man walking off the train with a noticeable limp, wearing dark pants, a dark shirt and a baseball cap.

Is this our guy? Rich thought.

Agent Michaels ran the tape back so he could concentrate on the subject from the moment he stepped off the train and the surveillance camera inside the Metro tunnel picked him up. The guy definitely had a limp but he never appeared to look up so the camera could get a picture of his face. Rich switched tapes to see the video feed from another camera where the turnstiles and ticket booth were located. Clearly visible on the second tape, the subject exited through the turnstiles and left the Metro station. Although the guy never allowed the camera to get a shot of his face, Agent Michaels could make a general description of the suspect.

Six feet tall, about 200 pounds, he thought. *Not much for now, but at least it's a start.*

Too late to call Jimmy O'Rourke, Rich needed to get home and get some sleep. Shutting it down for the night, he grabbed his briefcase and left for home, knowing he would be back at it first thing in the morning.

Rich rang Jimmy on his way into the office after a solid four hours of sleep.

"I may have something, Jimmy," he said into his phone as he headed down the I-395 exit ramp onto Massachusetts Avenue. "Meet me at my office and I'll show you what I've got."

"On the way," Jimmy replied.

Twenty minutes later Jimmy walked into Rich's office and slid a chair beside Agent Michaels' desk.

"What are we looking at?" asked Jimmy as he sat down and looked at the open laptop on Agent Michael's desk.

Rich pulled up the video shot he had discovered the previous evening of Justice Byers departing the Metro at DuPont Circle, presumably on his way to the theater. After allowing Jimmy to view it, he then grabbed the DVD from the Woodley Park station so Jimmy could see the person Rich now considered suspect number one in the murder of Supreme Court Justice Hayden Byers.

"Take a look at what I found last night," Rich said to Jimmy.

He clicked the *play* button on the video feed so Jimmy O'Rourke could see the suspect get off the train at Woodley Park and make his way out of the tunnel. Rich put in the second tape, which covered the ticket booth area, so Jimmy could watch the suspect again until he left the view of the surveillance camera and exited the Metro station towards 24th street.

"The guy definitely has a limp," Jimmy noticed. "Do you think he's our guy?"

"Right now, he is," responded Rich.

Michaels ran the Woodley Park tape forward to the time right after the murder occurred, looking to see if the guy with a limp returned. After several minutes of viewing, their suspect reappeared and entered the station.

"There he is," exclaimed Jimmy.

Sure enough, the same guy in all black clothing, walking with a discernable limp, could be seen going through the turnstiles into the train tunnel and boarding the Red Line train headed north. Jimmy took another look at the Metro map spread out on the desk.

"The next station to the north is Cleveland Ave, followed by Van Ness," Jimmy commented. "Slide the box over here and let me find the surveillance tapes for those stations. Let's see if we can pick him up getting off at one of those stops."

Jimmy unzipped his utility bag and removed his own laptop. After finding the tapes for the Cleveland Ave and Van Ness Metro stations, both investigators began viewing the tapes on their respective computers trying to find their suspect again.

In a matter of minutes, the two detectives found what they were looking for. Eight minutes after the Red Line train carrying their suspect departed the Woodley Park station, Jimmy and Rich saw him exit the train at the Van Ness stop. Once again, the investigators could not see his face because of the bill of his baseball cap and he never made the mistake of looking up at any of the cameras. They did notice, however, as he walked he constantly kept looking left, right, then behind.

"Well, if that's not our guy," remarked Jimmy, "why is he constantly checking his six?"

"Checking his six?" Rich asked with some bewilderment in his voice.

"Yeah," replied Jimmy. "Checking his six o'clock. You know, looking behind him."

"Got it," replied Rich. "He's definitely doing that."

"What's near the Van Ness station?" Rich asked.

"D.C. University is right there," replied Jimmy. "Don't know if we'll find any suspects there, though. The place is full of commie lovers. You can bet Byers would be a hero to most of the little minds of mush who attend that university."

"Do they have a Young Republicans chapter there?" asked Rich with a smile.

Jimmy laughed.

"Van Ness Street and Connecticut Ave are the two main thoroughfares running right by there," Jimmy added. "I guess he could've had his car parked there on the street. Maybe he got in his car and drove away." "Makes as much sense as anything else," said Rich. "Does the city have any street-level cameras up there?"

"Not that far north," replied Jimmy. "We have some street cameras in operation but they are primarily in the areas where most of the tourists hang out like on The Mall and near most of the monuments."

"Well, we know he uses the Metro," said Rich. "My guess is if we keep going over these tapes he may show up again somewhere else."

"Let me ask you something, Jimmy," Rich continued. "If you were going to handle this job, what are things you would do to make sure it went off without any hitches, and gave you the best chance of pulling it off without getting caught?"

"The first thing is surveillance," replied Jimmy. "I would want to follow Byers around for a while and see where he likes to go. Does he travel around by himself or with friends? What restaurants does he like to eat at? Stuff like that."

"Or maybe where he likes to go to catch a movie?" said Rich.

"Exactly," responded Jimmy.

"My guess is," continued Rich, "our guy did some extensive surveillance work on Byers prior to the killing. Remember, Byers thought he saw some guy with a limp following him a couple weeks before the murder. Our suspect is definitely a professional. He would not have wanted any surprises and he knew, or had a pretty good idea, Byers would be at the *Bijou*. Remember, Byers went there on a regular basis. There's more than a betting chance our suspect knew it as well."

"Probably why he didn't need to follow him when he got off the train at DuPont Circle," Jimmy added. "He probably knew Byers would be going to the theater and figured he'd just show up and wait for him to take his seat. He may have already been in there when Byers arrived."

"Which would explain why our guy got off at Woodley Park," said Rich. "He probably went to the theater ahead of Byers and just waited for him to come in. Brilliant."

"We're going to need more tapes," said Jimmy. "This guy probably made the same run at least a couple of times before the night of the murder. He would want to be familiar with every step he would take once he left the Woodley Park station and got to the theater and know every inch of the inside of the theater as well. If we keep looking, I'm betting he'll show up on another video feed in the weeks leading up to the murder."

"You're right," said Rich. "Why don't you head over to the Metro corporate office and let them know we're going to need more tapes. I'll get another subpoena to cover it and meet you there in about an hour."

"And don't forget about our golf date," Jimmy said to Rich. "You're looking like you could use a little diversion."

"Funny," replied Rich. "My wife told me the very same thing this morning."

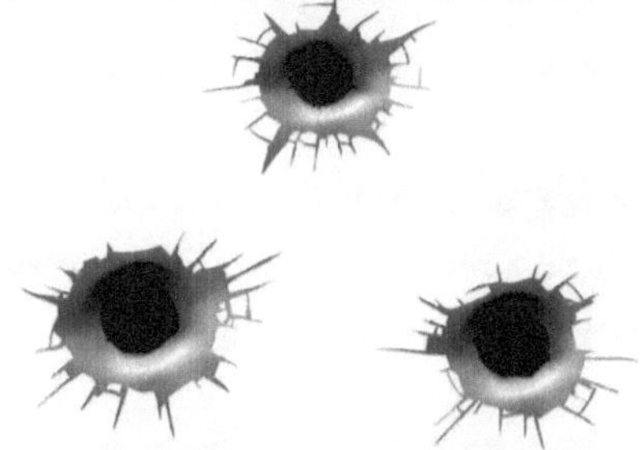

CHAPTER SIXTEEN

President Ferrell stood behind a podium directly outside the door leading into the East Room of the White House. Behind the President stood William Garrett, currently a sitting judge on the D.C. Federal Court of Appeals. About seventy-five members of the White House press corp were present to cover the President's announcement of his nomination of Judge Garrett to replace Justice Byers on the Supreme Court.

"Ladies and gentlemen," he began. "Several months ago, we learned of the tragic loss of Justice Hayden Byers, one of the greatest legal minds of the last century. While the circumstances surrounding his death continue to be scrutinized by the FBI, the vacancy on the Court can no longer go unfilled. The lack of finding of the investigation into the senseless murder of Justice Byers cannot be used as an excuse to postpone naming his replacement. I am here to announce to the American people I have settled on my choice to fill the vacancy.

"Judge William Garrett currently sits on the D.C. Federal Court of Appeals," he continued. "My predecessor, who happens to be a Republican, appointed Judge Garrett to his current position. For the past twelve years Judge Garrett has faithfully served his country as an appellate court judge, and in my view, is the best-qualified person in America to fill the current vacancy on the Supreme Court. Now, I have certainly heard some of the chatter coming out of Washington. Some have expressed strong feelings they think this nomination should be made by the next President. Somehow, because we are in the middle of an election season, these voices feel our government is not capable of functioning. I'm here to tell the American people this thinking is utter nonsense."

"The Supreme Court is too important of an institution to be left deficient simply because an election is underway," the President continued. "Of all the institutions of government which currently exist, the Supreme Court above all others should be completely devoid of politics. It will be almost a year before the next President is sworn in and I will not allow the nomination and confirmation of the next Supreme Court justice to be held up because of political rancor. It is for this reason I am submitting the name of Judge William Garrett to the United States Senate for their consideration, and I am asking them to perform the duties expected of them by the American people. Judge Garrett deserves a fair and impartial hearing by the Senate Judiciary Committee, followed by an up or down vote for confirmation by the entire Senate body. It is now my pleasure to introduce to the American people the man I hope will become the newest member on the United States Supreme Court, Judge William Garrett."

President Ferrell had certainly been accurate when he mentioned the fact Judge Garrett had been appointed to the D.C. Court of Appeals by a Republican President. Although not a far left liberal in the mold of Justice Byers, Judge Garret did not have the reputation of being a true conservative constitutionalist favored by most Republicans, particularly those on the Senate Judiciary Committee. Judge Garrett had been an abject disappointment to conservatives, one more in a long line of Republican appointees to the federal judiciary who failed to bring conservative philosophies to the bench. Like many other liberal judges throughout the country, Judge Garrett believed the U.S. Constitution to be a *living, breathing document* and should not always be applied literally, firmly believing changes in the American culture over the last two hundred plus years necessitated the U.S. Constitution change as well.

The biggest point of contention between Judge Garrett and conservatives will most certainly be his stated stance on American's Second Amendment right to *Keep and Bear Arms*. Judge Garrett had previously ruled in favor of a Washington D.C. law prohibiting citizens from carrying concealed weapons, regardless of whether they had obtained carry permits. The D.C. law he ruled on also prohibited any citizen of the District of Columbia from owning a handgun, even if the gun remained inside his or her own home. The restrictive D.C. gun law Judge Garrett favored only permitted its citizens to own long guns (rifles or shotguns), and mandated the guns be kept inside of one's residence.

Law abiding citizens were not permitted to transport their long guns from their place of residence unless unloaded. And to make matters worse for supporters of Second Amendment rights, the law also required citizens owning long guns to register their ownership with the D.C. Metro Police. The U.S. Supreme Court ultimately overturned the D.C. Court of Appeals' ruling on this issue, claiming the law clearly violated the rights provided to citizens in the U.S. Constitution. But Judge Garrett had exposed himself as an anti-gun, anti-Second Amendment jurist, putting his confirmation to the Supreme Court in serious jeopardy.

"Thank you, Mr. President," Judge Garrett said as he addressed the nation and the crowd of reporters covering the President's announcement. "On behalf of my family, I would like to take this time to tell you what a great honor this truly is. As a young lawyer growing up in the profession in upstate New York, I could never have dreamed of a day like today taking place. When I practiced law, I held judges in the highest esteem, although I didn't know at the time what a hard and important job they had. And then I became one. When that happened, I realized the lives of some of our citizens would literally rest in my hands. I never lost sight of this and have worked every day of my life in a manner designed to improve the lives of those citizens passing before my bench."

"As you mentioned, Mr. President," he continued, "your predecessor appointed me to my current position on the D.C. Court of Appeals. When the Senate confirmed me for the position, I thought I had reached the highest pinnacle possible in my professional life. It is why today I am so humbled you have placed your faith in me for this important position. I vow to you, and to the American people, I will work every day from this day forward to be worthy of the trust you have placed in me. Thank you all very much."

Judge Garrett stepped away from the podium and turned to shake the hands of President Ferrell and Vice President Hogue, who had joined the President for the announcement ceremony.

"Mr. President," shouted one reporter. "What do you think of your chances of getting Judge Garrett confirmed, especially with the political environment that exists right now?"

"This isn't about politics," responded the President as he tried to walk away without having to answer questions. "Let me put it this way," he continued. "I've done my job, now it's time for the Senate to do theirs."

The President waved off any more questions and walked into the East Room of the White House with V.P. Hogue and Judge Garrett behind him. The three of them sat down for coffee before continuing with the day.

"Tell me the truth, Eric," Judge Garrett said to the Vice President, whom he had become good friends with over the past few years. "If the Senate blocks me now, and you end up winning the presidency in November, can I expect to be back here again for another announcement?"

"Nothing personal, Bill," replied V.P. Hogue, "but this is your only shot. I hope you get confirmed, but no, you won't be back here again."

"Good to know where you stand, sir," Garrett replied to the Vice President as he stood to excuse himself before taking the first sip of his coffee.

After shaking hands with the President and Vice President, Judge Garrett walked out of the room.

"Good God Eric," Rob Ferrell said to his Vice President. "You're a cold SOB.

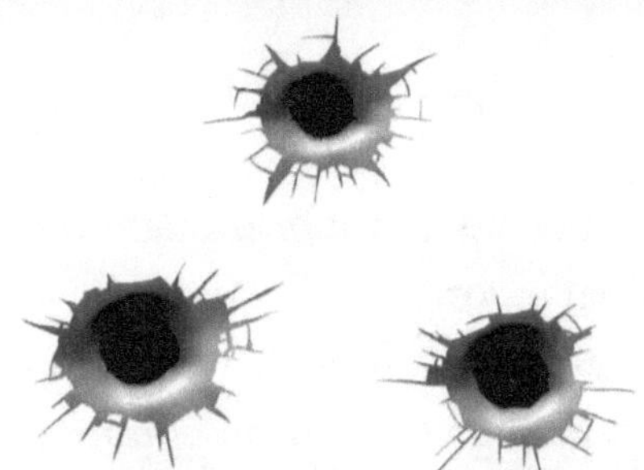

CHAPTER SEVENTEEN

There are many characteristics that go into making a good and effective investigative journalist. Being highly skeptical of those in positions of power and not accepting anything at face value are at the top of the list. This would be how anyone who knew Casey Dean would describe her. She had an innate ability to look at a set of facts and see things other reporters would miss. In all her years of covering news stories or doing interviews, she never accepted someone at their word, simply because they sounded sincere. She never accepted a set of facts as being all there was, even when it may appear to be nothing more to it. She always assumed there had to be more and that most powerful people were trying to hide something. Her gritty, persistent personality is what made Casey Dean a great reporter, and why she broke stories others would miss.

From the outset, when she first heard President Ferrell discuss the death of Justice Byers, she knew there had to be more to it. Sensing the President was attempting to hide something with his less than forthright comments from the start, she assumed he wanted to keep extremely embarrassing information from reaching the ears of the American people. Her inherent cynicism turned out to be well founded.

Additionally, she digested every news report written on the so-called assassination of CeCe Diamond, the head of the S.P.A., even reaching out to a fellow reporter with the San Francisco Chronicle who covered the story. Casey asked the reporter if he thought there could be anything missing from the initial reports.

"No, nothing at all," he answered. "It's pretty much cut and dry. The cops out here are telling us it's nothing more than your run-of-the-mill shooting. It just happens to be someone in the public eye, who engendered a lot of hate from a lot of people because of her stances on various issues. More specifically, I would say her ardent support of a cop-killer."

Pretty much cut and dry, Casey recalled the words of the San Francisco reporter. *Nothing is cut and dry*, she thought.

Casey Dean knew up to this point two high-profile murders had been committed within a few months of each other.

Actually, it had been three, but the death of Chris Dyess had been ruled a heart attack and only the *New Sons of Liberty* knew the whole truth.

One of the murders took place on the East coast and the other on the West coast. Both members of the political Left, it seemed this was the only thing the two victims had in common. This fact alone could not tie the murders together, but Casey had a nagging suspension they might somehow be connected. Because her instincts had proven her right so many times before, she would not dismiss them now. She knew she needed to dig deeper.

"Isn't this what investigative reporters are supposed to do?" she thought.

Casey spent the next day and a half researching everything she could to see if any connection between Justice Byers and CeCe Diamond existed. After reading every opinion the justice had written since his appointment to the Supreme Court, Casey went further back into his past to his time as a radical leftist representing the ACLU. She found legal briefs he had filed on behalf of environmentalist groups suing the federal government and looked at initiatives the Tides Foundation had supported during the time period he sat on their board. Everything she found on Justice Byers indicated to her his standing as one of the most fervid liberals who ever lived. No surprise, really, as a simple reading of his Supreme Court opinions would have told her that. After all, he never attempted to keep his political leanings a secret.

She decided to drive to New York and stop by the ACLU headquarters to poke around. Not knowing what exactly to look for, she figured at worst, if she came up empty, it would be a wasted day. No harm, she reasoned. God knows she had hit dry wells before.

It's certainly worth a try, she thought.

Casey drove to New York City and found the ACLU office building on Broad Street. Once inside the lobby, she identified herself to the clerk as a reporter from the Washington Chronicle. As good reporters are sometimes inclined to do, Casey lied to the desk clerk by saying she wanted to do a story about all of the good work done by the ACLU over the years and needed background information to augment her article. Summoned from one of the back offices, the ACLU press officer appeared, eager to meet Casey. He escorted her into a back room where reams of documents were housed chronicling the long history of the ACLU and the countless liberal causes they supported. Casey found volumes of documents with Justice Byers' name prominently mentioned, written during his time with the organization.

After more than three hours of tedious reading, Casey Dean came across a document that got her full attention. The ACLU had filed suit in federal court on behalf of an environmental group, suing the state of California to stop the construction of a highway. The building of the new roadway had been planned as a way of providing greater public access to the Monterey Peninsula. Alleging the construction of the highway would negatively impact the spawning habits of fresh water smelt indigenous to the area, the ACLU filed suit against the state to stop the project.

A typical liberal cause, she thought, *nothing out of the ordinary for this group.*

Her interest piqued when she saw the name on the document listed as Hayden Byers' administrative assistant, none other than CeCe Diamond.

She walked into the office of the press officer who had assisted her and asked him if he could shed any light on the matter.

"Actually," the press officer said to Casey, "I never knew she worked here. We've got all former employees archived in our HR database. Let me pull it up and see if I can find her."

In a few minutes, he found records archived of Ms. Diamond for the time period she had been employed by the ACLU.

"Okay," the press officer began. "This makes a little more sense why I didn't know we had her on our rolls. Apparently, she worked here for only a short period of time, less than a year it looks like. Nothing here indicates why she left. Maybe we weren't radical enough for her," he said with a smile.

"Thank you for your help," Casey told the press officer. "I think I've got what I need."

While driving back to Washington, she rang Agent Michaels on his cell.

"Rich," she said into her phone, "it's Casey. Can I meet you at your office in about two hours? There's something on the Byers case I need to discuss with you."

"Sure," replied Rich. "I'll be here. Just let yourself in. I'll let the front desk know you're coming."

Exactly two hours later Casey Dean walked into the FBI WFO and headed for Agent Michael's office.

"I found out something you might think is interesting," she said to Rich as she took a seat in front of his desk. "I'm not 100% sure there's anything to it, but I think it's definitely worth talking about."

"What've you got?" asked Rich.

"For the past few days I've been going over in my mind whether the Byers murder was random, or part of something bigger."

"Nothing random about it, I can tell you that much," Rich offered. "As you know his wallet and jewelry were still on his body, so we know it wasn't a simple robbery. The manner in which he died indicates to me someone specifically targeted him. You know I can't give you any specific details of the investigation, but as far as it being part of something bigger,

I honestly have no idea. You said you found something you thought I might find interesting. What is it?"

"Well," she began, "I think we can both agree Justice Byers' political leanings were, shall we say, somewhat to the left of center. Some might say way left of center."

"I think you're being kind, Casey," replied Rich. "I would describe him as a raging liberal. Perhaps even a lunatic."

"Now Rich," Casey implored, "let's not forget one person's raging liberal might be another person's conscientious objector. At any rate, I would have to acknowledge you are definitely not alone in your assessment."

"So, let's look at the murder of CeCe Diamond out in San Francisco," she continued. "One could certainly make the case her politics were in line with Justice Byers."

"Oh yeah," said Rich. "A raging liberal as well. We totally agree there."

"Well," continued Casey, "I did a little checking on her and what happened when she tried to give her speech in San Francisco. Now I'm not saying the two murders are necessarily related, at least not yet. But I couldn't help but wonder if something tied the two cases together."

"Boy," said Rich with a slight grin, "so everything I've heard about you is true."

"Just hold on now," Casey replied. "I'm not jumping to any conclusions. But I thought it curious that two of the most liberal people in America were murdered within a couple months of each other. It kept eating away at me they were somehow related. So, I decided to take a little trip up to New York and do some poking around at the ACLU headquarters. Don't forget, Justice Byers worked there for many years prior to his appointment to the Court."

"Yeah," said Rich. "I'm pretty sure that's why President Ferrell picked him for the bench. His left-wing views had always been aligned with our esteemed President."

"It's not too hard to figure out on which side of the political spectrum you fall," Casey said with a smile. "But I think you're probably right about why the President picked him. And here's something I bet you didn't know. CeCe Diamond once worked for Justice Byers at the ACLU as his administrative assistant. Only for a short time, mind you, but she nonetheless worked for the guy."

"You're shitting me," Rich responded with astonishment. "How come we didn't know that?"

"Because you're not as good at finding out obscure facts as I am," she said with a smile.

"Apparently not," he said. "I agree with you it's interesting, but I'm not sure it ties the two murders together."

"Okay," began Casey. "On its face, there appears to be no link between the two murders. I'll give you that. But I never take things at face value. You should know that about me."

"I'm beginning to get that impression," Rich said with a wry look on his face.

"Now, let's look at what we do know about the assassination of Ms. Diamond. She gave a speech in front of a crowd at the Golden Gate Park in San Francisco. After standing in front of a podium for only a couple of minutes, her guts were blown out by a high-powered rifle. The cops out there are saying it appears to be a local police matter, assuming some pissed off radical gunned her down for leading a rally in support of a scumbag cop-killer. Sounds reasonable so far?"

"So far," replied Rich. "Go on."

"But what if there's more to it?" she continued. "What if the rally had little to do with the motive for having her knocked off? What if the rally simply provided the killer with the perfect opportunity to take her out?

"Interesting so far," Rich remarked. "Go on."

"Then we have Justice Byers. A far-left radical liberal hated by those on the political Right."

"No doubt about that," said Rich.

"And CeCe Diamond. Also considered by many to be a far-left radical liberal hated by those on the political Right, a trait they both shared. And to make matters more interesting, they once worked together. Now, we both acknowledge Justice Byers died at the hands of a professional killer, right?"

"We're in agreement there," responded Rich. "But where's the tie to Ms. Diamond? I need more than their common political views."

"And I do as well," Casey replied. "So, let's look at her murder. The cops interviewed everybody in the crowd at the event, and nobody heard a gunshot, right?"

"That's right," said Rich. "Continue."

"The rifle slug that almost cut her in two came from a high-powered rifle. Hang on a second; let me check my notes. Here it is. The police report identifies the rifle slug as a 408. I'm assuming 408 denotes the caliber of the bullet which killed her?"

"Exactly," interjected Rich. "That caliber of bullet didn't come from a rifle used to hunt squirrels; I can tell you that. It most definitely came from a sniper rifle."

"Precisely," continued Casey. "It also means the shooter didn't need to be near the stage when he took his shot, which is why no one heard it when he fired."

"Which would mean," began Rich as he started to show more interest in Casey's theory, "the shot came from quite a distance away."

"Right, and what it tells me," Casey continued, "is the killer in San Francisco wasn't your run-of-the mill, pissed off, right-leaning extremist like the San Francisco police seem to think. An expert took the shot that killed her. Whether you can classify the killers of Byers and Diamond as professional assassins or not, I'm not sure. But one thing is certain, they were highly skilled in the art of murder, and I think at the very least we should consider the possibility the two murders are linked."

"Damn," replied Rich. "You might be on to something. Of course, if you're right and the two murders are tied to one another, it will change everything. The scope and impact of this investigation just got bigger. Even though it's only a theory at this point, and a plausible one I might add, my Director will want to hear it sooner rather than later. I better get over to his office as soon as possible and fill him in. He's not going to want to read about this in the paper, you can be sure of that."

"Of course, you'll keep me posted on this, right Rich?" Casey asked. "I'm going to want the exclusive on this."

"Absolutely, Casey," he replied with a grin. "Excellent work, I might add. You've given me a lot to think about."

"Just doing my job," replied Casey with another smile.

"Do me one favor, though," Rich said to Casey as she stood up to leave his office.

"Sure, what is it?"

"Just give me a heads up before you go to press on any of this," Rich replied. "My Director will not be pleased if he gets blindsided by one of your explosive headlines. At least let us be prepared to react to the public outcry sure to take place if this theory of yours gets out."

"You got it," said Casey.

As soon as Casey Dean left his office, Agent Michaels sent an interoffice request to the San Francisco FBI field office requesting a copy of the case file on the Diamond murder from San Francisco P.D. He received it via secure fax four hours later. There were no bombshells in the report and almost everything he read he already knew. No determination had been made as to exactly where the shot that took the life of CeCe Diamond came from, only that it had been taken from a great distance away. Rich Michaels now looked at his investigation in a different light. He got an appointment to see his Director and filled him in on his new theory regarding the two murders.

"I hope you're wrong," the Director told Rich. "But we have to consider all possibilities. I'll mention it to the President when I have my weekly briefing with him, but I don't want to cause undo alarm unless we have something more concrete. Stay on it and keep me posted.

"Will do, sir," replied Agent Michaels.

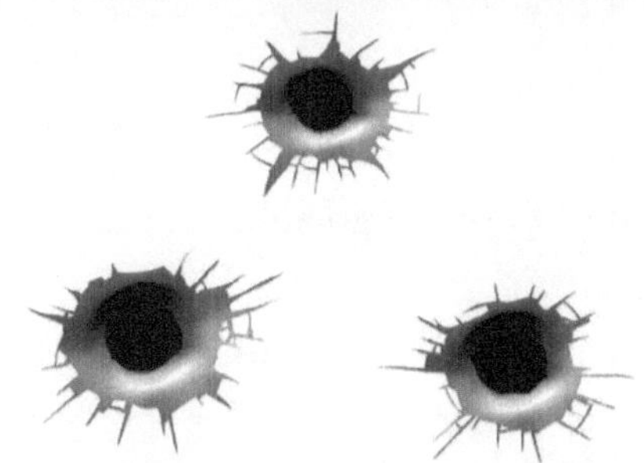

Chapter Eighteen

The Citadel, a military college located in Charleston, South Carolina, would host the second Republican debate between Governor Alan, Senator Smith and businessman Mark Wooddall. If Wooddall was to have any chance, he would need to land some body blows on his two competitors. It didn't take long for the first shot across someone's bow to take place once the debate began.

When answering a question put to the candidates by one of the debate moderators about jobs and the economy, Mr. Wooddall launched into an attack of both Governor Alan and Senator Smith.

"I am the only one on this stage," Wooddall began, "who has any clue how to create jobs in this country. Senator Smith is part of the Washington elite, having spent more than two decades in Washington, while Governor Alan is currently doing his best to ruin the economy of Indiana. There's a reason why our country's economy is in the toilet right now, and it's because of the policies pursued by the current administration. President Ferrell is more interested in increasing the number of welfare checks instead of increasing the number of paychecks. If I am elected, we're going to do things differently. My policies will be pro-growth policies designed to help the working middle class in this country, and nobody else on this stage has the ability to tackle our economy like I can. While my opponents in this race have spent their careers in politics, I have spent mine in the business world, creating jobs and making payrolls. While they are certainly fine individuals, not one of them has an inkling of how to go about creating jobs and getting our economy growing again."

"Governor Alan," responded the moderator. "I'll give you a minute to respond, followed by a minute from Senator Smith."

"Thank you," said the governor. "What Mr. Wooddall failed to tell you is he once testified before Congress in support of steel tariffs. Simply put, he is a protectionist. His support of those steel tariffs certainly padded his own personal bank account, but it also caused prices for the consumer to go up, resulting in a significant number of job losses. I don't think the American economy can afford to have someone like him in the White House. We need to create new, high-paying jobs, not laying off people which is what his policies will do."

"Senator Smith, your response?"

"Thank you," he began. "In addition to what the Governor said about Mr. Wooddall's policies, let me add there is nothing American about being an opponent of free trade. Something Mr. Wooddall apparently does not support considering his backing of those tariffs. Now, Mr. Wooddall also proudly claims he has always been a businessman. And as a businessman, he has only been concerned about the bottom line of his company and how best to maximize the profits of his investors and stockholders. So, if you happen to be one of those investors or hold some of his stock, then I'm sure you're happy with how he conducted himself when he ran his steel company. But being President is about caring about all Americans, not just a few."

"My policies for our economy are quite simple," Senator Smith continued. "We need to lower the corporate tax rate so businesses are able to expand. Once we do that, we will be on a path to significant job growth in this country again. Another important thing we need to do is cut the stifling regulations this administration has put on our companies that have hamstrung their ability to create good-paying jobs. We should be encouraging our job creators, not holding them back with all of these burdensome regulations. And lastly, we need an overhaul of our tax code. People should be allowed to keep more of what they make. Government has become too big and they need to get out of the way and let the free market be unleashed. If we can accomplish these things, our economy will have the potential to explode. My economic plan will result in a growth rate in our economy of between four and six percent, not the tepid one to two percent we have seen under the Ferrell administration. These are things I have always been in support of throughout my time in Congress."

"Thank you, Senator Smith," replied the moderator.

Expecting to shine on the topic of national security going into the debate, Senator Smith did not disappoint. As the only candidate on stage who had served in the military, his status as a war hero didn't hurt in a state filled with military families. South Carolina also is known for the many evangelical voters who live there as well. Senator Smith had the first group solidly in his corner, and many in the second group were beginning to come his way. Post-debate polls for the South Carolina primary showed Senator Smith gaining support, while Governor Alan was declining. As for Mark Wooddall, he was all but finished. He apparently needed someone to let him know.

Interrupting his campaign to go back to Washington, Senator Smith had pressing senatorial duties in need of his attention. The President had named a replacement to fill the vacancy caused by the death of Justice Byers, and it would be his job to chair the Senate Judiciary Committee tasked with reviewing the President's nomination. His committee would render a verdict on whether or not Appellate Judge William Garrett should sit on the highest court in the land.

No one at this point knew whether or not Judge Garrett's confirmation hearings would help or hurt the Senator's campaign. Knowing these were potentially treacherous waters, Senator Smith would play his role down the middle and appear to be fair and above board. Even though denying the President his Supreme Court pick was precisely his intentions, the Senator could not afford to be seen as a partisan hack predisposed on thwarting the nomination. Conservative Republican voters would relish his open opposition to Judge Garrett, which might help him in the primaries, but the all-important moderates and independents were the voters he needed to reach. Those blocs of voters would make the difference for him in the general election should he emerge as the eventual nominee. They would want to see him act in a fair and impartial manner, requiring a balancing act the Senator had performed hundreds of times since entering the political arena. He had gotten this far in politics by no accident, and he would now need all of his political skills to pull this off. There was no doubt in his mind he would.

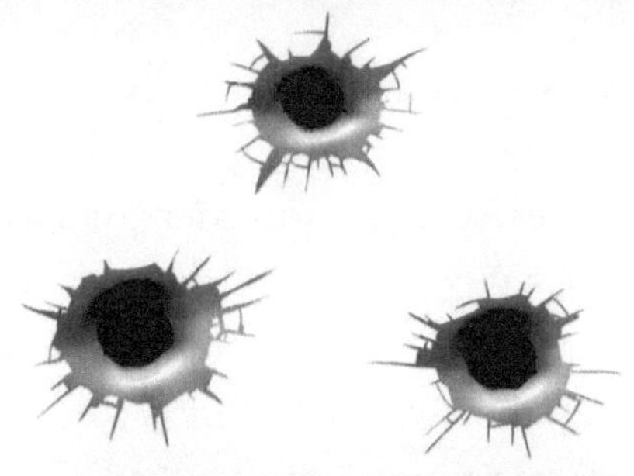

CHAPTER NINETEEN

D.C. Detective O'Rourke and FBI Agent Michaels had boxes of video surveillance tapes now at their disposal. Taking over one of the conference rooms in the WFO, they now had the use of several laptops to view the voluminous Metro tapes. Finding a video of a guy limping getting on or off a Metro train, amongst the tens of thousands of commuters captured by the system's video monitors, would be like finding a needle in a haystack. A long shot perhaps, but they knew criminal investigations are sometimes broken wide open when the investigator is able to uncover something normally missed by others. This would be their attempt at finding the needle. Knowing their suspect had used the Red Line Metro stations at Woodley Park and Van Ness, they concentrated their initial search on those stations and the ones in closest proximity.

Any criminal investigator worth his or her salt will tell you cases are sometimes made because of the sheer intellect of the investigator. Other times, however, it takes a tremendous amount of luck to break a case. Almost ten hours into the process of looking at stacks of video feeds, Rich and Jimmy got the lucky break they needed. In fact, it was a huge break.

"Hey Jimmy," said Rich. "Take a look at this."

Jimmy got up from his chair and walked to where Rich sat. According to the date and time stamp on the bottom of Rich's screen, the video feed came from the DuPont Circle Metro station recorded at 10:08

111

p.m., six days before Justice Byers' murder. As Rich played the video forward, they could see a guy getting off the train and walking with the other passengers towards the exit. Late in the evening, the crowd was relatively light. The guy they were looking at had a pronounced limp.

"Do you think he's our guy?" Jimmy asked.

"Take a look at him, Jimmy," Rich replied. "What would you say… maybe six feet, two hundred pounds or so?"

"Yeah, I'd say that's about right," Jimmy responded. "It could be him. Let's grab the tape from the other side and see if we can get him leaving the station."

Rich reached into the box beside his chair and found the videotape from the ticket booth and turnstile area of the DuPont Circle station. He slid a second laptop over in front of him and placed the DVD in so they could watch the two feeds side-by-side.

Fast-forwarding the second tape to 10:08 p.m., he hit the play button and let it run. Backing up the first tape to the point where the train pulled to a stop inside the station, they watched as the man with the limp stepped off the train and began making his way to the exit. Three or four times, they noticed, the man spun his head around as if trying to spot a tail.

"He must be our guy," said Jimmy. "He keeps looking around, definitely making sure no one is following him."

"Checking his six, you mean," said Rich.

"You got it partner," replied Jimmy with a smile. "Now you're catching on."

"Thanks," said Rich.

"Okay," said Rich as they both concentrated on the screen. "There he goes leaving the tunnel, now let's see if we can pick him up as he exits the turnstiles."

They moved their gazes to the second laptop. About thirty seconds of elapsed time later their suspect could clearly be seen limping along as he made his way through the turnstile, past the ticket booth and in the direction of the Q Street exit door.

Rich Michaels and Jimmy O'Rourke were smart and seasoned investigators, but they were also about to be the fortunate recipients of sheer dumb luck. As their suspect walked past the ticket booth and headed for the exit, Rich and Jimmy saw a quick flash of something passing in front of the video camera recording the shot they were looking at. A bird had flown into the Metro station terminal and passed over the heads of the commuters making their way to the exit. As their suspect walked along with the rest of the crowd in the direction of the Metro exit door, he instinctively did what every other passenger did; he looked up at the bird that had passed within a few feet of their heads. No more than three or four seconds from leaving the view of the camera recording the shot they were now looking at; their suspect gave the investigators the lucky break their case needed. When he looked up, the video camera got a clear shot of his face.

"Shit," exclaimed Jimmy. "Run it back. We got a shot of his face!"

Rich rewound the tape and hit the pause button just as their suspect looked up in the direction of the camera.

"Well, I'll be damned," said Rich. "I think we just got lucky."

After printing a still shot of their suspect's face, Rich turned to Jimmy and said, "I know who can help us with this. Go home and get some rest and let's meet back here around noon tomorrow. I'm going to stop by the Hoover building in the morning and see someone who might be able to do something with this photo."

"Sounds good, Rich," Jimmy replied. "My eyes can use the rest."

***

Deanna Mowery graduated from the Massachusetts Institute of Technology, more commonly known as M.I.T. Her field of study was in M.I.T.'s School of Applied Sciences, with an emphasis on the area of biometrics. This particular field of study refers to metrics related to human characteristics, and through the use of biometric authentication, can be used in computer science as a form of identification. As the world has become more automated through the uses of technology, law enforcement has begun taking advantage of technological breakthroughs in the area of biometrics to aid investigators in the surveillance of large groups of people. Due to advances in the area of science, the use of biometric identifiers has become more commonplace in the world of law enforcement to aid investigators in the labeling and describing of individuals.

After graduating number one in her class at M.I.T., Ms. Mowery received a Rhodes scholarship to attend Oxford University in Oxford, England. While there, she continued her studies of biometrics, with a concentration in the area of facial recognition. Generally speaking, a facial recognition system is a computer application programmed to identify a person from a digital image, usually produced from a video source or frame. Facial recognition computer software takes the digital image and maps the facial features present in the image. Facial recognition biometrics is similar in many respects to the biometrics used in fingerprint identification and eye scans.

Growing up in an upper middle-class household in Plantation, Florida, Deanna loved computers and technology. Her father, who once ran the computer system for Eastern Airlines, instilled in her a passion for both at an early age. After graduating high school with honors, Deanna enrolled at M.I.T. A prestigious university by all accounts, an education at M.I.T. came with a pretty high price tag. Although the recipient of some financial help through partial scholarships, Deanna would need to find other sources of income to foot the bill without piling up a mountain of student loan debt, something she had vowed not to do.

Once an All-State tennis player in high school, Deanna could have gotten a full ride to play tennis at any one of the dozen colleges in Florida offering her a scholarship. But technology and science was where her future lay and there was no better launching pad than M.I.T. Perhaps tennis, she thought, could help her get there.

After enrolling at M.I.T. for her freshman semester, Deanna decided to look for a part-time job to help cover the costs of her tuition. Walking into the office of the head pro at the Mount Auburn Tennis Club in Watertown, Massachusetts (a few miles from the M.I.T. campus),

Deanna applied for a position as a part-time tennis instructor. Besides making a few extra bucks to help pay for college, she thought, she could continue playing a sport she dearly loved.

Stunningly beautiful, Deanna had the innate ability to make a good impression any time she walked into a room. At five feet nine inches tall with radiantly bronzed skin, the result of hours spent outside on the tennis court, she had a perfectly toned body, with thigh and calf muscles taut as the strings on a banjo. Pulling her long, blonde hair behind her head into a ponytail, she walked into the office of the tennis pro, who jumped up from behind his desk to meet her.

"It's a pleasure to meet you," he said. "I understand you're interested in coming on board as one of our instructors." *If this young lady standing before me knows which end of the racquet to hold, I'm going to hire her*, he thought.

No doubt he thought of all the new bookings for lessons he would get from the young men in the area who would soon find a new passion for learning to play tennis.

"My name is Deanna Mowery," she said as she gave him a firm handshake. "I will be attending M.I.T. in the Fall Semester and need some extra income. I went to high school in south Florida where I played on the tennis team and made All-State my junior and senior year. I turned down several college scholarships to play in Florida because I wanted to attend M.I.T. I love the facilities here at Mount Auburn and think I would be a nice addition to your staff."

So do I, the pro thought, but didn't say out loud.

"Tell you what," he said, "let's go outside and hit the ball around and let me see what you got. We are always looking for good instructors."

It only took the tennis pro about five seconds to hire Deanna, especially when she whizzed a passing shot back across the net at him.

"I think you'll fit in quite nicely here," he told her. "I have a feeling your scheduling book is going to fill up in a hurry. Let's go inside and get some paperwork out of the way and get you on our schedule as soon as possible."

Besides helping to increase the revenue for the Mount Auburn Tennis Club, Deanna excelled in her studies at M.I.T. as she did with most other things in her life. While walking across campus one day during her senior year, a representative of one of the big New York City modeling agencies, on campus attending freshman orientation with his son, approached her. Struck by her incredible beauty, the modeling rep asked Deanna if she had ever considered pursuing a career in modeling. After handing her one of his business cards, he encouraged her to call him if becoming a model interested her.

"You're what we call in the business *a can't miss*," the rep said as they went their separate ways.

Although flattered by the offer, Deanna had no intentions of changing the direction of her life as her graduation from M.I.T. approached, as well as her stint at Oxford. Her future would be in the field she loved and posing in front of a camera did not fit into those plans. Following graduation from M.I.T. and the conclusion of her studies in Oxford, England, Deanna moved on with the next chapter in her life.

Now a high-ranking employee of the FBI, Deanna worked in the Science and Technology Branch (STB) at their headquarters building on Pennsylvania Avenue in Washington, D.C. Overseeing the Operational and Technology Division within the STB, Deanna's unit provided special agents with forensic science, applied technology and identification support. Her area of expertise, of course: facial recognition technology.

***

Right before 9:00 a.m., Rich Michaels walked into the Hoover Building and straight to Deanna's office, knocked on her door and invited himself in.

"I didn't know if I'd catch you here this early," Rich said with a smile as he took a seat in front of her desk.

"Yeah, right," she replied. "I don't get to keep agent hours like you, Rich. I'm usually here before seven and I'm lucky if I get back to my apartment by dark. What's up?"

"It's the Byers case," he said as he reached into his briefcase and pulled out a large manila envelope containing a still shot of the primary suspect in Justice Byers' murder. "We were able to capture this shot from one of the surveillance cameras mounted inside a Metro station. Right before walking out the exit door, he looked up suddenly when a bird flew in the station and over the top of his head."

"Lucky break there," Deanna commented.

"Don't I know it," Rich said in response. "This guy is cautious and seems to be always looking for a tail. We've gotten several shots of him before but he always wore a hat and never looked up. Thank God for the timing of the bird. Anyways, I hoped you could work some of your magic on this guy's face. See if maybe we can figure out who he is."

"Sure thing," Deanna replied. "I'll get my team on it right away. You know how this works, right?"

"To be honest with you, not exactly. I didn't go to M.I.T. In fact, I barely made it through F.S.U. How about giving me a quick tutorial so at least I can sound like I know what I'm talking about if anyone asks."

"No problem," Deanna said with a smile. "Basically speaking, every face, every fingerprint, every voice has specific biometric characteristics. Our facial recognition software will analyze and map the characteristics in your suspect's face. Eye shape, distance between pupils, distance between ears, length and shape of nose, shape of jaw, things like that. After the mapping is complete we will be able to classify his face based on all of those criteria. Once this classification is made we'll start the process of trying to put a name to his face. With millions of photos on file, our first step will be to eliminate all the photos we have not similarly classified as your suspect. Make sense?"

"So far," Rich replied. "Not unlike the way fingerprints are classified, right?"

"Exactly," she said. "Maybe you did learn something in Tallahassee after all."

"Now once the mapping and classification are complete," Deanna went on, "we can pull up photos of people with criminal records and separate out only those similarly classified as your suspect. Obviously, your guy is a white male so the first thing we'll do is eliminate anyone female, black, Hispanic, Asian, etc. Once done, we'll have a more manageable group of potential matches. That's when the fun begins. Someone, or in this case several some ones, will have to look at each potential candidate with their own eyes and hopefully find a positive match."

"What if there's no match?" Rich asked. "Maybe our guy has never been arrested. What would the next step be then?"

"Good point, Rich," Deanna replied. "A distinct possibility. Checking the photos of people who have a criminal record, though, makes the most sense. At least initially it does. If that comes up empty, we can move on to other areas where we have access to facial photos. For example, we can pull up driver license photos from all fifty states. After that we start looking at I.D. photos of state employees, federal employees, passports and military people. Essentially, anywhere someone had his or her picture taken for a photo I.D. we'll have access to it. Now, the potential pool of candidates is quite large and this will take some time, but at least we have a starting point. My unit is pretty good at what they do so I think there's a decent chance we can put a name to this guy's face."

"Tell you what I'll do," continued Deanna, "I'll have my team do all of the computer analysis I previously described. Once all of that is done, I will need you to send over a few of your research analysts to do the tedious part of looking at all of the potential matches and make a comparison with this photo you brought with you. Who knows, we might get lucky."

"Sounds good," Rich said as he got up to leave Deanna's office. "Just call me when you're ready and I'll send some people over. Thanks."

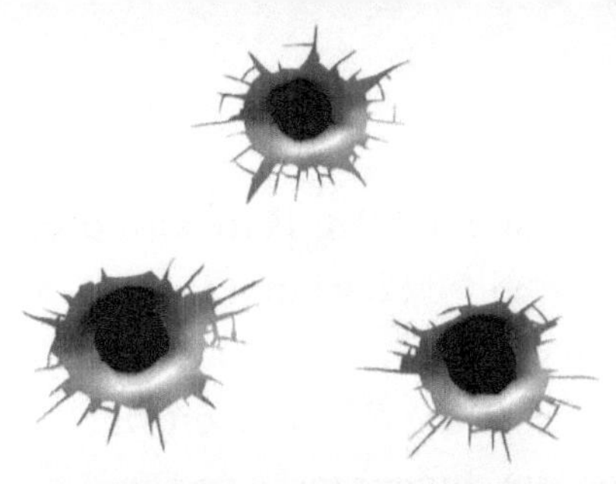

CHAPTER TWENTY

Senator Smith had come off the campaign trail and returned to Washington to chair the committee hearings considering the President's nomination to the Supreme Court. Campaigning for the presidency can be extremely hard and time-consuming and any time a candidate is not campaigning there is the potential for a missed opportunity to connect with a potential voter. Senator Smith, however, found himself in a precarious position.

Not wanting to give ammunition to his Republican challengers by having them accuse him of abdicating his responsibilities as a U.S. Senator, he felt it imperative to chair the Senate Judiciary Committee hearings on the Supreme Court nominee. This wasn't the same thing as leaving the campaign trail to cast some irrelevant vote on something most people couldn't care less about. These hearings would be followed by millions of Americans on T.V. and the Senator knew how he conducted himself at the hearing, every question he asked and every ruling he made as the committee chairman, would be looked at through a political lens. Americans paying attention to the hearings were sure to get a sense of what kind of President Senator Smith would make by how he ran his committee and how the committee treated Judge Garrett.

After being sworn in to testify before the Committee, Judge Garrett had the opportunity of making an opening statement. He talked about his personal background and the love of the law instilled in him through various mentors who helped shape his character throughout his life. Publicly thanking President Ferrell for placing his confidence in him, the judge acknowledged how humbled and honored he felt to have received the President's nomination to the Court.

Attempting to placate the Senators on the committee who would ultimately decide his fate, Judge Garrett assured them he took seriously his fiduciary duties to uphold the Constitution. Knowing his audience of Senators before him as he did, the judge did his best to assuage any doubts his job as a Supreme Court justice would be to always follow the Constitution and not attempt to make new law or change an existing one when a particular issue came before the Court. Winning confirmation before this committee, he rightly concluded, would hinge on this.

The other Republican Senators on the committee were cognizant of the fact their committee chairman was currently in the running to become the next President of the United States. Although they would be involved in the hearings and would take their respective time at the microphone to ask questions, they all agreed whatever sound bites made the nightly news needed to come from Senator Smith.

No Republican on the committee, or any of the Democrats for that matter, had any illusions of what the committee would ultimately decide. Republican voters across America would not stomach a Republican-controlled Senate Judiciary Committee confirming another Ferrell nomination to the Supreme Court. Knowing this, the Democrats had no problem pointing out they thought the hearings were nothing more than pure theater. Before questioning began, the ranking member on the Democrat side accused the Republicans of being insincere and said the hearings now underway were nothing more than a sham.

"Mr. Chairman," the top Democrat on the committee began, directing his remarks at Committee Chairman Smith, "you'll have to pardon my cynicism here, but the exercise this committee is about to undertake is spurious at best and downright dishonest at worst. Judge Garrett is a fine man and preeminently qualified to sit on the Supreme Court. He is more than worthy of receiving fair treatment by this committee and I hope you will conduct these hearings in a manner consistent with the high ideals this august body demands."

"Thank you, Senator," Chairman Smith said in response. "I think we are all in agreement Judge Garrett deserves a fair hearing and it is my responsibility to see he gets one. A responsibility, I might add, I take seriously. But let me be clear from the outset. This committee is not a rubber stamp for the President. Judge Garrett, or anyone else who appears before this committee, will receive a fair hearing. The determination of whether or not his nomination is voted out of committee and on to the Senate floor for a full up or down vote will be decided at the appropriate time and only after this committee has done its job of thoroughly vetting this nominee."

It struck the perfect tone. Not an amateur when it came to politics, Senator Smith let independents and moderates know he would be fair and non-partisan. The conservatives watching wanted no part of having Judge Garrett confirmed and were sure to interpret the Senator's remarks slightly differently. Voters sometimes hear what they want to hear, as Senator Smith certainly knew.

The crack staff working for the Republicans on the Judiciary Committee left no stone unturned in their background research of Judge Garrett. The text of a speech he had given several years earlier at an American Bar Association (A.B.A.) conference indicated Judge Garrett was not as robust in his defense of the Constitution as he now tried to portray. Speaking to his audience of A.B.A. attorneys, the judge talked about how he believed the Constitution should not be viewed as if cast in stone, but instead, should be looked at as a living, breathing document. Constitutional purists view this position as dubious at best; not believing in the notion that the Constitution is flexible and subject to change based on what is going on in the culture of the country at any given time.

In another speech the committee staffers uncovered, Judge Garrett talked about the need of the United States Supreme Court to look at what judiciaries in other countries were doing when it came time for them to render judgment in certain cases.

"We cannot be an island," Judge Garrett declared in his speech. "The United States is part of the global community and we should not withdraw from it. Our laws, and the temperance of our judiciary, should not discount what legal advances are being made in other countries within the global community. The actions of our courts should, at the very least, place some consideration on these outside factors when making decisions."

The issue most front and center with the Republican committee members unmistakably would be the judge's view on the Second Amendment. Fodder for an all-out Republican assault on Judge Garrett's nomination, his decision and opinion regarding the D.C. gun law case provided the opponents of his nomination the most ammo. His defense of his prior ruling was tepid at best.

"I fail to see," began Senator Smith, "how you can be viewed as anything other than an opponent of the Second Amendment. Your ruling and opinion are quite clear. Many of us believe the Second Amendment means exactly what it says. When it says, and I quote, "*The right of people to keep and bear arms shall not be infringed,*" that is exactly what the framers of our Constitution meant. Your ruling is in direct conflict with this and no attempt by you to project some nuanced position can change the facts."

The Democrats on the committee continued to defend Judge Garrett at every turn and constantly reminded anyone paying attention the Republicans were being unfair and disingenuous in their treatment of the nominee. Adept at appearing above board, Senator Smith performed his chairmanship duties flawlessly. No Republican, either inside or outside of elected office, would suggest publicly the fix was in on Judge Garrett's confirmation; although it most certainly was.

Some pundits on television, especially those over at MSNBC, had no problem stating categorically the Republicans on the committee, especially their chairman, had no intentions of confirming Judge Garrett. According to them, the hearings were rigged from the start and predicted the Senate Judiciary Committee would not even move his nomination out of committee, much less provide the nominee a full vote in the Senate. Even the majority of the punditry on the Fox News

Channel agreed the nomination had no chance and might not make it out of committee for consideration before the entire Senate.

Of little surprise to most, and to the glee of everyone opposed to President Ferrell, Judge Garrett's nomination to the Supreme Court died in committee. On a party-line vote, the Republican-controlled Judiciary Committee summarily killed his nomination, failing to provide the judge with the opportunity of having his nomination debated on the Senate floor before the entire Senate body, though it would not have made any difference in the final outcome. Not one Republican Senator had voiced support for the nomination and since they currently enjoyed majority status, no path existed for the judge to be confirmed.

Following the vote killing Judge Garrett's nomination, Senator Smith addressed the committee room and more importantly the voters watching on T.V.

"The Senate Judiciary Committee," he began, "has discharged its duties faithfully and provided to the nominee a fair and impartial hearing. The committee has found the nominee's positions as they relate to his fiduciary duty to uphold the Constitution are, at best, lacking. It is precisely for this reason our committee will not move his nomination forward. It is our belief a full up or down vote by the entire Senate body will not change the ultimate outcome of this nomination. Based on the decision of this committee, this matter is now closed."

Senator Brian Smith could not have helped his campaign for the Republican nomination more if he had been on the campaign trail holding rallies and town hall meetings. His performance at the hearing on Judge Garrett and the sound bites that made it on T.V. were politically brilliant, and he didn't have to spend one red cent on T.V. or radio ads. As he began preparation for the next round of primary contests, his campaign seemed to be picking up steam. He would be hard to stop.

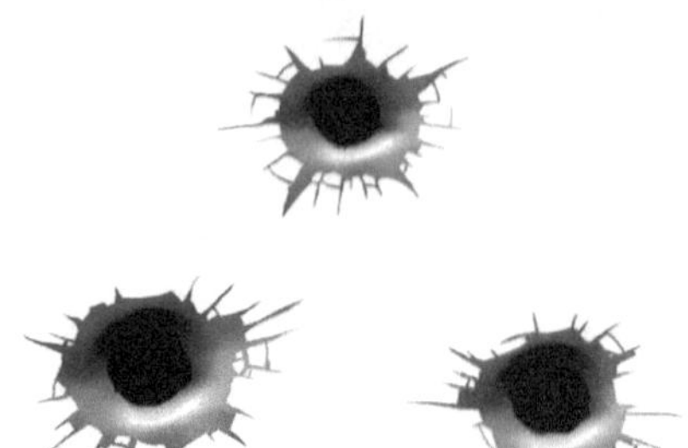

CHAPTER TWENTY-ONE

The *New Sons of Liberty* consisted of like-minded men who shared a common purpose. Intent on striking a debilitating blow against the liberal forces undermining the freedoms and liberties that had made America a great country, they were willing to use any and all means necessary to accomplish this common goal. Although it would be impossible to wipe out everyone with whom the *Sons* viewed as enemies, Jupiter felt the time had come to make an even bolder statement in their pursuit of liberty. Time for their adversaries to know a battle had been waged against their way of life and it would be a relentless crusade knowing no bounds. After meeting with Apollo to discuss ideas about how to ratchet up the intensity of their efforts, a hastily put together meeting of the *Sons* convened. All five members were present as Jupiter addressed the group.

"Thank you all for coming on such short notice," he began. "Apollo and I thought it important to discuss a bit of business we feel has a sense of urgency and must be addressed sooner rather than later."

"We're all ears, Jupiter," Orcus chimed in. "What's on your mind?"

"I'm sure all of you watched the Senate hearings a couple of weeks ago on Capitol Hill," he said.

"Are you're talking about the hearings on douche bag Garrett?" asked Janus.

"Absolutely," replied Jupiter. "After the hearings concluded, Senator Riley made his usual comments about how the Republicans are nothing but a bunch of obstructionists. I expected no less. We've settled on him and he will hear from us in due time. But for the moment, I think we need to put him on the back burner. We believe there is a more pressing issue and it's something we don't think can wait. If we all reach agreement, I'd like for us to move on this as soon as possible."

"What is it, or should I say, who is it?" asked Janus.

"Mark Hayes, one of those talking-head bastards over at MSNBC," Apollo replied.

"Oh, I hate that son-of-a-bitch," said Neptune.

"Yeah, me too," added Janus. "He's no friend of ours; I can tell you that."

"Look," continued Jupiter, trying to refocus the group on the matter at hand, "here's what we've got. Since the hearings on Judge Garrett concluded, Hayes has been out they're parroting the liberal line about how conservatives and Republicans were putting on a show with the committee hearings. He keeps saying the Republicans intended all along to torpedo the President's nominee and the hearings were a total sham on the American people, a complete farce in his words. Normally I wouldn't care too much about anything this idiot had to say on his show. God knows nobody watches him anyhow. But some of his rhetoric is starting to take hold amongst the major media outlets. And to top things off, he's now touting a special he's going to run on his network. According to him and the promos they are running, this *special* of theirs is going to expose the hypocrisy of conservatives."

"In other words," chimed in Apollo, "it's going to be nothing more than a hit piece on Republicans."

"So, I got to thinking about something Neptune brought up at our last meeting," Jupiter continued. "He said something about sending a message. Now I don't think if we hit Hayes his network is going to scuttle their story. On the contrary, I think some of the brass over there will be more excited about running the piece, hoping for a little boost in their ratings. Frankly, I don't give a shit about that. But what I do think is important, at least from our standpoint, is sending a message to other reporters out there. If others are inclined to run hit pieces on

Republicans filled with lies and half-truths, then I want them to know what's about to happen to Hayes might happen to them as well. It will give some of them, or hopefully all of them, pause before they go down the same road. We can't let assholes like Hayes spew their venom and lies on the American public with impunity. They must be held to account. Your thoughts?"

They went around the room and each man agreed Hayes would make a worthy target for their cause.

"I want Apollo to run point on this," Jupiter told the group. "He's done some preliminary work on Hayes and I want him to get the rest of you guys up to speed. Apollo, the floor is yours."

"Thank you," Apollo said as he stood to address the group.

"As Jupiter mentioned, I've done some preliminary stuff on this asshole. This is what I found out so far. He's got an apartment on West 57th Street in Manhattan where he generally stays during the week while he does his Monday through Friday show. He usually leaves the city on Fridays to go to his home in the Hamptons and drives back into the city on Monday mornings. He drives a black 2015 Lexus that he parks in the parking deck of his apartment building. Most weekday mornings he leaves his apartment and drives down 57th, turns south on Avenue of the Americas, and left onto West 49th Street. About two blocks later he makes a left-hand turn into the parking garage at 30 Rockefeller Center where the NBC offices are located. He takes this same exact route into work every day from what I can tell. I'd like to see it happen as close to the NBC building as possible for maximum effect. This T.V. special of his is set to run on Thursday night at eight o'clock eastern, which is why Jupiter and I feel this mission is time sensitive. I say we make this thing happen that afternoon, the same day of the broadcast."

"What'd you have in mind, Apollo?" asked Orcus.

"I'm thinking we could get Janus into his apartment parking deck around two or three on Thursday morning," Apollo replied, spitting out a well-used wad of tobacco and replacing it with a fresh one. "His parking spot is on the second level. Once you're in there, locate his car and place an explosive device underneath it, somewhere out of sight.

You should be able to tape it to the undercarriage. Neptune, I want you to find a parking spot alongside 57th and wait for him to leave for work later in the morning. Once he pulls out onto 57th, get in behind him and follow him all the way to his office building. The detonator will be radio-controlled so you'll be able to hit the switch at any time along the way. Try to stay within four or five car-lengths behind him and you should be fine with the signal. Much further and you may be out of range.

Now the blast will go straight up and straight down, so except for a nice big hole in the asphalt, you shouldn't have to worry about collateral damage. Make sure you hit the button before he goes through the security gate at the NBC building. Try to get him right outside their building, somewhere on the street where it will cause the most chaos. If you wait for him to turn onto West 49th, you can continue on the Avenue of the Americas and not make the turn behind him, just hit your switch as you pass through the intersection at 49th. Once the charge goes off, hall ass down the Avenue and get the hell out of there. All of the commotion will be behind you, so you should be able to get out of there with no problem."

"Sounds good," Neptune said. "What about Janus? After he places the charge under the car, do you want him to hang around and get in with me?"

"Absolutely not," Jupiter interjected. "Once you've done your part, Janus, I want you to head back here. We don't need our assets unnecessarily exposed. You can handle your part, Neptune, by yourself. And if something does go horribly wrong, you know what to do."

"I've got my pill right here," Neptune said as he patted his shirt pocket.

The *Sons* went over every possible detail of the task ahead. Although they had five days before execution of the mission, they decided it would be prudent for Janus and Neptune to get to New York as soon as possible. Janus would need to get familiar with the apartment parking deck at Hayes' complex and Neptune would need to get familiar with the route from Hayes' apartment to the NBC building at 30 Rock.

Although no more than a couple of miles, Neptune needed to see what the traffic flow would be like on the route during the time Hayes generally left for the office, usually around 10:00 a.m.

Janus and Neptune drove separately to New York and spent sufficient time preparing for their mission. Each felt ready; comfortable they would be able to pull it off without a hitch.

While simple in its design, the explosive device Janus would place underneath Hayes' car would be devastatingly lethal. His bomb was made from two metal pipes, an inch and a half in diameter and cut to nine inches in length, the ends threaded so metal caps could be screwed on. After packing the pipes with black powder and screwing on the caps, Janus inserted fuses through tiny holes drilled in the ends of two of the caps. Once inserted, the fuses were tied together and connected to a radio-controlled detonator. Janus used a strand of black duct tape to bind everything together.

At precisely 2:15 a.m. on the morning of the mission, Janus entered the parking deck of Hayes' apartment complex wearing black sneakers, black pants, a long-sleeved black pullover and a black ski mask. His apparel would obscure his features from the surveillance cameras present inside the parking garage and make it impossible for law enforcement to identify him once they got around to viewing the tapes. By that time, the job would be completed and he would be long gone.

After quietly slipping into the parking area where the 2015 Lexus was parked, Janus crawled underneath the car, used more duct tape to secure the pipe bomb to the undercarriage, and then activated the transmitter connected to the fuses. Twenty minutes later he pulled onto I-95 and headed south back towards D.C.

While Janus carried out his part of the mission, Neptune sat seated behind the wheel of his car parked alongside 57th Street with a clear view of the exit ramp of Hayes' parking garage. Reclining his driver's seat so his head would be out of view, Neptune set the alarm on his watch so he wouldn't make the mistake of falling asleep and miss Hayes when he pulled out of his garage. At 9:48 a.m. Neptune spotted his target as

Hayes' car departed the parking garage and pulled out onto 57th Street, presumably in route to the NBC building at 30 Rock.

As Hayes' car passed by, Neptune pulled out and got in behind him, careful to keep a distance of four to five car lengths. As Hayes made his turn onto Avenue of the Americas, Neptune noticed the light at the intersection turn from green to yellow. Not wanting to get caught by the light, Neptune sped up so he wouldn't be forced to stop and lose his visual on Hayes. Although he knew he had time to make it through the intersection before the light turned red, a New York City transit bus coming from the opposite direction rushed through the yellow light and turned in front of Neptune, apparently thinking Neptune would stop for the light. Having to step on his brakes to avoid a collision with the bus, Neptune had to wait a few seconds before completing his turn and continuing. Unfortunately, the bus he almost collided with was now between him and his target and traveling at a slow rate of speed.

Flushed with panic, Neptune knew if he didn't get around the bus, Hayes would make the turn onto 49th Street and he would be too far back to detonate the bomb. Gunning his accelerator to pass the bus, Neptune narrowly avoided a head-on collision with another vehicle coming in the opposite direction, while losing sight of his target. As Neptune reached the intersection at 49th Street, he looked to his left hoping to spot Hayes' car. When he didn't see it, he decided to make the turn onto 49th Street instead of continuing down the Avenue, as he had originally planned. Attempting to catch up to Hayes before he reached the turn lane into the NBC building, Neptune sped up hoping to reacquire a visual on his target. As he neared the turn lane for the NBC garage, Neptune looked to his left and saw Hayes' car stopped beside the guard gate at the garage entrance. A uniformed NBC guard was leaning into Hayes' car, no doubt checking his I.D. before allowing him to enter.

Neptune had missed his opportunity. He knew if he hit the switch now, he would most certainly kill the innocent guard, not something he, nor any of the other *Sons* could tolerate. Knowing he had failed in his mission, he got out of there as fast as possible. He could do nothing now but go back home and try to explain to his colleagues what happened.

Jupiter, Apollo, Orcus and Janus were at their respective homes watching T.V., each expecting a news bulletin to flash on the screen announcing an explosion at the NBC headquarters building. At 10:00 a.m., no bulletin. At 10:15 a.m., still nothing. By 10:30 a.m. they all had a sinking feeling something had gone wrong. At that moment Jupiter received a text from Neptune, and it wasn't the text he had been expecting.

It read: *liberty failed–NSOL, Neptune.*

Uh oh, thought Jupiter. *The shit is about to hit the fan.*

At 10:53 a.m. the MSNBC news program on air ran a banner across the screen that read: *Breaking News.* Jupiter leaned in to listen.

"A few short minutes ago," began the reporter, "security personnel at the NBC headquarters building in Manhattan discovered a pipe bomb taped to the underside of a car being driven at the time by MSNBC News host Mark Hayes."

Virtually every office building in Manhattan had been under heightened security efforts due to the never-ending threat of terrorist attacks. After Hayes showed his NBC I.D. at the guard gate entering the parking garage, a second security guard came over for a security check of his car. After extending a long pole with a mirror attached to look underneath the car, the guard discovered the explosive device Janus had taped to the undercarriage.

Every news outlet in America now ran with the story.

TV news host Mark Hayes targeted for assassination became the line most used to introduce the story.

"Hayes," said one of the hosts on MSNBC "could not be reached for comment." No doubt too shaken and upset to appear on camera.

FBI Agent Rich Michaels sat behind his desk when another agent came out of a conference room where a TV had on the story.

"Rich," the other agent said to Michaels, "get in here. You've got to see this."

Agent Michaels went into the conference room and watched the report for about ten minutes. Pulling his cell phone out of his pocket, he dialed the number to Casey Dean.

"Are you watching this?" he asked her.

"I've got it on now," she replied.

"You nailed it, Casey," he told her. "Damn, I had my doubts but you were dead-on with this one."

"I wish I wasn't," replied Casey. "For once in my life I wish I had been wrong. By the way, I'm giving you the heads up I promised. This thing with Mark Hayes makes it more likely than not our theory about these murders has merit. I'm going with my story as soon as I can get it run by my editor. Look for it to come out as early as tomorrow."

"Thanks for the early notice," Rich replied, "I'll let the Director know it's coming out. He's going to want the President to have a heads up on this as well. I'm sure it's going to create a firestorm."

Casey Dean's front-page story in the Washington Chronicle the next day had the same effect as pouring kerosene on an already raging fire. Every news story in America led with what almost happened to Hayes outside the NBC studios in downtown New York City. Casey's story ratcheted everything up to another stratosphere. Positing her theory that the attempted assassination of Mark Hayes could be tied to the murders of both Justice Byers and S.P.A. head CeCe Diamond, Casey contended in her article a conspiracy actively targeting liberal Americans for assassination could be in play. The only thing her story missed was the inclusion of the *heart attack*, which took the life of another raging liberal, Chris Dyess.

***

Several days after the attempted assassination of Mark Hayes, Rich Michaels sat at his desk trying to make heads or tails of where his investigation might be going. Leaping up from his desk, he sprinted out of the office and into his car for the quick drive over to the Hoover building. Deanna Mowery had phoned Rich to tell him they had a positive I.D. on his suspect.

"What'd you find, Deanna?" Rich asked with exasperation as he stepped into her office, completely out of breath.

The photo of Rich's suspect from the Metro station camera sat on Deanna's desk, lying next to another photo of a man in military dress blues.

"Master Sergeant Steve Lick," she said with a smile as she tapped the second photo with her finger. "He's your guy."

"How'd you find him?" Rich asked.

"We came up empty on all of the photos we had of known criminals," she began. "So, we started scouring the databases of government people, all of whom had ID photos on file. No luck there either. Then we decided to look at military ID photos. I called over to the Pentagon and they were very helpful. That's when we found this guy."

"What do we know about him?" Rich asked.

"Special Forces," she replied. "Served in Iraq. His file says he trained as a sniper, and if that's not interesting enough, here's something else. He got wounded in battle. Apparently, he had been riding in a Humvee when it ran over an IED. The explosion ripped through the bottom of his vehicle and blew off part of his leg. After the V.A. fitted him with a prosthetic, he received an honorable discharge."

"Holy shit!" exclaimed Rich. "Where is he now?"

"Would you believe he lives right here?" she asked with a sly smile. "The Pentagon mails his disability check to an address in Woodbridge, Virginia."

"Damn, Deanna," Rich replied. "I knew you were good, but this is ridiculous. It must be difficult for you, all of the pressure and all."

"What are you talking about?" She had a quizzical look on her face.

"Beauty AND brains?" He responded with a smile.

"Get the hell out of my office!" She had to laugh.

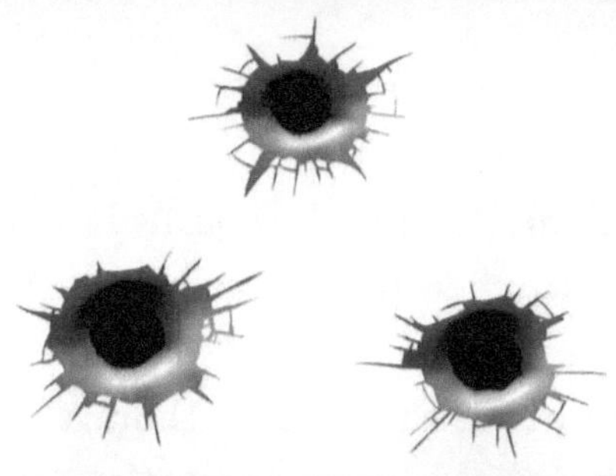

Chapter Twenty-Two

White House Press Secretary Michael Thomas expected his daily White House briefing to be anything but routine. White House pressers this far into a President's term, especially when it's a second term, tend to be less confrontational. Mr. Thomas had been doing it for more than seven years and by now had built up a fairly cordial relationship with the reporters covering the White House, the banter back and forth mostly civil. On this particular morning, however, the White House press corps would not be placated with dodged answers or less than forthright statements coming from the President's mouthpiece.

Mr. Thomas began by informing the reporters the FBI Director had earlier met with the President to inform him the FBI would be expanding their investigation into the murder of Justice Byers, considering the possibility it might be tied to the murder of Ms. Diamond and the attempted murder of news reporter Mark Hayes. Alluding to the recent article in the Washington Chronicle by Casey Dean, Mr. Thomas also suggested the three separate crimes might be part of a larger conspiracy to target liberal Americans for assassination.

"The President believes," Mr. Thomas commented as he took a deep breath, "it is entirely possible the reporting in the Washington Chronicle has merit. And like most Americans, the President is appalled at the notion holding political views contrary to conservative orthodoxy can somehow justify the violent actions we have witnessed against these individuals. This is America, and Americans have the right to practice their religion or practice their politics as they see fit. No one should be targeted for having views different from someone else's."

A reporter raised his hand and Mr. Thomas nodded. He stood to ask the first question.

"But Michael," he began, "Democrat political leaders, including the President himself, have suggested policies some Republicans have voiced support for have either been racist, homophobic or perhaps misogynistic. Don't you think rhetoric like that could have led to the reaction apparently some have taken against your side?"

"I think your question is totally absurd," Thomas forcefully responded. "There is no justification for what has happened. Political differences should be settled at the ballot box, not at the point of a gun. Conservatives are free to air their differences with the President, but they are not free to take matters into their own hands and exact retribution against those with whom they disagree."

"How do you know these crimes were committed by conservatives?" the next reporter asked. "Does the FBI have any suspects?"

"I'm not saying these crimes were necessarily committed by conservatives," Thomas said, trying to walk back his last comment. "I'm saying, political discourse should involve an exchange of ideas between two points of view and should never resort to violence when trying to settle those differences. And as far as the FBI investigation goes, the Director has assured the President the Bureau is fully engaged in this investigation and they will let no stone go unturned in solving this case."

"Does the President see any connection with these crimes to the Senate's recent rejection of his nomination to the Supreme Court?" asked another reporter.

"With regards to the Republican-controlled Senate's rejection of Judge Garrett," began Thomas, "the President is obviously disappointed the Senate once again has failed to do its job. Judge Garrett, by all accounts, is eminently qualified to sit on the Supreme Court. The President, and I think most clear-thinking Americans, saw what the Republican Senators did as partisan politics at its worst. The Senate abdicated their responsibility in order to score political points with the base of their party. I think it's reasonable to assume they did this in the misguided hope it will increase turnout for them on Election Day. I'm not sure anyone can argue with this assessment. And to add, I think it is shameful the Republican-controlled Senate has denied a good man an up or down vote when he surely earned the right to have it. I think most Americans would agree as well."

"But Michael," the same reporter continued, "does the President believe Senator Smith orchestrated the Senate's rejection of Judge Garrett because he is running for President? Obviously, if Senator Smith wins in November, he will get to pick his own nominee."

"I'm saying," responded Thomas with a heightened level of irritation in his voice, "the President believes his nominee to the Supreme Court worthy of a fair hearing and should have received an up or down vote in the Senate. Denying him the vote smacks of politics. I have no idea what the motivation of Senator Smith is and whether or not he orchestrated anything. I'm saying Judge Garrett did not receive fair treatment and the Senate did a disservice to the American people by not holding a vote on his nomination."

Senator Smith couldn't help but smile as he sat in his senate office watching the White House presser on television. The Democrats were starting to panic, he believed, as Michael Thomas did not summarily reject the notion of the supposed conspiracy being tied to the desire for Republicans to gain back control of the White House. Now in the race for the presidency, the Senator would need to stay above the fray and display an unequivocal rejection of any violence taken against anyone for political reasons. Amy Killen, his political advisor and campaign chairwoman, had been telling him for weeks his best chance to win the nomination would be for him to appear *presidential*, which is exactly what he had been doing.

"Don't stoop to their level," Ms. Killen advised Senator Smith. "Let the other guys get down in the mud. The voters are looking for a mature, steady hand. We win if you maintain the course," came her sage advice.

As Senator Smith left the Russell Building to head back out on the campaign trail, he stopped to talk to reporters who wanted his reaction to the latest news.

"Senator Smith," a reporter asked, "what's your reaction to the case being made that the murders of Justice Byers and Ms. Diamond, and the attempted assassination of Mark Hayes are somehow related?"

"I have complete faith in the FBI Director to get to the bottom of it all," he replied. "I have no opinion on whether or not they are connected. Obviously, I am not privy to what the FBI knows. The best thing for me to do, and everyone else for that matter, is let the FBI do their job. I have read some of the reporting done in the Washington Chronicle concerning this case and it seems to me their reporting has provided some validity to the notion there is an effort by someone to silence voices of dissent. Now, I have no independent knowledge of that, I'm only basing this on what I've read. But I can tell you this, the FBI is the finest law enforcement agency in the world and I have no doubt they will figure this out."

"I will also add," the Senator continued, "for once, I agree with the President on something. And it's this. We should not be settling our political differences with violence. I have been running a positive campaign since I announced my candidacy for President and I don't plan on changing. My campaign has been based on ideas I believe are best for our country. The Ferrell-Hogue administration has been a total disaster and we are seeing more evidence of this every day. Their policies continue to hurt the average American and the rhetoric we are now hearing from the Hogue campaign has been nothing short of divisive. One would have to assume the Vice President has decided the best way for him to get elected is to demonize his political opponents and divide Americans along racial and socioeconomic lines. Appealing to the lowest common denominator of the electorate is not a winning strategy and I don't believe Vice President Hogue will be successful in this regard. As candidates for public office, we should be striving to lift people up, not tear them down."

"Senator Smith," another reporter began, "both the President and his press secretary have made statements regarding the Judiciary Committee hearings on Judge Garrett. Both have suggested your committee did not carry out its duty and, in fact, have let down the American people. Do you care to comment on their characterization of what your committee did?"

"I'd love to," began the Senator's response. "I am proud of the role we played in the process. I think the hearings held on Judge Garrett's nomination showed the American people how wrong the President's choice turned out to be. While he may be a fine and decent man, he does not belong on the Supreme Court and I think our hearings proved that. Politics had nothing to do with it. If the President had sent us a nominee who believed in the primacy of the Constitution as written, he would have received a confirmation vote in the Senate. But the President chose to send us a nominee who does not believe in following the Constitution as written, and his nomination should have been rejected. And for that, neither I nor anyone else on the committee has anything to apologize for. We did our job."

Senator Smith walked away from the reporters telling them he needed to get back on the campaign trail. Several rallies had been scheduled for some of the thirteen states that would be voting on Super Tuesday. A strong showing by his campaign would go a long way to securing the Republican nomination and the exposure he received at the Judiciary Committee hearings definitely boosted his campaign, at least in the eyes of Republican voters. And right now, they were the only ones who mattered. Once he secured the nomination, he would worry about the general election and what he needed to do to attract the independents and moderates, and perhaps even a few Democrats.

Although primary elections for the Democrats were still underway, Vice President Hogue's campaign had begun to pivot towards general election mode. With his nomination virtually assured from the start, the vote on Super Tuesday would most likely put him over the top in terms of delegates needed for him to officially secure the Democrat Party's nomination. His problem, becoming more apparent by the day, would be how the Vice President could generate enthusiasm from the Democrat voters he will need in November.

The paltry low turnout of Democrat voters in their nominating process could logically be attributed to Hogue having no legitimate competition. At least that's how the Democrats were spinning it. When the general election takes place in November, they surmised, their turnout will return to normal. V.P. Hogue continued to try and make the case he needed to be elected so Republicans could not undo all of the good things the Ferrell-Hogue administration had accomplished on behalf of the American people. Convincing voters of what those great accomplishments were, however, had become problematic.

Believe what I'm telling you, not your lying eyes, seemed to be the unofficial slogan of the Vice President's campaign, as more and more Americans were having a hard time believing things were as great as they were being told. Like most Democrats in national elections, Hogue counted on the votes of people Republicans would describe as *low information voters*. If the American people knew how bad the Ferrell policies had been for the country as a whole, he wouldn't stand a chance of getting elected dogcatcher, much less President of the United States. An ignorant electorate is what he needed to achieve victory and his strategy would be the usual Democrat formula in national elections: promise everything, deliver nothing and hope enough people will go to the polls and vote who don't have a clue about what's going on in the world. Unfortunately for the country, this strategy had worked many times in the past.

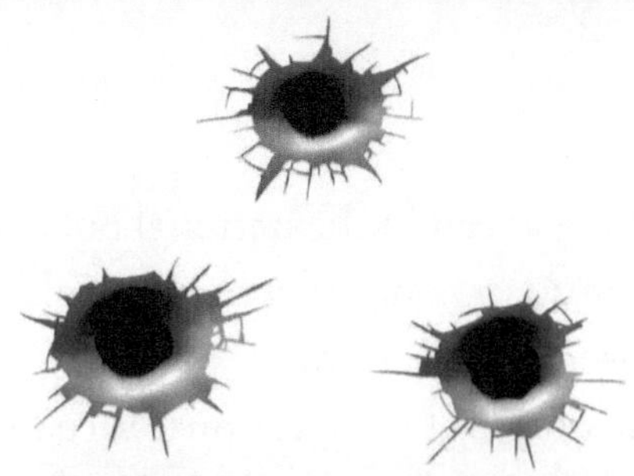

Chapter Twenty-Three

With President Rob Ferrell's final year in office drawing to a close, the country was enjoying relative peace with the possible exception of the political battles raging as Democrats tried to hold onto the White House and possibly win back one or both houses of Congress. The economy was not doing nearly as well as many thought it should, but most Americans seemed willing to give the President a pass. With an overall job approval rating of 51%, not too bad for the final year of the President's second term, Rob Ferrell was viewed by most as having things pretty much under control. At least that's what he kept telling them.

President Ferrell continued to try and make the case to the American people, if he didn't have to work with a recalcitrant congress controlled by those pesky Republicans, his administration could have gotten more done on behalf of the nation. For years the President and most Democrats complained that income inequality, which had gotten worse under the Ferrell administration, had been caused by greedy corporate elites who kept ripping off hardworking Americans so they could line their own pockets. It made no sense, of course, but it didn't seem to matter. The Democrats kept saying it and seemed to always get away with it. No surprise, really, since they had a willing accomplice in the main-stream media, unwilling to call them on their ridiculous babble.

The President kept doing everything he could to pave the way for his successor, whom he hoped would be his Vice President, Eric Hogue.

V.P. Hogue kept polling ahead in the national polls against both Senator Smith and Governor Alan, one of whom would be his Republican opponent in the November election.

In the political history of U.S. elections, Vice Presidents running to succeed their bosses have tried to put daylight between themselves and the Commander-in-Chief under whom they served. The reasons for this were varied. Perhaps the sitting President had low approval numbers at the conclusion of his term, or there were significant policy differences between the two. Usually, however, the Vice President running for a promotion wanted to show the voters he was his own man; independent and in possession of a certain level of gravitas voters were looking for in a President.

Vice President Hogue, however, differed in this regard. Inextricably linked to President Ferrell, the Vice President did not believe creating distance from him would improve his prospects. Hogue needed the President's help and, more importantly, he needed the *Ferrell coalition* of voters that twice elected him to the highest office in the land.

The Vice President kept active on the campaign trail as the date of the Democrat Convention drew closer, to be held at the Pontiac Silverdome in Detroit. Wanting to walk into the convention hall at the Silverdome with the wind at his back, the V.P. calculated his best chance for victory would be to be seen with President Ferrell as much as possible.

The presidency, no matter who occupies the office at the time, is the ultimate platform for national exposure. Eric Hogue knew being seen standing side-by-side with the President would give the appearance of his readiness to simply step into the job. The downside to this, however, would be if a confluence of events occurred which tarnished the luster of the sitting President.

Vice President Hogue had come back to Washington to stand with the President in the Rose Garden as he welcomed a large contingent of Muslim-American Imams. The purpose of the photo-op was for the President to portray how much love and respect he had for the Muslim community. Since the 9/11 attacks on America by Islamic radicals engaged in a *jihad* against the West, several terrorist attacks around the world had been tied to Muslim extremists.

In spite of the overwhelming number of these attacks committed by them, President Ferrell had consistently refused to acknowledge a terrorist problem existed within the Muslim community. Instead, it had been his position to constantly remind Americans and the rest of the world, the Muslim religion is one of peace, and any comments to the contrary were nothing more than religious bigotry.

He continually asserted ISIS and Al-Qaeda were terrorist groups that hijacked the religion of Islam and their acts of terrorism were not tied to the religion of Islam and the hundreds of millions of peace-loving Muslims around the world. Except for a few isolated instances where radicalized Muslim Americans committed acts of violence, America had been relatively free from acts of terrorism. Even in those few instances, President Ferrell refused to acknowledge the Muslim religion had anything to do with the violence. This, despite the fact irrefutable evidence existed indicating the perpetrators were followers of Islam, had been radicalized into waging *jihad*, and had pledged their allegiance to ISIS.

"Ladies and gentlemen," the President said to the crowd gathered in the Rose Garden, "I am honored to stand here with some of the leaders of the Muslim-American community. There has been an effort by some in this country, many of them in positions of political leadership (meaning Republicans), to cast aspersions on a great religion. As I have said many times in the past, the religion of Islam is a religion of peace. Acts of violence we have seen committed throughout the world by those claiming to be Muslims, are in fact acts of violence committed by common terrorists who have nothing whatsoever to do with the religion of Islam. Any claim to the contrary is simply not true. The United States of America is not at war with Muslims. Terrorists belonging to ISIS and Al-Qaeda have attempted to hijack a peaceful religion. I will not give credence to the notion they are somehow part of the religion. They are not. While ISIS is a problem in the Middle East and in parts of Europe, they are not a threat to our homeland in the United States. As a matter of fact, their sphere of influence is on the decline as more peace-loving people around the world reject their hateful ideology. As Americans, we must all reject the efforts of extreme elements in our country to tie radical terrorism to the Islamic religion."

From a political standpoint, Vice President Hogue considered it a homerun for his campaign, as he relished the idea of being portrayed as an American leader who welcomed all people, regardless of background, into the fabric of this country. Like most other Democrats, however, he favored open borders. While he could never come out in favor of illegal immigration, nonetheless, he supported no national effort to curb it. Viewing all illegal immigrants as potential Democrat voters, he would not take part in doing anything to reduce those numbers.

Like the President himself, V.P. Hogue considered Muslims to be the latest group of people victimized by those he considered religious bigots. He wanted to be seen standing up for them, in hopes doing so would garner him more votes. The picture of him standing with the President as he welcomed Muslim leaders to the White House, decrying religious bigots wherever they existed, was pure political gold, he thought. Unfortunately for him, the optics would soon take on new meaning.

About the same time the President addressed those in the Rose Garden, a young man and woman stepped off a Greyhound bus pulling into a covered parking area outside the Mall of America. The Mall of America is the largest shopping mall in the U.S., located in Bloomington, Minnesota, a suburb of Minneapolis, the hometown of President Ferrell. Minneapolis is also where preliminary plans were underway to build Rob Ferrell's Presidential Library.

In spite of warm temperatures, the man and woman were wearing large long-sleeved jackets, zipped all the way up in front. As they entered the mall, they made their way to the large and crowded food court area. Once there, they separated and walked to opposite ends of the room. A witness later stated the man shouted *Allahu Akbar,*" right before he and his female companion simultaneously triggered explosive bomb vests they each wore under their jackets. The explosions killed twenty-six innocent people along with the two terrorists.

Within hours of the attack, FBI investigators positively identified the couple as a brother and sister from New York City. After securing a search warrant for the terrorists' New York apartment, the FBI raided their residence and found bomb-making material and emails on their computer directly linking them to ISIS. When investigators dug a little further, they discovered the terrorists were members of a local Mosque in Queens, New York. In an ironic twist, the leader of this Mosque happened to be one of the Imams that stood with President Ferrell and Vice President Hogue in the Rose Garden the day the attack took place.

President Ferrell, and by extension Vice President Hogue, looked like utter fools. If the majority of the electorate had not yet been engaged in the two primary contests underway before this, they were certainly paying attention now. This was potentially catastrophic for the Hogue campaign. The President, of course, voiced his outrage at what happened and expressed his condolences to the victims and their families. He did his best to convince Americans yet again the horrendous attack on shoppers at the mall in Minnesota had absolutely nothing to do with the religion of Islam.

The American people were having none of it. They were sick and tired of a spineless President who still refused to acknowledge the problem festering throughout the world, one that had struck us here in our own backyard.

National security moved to the top of everyone's list as the most important issue of the campaign season. From a purely political point of view, while the events at the Mall of America dealt a vicious blow to V.P. Hogue's chances of succeeding President Ferrell in the White House, it bolstered the chances of Senator Brian Smith. From the beginning of the campaign season, Senator Smith received the highest marks when it came to issues of the military and national security. With the terrorist attack fresh on the minds of primary voters, his standing in the Republican field reached new heights. Governor Alan and businessman

Mark Wooddall were still in the race but the outcome of the Republican contest became a *fait accompli*.

Senator Smith dominated the primary contests held on Super Tuesday and followed up those victories with more dominating performances in later states. The majority of the Republican Party began to coalesce behind his candidacy, as the time had come for the Party to come together in preparation for the general election. Nobody on the Republican side had any illusions the terrorist attack had destroyed any chance for a Hogue victory, cognizant that by the time the November election rolled around, the wounds to the American psyche caused by the events at the Mall of America would not be quite as fresh. President Ferrell, of course, would still be President and would use the power of his office to help V.P. Hogue. Senator Smith and the Republican Party were not about to underestimate the President's ability to sway voter sentiment in the direction of his Vice President.

What Senator Smith couldn't know, however, was his campaign would soon get a boost from the unlikeliest of places: the Rob Ferrell administration itself. Two months after the terrorist attack that took the lives of twenty-six innocent Americans, President Ferrell spoke to the nation in a prime-time address from the Oval Office. An address he felt necessary to stem the tide of dissent seemingly building against him over his foreign policy in general, and his indifferent response to the terrorist attack in particular.

"My fellow Americans," he said to the nation as he began his primetime address. "The tragic events that unfolded near my own hometown were nothing short of a national tragedy. As our nation continues to grieve the loss of innocent life, we must not give in to the misguided urge by some who have called for our nation to react in a manner not consistent with our ideals as Americans. Some have called on me as your Commander-in-Chief to launch military strikes in the Middle East as retaliation for what happened at the Mall of America. Many of these voices seem to infer America is somehow at war with the Nation of Islam. We are not. The two people who committed the horrific acts we saw in Minnesota claimed an alliance with the terrorist group known as ISIS. A group that is not representative of the hundreds of millions of peace-loving Muslims around the world."

"We must resist the urge," the President continued, "to risk the lives of our brave men and women in uniform for the sole reason of seeking revenge for those whose lives were tragically and needlessly lost in this senseless attack. As I have stated many times in the past, I will not commit our troops to military attacks on the other side of the globe, hoping to wipe out the forces of ISIS, when doing so would risk the indiscriminate killing of innocent Muslims, as well as the lives of our American soldiers. ISIS is the enemy, not the religion of Islam. I will continue my strategy of using our military might to contain ISIS and will refuse the call by some to get our country bogged down in another ground war in a far-off land where the lives of American troops and innocent Muslim citizens are put at risk. I will not provide the forces of ISIS another recruitment tool in their efforts to attract followers to their cause."

Four-star Army General J. Gordon Shirley, the President's selection to be Chairman of the Joint Chiefs of Staff two years earlier, watched the President's address from his office in the Pentagon. Steam literally billowed from his ears as he listened to the President's address. For more than eight months the General had been recommending to the President he take a more active role in his efforts to hunt down and destroy ISIS. General Shirley and other military leaders had been telling the President for months if the U.S. did not begin a major military offensive against ISIS in the Middle East, they were certain to bring their fight against us to our own backyard. Which is exactly what happened as evidenced by the attack on Americans inside the Mall of America. Yet, here was the President on national television, once again refusing to acknowledge the obvious. Unable to stand it any longer, General Shirley showed up at the White House first thing the following morning.

"You seem upset General," the President sarcastically commented to General Shirley when he walked into the Oval Office.

General Shirley shook the hands of the President and Vice President Hogue, also in attendance, before sitting down on the couch in front of the President's desk.

"Mr. President," the General began, "with all due respect, sir, but what the hell are you doing? What in God's name were you trying to accomplish with that bullshit speech last night?"

"Hold on, Gordon," V.P. Hogue said as he jumped to the defense of his boss, "let's not lose sight of the fact you're speaking to your Commander-in-Chief."

"Mr. President," General Shirley said as he began to calm down, "the Joint Chiefs and I have been telling you for months something like this would happen if we didn't take a more aggressive stand against ISIS. You said in your address to the nation last night you are afraid of us being used as a recruitment tool for them. I hate to tell you this, sir, but a year ago they had a handful of followers. Six months ago, they had maybe five thousand. Today their numbers are upwards of eighty thousand and they're spread out in more than thirty countries. Isn't it obvious to you they are not having any trouble attracting new members?"

"That's not the only issue, Gordon," the President responded. "As you know, when I came into office I told the American people I would stop getting us into needless ground wars in the Middle East. I don't plan on going back on that promise."

The General would not back down.

"Then can you please explain to me, what the hell good is it for us to have the mightiest and most capable military in the history of the world, if we're not going to use it to destroy our enemies? They sure as hell are intent on destroying us."

"Our enemy is not the Muslim world," the President said. "ISIS is a bunch of rag-tag wannabees who have some perverted view of their religion. They do not pose an existential threat to our homeland and I'll be damned if I'm going to act like they do."

"Those rag-tag wannabees, as you call them," the General responded with more than a tinge of exacerbation in his voice, "just murdered twenty-six Americans in a damn shopping mall. I bet their families would disagree with your assessment of their capabilities."

"You're out of line, Gordon," V.P. Hogue interjected.

"I'm calling it like it is, Eric," General Shirley replied as he returned his glare to the President.

"Look," the General continued. "You put me in this position to do a job. Part of my job is to advise you on matters pertaining to the military. So, I'm telling you once again, and as forcefully as I know how, we must take the fight to them. This dithering has got to stop. If we are not going to protect the American people, then we ought to be honest and tell them the truth."

"Damn it, Gordon," the President shouted back at his top military adviser, irritated his strategy had been questioned. "That's bullshit and you know it. Maybe you've forgotten who the damn President is. So, let me remind you. I'm the one who gets to set our foreign policy with regards to the use of our military, and you're the one who gets to carry it out. Now if you're not prepared to do that, perhaps I need to get someone who will."

"Mr. President," General Shirley retorted without hesitation, "it is your privilege to relieve me anytime you want."

"Now come on, Gordon," the President replied, trying to relieve the tension escalating in the room. "I don't think it needs to come to that. I put you in this position because I know you're the best at what you do and I appreciate your advice. I always want you to give it to me unfiltered. But don't expect me to change my strategy. Now I know you may not like it, but my decision on this is final and you're going to have to live with it. Let's just say you and I will agree to disagree on this and leave it at that."

General Shirley left the Oval Office more frustrated than when he walked in. Unfortunately, the results of his meeting with the President and Vice President were pretty much what he had anticipated. There was no getting through to either of them, he thought, and he was getting pretty damned tired of trying.

The General's aide, waiting outside the door to the Oval Office, snapped to attention when the General and the Commander-In-Chief appeared in the doorway following the conclusion of their intense encounter. After shaking hands with the President and Vice President, General Shirley saluted his Commander-In-Chief and left the White House in the company of his aide.

"That weak son-of-a-bitch is going to get us all killed," General Shirley commented to his aide once they reached the outside grounds of the White House. "And his lackey Hogue is no better. The smug bastard sat there the whole time drooling on himself. He's as misguided as his boss. God help us if he wins in November."

"Do you think he'll win?" the General's aide asked.

"Not if I can help it," replied General Shirley.

Three days after his meeting with the President and Vice President, General J. Gordon Shirley announced his immediate retirement from service. The announcement came as a surprise to the administration and a gut punch to the Vice President. The optics of the timing of the General's retirement did not look good. As the highest-ranking military officer in the country, the General made no secret his stepping down was in direct response to the tepid way the President had been handling the threat of global terrorism most Americans believed existed.

Frankly speaking, President Ferrell couldn't care less about General Shirley stepping down, preferring someone in office who didn't question his decision-making. V.P. Hogue, on the other hand, became concerned about how it might impact his race for President. Needing things to go as smoothly as possible between now and the November election, the Vice President could ill afford any turmoil existing at the highest levels of government. The embarrassment to the administration caused by the sudden resignation of General Shirley was exactly what the Hogue campaign did not need.

"That son-of-a-bitch cut my throat," V.P. Hogue said to one of his staffers after the General's announcement.

Two weeks later, the Vice President's campaign efforts would take yet another blow. Only this time it would come in a much subtler way and at the hands of the *New Sons of Liberty.*

***

"Fred, this is Eric," the Vice President said after placing a call to his friend Fred Stein. "It's been a bad couple of weeks. I need to know you've got things under control down there. As I'm sure you are aware, Ohio is going to be crucial."

"Don't worry Mr. Vice President," Stein replied. "We're working hard down here. I'm sure Ohio will go our way."

"It better," the V.P. responded before hanging up his phone.

Fred Stein had become a critical player in the Vice President's hopes of winning the state of Ohio in the general election. As a community organizer, Stein had worked to influence government, corporations and other institutions in order to better the lives of those in his community who were otherwise powerless to do so on their own. In reality, he was nothing more than a political hack, stopping at nothing to see Democrats elected to public office.

What Stein had been working on for several weeks in furtherance of the Hogue campaign, went unsaid in his phone conversation with the Vice President. Several large cardboard boxes sat on the floor beside Stein's desk in his office on St. James Avenue in Cincinnati. The boxes contained thousands of absentee ballots Stein and his staff had planned on filling out for the upcoming election. The names of the voters who were going to cast those ballots, most assuredly for Vice President Hogue, had not yet been determined. Three of Stein's staff members had gone to the Calvary Cemetery on Duck Creek Road to obtain the names to go on those ballots. Fred Stein had been counting on a position in a Hogue Administration and didn't want to leave anything to chance.

Janus had used a fake I.D. when checking into the Spring Hills Suites on Eden Park Drive, a couple of blocks from Stein's office. Posing as an insurance salesman, he spent two and a half weeks keeping an eye on Stein, working out in the hotel gym, and chasing skirts at *O'Malley's In the Alley,* an Irish pub in downtown Cincy.

Following Stein around for seventeen days had become tedious for Janus, with the exception of one particular place Stein liked to visit. The 4Play Club and Lounge on Sycamore Street was apparently Fred Stein's favorite place to go and unwind after a grueling day of strong-arming local businesses and government officials. Janus rather enjoyed this part of his assignment and paid for several lap dances inside the club so he would *fit in*. Stein, Janus noticed, regularly visited one of the VIP rooms each time he went there.

"Honey," Fred said to his wife on the phone before wrapping up for the day, "I've got a couple more meetings before I'm done. I should be home pretty late so don't wait up. I'll grab something to eat between meetings."

Janus watched from across the street as Stein hung up the phone, locked the office front door and got into his car to leave. As soon as Stein made a turn onto Columbia Parkway, Janus knew where he was headed. After watching Stein enter 4Play, Janus parked his car five blocks away and walked to the club. Grabbing his usual table near the back, Janus could see Stein sitting near the stage up front. Already working on his second glass of bourbon, Stein got up from his table when a tuxedoed employee came over to escort him to one of the VIP rooms. Janus made note of the door adjacent to the VIP rooms, leading to the back alley behind the club, where he would make his escape after completing his mission.

Knowing Stein usually took between thirty and forty minutes to conclude his *business* inside the VIP room, Janus waited at his table a good fifteen minutes before making his move in that direction. Before rising, Janus removed a Sig Sauer P320 9mm pistol, with the serial numbers removed, from his waistband and held it underneath his table as he screwed a silencer onto the muzzle.

After sliding the weapon underneath his shirt, he rose from his table and began walking towards the VIP room where he had seen his target enter. Assuming there would be surveillance cameras inside the club, he disguised his appearance by wearing large, black-rimmed glasses and a black beanie. The three weeks' worth of facial hair growth would further mask his identity and would be shaved off as soon as he returned to his hotel room after taking care of Mr. Stein.

Before approaching the VIP room containing his target, Janus went inside the men's room and removed his phone from his pocket. Dialing the number to the 4Play club, Janus told the person answering the phone a fight had broken out between two drunken guys outside the club's front door and they'd better send someone outside before the fight got out of hand. After giving the bouncers inside enough time to leave their posts and go outside to see about the fight, Janus departed the restroom and made a beeline to Stein's VIP room.

Drawing his pistol from his waistband, Janus gave the door a swift kick splintering the wooden doorframe around the door's latch. The door slammed open, scarring the hell out of Stein and his female companion and exposing Janus to a sight he knew would haunt him forever. Fred Stein stood facing the door, completely naked with his hands stretched out to the side and secured with leather straps to eye bolts on the wall. Janus would later joke to Neptune it reminded him of Jesus hanging on the cross.

In addition to Stein being tied up, he had a bright orange plastic ball shoved in his mouth so he couldn't talk and a long black scarf covered his eyes. Most likely startled by the sound of the door crashing in, Stein began making indiscernible muffling sounds with his mouth. The female, apparently in the role of a dominatrix, wore only spiked boots and a black leather bustier.

As soon as the door crashed in, the leather *cat-o-nine tails* whip she had been using to *punish* her perverted client went flying across the room as she fell face down on the floor screaming. Unable to accurately describe the person who broke into their room, she would later tell the cops the man was a black male wearing a ski mask. With his blindfold intact, Fred Stein never saw what hit him. Raising his pistol to eye level, Janus unloaded his 15-round magazine into Stein's chest before dropping the gun at Stein's feet and leaving through the back door.

Back inside his hotel room twenty minutes later, Janus pulled the *burner* phone out of his pocket he had used to make the bogus call from the men's room and typed out his text message to Jupiter: *liberty prevails–NSOL, Janus.*

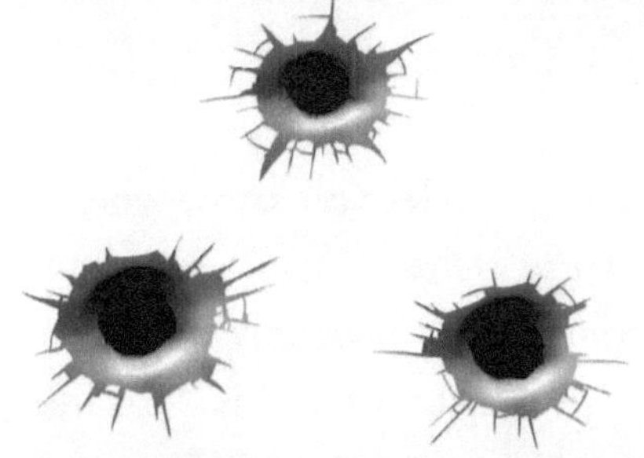

CHAPTER TWENTY-FOUR

Rich Michaels and Jimmy O'Rourke sat around a conference table at the FBI's WFO. Open before them sat the case file on the Byers and Diamond murders, and the attempted assassination of Mark Hayes. Now fully convinced of the existence of a conspiracy to eliminate American leftists, the investigators would be adding the name of Fred Stein to the file. Rich Michaels would travel to Cincinnati later in the day to talk with the local police about the murder of Fred Stein inside the 4Play Club and Lounge but did not expect to find anything shedding new light on their investigation. The female witness, *working* on Stein moments before he was killed, would be absolutely no help. To make matters worse for the police, the surveillance cameras inside the club hadn't been working for over a month.

"Other than pure speculation," Jimmy said to Rich, "do we have anything concrete making the connection? It's certainly an interesting theory, and not one I am prepared to refute, but I'd sure like to have something concrete to tie them together."

"I totally agree," responded Rich. "Let's go over what we have and talk about what our next move should be. Let's start with Byers. We know a professional killed him, or at least someone savvy enough to commit the murder in a theater where other people were present and walk out without being noticed."

"And let's not forget," added Jimmy, "he did it without leaving a speck of evidence behind."

"Precisely," said Rich. "I'll let you know when I get back from Cincy if I find anything of use there. I spoke to our Cincinnati office this morning and they told me it's probably a wasted trip, but I still need to go. These guys are professionals and it's not likely they left anything behind. In the meantime, while I'm gone I want you to concentrate on what we do have that's promising. Now, the judge twice wrote in his journal, within a couple weeks of his murder, about the guy with a limp following him. Hopefully, it's the guy we spotted on the Metro tapes. And now, thanks to my new best friend Deanna, we think we have a positive I.D.," Rich said as he dropped the picture of Steve Lick on the table in front of Jimmy.

Spinning the photo around for Jimmy to see, Rich declared they now had a suspect in the case.

"Deanna and her people were phenomenal," Rich told Jimmy. "We think this is the guy we are looking for."

"Who is he?" asked Jimmy as he picked up the photo and began studying the face of their suspect.

"Steve Lick," said Rich. "Or to be more specific, Master Sergeant Steven Lick, former member of the 5th Special Forces Group out of Ft. Campbell, Kentucky. His military file indicates he trained as a sniper and had several kills over in Iraq. He lost part of his leg when his Humvee ran over an IED buried in a dirt road. After the Army fitted him with a metal leg, he received his honorable discharge and now lives a little south of here in Woodbridge, Virginia. According to the Pentagon, his address on record is 1655 Triad Court. It's where they mail his disability check every month."

"It certainly ties into the killing of Ms. Diamond," Jimmy commented. "Based on what we know about the Diamond hit, the shot taking her out would have been child's play for someone with his skill set."

"Agreed," responded Rich. "But he can't be the only one capable of making that shot. If we're right on this conspiracy angle, there's no way Lick acted alone. There have to be others involved."

"Maybe other former soldiers," Jimmy opined. "Most of these military guys have a hard time putting their faith and trust in others who are not like them. Or at least not in people who haven't shared some of their same experiences."

"Now you're thinking like a seasoned investigator," Rich said with a smile.

He pulled out and opened another file folder.

"I got this from the Pentagon this morning," Rich began. "It's a file on Lick's entire unit, at least those who were in his unit during his service period. Most are still active-duty and don't appear to be of any interest to us, but a couple of them received their discharge about the same time as Lick."

Seven names were on the list of Lick's former unit who were no longer on the military payroll. The former Battalion Executive Officer, Major Bill Allen, Sergeant Hal Masters, and Sergeant David Kyle were among the names on the list.

"The only other sniper in his unit is this guy right here, David Kyle," Agent Michaels said pointing to the official military photo of Sergeant Kyle. "I've got some of our research analysts trying to run down locations of each of these other men. We're running their social security numbers and checking state driver license databases to see if we can find them. Hopefully their research will turn up something soon and we can get some locations for them."

"In the meantime," said Jimmy, "we need to start keeping an eye on Lick. Right now, we don't have anything to charge him with and if he gets wind we're on to him, he'll go underground. We're going to have to be extremely careful not to tip him off."

"Agreed," replied Rich. "After we finish up here why don't you take a trip to Woodbridge and do a cursory drive-by. See what the lay of the land looks like and pick out a few good spots to sit so we can watch his house and be able to pick him up when he leaves."

"Sounds good," said Jimmy. "Now what about Hayes. I'm assuming Lick, as well as any one of these other guys, could have easily managed making the bomb found taped to the undercarriage of his car."

"No doubt about that," replied Rich. "All of these guys would have been highly trained in the use of explosives. What I still can't figure out is why the bomb never went off."

"Maybe the trigger device failed," Jimmy suggested.

"The detonator didn't fail, Jimmy," Rich said. "Our lab guys told me the bomb was hot and the detonator connected to the fuse active. For whatever reason, the guy holding the trigger didn't hit the button."

"Maybe he grew a conscious," Jimmy said with a laugh.

"Not likely," replied Rich.

"Yeah, you're probably right. One thing's for sure, though," said Jimmy.

"What's that?" Rich asked.

"Mark Hayes is glad he didn't hit the button."

Rich smiled in response.

"I'll head south and get back to you when I've scoped things out," Jimmy said to Rich as he got up to leave his office. "Have fun in Cincinnati. Hey, do you think you can bring me back a jug of Gold Star chili? I hear it's pretty good."

"I'll see what I can do," Rich replied with a smile. "See you when I get back."

Jimmy got in his car, drove the thirty miles down I-95 and got off at the Gordon Blvd., Hwy 123 exit for Woodbridge. After making a turn onto Old Bridge Road, he drove a few miles further through the heart of Woodbridge until he found Triad Court. Finding a spot at the end of Lick's street where he could set up for surveillance, Jimmy backed his car in amongst others parked on the street and began keeping a watch on Lick's house.

Jimmy had done this too many times in his long career to count. Television shows and movies about cops always make it seem their life on the job is full of excitement. The reality is an investigator sometimes must spend countless hours sitting behind the wheel of a car simply waiting for a suspect to move. And even when he does move, he may be doing nothing more than going to the gym, the grocery store, or out for a movie. Days, even weeks, can be spent sitting on surveillance waiting for a suspect to do something the investigator can use in his or her investigation. All too aware of this, Jimmy knew it needed to be done. Right now, Steve Lick was the only suspect they had, and if they were going to get a break in this case, Lick would have to be the one to provide it.

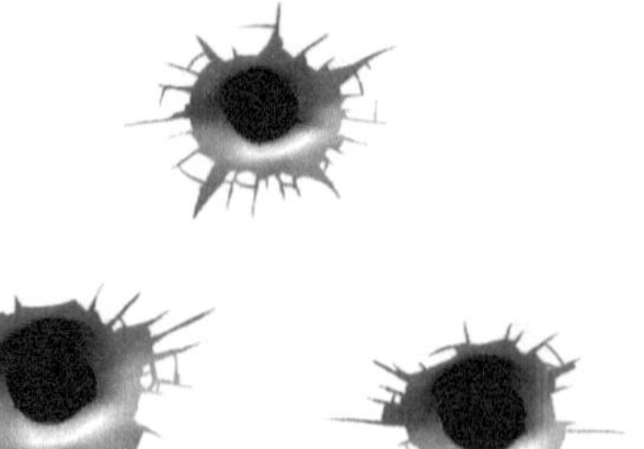

CHAPTER TWENTY-FIVE

The Republican Party had scheduled their nominating convention in Indianapolis, Indiana, inside Lucas Oil Stadium, home of the NFL's Indianapolis Colts. With a capacity of 70,000, the venue would be big enough to hold what the party leaders hoped would be a grand affair. Both political parties liked holding presidential conventions in states deemed to be swing states in the general election, hoping the extravagance of such an event might help influence the voters in the state to side with their candidate. Indiana enjoyed the distinction of being considered a red state, meaning it usually went to the Republicans, and its close proximity to Ohio added even more importance. Well aware of the fact no Republican has ever been elected to the White House without winning Ohio, the Republicans knew how critical the state would be in the general election if they were going to reclaim the White House.

Senator Brian Smith's campaign had picked up a head of steam following the terror attack at the Mall of America because of the importance now being placed on matters of national security. An issue squarely in the middle of the senator's proverbial wheelhouse, the perception voters had of how Senator Smith would combat the growing problem of terrorism proved instrumental in several decisive victories over Governor Alan in the race to secure the nomination.

Businessman Mark Wooddall ran a respectable campaign but never became a factor in the final outcome. Suspending his campaign after finishing a distant third in most of the Super Tuesday contests, Mr. Wooddall lined up behind the candidacy of Senator Smith.

Governor Alan also received credit for running a respectable campaign. Although one of the Super PACs supporting the governor ran negative ads against Senator Smith, they did little to dissuade the voters supporting the Senator. Governor Alan even renounced one of the ads, telling his supporters his campaign wanted only to portray a positive image. He would not get in the gutter in the hope doing so would bolster his chances of winning the nomination. "I will not take the low road to the highest office in the country," he proclaimed on many occasions.

A decent man by all accounts, Governor Alan received praise for the positive and uplifting nature of his campaign and saw his popularity numbers amongst his Indiana constituency soar as a result. The manner in which he conducted himself throughout the campaign also gained him favor from Senator Smith. When the Senator garnered the necessary number of delegates to make him the presumptive nominee, Governor Alan effusively praised Senator Smith and encouraged all of his supporters to join him in rallying around their Party's newly minted nominee. No doubt Governor Alan felt doing so would increase his chances of receiving the number two spot on Senator Smith's presidential ticket.

When it became apparent he had won the Republican nomination, Senator Smith began discussions with his top advisors about the all-important selection of a running mate. Conventional wisdom held nobody ever voted for President based on who sat in the number two position, but a bad pick could potentially be hurtful to the prospects of winning and Senator Smith knew this.

Presidential candidates always consider whether or not a prospective running mate can add a crucial state to the win column in the general election. As evidenced by his win over Senator Smith in the Ohio primary election, Joel Alan demonstrated the degree of his popularity in the Buckeye state as well as his own state of Indiana. With this being a critical factor in Senator Smith's decision about whom to choose as his

Vice President, he announced to the American people two days before the start of the Republican convention he had selected Governor Alan to be his running mate.

Standing in front of a raucous crowd outside Lucas Oil Stadium, Senator Smith introduced his choice of running mate to the nation.

"Ladies and gentlemen," he said, in front of a bank of T.V. cameras and microphones, "it has been the greatest honor of my life to run for the presidency of the United States. The campaign has been long and difficult, with too many eighteen-plus hour days for me to count. But everything we have done so far has brought us to this point. In a couple of days, in this beautiful stadium behind me, the Republican Party will choose its nominee for President. I cannot tell you how important it is for the future of our country that we win in November. The Democrats will meet in Detroit in a few weeks to nominate their candidate for President and will try to convince the American people their candidate, Vice President Eric Hogue, is the person most qualified to assume the mantle of power belonging to the office."

"I am here today to tell you nothing could be farther from the truth," Senator Smith said. "Vice President Hogue has been part of an administration that for eight long years has defied the will of the people. The Ferrell-Hogue administration has snubbed their collective noses at all of us. Through illegal and unconstitutional executive actions, they have essentially shredded the greatest document ever devised by human hands: The Constitution of the United States. Vice President Hogue has been campaigning for the last year telling the American people if we'll give him the chance, he knows what needs to be done to fix the problems in this country. He says we have a problem with income inequality and the wealth gap in this country is out of control. What he doesn't tell you is they have both gotten significantly worse over the past eight years while he and his boss, President Ferrell, have been in charge."

"He says too many jobs are being exported overseas," he continued, "and he will be able to bring those jobs back to America. What he won't tell you are too many Americans have lost their jobs, and fewer have been created since he and President Ferrell were elected eight years ago. He claims many Americans are not paying their fair share of taxes but won't tell you working Americans are now paying the highest percentage of the total tax burden in the history of this country. The National Healthcare Act this administration shoved down the throats of the American people has been the greatest job-killer of our lifetime. Instead of lowering healthcare costs, which President Ferrell and Vice President Hogue promised, their healthcare law raised premiums on every hardworking person in America."

Every cable news channel in America ran Senator Smith's speech live, as the crowd of supporters in attendance continually interrupted his delivery with voracious applause and shouts of, *USA! USA!*

"As if their domestic policies haven't hurt our country enough," he continued, "the foreign policy of the Ferrell-Hogue administration has been worse. Radical Islamic terrorists have declared war on us, yet this administration has refused to acknowledge there is a problem. They have coddled the terrorists because they are afraid of hurting their feelings. They refuse to bomb our enemy because they are afraid doing so would hurt the environment. They refuse to stand with our closest ally in the Middle East, Israel, because of fear the Arab states who already hate us, will hate us even more. To put it bluntly, Rob Ferrell and Eric Hogue are afraid of almost everything, including their own shadows. America must no longer project fear to the rest of the world. Instead, we must project strength. It is the only way we will regain the respect we have lost under this administration. Being liked by others is a desirable endeavor but being respected is paramount. Our friends no longer trust us, and our enemies no longer fear us. Things must change if we are going to continue to be an influence for good in this world."

The crowd cheered even louder as Senator Smith hit all the right notes. The loudest applause, however, would be saved for his next comment.

"It is now my distinct pleasure and personal honor to introduce the next Vice President of the United States: Joel Alan, the Governor of the great state of Indiana."

The crowd went ballistic as Governor Alan shook the hand of his soon-to-be running mate and approached the podium. After waiting a full minute and a half for the applause to die down, he made his brief remarks to the crowd.

"Thank you, Senator Smith," he began. "What an honor it is for a middle-class kid from Fort Wayne, Indiana, to stand before you today as potentially the next Vice President of the United States. This election will possibly be the most important Presidential election of a generation. Senator Smith has demonstrated throughout this campaign he is undoubtedly the leader this country needs at this important time in our history. Vice President Hogue says he wants to be the third term of President Ferrell. In other words, he wants to continue the policies that have made us weaker economically, and perhaps more importantly, weaker on the world stage. I'm not sure our great nation can withstand another term from this bunch."

He waited for more applause and cheering to wane before continuing.

"Not so long ago, Vice President Hogue stood beside the President in the Rose Garden and announced to the world their foreign policy initiatives had neutralized the threat of ISIS, and because of their leadership, our enemies were either contained or on the run. According to them, those of us concerned about the threat of terrorism inside our own country were nothing more than religious bigots. In their view, we are wrong because we are willing to acknowledge the obvious reality that religious zealots, who claim allegiance to Islam, want to kill us. Within twenty-four hours of the President and Vice President's embarrassing display of feckless ignorance, the terrorists they claim are no threat to us, killed more than two dozen of our fellow citizens in a terrorist attack in Minnesota."

"This country," he continued as his speech wound down, "may not survive another four years like the past eight. The damage a Hogue administration would inflict on America would be catastrophic and must be rejected. At this time in our nation's history, the one person most capable of providing the type of leadership we need to keep our homeland safe and regain the respect lost by the current administration is

Senator Brian Smith. I am grateful and humbled by the honor bestowed on me today and I pledge to you, the American people, I will work harder than I ever have at helping Senator Brian Smith become the next President of the United States. Thank you for coming out today in support of the Senator and myself, and may God bless the United States of America."

Senator Smith stepped forward and grabbed the hand of Governor Alan as they soaked up the applause. Raising their hands high above their heads, they waved to the adoring throng of supporters. The wives of the candidates also stepped forward to join their husbands on stage, as all four appeared to enjoy the adulation bestowed upon them.

No Presidential campaign is easy and the two candidates would not take anything for granted. They would work as hard as they possibly could to earn every vote. In two weeks, the Democrats would be nominating their candidate, Vice President Hogue, at their convention in Detroit. Although the V.P. would probably get a minor boost in the polls as most nominees do coming out of their respective conventions, he and most Democrats with a clue knew their prospects for winning the White House were bleak. With an anemic growth rate of one and a half percent and virtually no new jobs being created, the American electorate had become exasperated with an administration more concerned with political correctness than of growing the economy and keeping its people safe. Voters would be looking for someone with a spine to become the next occupant of the Oval Office, as Democrat hopes of remaining in power were fading fast. Riding high with improving prospects for victory in November, the Smith-Alan ticket could not have looked any better.

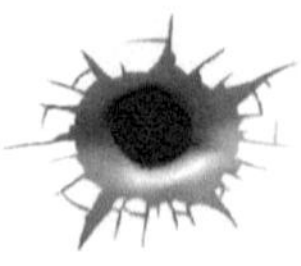

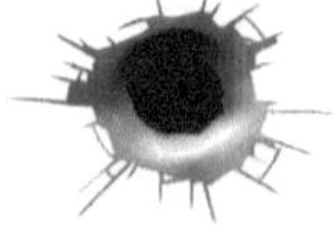

Chapter Twenty-Six

Neptune was still reeling from what he considered to be his failed mission in New York City, although the rest of the *Sons* understood why his mission had failed. To a man, they all told Neptune he ultimately made the right decision in opting to not detonate the bomb under Hayes' car. None of them would have been okay with the collateral damage of an innocent guard being killed along with Mr. Hayes.

Neptune now had a new mission and he vowed not to fail again.

Democrat Senate leader Edmund Riley lived in a modest 1500 sq. ft. apartment in the *Capitol Hill Arms* apartment complex located on Massachusetts Avenue. Only seven blocks from his third-floor apartment to the Capitol, Senator Riley preferred to walk to work on days when the weather permitted. For the immediate future, however, it would no longer be possible due to the security concerns surrounding members of Congress (especially liberal members of which Riley surely belonged). The Capitol Police assigned some of their officers to protection duty for Senator Riley whenever he left his apartment or wandered outside the confines of the U.S. Capitol building. He tried convincing the public he didn't worry about being targeted by the killers, who according to media reports were after American liberals. Although it may have been his public stance, the Senator did not want to take any chances and gladly accepted the police protection provided him.

The murders of Justice Byers, Ms. Diamond and Fred Stein, as well as the failed assassination attempt on Mark Hayes had gotten Senator Riley's attention. The wall-to-wall media coverage of a possible right-wing conspiracy targeting liberals didn't help either. As of late, he tried to not be as loud and boisterous in his defense of liberal causes as he normally would. This change in attitude, however, would not save him. He had earned his spot at the top of the *New Sons of Liberty's* hit list and nothing he could do or say would change it.

For the past week Neptune had been watching Senator Riley come and go from his apartment from a vantage point across the street in Stanton Park. Living alone, Riley usually left his apartment around 8:00 a.m. and got into a waiting Capitol Police squad car for the seven-block drive to the Capitol building. Each night, usually between seven and eight o'clock, another squad car would deliver the Senator back home.

At about 6:00 p.m. on the day the *Sons* had agreed the hit on Riley would take place, Neptune walked up the staircase inside the *Capitol Hill Arms* apartment building. Assuming there would be security cameras inside the Senator's apartment building, Neptune carefully concealed his identity. Normally clean-shaven, he had grown out his facial hair and wore a Washington Nationals baseball cap pulled low on his forehead. A nametag hung from his shirt pocket that read: *Capitol Hill Arms Maintenance*. The nametag, he felt, would make him look like he belonged inside the building should he bump into another resident. Fortunately, he encountered no one. With an hour to complete his part of the mission, he knew if everything went according to plan he would be in and out of Riley's apartment in less than twenty minutes.

Just take your time and don't rush this, he thought. *Everything must go right.*

Approaching the Senator's front door in a hall area where three other apartment doors were present, Neptune reached into his pocket and retrieved a set of lock-pick tools. It took him about six seconds to pick the lock and enter the apartment.

Once inside, he walked over to a bookcase standing against the living room wall and facing the front window, with a direct line-of-sight to

Stanton Park across the street. Reaching again into his pocket, Neptune pulled out a small block of Composition C-4 plastic explosive. With a texture similar to modeling clay, C-4 can be molded into almost any shape one desires. After removing one of the books from the bookcase, Neptune molded the C-4 around the back binding of the book and put it back on the shelf from where it came. Once the book had been replaced, he removed a tiny round infrared reflector from his pocket and pressed it into the molded clay.

Walking into the kitchen, Neptune slid the gas stove away from the wall far enough so he could step in behind it and have access to the gas line running from the wall to the back of the stove. Kneeling between the wall and stove, Neptune retrieved another item from his pocket critically important to the success of this mission: a sealed glass vial containing nitric acid. The colorless and odorless liquid, when applied in concentrated form, would eat through metal as the liquid received exposure to air and began its oxidation process. Crouching down further, Neptune secured a glass container underneath the metal gas line protruding from the wall. After slightly bending the metal line so it rested on the bottom of the container, he unsealed the vial of nitric acid and poured its contents into the glass container, making sure a portion of the metal gas line was completely submerged. The nitric acid immediately began eating through the metal gas line and in about three to four hours would completely eat through, rupturing the line and causing gas to fill the apartment.

Having flawlessly completed his part of the mission, Neptune slid the stove back into its original place and left, with nothing more for him to do but wait. Orcus would handle the next part of the mission later in the evening.

The communications director for the Democrat National Committee had recently announced Senator Riley would be giving the keynote address at the Democrat convention scheduled in Detroit. As one of the Vice President's closest and dearest friends, many insiders believed Senator Riley would have his pick of Cabinet positions in a Hogue administration, should the Vice President be fortunate enough to prevail in November. This day, however, belonged to the Republicans as most of the political attention was on them and their convention in Indianapolis. Senator Brian Smith would be officially accepting the Republican nomination for President sometime around nine-thirty later in the evening.

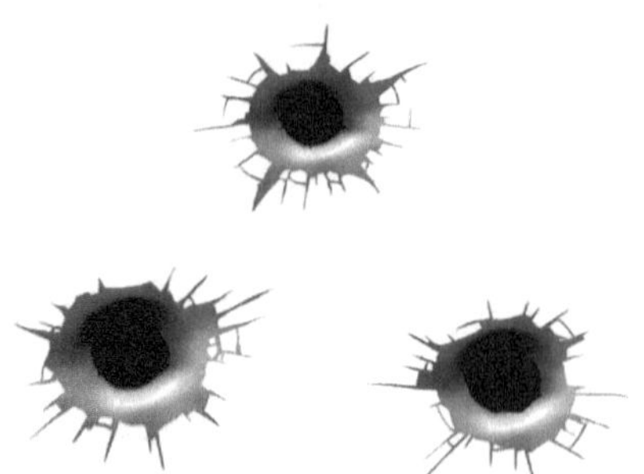

CHAPTER TWENTY-SEVEN

Jimmy O'Rourke and his partner Charlie Bass had been swapping off surveillance duties on Steve Lick's house for the past several weeks without seeing anything of importance. Lick seemed to be fond of going to his gym on Smoketown Road and hanging out at a sport bar adjacent to the Potomac Mills mall. Most of his travel time he spent in and around his home in Woodbridge, except for one day trip to the Walter Reed Medical Center in Bethesda, Maryland, purportedly for a physical therapy session.

With a family vacation trip to the Outer Banks of North Carolina planned, Charlie Bass would be unavailable for the next two weeks, leaving Jimmy with sole responsibility of keeping an eye on Lick until he returned. With nothing better to do one afternoon, Jimmy decided to hop in his car and take a drive down to Woodbridge and set up once again at Steve Lick's house. Assuming it would probably be another wasted effort, he nonetheless phoned Rich Michaels to let him know his intentions.

"Hey Rich, it's Jimmy," he said into his phone. "I'm heading back down to sit on Lick's house again. I'll let you know if I see anything interesting."

"Sure thing, Jimmy," Rich replied. "I've got a meeting with the Director on where we are on this case. I wish I had something new to report to him, but I'm afraid he's going to be disappointed. Seems like things have quieted down. I'll give you a call a little later. Have fun."

"Oh, you know I will," Jimmy sarcastically replied.

After sitting on Lick's house for five hours and seeing absolutely nothing worthwhile, Jimmy decided to call it a night and head home. Now past dinnertime, his suspect had been inside his home since returning from a trip to the grocery store and Jimmy's stomach had begun to growl. His wife phoned to tell him by the time he made it back home she would probably be in bed but would leave some supper for him on the stove.

"Pot roast," she told him.

"Thanks, honey, that sounds great. I'll see you in the morning."

About the time Jimmy cranked his engine to head north, Steve Lick's garage door began to open. A few minutes later Jimmy pulled onto Old Bridge Road behind Steve's car and headed towards the interstate. With nothing of substance to report, he didn't feel a need to call Agent Michaels.

Probably another wild goose chase, he thought.

He couldn't have been more wrong.

Pulling onto the I-95 north on-ramp, Steve Lick began driving towards D.C. with Jimmy on his tail. Maintaining a good distance behind Lick so not to be noticed, Jimmy observed his suspect take the off-ramp for the 14th Street exit. He grabbed his phone and dialed Rich's number.

"Hope I'm not disturbing you, Rich," Jimmy said.

"Just sat down to eat a late supper," Rich replied. "Anything happening?"

"I figured I'd wait to call when our guy did something interesting," Jimmy said. "I didn't think you needed to come out unless I needed you. Right now, I'm following him into the city, getting off at 14th Street as we speak. I'll keep you posted if I see anything, so keep your phone handy and I'll get back to you if anything happens."

"Thanks Jimmy," Rich replied. "I'll take this to go and head your way. If you're going to be out this late, I ought to be out there with you. I'll give you a shout when I'm close. Should be no more than an hour."

"Sounds good," Jimmy said.

Steve Lick turned off 14th Street onto Constitution Avenue and parked his car along the road near the Smithsonian Museum of Natural History. Jimmy pulled off as well and parked fifty yards behind Lick, watching as his suspect got out of his car carrying what appeared to Jimmy to be a rolled-up blanket or tarp. Lick headed in the direction of the Federal Triangle Metro station, walked down the stairs into the train tunnel and waited on the platform for the next Blue Line train. Due to the late hour, Jimmy became concerned there were not enough people to blend in with to keep his presence concealed from Lick. Knowing Lick to be ever conscious of a potential tail, Jimmy stayed as far back as he could so not to be spotted. Before entering the underground tunnel of the Metro station, Jimmy pulled out his phone and dialed Rich's number while he still had a signal.

"Rich," Jimmy quietly said into his phone. "He parked his Taurus right beside the Natural History museum on Constitution Avenue. I'm about to follow him into the Federal Triangle Metro station. It looks like he's set to get on the Blue Line heading further north into the city. I'm going to lose you when we're inside the tunnel but I'll call you with our location as soon as we stop and I can get a signal again."

"Okay," replied Rich. "I'm on the way."

Agent Michaels had no idea where they were headed so he figured he would drive to the city and wait to hear back from Jimmy. Steve Lick sat down by himself two train cars in front of Jimmy, who could still see him through the front windows of his car and the next. When they pulled into the Capitol South Metro station, Lick got up from his seat and exited the train with Jimmy following at a safe distance. Keeping with his standard practice, Steve Lick constantly looked behind and to his left and right as he walked. He had no reason to think someone could be following him, but old habits are hard to break. Well aware of Lick's habit, Jimmy continued to stay as far back as he could.

Lick walked up the stairs of the Capitol South Metro station and out onto C Street, turned north, and began walking up 2nd Street, rolled up blanket tucked securely under his arm. Once outside, Jimmy took out his phone and dialed Rich's number.

"We got off at the Capitol South station," he reported. "He's walking up 2nd Street right now heading towards Maryland Ave. He doesn't appear to be in any kind of a hurry. He's got a large blanket rolled up under his arm but I can't tell what's in it. I'm staying way back so he doesn't spot me. I'll call you back in a few."

"Got it," replied Rich. "I'm maybe twenty minutes away. Keep me posted and don't take any chances. Whatever he's up to, he's sure to bolt if he figures out you're following him."

"No doubt about that," replied Jimmy.

When Lick reached the intersection of Maryland Avenue and 2nd Street, he turned right on Maryland and headed towards Stanton Park. A vacant building on the southwest corner of Stanton Park was his intended destination.

Once a small apartment complex, the building had been bought by an investor who wanted to convert it into high-dollar condos. One of the top floor units on the west side of the building had a perfect sight line into Senator Riley's third floor apartment window three hundred yards away. A little past nine in the evening, the street traffic was light. Jimmy got extremely worried he would either be spotted by Lick if he followed too close or would lose him if he stayed back too far. He erred on the side of staying back knowing his target would abort his plans if he spotted a tail.

At this moment, six hundred miles west, the crowd at Lucas Oil Stadium erupted in a frenzy. Governor Alan had finished giving a speech to the Republican delegates gathered to officially nominate him and Senator Smith as the Republican ticket for President. Humbly accepting the nod from Senator Smith and the delegates in attendance to be the number two on the ticket, the Indiana governor told the delegates, as well as millions watching at home, how he and Senator Smith would bring sanity back to government. He talked about the failures of the Ferrell-Hogue administration and how the country could not afford four more years of what the previous eight had been like. Only Senator Smith, he said, could right the ship and he felt pride and honor to have been selected to work beside him.

The Arizona Governor, who had given his endorsement to Senator Smith early in the primary season after officially dropping out of the race, had been selected to give the keynote address. His early endorsement of Senator Smith endeared him to the Smith campaign and earned him the coveted speaking slot.

Steve Lick, ever cognizant of a potential tail as he walked, reached the vacant building adjacent to Stanton Park. Spotting the bolt cutters Neptune had left for him hidden in some bushes outside the back door, Lick cut through the chain securing the door, dropped the chain and bolt cutters on the ground, and quietly stepped inside. Unfortunately for Jimmy, he no longer had a visual on Lick and never saw him enter the building. Staying as far back as he could to avoid being detected, Jimmy lost sight of Lick somewhere around the intersection of 2nd Street and Maryland Avenue. He called Rich to give him an update.

"Rich," Jimmy whispered into his phone, "I lost him around 2nd and Maryland. There's nobody around so I had to stay back so he wouldn't see me. I'll keep looking and try to relocate him. Just come to 2nd and Maryland and park on the street. We'll be somewhere between there and Stanton Park. Keep this line open and I'll let you know as soon as I find him again."

"Roger that, Jimmy. I should be there in about fifteen."

Steve Lick made his way into the vacant building and climbed the steps to the top floor. Walking to the window overlooking Stanton Park, he now had a direct sightline into Senator Riley's third floor apartment window. Lick checked his watch. If Neptune had done his job, of which Steve had little doubt, the acid had been working on the gas line in his apartment for a little over three hours. In preparation for this mission, the *Sons* had been meticulous in testing precisely what effect the nitric acid Neptune had taken into Riley's apartment would have on the metal gas line. Every test they ran had virtually the same results. The acid would eat through the metal in a little under three hours, rupturing the line and causing the gas to be dispersed throughout the Senator's apartment.

Senator Riley, doing what he normally did at this hour of the night, reclined in his bed watching coverage of the Republican National Convention on T.V. Disgusted at what he heard being spouted from the podium in Indianapolis, he seethed with anger as he watched Senator Smith prepare to receive his party's nomination.

"What a bunch of horse shit," he said out loud, as he waited for Senator Smith to take the stage and give his acceptance speech.

He knew Senator Smith extremely well from their many years together in the Senate. U.S. Senators traditionally adhere to an unwritten rule discouraging Senators from making negative public comments about fellow Senators. Obviously, it's not a rule always followed. Senator Riley, however, is from the *old school* and for the most part has declined to make public comments critical of his colleague from the other side of the aisle. That would soon change, he surmised, once Senator Smith received his party's nomination to be their candidate for President. As soon as that happened, Senator Smith would become the Democrat Party's number one enemy and then, all bets would be off. Senator Smith would be fair game for whatever attacks Senator Riley and his Democrat colleagues could come up with.

Steve Lick unrolled his blanket and removed a Barrett Model 98B bolt-action sniper rifle and chambered a single .338 caliber Lapua Magnum round into the breach. Confident there would be no need for a second round, Lick rested the twenty-seven-inch barrel on the windowsill of the open window in front of him. After turning over an empty five-gallon paint bucket to use as a seat, he sat down behind his rifle, leaned forward, and peered through the infrared scope mounted on top of his gun. Once he adjusted the scope, Lick could plainly see into the living room of Senator Riley's apartment three football fields away.

Having done this more times than he could count, Lick continued to peer through the scope as his breathing began to slow. The tiny infrared reflector, pressed into the C-4 molded around one of the books on the Senator's bookshelf, illuminated in Lick's scope. He began increasing pressure on the trigger, careful to keep the crosshairs in his scope trained on the tiny light.

Jimmy O'Rourke had made it to Stanton Park and did his best to conceal his presence by hiding behind various trees and bushes lining the park. Frustrated because he had not yet reacquired his target, he sat completely still on a park bench and did a slow 360-scan to look for any movement that might be Lick. He then noticed what appeared to be a vacant building adjacent to the park with an *Under Construction* sign planted in the front yard. Standing up from the bench, he headed in the direction of the building. As he reached the backside of the building, Jimmy noticed the bolt cutters and broken chain Steve Lick left lying on the ground in front of the door.

"Rich," Jimmy said on the open line he had maintained with Agent Michaels, "I'm at the back of this vacant building right next to Stanton Park on the southwest corner. The chain locking the door has been cut. The bolt cutters are right here on the ground. I'm going inside to check it out."

Not wanting his phone to give away his position should Lick be inside, Jimmy turned it off and put it in his pocket. He never heard Rich tell him to wait on him before entering the building.

Senator Riley, oblivious to the gas now completely enveloping the kitchen and living room area of his apartment, continued talking out loud to his television, cursing the dribble now coming from the Governor of Arizona.

"What a bunch of bullshit lies," he shouted at the screen.

I know Senator Smith better than anyone, he thought. *And starting tomorrow I'm going to start letting people know exactly what I really think of him.*

Unfortunately, the Senator would not be able to keep his vow.

The silencer Steve Lick had attached to the end of his rifle completely muffled the sound of the shot. The copper-jacketed .338 round exited the muzzle of his weapon at 3,100 feet per second. Taking less than one quarter of a second to break through the living room window glass of Senator Riley's apartment, the bullet impacted the C-4 molded to the back of a book on his bookshelf. The C-4 by itself might possibly have done the job, but the explosion, in concert with a room filled with natural gas, proved absolutely devastating, completely obliterating the entire apartment and everything inside. Senator Riley never had a clue what hit him. Investigators would ultimately find pieces of his body strewn about the apartment, as well as the street below.

The sound of the explosion startled Jimmy O'Rourke, by now making his way into the building. He accidentally knocked over a sawhorse supporting several 2x4s resting on top when the muscles in his body flinched at the sound of the explosion. Steve Lick, attempting to make a quick departure from the building, heard the commotion Jimmy had made below him. Picking up a large screwdriver he spotted lying on the ground, Lick quickly and quietly moved to a hiding place behind the open door into the room. As he stood completely still listening intently for any sound from below, Lick could hear the faint muffle of footsteps coming his way.

Not sure at this point what had happened, Jimmy only knew a huge explosion occurred somewhere across the street, with no idea a rifle shot from the room he now approached had set off the explosion. He never heard the gunshot because the silencer on Lick's rifle had muffled the sound of the shot. Although he had discovered the cut chain securing the back door, for all he knew it could have been some homeless guy looking for a place to crash or vandals looking for something to steal. Jimmy wanted to finish a quick sweep of the vacant building before investigating the explosion.

As he reached the top of the stairs, he squinted trying to see inside the darkened room. For a moment, he stood still and listened but could hear nothing. In the blink of an eye, Steve Lick emerged from behind the door, taking Jimmy O'Rourke by complete surprise. Jimmy had no time to react as Lick plunged the screwdriver into Jimmy's mid-section, below the center of his ribcage. The nine-inch length of tungsten steel penetrated Jimmy's body with such force the tip of the Phillips head screwdriver poked through the skin in his back.

As he began falling, Jimmy found himself staring into the face of the man he had been watching for so long. With the handle of the large screwdriver sticking out the front of his chest, Jimmy crashed violently to the floor, completely incapacitated. Quickly descending the stairs to make his escape, Steve Lick exited the building.

Rich Michaels reached the edge of Stanton Park as the explosion occurred and instinctively dropped to the ground when the blast went off. Although a hundred and fifty yards away from Senator Riley's apartment when it vaporized, he nonetheless was splattered with small pieces of glass and tiny chunks of concrete. Like Jimmy, he had no idea a rifle shot from the vacant building had set off the explosion but did know Jimmy was about to enter the building when they lost phone contact. Quickly getting up off the ground, Rich ran to the back of the vacant building and noticed the cut chain and bolt cutters Jimmy had mentioned before losing contact.

"Jimmy," Rich shouted as he came through the door. "Jimmy, are you in here?"

Eerily quiet, Rich stood still listening for any response from Jimmy. None came. Racing up the stairs to look for his friend, Rich found Jimmy on the ground, the handle of the screwdriver protruding from his chest. He nudged Jimmy and shouted, "Jimmy! Can you hear me?"

Unconscious and showing no signs of life, Jimmy gave no response. Not knowing if he was alive or dead, Rich leaned in and placed his right cheek against Jimmy's nose and mouth, longing to feel even the faintest of breaths. Placing his index and middle finger on Jimmy's carotid artery, he prayed to feel a pulse. Although faint, the pulse was there.

At least he's alive, Rich thought.

Jimmy slowly opened his eyes and could see the concern on Rich's face. As he began to move his lips, Rich leaned in closer to hear what his friend had to say.

"It's Lick, get to his car on Constitution...." Jimmy whispered before passing out again.

After calling the paramedics, Rich reached out to a member of his surveillance team he had activated when he first lost contact with Jimmy at the Federal Triangle Metro station.

"I'm inside a vacant building next to Stanton Park," Rich said. "Jimmy is hurt bad but I think he'll make it. I'm going to stay with him until the paramedics get here. Go find Lick's car on Constitution Avenue. It's a dark blue Ford Taurus, parked somewhere near the Natural History museum. Just hang back and see if he shows up to his car. If he does, take him down."

"Roger that," came the reply from one of the agents responding to Rich's urgent request for assistance.

Steve Lick made his way back to the Metro station and got on the Blue Line train, wanting to get back to his car as soon as possible. He had no idea who he had stabbed and frankly didn't care. He knew he needed to get out of town as fast as possible and decided that getting to his car would be his best option. Lick had no idea Rich and Jimmy had been on to him for several months and made the mistaken assumption nobody knew about his car parked on Constitution Avenue. While riding the train back to his car, Lick took out his phone and typed in his message to Jupiter. He'd send it as soon as he reacquired a signal above ground.

Unbeknownst to Lick, a team of federal agents sat in wait for him near his car. As he reached the top of the stairs at the Federal Triangle Metro stop, Lick removed his phone from his pocket and pressed the *send* button before dropping it in a sewer grate outside the Metro station and heading straight for his car.

As he crossed Constitution Avenue, he reached in his pocket for his car keys and quickly looked around for anything that might give him alarm. He didn't see the two FBI agents lying down in the back seat of the car parked directly in front of his, or the two agents hiding behind the hedge lining the sidewalk in front of the Natural History museum. As Lick got behind the wheel of his Taurus, the agents made their presence known, rushing his car with guns drawn and shouting for him to put up his hands.

All five members of the *New Sons of Liberty* had talked about what they would do if ever caught in this exact predicament, having each vowed never to be taken into custody. This became Steve Lick's moment of truth. Realizing he had been caught with no chance of escape, he knew exactly what his next move would be. As the agents moved in closer to his car, he reached into his left breast pocket and removed the tiny white pill he always carried with him on every mission for the *New Sons of Liberty*. He had done his part, he reasoned, having served his country honorably. Satisfied in knowing he had fulfilled his responsibility to the cause and had performed his final mission in the defense of liberty with honor, Lick placed the cyanide pill in his mouth. As pieces of glass sprayed across Steve Lick's body, the result of his passenger window being kicked in by one of the agents, Lick crushed the little white pill between his teeth.

***

The cacophony of chants inside Lucas Oil Stadium had reached a crescendo, as hundreds of *Smith-Alan* signs waved amongst the crowd of Republican delegates. Several colorful beach balls were being smacked and punched above the heads of the rapturous supporters. Knowing the time had come for the main event, the crowd anxiously awaited to hear from the man who would soon restore the Republican Party to prominence by regaining control of the White House.

Brian Smith stood off stage waiting for the moment. After more than a year of campaigning, Senator Smith had put more time and effort into his run for the White House than any other endeavor he had undertaken in his life. Tonight would be the payoff for all the work.

Knowing the Democrats and Vice President Hogue were not about to give up the presidency without a fight, Senator Smith understood from this point forward he would have to be disciplined and focused, aware the political winds were clearly at his back. The Democrats would be holding their nominating convention in a couple of weeks and would probably get a short-lived boost from it, but no doubt the country wanted change in leadership. President Ferrell's final year in office had not gone well and his diminishing poll numbers were having a direct effect on his Vice President's chances for victory in November. Senator Smith and the Republican Party knew the election was within their grasp. Essentially, theirs to lose and Brian Smith had no intentions of screwing it up.

"And now, ladies and gentlemen," the Arizona Governor shouted into the microphone as he concluded his speech, "this is the moment you have all been waiting for. So, without further ado, it is my pleasure to introduce to you the senior Senator from the great state of New Jersey, and the next President of the United States of America…Senator Brian Smith!"

The crowd erupted even louder, rocking the stadium with foot stomping in anticipation of hearing from the nominee. As he allowed the cheering and clapping to reach a climax, Senator Smith paused for a moment before making his entry onto the stage. Before stepping out from behind the curtains adorning the stage to greet his throng of supporters, the Senator and soon-to-be Republican Presidential nominee felt the vibration of his cell phone inside his suit breast pocket.

As he reached to retrieve his phone, the curtains were swept open for him to take the stage. Stepping into view of the crowd of Republican delegates, Senator Smith quickly looked at the text before returning his phone to his pocket.

A short text, it simply read: *liberty prevails–NSOL, Orcus.*

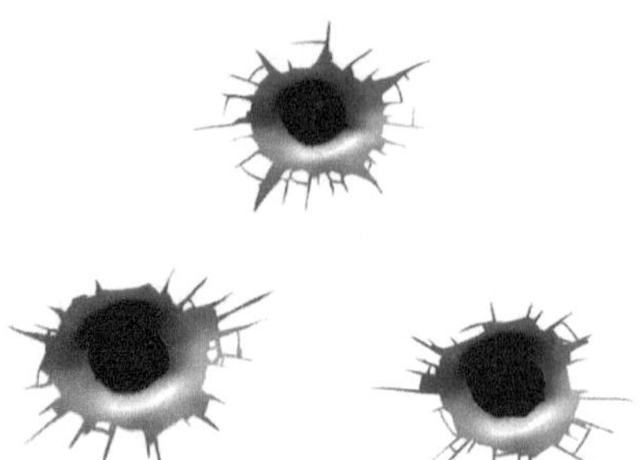

Chapter Twenty-Eight

Article II of the U.S. Constitution requires the President of the United States to "*periodically report to the Congress on the state of the union.*" Traditionally done in late January or February each year by the sitting President, the speech to Congress and the nation this year would be delivered by newly inaugurated President Brian Smith. Since a newly elected President cannot officially report on the *state of the union*, the speech is given and simply referred to as an *Address to a Joint Session of Congress*. President Smith's first major address to the country as President since his inauguration, his address will involve all of the normal pomp and circumstance associated with previous State of the Union addresses.

The American people had a sense of where the new President's priorities lie based on his campaign. His victory over the sitting vice President was overwhelming, as he won thirty-eight states and almost 350 electoral votes. A complete and total repudiation of the liberal policies of the previous administration, President Smith had a clear mandate to pursue the policies he espoused during his campaign.

The House and Senate Sergeant at Arms stood in the doorway of the House Chamber to announce the President's entry.

"Mister Speaker, the President of the United States," shouted the Sergeant at Arms as Brian Smith entered the House Chamber, greeted by a standing ovation of Congress, as well as other guests invited to hear the address. Slowly making his way down the aisle to the podium,

President Smith shook hands with dozens of congresspersons and Senators, soaking up the applause and adulation being heaped upon him. Finally reaching the podium, he handed a copy of his speech to the Speaker of the House and shook the hands of the Speaker and Vice President Joel Alan, both of whom would be seated behind the President during the speech.

"Members of Congress," began the Speaker, as he gaveled in the beginning of the session, "I have the high privilege and distinct honor of presenting to you the President of the United States." Another five minutes of applause and cheering erupted before President Smith was ready to begin his address to Congress and the nation, noting a litany of legislative priorities his administration would undertake. After explaining he would pursue an agenda of tax cuts and regulation reform to get the economy out of the doldrums of the past several years, he made clear his intentions regarding the threat of global terrorism.

"We have seen an unprecedented rise in terrorist activity, and as a nation we have not done enough to combat it. The role of the United States in addressing the problem of terrorism should be one of leadership. Leading from behind will no longer be the policy of the United States." The entire House Chamber erupted as most members of Congress, including some Democrats, rose to their feet and applauded. It took three full minutes for the applause to die down.

"For the past several years the threat of Islamic terrorism throughout the world has escalated," the President continued, "and too often we have sat back in dismay at the carnage left behind by these savages, purporting to carry out their deeds in the name of their religion. It is high time we say to peace-loving people all around the world, including the peaceful followers of Islam, *enough is enough*. Let us all stand together and reject the forces of hate and violence, responsible for the taking of so much innocent life."

Once again, everyone rose in unison to applaud, this time including all of the Democrats. There would be time to disagree with this President in the future regarding his legislative pursuits, but the nation was united around the idea of doing something to eradicate the scourge of terrorism, and every Democrat in the House Chamber listening to the President knew it. "The terrorists, as well as the nations who support them, have declared war on the United States," President Smith continued, "and until now we have not acknowledged this fact. So, let me be clear. This lack of acknowledgment ends tonight."

The audience let out with another eruption, this one louder and longer than the last.

"I want nations around the world to know, if you stand against terrorism, the United States will stand with you. You are either with us in this global crusade or you are with the terrorists. The war against ISIS and other affiliated terrorist organizations will not be a conventional war and will not be fought in a conventional fashion. When I campaigned for this office I told the American people it would be the highest priority of my administration to wipe ISIS off the face of the earth and this is exactly what I intend to do."

A few weeks earlier, President Smith's inauguration speech received rave reviews in terms of its tone and the expressions of unity he would seek in his effort to bring the country together. His speech before the joint session of Congress was more about letting the country and the world know exactly where Brian Smith stood with regards to how he would run his administration.

Full of substance, the speech would be viewed favorably by those concerned about how the new administration would tackle the economic malaise resulting from the previous administration, and what the President would do about global terrorism. The devil, of course, is always in the details, and some of what President Smith had in mind he could not share. Namely, how far he would go in pursuit of victory in the war against terrorism. The meeting scheduled for the following morning with his CIA Director would indicate how far he would go.

***

As a newly minted second lieutenant, graduating with honors from the U.S. Military Academy at West Point, J. Gordon Shirley's first taste of battle occurred at the tail end of the Viet Nam War. Over the next thirty plus years, his precipitous rise through the ranks of the U.S. military, due primarily to his keen intellect and political skills, culminated in his elevation to Chairman of the Joint Chiefs of Staff under President Rob Ferrell.

General Shirley had a major falling out with his former boss over President Ferrell's obvious lack of commitment to fully engage the military in the fight against Islamic terrorism. On the heels of a terrorist attack on innocent shoppers at the Mall of America, followed by the cowardly and tepid response by President Ferrell, General Shirley resigned in protest. The public humiliation caused by the resignation embarrassed the President and dealt a major blow to the candidacy of Vice President Eric Hogue, running to succeed President Ferrell. At General Shirley's retirement ceremony, then-Senator Brian Smith had a private and illuminating conversation with the General, which revealed where General Shirley stood regarding the efforts being made by his country to go after radical terrorists.

"It makes me sick to my stomach," he told Senator Smith, "to see how weak and feckless this administration has been in taking on the terrorists. I'm tired of all the political correctness infecting this White House and how we're supposed to treat these savages with kid gloves. What we should be doing is meeting their savagery with some of our own. These bastards are cutting off people's heads and drowning them in steel cages, for God's sake, and we're supposed to be worried about how we go after them? It's asinine if you ask me, Senator, and if you get into office I hope you will have a better understanding of what we're up against than the buffoon-in-chief we have now or his lackey Vice President. God help us all if that spineless bastard wins."

The conversation left an indelible mark in Brian Smith's mind, and following his victory in the Presidential election, put General Shirley's name near the top of his list of those he would consider for important jobs in his administration. Acknowledging the contribution made to his own candidacy by the General's act of defiance to the President he once served, and remembering the sentiments privately expressed to him by the General at his retirement ceremony, President Smith reached out and tapped General Shirley to serve in his administration as head of the CIA.

***

"Good morning Mr. President," General Shirley said as he shook the President's hand and took a seat in front of the President's desk in the Oval Office.

"Thanks for coming by, Gordon," President Smith replied, as he moved from behind his desk to take a seat beside the General. "I asked you to stop by this morning to make sure we have a clear understanding of my commitment to go after ISIS and rid the world of these savages."

"I share your commitment, Mr. President," General Shirley responded.

"That's good to hear, Gordon," said the President. "I never had a doubt about your resolve, General. Which is precisely why I picked you for this position. Now, I think we would both agree this war, if we are really going to win it, will require unconventional means, the heart of which will revolve around raw intelligence. I'm sure you are aware having a strong military presence will not be enough. These bastards are spread out in over thirty countries and carpet-bombing the shit out of them, while it may damage their organization, will also inevitably take the lives of hundreds of thousands of innocents. That's not something I'm willing to do, especially when I believe there's a better way. As I said before, it's going to take unconventional means, General. We may be required to use strategies and tactics heretofore regarded as, shall we say, *unseemly*, perhaps even *barbaric*."

"I am fully committed, Gordon, to utilizing every means at our disposal to hunt down every ISIS leader we can identify and eradicate them from the face of the earth, and I am placing no restrictions on you to accomplish this. These people are savages, Gordon, and sometimes it takes a savage to defeat a savage, if you get my drift."

"On this point, Mr. President, you and I are in total agreement," General Shirley replied.

"Thank you for coming by Gordon," President Smith remarked as he rose from his chair, indicating the meeting was ending. "By the way, Gordon," the President added, "I'm sure you are familiar with the phrase *plausible deniability?*"

"I am, indeed, Mr. President," General Shirley responded.

"Good," said President Smith. "I want to make sure we are on the same page. I have complete faith in your ability to make the right call on how best to attack this cancer. As I'm sure you can appreciate, there may be some things undertaken I don't want directly connected to this office."

"Absolutely, sir," the General replied. "I appreciate your confidence in me. I don't plan on letting you down."

The President and his CIA Director were clearly singing from the same sheet of music. Although unsaid, both men were in full agreement; actions would need to be taken that were outside the bounds of current U.S. law if innocent lives were to be saved from the bane of Islamic terrorism. General Shirley was a true patriot and not afraid to get his hands dirty in his efforts to defeat enemies of the freedoms and liberties he had dedicated his life to preserve. Now would not be the time for half measures. Nothing he had done in his life up to this point indicated his resolve would be anything but steely, and he wasn't about to change now.

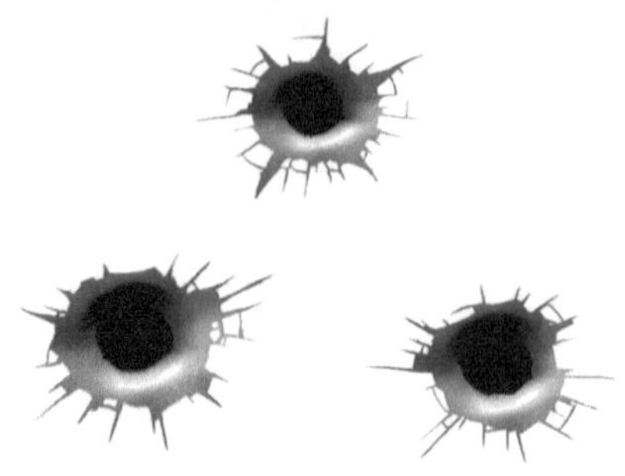

CHAPTER TWENTY-NINE

It was hot. Damn hot. A *Ghillie* suit covered the body of David Kyle, adding about fifteen degrees on a day when the temperature in the shade easily reached a hundred. Made from strips of light brown burlap, designed to blend into the surrounding environment, his suit made his presence undetectable. Unfortunately for Kyle, the nearest shade was miles away. Walking nearly two miles across desert-like environs from the northeast corner of Israeli-occupied Golan Heights, Kyle lay still across a large boulder overlooking the Syrian village of Hadar, as the sun relentlessly pounded his body.

After maintaining his position for nearly four hours, his two-liter bladder pack of water nearly dry, every square inch of his frame dripped with perspiration. Regardless of the elements, David Kyle knew he would need to maintain his position until the mission he was on reached its inevitable conclusion. Peering through the scope mounted on his Barrett M98 sniper rifle, Kyle had a perfect view of the Hadar village market where local citizens were doing their afternoon shopping for clothes, prayer rugs and smoked salmon. Located in the middle of the market, under a large white canopy, sat a set of picnic tables, approximately three quarters of a mile from where Kyle lay. David Kyle had been specifically recruited for these types of missions. Several months earlier his close friend and former commander Bill Allen, now the President's most trusted advisor, lured him back into the service of his country. Assured his unique skill set would be desperately needed in

America's covert battle against global terrorism, David Kyle had been brought on as a *contract* employee of the CIA, assigned to work directly under his controlling agent, Chris Roth.

***

For the past few years Roth had been posing as a commercial fisherman, operating a fishing trawler on Lake Tiberius, near the southeast border of Israel. His real job, however, has been to gather whatever information he can about the activities of ISIS fighters and leaders enjoying free reign in and around western Syria.

As ISIS has been allowed to grow and strengthen, the Syrian President and his regime have become allied with the terrorist group, primarily because their real fight is against the Free Syrian Army and the Nusra Front, both organizations trying to overthrow the current ruler and take control of the country. Because of their desire to have safe havens from where they can operate unmolested by the local regime, ISIS has shown itself to be a willing partner of the Syrian government. A highly paid and well-placed source of Chris Roth's informed him of a meeting set to take place under the white canopy between a Syrian General and two high-ranking ISIS leaders, Mahir Rachman and Abu Khan.

Rachman and Khan were the masterminds behind a devastating terrorist attack a year earlier at the Amsterdam Centraal, the largest train station in The Netherlands. In the attack, five ISIS sympathizers, convinced by Rachman and Khan of their afterlife with seventy-two of the most beautiful virgins imaginable, exploded suicide vests inside the crowded Amsterdam train station. The explosion killed sixty-seven innocent people, nine of whom were American citizens part of a tour group on their way to visit the home of Anne Frank.

***

The mission plan Chris Roth and his team had put together, while simple in concept, would require impeccable timing and execution for it to succeed. The vehicle in which the Syrian General traveled was enroute to Hadar from his military compound in Damascus. Since the moment he pulled out of the Presidential palace, the General had been under the watchful eye of a CIA drone flying five miles above the earth. David Kyle's headset began to crackle.

"Alpha Two this is Eagle Eye. Target is heading your way, about two clicks out from your location. ETA less than ten mike," came the words from the drone operator located in an underground bunker a hundred miles away from Kyle's position.

"Roger that," responded Kyle. "I've got him."

Kyle could see the black SUV carrying the General through his riflescope as the vehicle made the turn onto a dirt road leading to the Hadar market.

"Alpha Two to Alpha One. Are all assets in place?" Kyle asked Roth, the mission commander.

The assets he referred to were seven CIA operatives who were shopping in the market, near the picnic tables under the canopy. Two of the assets were carrying hypodermic needles loaded with large doses of Ketamine, a drug used as a surgical anesthesia. Four other assets had relatively small hand-held smoke bombs, the purpose of which would be to hide their escape once the mission concluded. The seventh and final asset was CIA Agent Chris Roth, who sat behind the wheel of an idling pick-up truck, loaded with wooden crates filled with olives, sugar beets and lentils, all staples of a typical Syrian shopping bazaar.

"Alpha Two this is Alpha One. Assets are in place. Standby for a go-no go."

"Target vehicle coming to a stop," Kyle responded, as he observed the SUV stop near the white canopy.

The General departed his vehicle and made his way to the picnic tables under the canopy. Staying behind the wheel of the SUV, the driver watched as his boss walked over to the picnic tables and took a seat. A few moments later, two men, presumably Rachman and Khan, emerged from the crowd of shoppers and joined the General under the canopy. Rising to greet the two men, the General shook their hands and motioned for them to take a seat.

The purpose of the meeting, according to Roth's highly reliable source, would be to arrange the transfer of funds from the Syrian government to ISIS leaders. Funds destined to be used to finance a terrorist attack ISIS planned to carry out in Brussels, Belgium within a week. This highly placed source, a mid-level ISIS leader himself, had concluded selling information to the CIA to be far more profitable and personally beneficial than any satisfaction he would receive from striking a blow against a bunch of infidels who had never done anything against him or his family.

As the three men continued to talk, Roth radioed to his men to begin moving closer to the canopy. He gave one more transmission to let David know he could execute at will.

"Alpha One to Alpha Two" he said into his mic, hidden under the lapel of his shirt. "Go when ready."

Since the General had taken his seat under the canopy, Kyle had maintained sight of his target, keeping the crosshairs of his scope trained squarely on the center of his forehead. Moving his right index finger from the trigger guard to the trigger, he began to slowly exhale as he applied more pressure to the trigger. The silencer, attached to the muzzle of his rifle, would mute the sound of the shot and prohibit anyone in the market area from knowing where the shot came. Without the silencer, the shot would ring out and echo off the rocks around him, exposing his position and possibly jeopardizing his escape back across the desert.

The rimless bottleneck .338 Lapua Magnum round Kyle had chambered into the breach of his rifle, exploded as the hammer struck the firing pin, sending the copper jacketed bullet down the barrel of his rifle towards his target. The bullet struck the Syrian General about an inch below his left eye, blowing blood, brains and bone fragments out the back of his skull. Kyle immediately racked in a second round and adjusted his aim to the black SUV, located about fifty feet from the canopy. The General's driver opened his door and barely got one foot on the ground before Kyle's second round passed through the open driver's door window, striking him right below his Adam's apple. He slumped to the ground, blood gushing from the fist-sized hole in his neck.

A second after the General's head recoiled backwards from the impact of the shot, Roth's men quickly rushed the picnic tables. As their smoke grenades ignited amongst the crowd of shoppers, the two men holding hypodermic needles containing Ketamine lunged at Rachman and Khan and plunged the needles deep into their throats, trying to get the drug directly into their carotid arteries.

Rachman and Khan briefly wrestled with their captors before losing consciousness and collapsed to the ground. As Roth pulled his truck beside the white canopy, all six of his men grabbed the seemingly lifeless bodies of Rachman and Khan and threw them in the back of the truck. Roth then floored the accelerator as his men jumped in and proceeded to make their escape. No more than sixty seconds had elapsed from the moment the bullet struck the General's head to the moment Roth pressed the gas to get away. The mission had been flawless.

"Alpha One to Alpha Two," Roth said into his radio as they sped along the dirt road taking them out of Hadar. "Well done, my friend. Beers will be on me."

David Kyle had begun making his way back across the desert and in the direction of the friendlier confines awaiting him on the Israeli side of the Golan Heights.

"You got it, man," Kyle replied. "It may take half a case to replenish the fluids I just lost."

Chris Roth smiled as he continued to drive away.

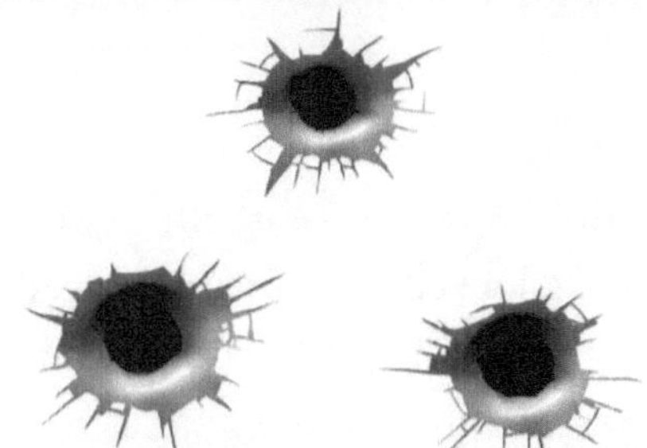

CHAPTER THIRTY

With a population of a little over a half million, Port Said, located in northern Egypt along the banks of the Mediterranean Sea, is frequently visited by small merchant ships importing goods into the Egyptian economy. Dock workers, used to seeing a variety of ships and boats unload various-sized cargo containers on their docks, saw nothing out of the ordinary when Chris Roth pulled his boat into the Port Said harbor and began unloading two large wooden crates.

The contents of those crates, however, were not anything related to goods being introduced into the Egyptian economy. Instead, the crates contained the unconscious bodies of Mahir Rachman and Abu Khan, two of the most vicious terrorists alive and seminal figures in the hierarchy of ISIS, the world's most dangerous terrorist organization.

After loading the crates into the back of a van, Roth and three of his men drove to a plain brick building located near the Gianola fish market in the center of town. Although disguised as part of the fish market where fresh catch was sold, the building was actually a *safe house* under the control of the Mukhabarat, Egyptian's equivalent to the CIA.

A six-inch thick reinforced metal door led down to the basement, which contained several separate rooms, all equipped with soundproofing on the walls and ceilings. Pausing for a moment outside the door, Roth waited for the buzzing sound to let him know the door had been unlocked. He pushed open the door and held it for his men who were using two dollies to transport the crates. Once they reached the basement, two more locked doors were buzzed open, allowing the men to deposit the crates containing Rachman and Khan in the separate rooms that would become their homes for the next few days. "Let's unload those crates," Roth ordered. "It'll be a few more hours before they come to. We've got time to grab something to eat."

***

A Presidential executive order originally signed by President Ford in 1976, and subsequently expanded by President Carter two years later, expressly prohibited any U.S. government intelligence official, or anyone acting on behalf of the U.S. government, from being party to an assassination. While some would argue such an order would not apply in time of war (and the U.S. was surely in the midst of a war against radical terrorist groups like ISIS), the mission carried out by Chris Roth and his team at the Hadar shopping market could be viewed by many as a direct contravention to the prohibition against assassinations.

What he was about to participate in would definitely put himself and his agency in hot water if ever made known, especially in light of the fact the U.S. Congress made it illegal for U.S. agencies and their agents to engage in torture. The only people outside of Roth's team who knew his whereabouts and what he had been doing for the past couple of days was his CIA Station Chief in Beirut, Lebanon and General J. Gordon Shirley, Director of the CIA.

***

As Rachman slowly began to regain consciousness, he awoke to find himself secured to a metal chair, a leather strap tight around his chest and fastened to the back of the chair. His hands and feet were secured as well. As the room began to come into focus, he shook his head back and forth several times trying to shed the cobwebs. When his vision cleared, he saw Chris Roth standing in front of him. Roth, a fluent Arabic speaker, would not need a translator for the interrogation about to commence.

192

"Mahir Rachman," Roth began. "My name is Jonathan Reed (the bogus name he currently used) and you are now my prisoner." Roth walked to the other side of the room to a wall switch in front of Rachman. As Roth held the switch in the *up* position, a set of motorized roll-up shades began to rise, exposing a large window between his room and the next. Once the shades were fully raised, Rachman could look into the other room and see his friend and colleague, Abu Khan. Similarly seated and bound to his chair, Khan began moving his head around as the effects of the drugs were starting to wear off.

"Don't worry, he can't see you. This is a two-way mirror," Roth said to Rachman as he tapped his finger on the glass. "Look Mr. Reed, or whatever your real name is," began Rachman. "I know who you are, but I'm not sure why you're wasting your time with me. What is it you expect to get from me?"

"Information, Mr. Rachman," Roth replied. "And I can assure you I am willing to stay here for as long as it takes and do whatever is necessary to get it. Whenever I go after something, Rachman, I usually get it, so I suggest you cooperate. Believe me, it will make your stay with us far more enjoyable."

"Like I've already told you," Rachman responded, "you're wasting your time. Whatever information you are looking for, I can't possibly help you. You must have me confused with someone else."

"Bullshit, you piece of scum," Roth said as he leaned in and pressed his nose an inch from Rachman's face. "I know exactly who you are and what you're capable of. I saw some of your handy work in Amsterdam. Tell me shithead; does it make you feel like a man to kill innocent women and children? Do you really think Allah is happy with you when you murder some of His children?"

"What can you possibly know about Allah," Rachman forcefully replied. "You know nothing about our way of life or our religion. Allah smiles down on us whenever we rid the world of infidels like you! Of course, I am not familiar with what you say happened in Amsterdam, Mr. Reed. But if it resulted in the destruction of infidels, then all I have to say is: *Praise be to Allah.* Just what is it you think I know, Mr. Reed, that has resulted in my illegal incarceration?"

"I want to know about Brussels, Mr. Rachman," Roth replied.

"Unfortunately, you have been the recipient of bad information, Mr. Reed," said Rachman. "I'm afraid I don't know anything about Brussels."

"Well," said Roth as he turned to walk out of the room, "how about I give you a little time to think about it."

This was not the first interrogation Chris Roth had participated in and he knew going in neither Rachman nor Khan would talk, at least not initially. This would take some time, he surmised, but unfortunately, he didn't have a lot of it to waste. For now, Roth would let Rachman and Khan sit and sweat it out while he made arrangements for the next phase of his interrogation.

The next two days were something less than pleasant for the two ISIS leaders as they sat restrained in their chairs, enduring the heat from multiple incandescent light bulbs staying on round-the-clock. Denied food and water, neither had access to a bathroom and whenever either man appeared to be dosing off in their chair, their *babysitters* would pipe in *Guns N' Roses* to keep them awake. Roth did not know exactly when ISIS planned their attack in Brussels, but he knew it to be imminent. Getting the information needed would take time, and the clock was ticking.

Fifty hours into their detainment, two of Roth's men entered Rachman's room and untied him from the chair. Barely able to stand without assistance, Rachman was escorted into the restroom where his pants and underwear were removed while being held under the shower to wash off the human excrement he had been sitting in for the past two days. Now naked from the waist down, Rachman's captors escorted him back to his room, securing him again to the metal chair. Only this time there was a slight deviation from when he first entered the room. Rachman immediately noticed the strange looking device sitting on the table in front of him.

"It's called a *picana*," Roth said to his prisoner, as Rachman stared at the device before him.

A *picana* is a wand or prod which delivers a high voltage, but low current electrical shock. The bronze tip of the device has a rubber insulated handle and is connected by wire to a control box with a rheostat, allowing the operator to raise or reduce the amount of the voltage output. This particular *picana* was powered by two car batteries wired to the control box. Rachman smiled at Roth as he attempted to get comfortable in his chair.

"You must think I am stupid, Mr. Reed. I know what you are allowed to do to me and I also know what you are NOT allowed to do. I'm afraid this stunt of yours is not going to work. Like I told you before, you are wasting your time. Anyways, Mr. Reed, you must know we train for this. We are well aware of the tactics used by the CIA and how to defeat them, so if you insist on wasting your time and mine, by all means go ahead."

Roth knew Rachman was telling the truth. Prior to the current Presidential administration in Washington, the U.S. endured eight years of an uber-left administration who spent a great deal of time apologizing to nations around the world for America's perceived mistreatment of others on the world stage. The treatment of prisoners at Abu Ghraib and the use of water boarding to extract information were most often cited in this condemnation.

In addition to water boarding, many of the interrogation techniques used by U.S. intelligence agencies for the past half-century were exposed to public scrutiny and criticized by the previous administration. Unfortunately for the intelligence community as a whole, this exposure resulted in the enemies of America knowing a lot about what interrogation techniques were considered *acceptable*, and which ones were not.

"Unfortunately for you, Mr. Rachman," Roth responded, "we've had a change in administrations in our country and I think you will find our policies regarding the treatment of prisoners has undergone a substantial revision."

Chris Roth knew from the moment the meeting took place under the white canopy; Rachman would be the primary focus of this interrogation. Rachman, with Khan standing behind him, approached the Syrian General first and extended his hand, indicating Rachman's higher status in the pecking order. Unfortunately for Khan, this observation made him expendable.

At this point the only thing Rachman could be sure of was his captors held him in a secure location, probably underground, in a room with soundproofing covering the walls and ceiling. He had no idea of the building's location, or even in what country it sat. This would become apparent to him when Roth raised the shades so Rachman could see into Khan's room.

Unable to mask the sense of panic as it washed over his face while looking into Khan's room, Rachman seemed frozen when he saw the man standing in front of his colleague. The uniform and insignia on the man's shoulder patch identified him as an officer with the Egyptian General Intelligence Directorate, commonly referred to as the Mukhabarat. Known as brutal savages in their treatment of ISIS fighters, the Mukhabarat had a well-earned reputation for using extremely inhumane tactics to extract information. Rachman realized how drastically worse things had gotten for himself and Khan.

"You were right about one thing Mr. Rachman," Roth said. "There are certain things I am prohibited from doing in my attempt to gain information from you and Mr. Khan. Unfortunately for you and him, though, the Mukhabarat is not limited by those same restrictions."

"We know you are planning a terrorist attack in Brussels in the immediate future," Roth continued, "and it is my intention to find out everything you know. Perhaps we will get everything we need from Mr. Khan, which will make further detention of you unnecessary. But I somehow doubt this will be the case. For the time being, why don't we both sit back and watch as our Egyptian friend goes to work."

Like Rachman, Khan had also been taken into the showers, cleaned up and returned to his room sans clothing from the waist down. A second *picana*, identical to the one in Rachman's room, sat on the table in front of Khan.

With water still dripping from Khan's scrotum, the Egyptian placed the end of the bronze wand underneath Khan's testicles. For the next two hours Rachman watched as his fellow ISIS patriot was subjected to the excruciating pain of having his balls shocked by the electrical current emanating from the *picana* operated by the Egyptian intelligence officer. Each time the Egyptian turned up the dial on the rheostat, delivering an increase in the flow of electricity, Khan's head snapped backwards as he screamed in pain. Rachman could only stare; assured in the knowledge this level of pain would surely be visited on him shortly.

As they continued watching the interrogation through the two-way mirror, both Roth and Rachman watched as the Egyptian removed the copper wand, placed it on the table and then walked out of the room. A few moments later he knocked on the door and entered Rachman's room.

"He's telling us he knows nothing," the Egyptian said to Roth in front of Rachman. "It's obviously a lie, but we might want to think about moving on to the next step."

"I agree," replied Roth. "But first let's give Mr. Rachman a chance to save his friend from more discomfort," as he turned his gaze to Rachman. "What do you say Mr. Rachman? You can save your friend from additional pain if you tell us about what you have planned for Brussels. And understand something Mr. Rachman; we are not going to let either of you go until we have confirmed you're telling us the truth. So, what do you say, is there anything you want to tell us?"

"I've already told you," Rachman said emphatically, "I don't know what you're talking about."

"Very well then," said Roth, nodding to the Egyptian. "Go ahead with your next step."

Assuming he was about to witness more of the same treatment to his friend Abu Khan, Rachman let out a sigh and leaned back in his chair. In a matter of minutes, he would realize his expectations were grossly wrong. When the Egyptian reentered Khan's room moments later, he carried with him a rope under his arm. Sliding a chair across the room to use as a step stool, the Egyptian stood on the chair and fed one end of the rope through a large eyebolt secured to one of the rafters in the ceiling. Stepping down from the chair, he began fashioning a noose at one end of the rope. Roth shifted his eyes to Rachman to gauge his reaction to what they were observing. Rachman's facial expression had not changed. After completing the noose, the Egyptian walked over to his prisoner and placed the noose around Khan's neck, sliding the knot downward so the loop fit tight under his chin.

Two of Roth's men, who had been waiting outside the door of Khan's room, entered and along with the Egyptian, grabbed the free end of the rope. In unison, the three men began pulling on the rope, causing Khan's body, still strapped into his chair, to slowly be lifted off the ground. When the bottom of Khan's chair reached about two feet above the floor, the end of the rope was tied off to another eyebolt attached to the brick wall, indicating this interrogation technique had been used in this room before. As Khan's body began to flail about, the Egyptian and the other two men left the room, closing the door behind them. Rachman could only stare as he watched his friend die an agonizing death before his very eyes.

"I want you to understand something, Mr. Rachman," Roth said as he lowered the shades on the two-way mirror. "What happened to your friend will surely happen to you if you don't tell me what I want to hear. Only in your case, the duration of the pain to be inflicted on you will be much longer and will include some other techniques our Egyptian friend is anxious to use. But make no mistake, the only chance you have of getting out of here alive is if you cooperate. No more bullshit about not knowing anything about Brussels. We know your group is planning a major attack in the next few days and you're going to have to tell me what it is if you expect to live. And I'm going to need specifics about where and when, so keep in mind Mr. Rachman, anything you tell me will have to be verified before we let you go."

"What guarantee do I have that you will let me go if I tell you what you want to hear?" asked Rachman.

"You're going to have to take me at my word, Mr. Rachman," Roth responded. "But I can guarantee you this, if you don't talk you will die a painful death in this very room. Our Egyptian friend is outside the door anxious to get started, so I suggest you make up your mind quickly."

Rachman had no doubt about his imminent demise. Any chance he had of walking out of this dungeon alive, albeit small, rested on whether or not he would expose the attack his group had planned for Brussels. Attempting to stall for more time and call Roth's bluff would be fruitless, as he had witnessed what his captors were capable of doing. Rachman's decision had become clear: tell Roth what he knew or die a very painful death at the hands of the Mukhabarat officer waiting to work on him. The desire to stay alive can be a strong motivator when attempting to reach a decision such as this. Rachman, with no assurances from his captors his cooperation would save his life, figured his only chance, regardless of how remote, would be to tell the CIA agent what he wanted to hear.

"Very well, Mr. Reed," Rachman began. "You win."

"I had every intention of winning, Mr. Rachman."

While not complicated, the ISIS plan Rachman spelled out for Chris Roth over the next twenty minutes comported with the desire of ISIS terrorists to inflict casualties on small groups of innocent people, keeping their terrorist activities front and center on the world's stage. According to Rachman, an ISIS soldier would drive a van loaded with explosives into a crowd of people attending a concert at Brussels Park, near the Royal du Parc theater in downtown Brussels on Sunday. Roth immediately verified that a musical concert was scheduled for the following Sunday as part of a cultural event where thousands were expected to attend.

While keeping Rachman on ice over the next few days in his cell, Roth left some of his team behind to babysit Rachman and flew to Brussels to coordinate with the Belgium Federal Police force on stopping the impending terrorist attack.

With over a hundred plains-clothed federal police officers encircling the Royal du Parc on the day of the concert, hundreds of visitors began filing into the park, taking their seats on blankets and chairs on the grassy field where the concert would take place. Fifteen minutes into the opening act, one of the federal police officers at the southwest corner gate of the park, radioed to his commander a white van with placards on the doors, which read *Brussels Caterers,* turned into the park and stopped at his gate.

Several other officers rushed to the location and approached the van, pulling the driver out and holding him while the van could be searched. When the officers opened the passenger-side door, they noticed an ignition switch lying on the front passenger seat, connected by a long wire to two tons of explosives packed into the back of the van.

Rachman's information had been accurate and the interrogation, which revealed the ISIS plot, had prevented the killing of several hundred people in the park. Roth could not have been more pleased.

But like most operations involving the CIA, nobody outside of a very small group of people would ever know of his involvement. The Brussels news reports later in the evening would report the Belgium Federal Police had thwarted an attempted terrorist attack at the Royal du Parc, with no mention of how or where they received the information upon which they acted.

Unfortunately for Rachman, giving up the operation wasn't going to save him. He probably knew it all along, but figured he had no other option than to give his captors what they wanted. Roth called one of his team members still keeping watch over Rachman and told him what happened in Brussels.

"We're done with Rachman," Roth told him. "Tell our Egyptian friend to finish up and thank him for his assistance."

"Roger that," came the reply.

The Mukhabarat would never let an ISIS leader go free once he had been captured. At the very least, Rachman's cooperation saved him from hours or even days of extreme pain. The Egyptian simply walked up behind Rachman as he sat tied to his chair and placed the muzzle of his pistol to back of his head. Knowing his inevitable fate, Rachman closed his eyes as the Egyptian squeezed the trigger.

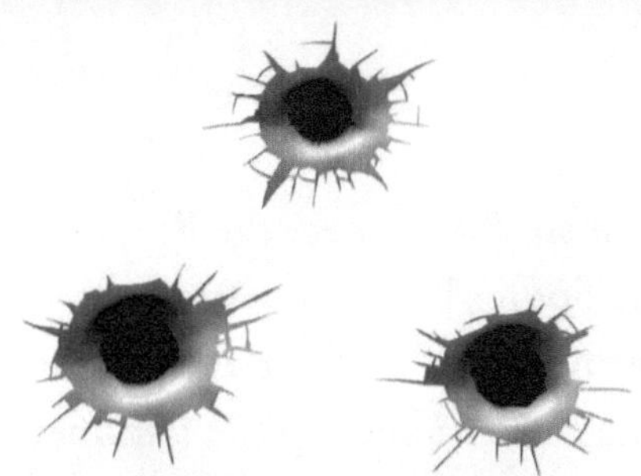

Chapter Thirty-One

Retired Army Major Bill Allen hated politics, as well as most of the politicians he had encountered throughout his adult life… save one. Throughout his military career he was the kind of leader who could be counted on to identify a problem, devise a plan to address it, and carry out the plan with an unmitigated steadfastness, usually resulting in a successful resolution. Blindly loyal to the man he now served; his official title was *Counselor to the President.*

Those within the inner circle of the Smith administration knew of the high regard in which Major Allen was held by the new President and how he was probably the last person on earth any of them wanted to cross. The power and influence Bill Allen had, because of his close proximity to President Smith, caused a majority of White House staffers to shutter whenever he walked into a room.

A young assistant assigned to the White House press office found out the hard way Major Allen was the wrong person to get sideways with. Trying to impress a young lady on the phone of his importance within the new administration, the assistant made the mistake of lounging back in his chair with both feet parked squarely on top of his desk while he chatted. Fifteen minutes after Major Allen walked in and observed the young man's posture, the assistant had all of his possessions in a cardboard box, having been reassigned to a small cubicle at the Commerce building on 14th Street.

Bill Allen's job was simple: protect the President at any cost and take care of issues on behalf of his boss, no matter how unseemly, which were beneath the dignity of the office for the President to handle himself. Everyone knew of the close friendship the two men had shared over the past two decades but obviously knew nothing about their involvement with a small group of men known as the *New Sons of Liberty*.

Bill Allen had earned his position in the President's inner circle and President Smith knew he could rely on his friend to watch his back and do everything within his power to keep anything damaging from reaching the Oval Office. No President can know what slings and arrows will eventually come his way, but they indeed will come. President Smith could not have a better man to protect him from such things than Bill Allen.

Military soldiers, especially those who shared the experience of having gone into battle in defense of their country, enjoy a special and unique bond because of their common experience. Such was the relationship between CIA Director Gordon Shirley and the President's right-hand man, Bill Allen. General Shirley had adamantly conveyed to the President his resolute commitment to their mutual desire of eradicating Islamic terrorists, and Major Allen's commitment was likewise immutable.

Mr. Allen had driven from the White House out to Langley to convene a meeting he requested with the CIA Director, to discuss strategy on how to go after the terrorists. Major Allen had brought along a close friend of his whom he fervently believed could contribute mightily to those efforts.

"Good afternoon, General," Major Allen said as he entered the office of the CIA Director, extending his hand. "This is the young man I told you about, David Kyle."

"Pleasure to meet you, son," General Shirley said to Kyle as he shook his hand. "Please, have a seat. I'd like you two to meet Chris Roth," he said as he motioned to Roth on the other side of the room. "He's one of the best guys I have in the field and he knows more about the problem we're facing in the Middle East than just about anybody."

Assigned to the region for the past ten years, Roth agreed with his boss that bringing on someone like Kyle would be helpful. A graduate of Troy University in Alabama, Chris Roth began his federal career as a second lieutenant in the Air Force Intelligence, Surveillance and Reconnaissance Agency located at Lackland Air Force Base in Texas. Following the conclusion of his obligated service with the Air Force, Roth was hired by the CIA and reported for training at the Federal Law Enforcement Training Center in Brunswick, Georgia. Prior to his deployment to the Middle East, he received advanced training at Langley, including an immersion Arabic language program where he became a fluent speaker.

He had a well-earned reputation as a stellar intelligence officer and his ability to recruit and cultivate sources of information in the region was renowned. General Shirley would be ramping up the Agency's endeavors relating to their efforts to combat terrorism and he wanted Chris Roth to be an integral part of this strategy. Roth would not let his Director down, or for that matter, his country. He wholeheartedly signed on to do whatever is necessary to wipe ISIS off the face of the planet.

Bill Allen came up with the idea to use Kyle as a contract employee of the CIA. Possessed of a skill set Allen thought beneficial to the war on Islamic terrorism, Allen believed Kyle's abilities and expertise would be helpful in those efforts. Leading a team of intelligence personnel who would be taking a more aggressive stance against the scourge of terrorism, Roth happily accepted David Kyle as the newest member of his team.

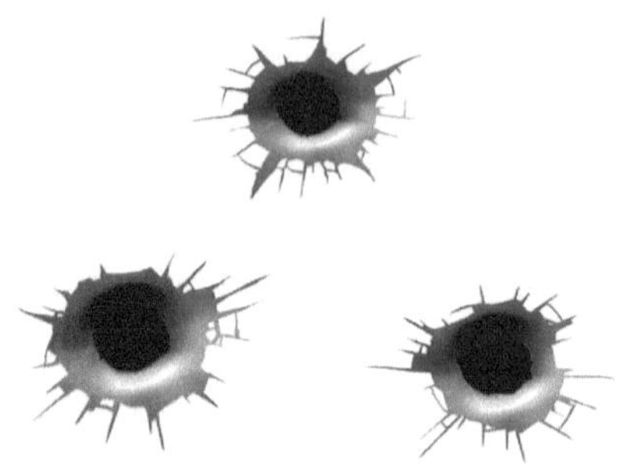

Chapter Thirty-Two

Steam continued to billow over the top of the shower stall as Deanna Mowery reached down and turned off the water. Stepping out of the shower onto the heated marble floors, she retrieved a towel hanging from one of the brass-plated towel racks. After drying off, Deanna slipped into one of the two complimentary two-hundred-dollar bathrobes provided to guests staying at the Ritz-Carlton Hotel. Located adjacent to the Fashion Centre at Pentagon City Mall in Arlington, Virginia, she planned on visiting some of the upscale shops after checking out of her five-hundred-dollar-a-night room. The shopping would wait, though, as the man seated on the bed in the adjoining room, adorned in the other bathrobe, had things on his mind which had nothing to do with shopping.

Kevin Pearson, Deputy Attorney General of the United States, had managed to keep his number two spot at the DOJ after President Smith's new Attorney General had been confirmed. Pearson had been known to be apolitical and President Smith's gesture of leaving him in his post as Deputy AG was seen as a smart political move. Pearson and Deanna had known each other by reputation, but never actually met until a mutual friend introduced them at one of the inaugural balls the night of President Smith's inauguration. They began quietly dating soon after, and for the past several months had been meeting at the Ritz-Carlton, usually on Friday nights, closing out their stressful workweeks with a little R-and-R. The two lovers agreed that making their *liaison* known would be beneficial to either, assuming the exposure would complicate their professional relationship.

A two-hundred-dollar bottle of Dom Perignon Champagne sat chilling in an ice bucket on the nightstand as Deanna walked out of the bathroom. Slowly sauntering across the floor with an impish smile on her face, Deanna released the tie holding the front of her robe together and let it drop to the floor as she reached the light switch on the wall, dimming the overhead lights. Filling two glasses from the bottle of champagne, Pearson handed one to Deanna as she approached the side of the bed where he sat. Unable to avert his gaze, Pearson's eyes darted up and down from Deanna's silky toned inner thighs to her magnificent alluring breasts, now inches from his face. Her bronzed skin, still damp from the shower, glistened in the faint light of the room.

"See anything you like?" she asked with a demure look on her face.

"I like everything I see," Kevin said, rising from the bed and loosening the front of his robe, pressing his chest against hers.

Setting her glass of champagne down, Deanna reached for a small bottle of body moisturizer and unscrewed the cap.

"Do you mind rubbing me down?" she asked as she handed the bottle of lotion to Kevin, sliding the robe over her shoulders and letting it drop to the floor. "My skin feels a little dry."

Kevin smiled as Deanna slid past him, spreading her nude body across the bed in anticipation of the full body massage he would graciously provide.

An hour and a half later, as their bodies lay entwined under the thousand-thread sheets on their bed following another incredible session of lovemaking, Deanna's phone began to vibrate on top of the dresser.

"Damn," Deanna said as she rolled off the bed, reaching down and retrieving her robe from the floor. "Don't they know I need some off time, too?"

Recently promoted to Executive Assistant Director of the Science and Technology Branch at FBI headquarters, Deanna Mowery had been appointed by the FBI Director to sit on the FBI's recently formed Executive Committee to Combat Domestic Terrorism. The committee's purpose would be to realign the Bureau's approach in combating domestic terrorism, a direct response to President Smith's commitment to aggressively pursue a strategy of eradication, as opposed to the strategy of containment sought by his predecessor.

"More committee stuff?" Kevin asked as he too rose from the bed and began getting dressed, confident in the fact their secret rendezvous had concluded.

"Yeah, looks that way," she replied. "The boss wants to get together right away. Sounds urgent."

Deanna dressed and before leaving their hotel room, walked over to Kevin and planted a long kiss on his mouth, while reaching down with her left hand to softly caress his *manhood.*

"Why don't you relax for a couple of hours while I go to my meeting," she told him with a smile as she gently gave him a squeeze, "and when I come back I'll see if I can put some life into him again."

After walking into the Hoover Building, FBI's national headquarters on Pennsylvania Avenue in downtown D.C., Deanna bumped into her good friend, FBI Agent Rich Michaels. Agent Michaels, with the help of Deanna and her facial recognition expertise, had broken open the case involving the assassination of Democrat Senate leader Edmund Riley over a year earlier. Former Army Special Forces Sergeant Steve Lick had been identified by his investigation as the assassin.

In addition to the murder of Senator Riley, blown to smithereens by a gas explosion in his apartment, Lick had also been the primary suspect in the murder of Supreme Court Justice Hayden Byers. Identifying Lick by the use of surveillance photos, which captured him leaving a Metro station prior to the Byers killing, Agent Michaels also believed Lick to be complicit in the murders of at least two other left-wing liberals, as well as the attempted assassination of a well-known talk show host. Unfortunately for Agent Michaels, his investigation hit a dead end when Steve Lick swallowed a cyanide pill as agents moved in to arrest him following the Riley murder. Always believing Lick did not act alone, Agent Michael's investigation could never identify other co-conspirators, as the investigative trail went cold after Lick's death.

Deanna Mowery strongly advocated the naming of Rich Michaels as lead agent in the FBI's national counterterrorism task force, a recommendation heartily endorsed by the Director.

"Nice to see you again, Rich," Deanna said, extending her hand as they both waited on the elevator to take them to the committee meeting with the Director.

"You too," replied Rich. "I hope I didn't pull you away from something important. Surely you had better plans for a Friday night than to meet back here?"

"Oh, so you're responsible for this meeting?" she said with a smile. "Don't worry about me, you should know I don't have much of a life outside of this building."

Reaching the third floor, the elevator doors opened as Deanna and Rich exited and made their way to the large conference room where the committee meeting would convene. Taking their place at the twenty-foot-long oak conference table, Deanna and Rich joined the rest of the committee, comprised of five other high-ranking FBI Assistant Directors, as the FBI Director called the meeting to order.

"Let's get right to it," the Director said. "I met with Agent Michaels earlier today and he has information I feel needs to be brought to the attention of this committee. Rich, why don't you come up here and fill everybody in on what you've been working on."

"Thank you, Mr. Director," Rich said, rising from his chair and moving to the front of the room. Setting his briefcase down on the table, Rich removed an 8x10 photo and passed it around the table.

***

Prior to the terrorist attack on September 11, 2001, several foreign intelligence agencies, including our own CIA, identified some of the 9/11 hijackers as al-Qaeda operatives. Had this information been known to domestic law enforcement agencies, it is possible they could've been flagged before boarding the planes they eventually commandeered and flew into the World Trade Center, the Pentagon, and a Pennsylvania field, in the worst terrorist attack in our nation's history. At that time, a proverbial *wall* existed between foreign and domestic intelligence agencies, which prohibited the sharing of information between the CIA and U.S. domestic agencies, primarily the FBI.

By law, the CIA's intelligence gathering operation is restricted to gathering only foreign intelligence and is not permitted to spy on individuals inside the United States. In addition to this moratorium on domestic spying activity, prior to 9/11 the CIA was reticent regarding the sharing of information and/or sources with other agencies, whether in or out of the U.S.

As a result of the breakdown within the intelligence community, many surmised the 9/11 attacks could have been prevented. U.S. government law enforcement and intelligence agencies made a concerted effort to remove this *wall,* which prevented the sharing of intelligence prior to 9/11, in hopes of thwarting future terrorist attacks. This intelligence *fusion,* located and controlled at the Department of Homeland Security, allows for a centralized gathering of incoming intelligence and subsequent dissemination of such information to any and all agencies equipped to use it in the protection of our homeland. This new relationship between U.S. intelligence agencies formed the basis for the briefing FBI Special Agent Rich Michaels would give to the committee.

***

"The photo going around the table," Agent Michaels began, "is of a man named Adnan Mustafa. He entered the U.S. four years ago on an H-1B visa to teach science at Morgan State University in Baltimore. He is also a prominent member of the Allah Haku Mosque in Highlandtown, a small community east of downtown Baltimore. According to intelligence we received from our counterparts at CIA, Mustafa has been in contact with suspected ISIS operatives in the Middle East and has met with them on at least three occasions over the past twelve months. Two of the meetings took place in Dubai, and another in Haima, Oman, where he has a home."

"I spoke with Immigration and a passport check confirmed he did take those trips, all within the past year. Since we got this information, we've had Mustafa under 24/7 surveillance. In the past two weeks Mustafa has spent one hundred percent of his time at three places: his apartment, located in northeast Baltimore, Morgan State University where he teaches and his mosque. Two days ago, he backed a panel van up to the basement door of his mosque where he and two other men spent about twenty minutes unloading the van into the basement. The open doors of the van had our view completely blocked so we couldn't see what they unloaded but based on how the van rode when he pulled in, it contained something heavy."

"Any ideas about what he may be up to?" asked one of the Assistant Directors.

"According to my counterpart with the Agency," Rich replied, "the NSA picked up some chatter coming out of Iran indicating they are expecting something to happen within the next two weeks. Based on what we know about Mustafa's background, we think they could be planning an attack on one of our electrical grids using an EMP."

"An EMP?" asked another committee member. "What's an EMP?"

"Electromagnetic Pulse," replied Rich. "Basically speaking, it is a short burst of a massive amount of electromagnetic energy. At high enough levels, and if strategically placed near a large electrical power plant, an EMP blast could knock out an entire electrical grid, in essence cutting power to everything within a hundred miles or so. A little less, perhaps, depending on how ambitious the terrorists are. Think of a lightning strike times ten. That's about what we might be looking at in terms of how much electromagnetic energy can be produced by one these blasts."

"And by the way, this is not a new phenomenon. This type of attack has been talked about within the intelligence community for the past several years. A few installations, like NORAD for example, have been planning for it by moving vital equipment to underground bunkers inside Cheyenne Mountain and building shields around the equipment designed to deflect the electrical pulse. Similar defensive measures are much harder to do, if not impossible, when talking about electrical power plants responsible for generating electricity for entire cities. Washington D.C. is on its own power grid and most of its electrical equipment is shielded. They also have a pretty sophisticated backup system so we don't think D.C. would be a likely target for this kind of attack. More than likely the terrorists would want to hit a major U.S. city, knocking out power to a million or so people. Such an event could be catastrophic, leading to widespread looting, food shortages and general mass chaos."

"What's next Rich?" Deanna asked. "Where do we go from here?"

"My team has already begun working on an affidavit for a search warrant for the Allah Haku Mosque," Rich replied. "We think it will be ready to go in a day or so."

The Director chimed in. "Let's not lose sight of the fact this is potentially a very sensitive situation, Rich. FBI agents crashing in the door of a mosque will not be viewed favorably if we screw up and not find anything. On top of that, we have to be extremely careful in not revealing the source of our information. As much as you can, keep our coordination with the CIA out of your affidavit. We need to stay under the radar as much as possible."

"Understood, sir," Rich responded. "We think we're going to be okay on that front. Let's hope DOJ gets on board and doesn't give us any push back."

"I may be able to help you there," Deanna said. "I have a pretty good contact over at DOJ. I'll do what I can to make sure they look favorably on your application for a search warrant. When do you anticipate sending it over? I want to give my contact a heads up so he knows what's coming."

"It'll be ready first thing on Monday," Rich replied. "Any help you can give us will be greatly appreciated."

"No problem," Deanna replied.

An hour later Deanna returned to the Ritz, sans clothing and in the arms of her very influential DOJ contact. There would be no problem,

Kevin Pearson assured Deanna, as the DOJ would happily to do its part in helping the FBI stop a possible terrorist attack.

"Now let's get to a more pressing issue," Kevin whispered to Deanna, smiling as he pulled her body on top of his, clasping his hands behind her lower back. "It's hard to think about work right now."

With a devilish laugh, Deanna leaned in and planted a long kiss on Kevin's lips. "Did you just say it's hard?"

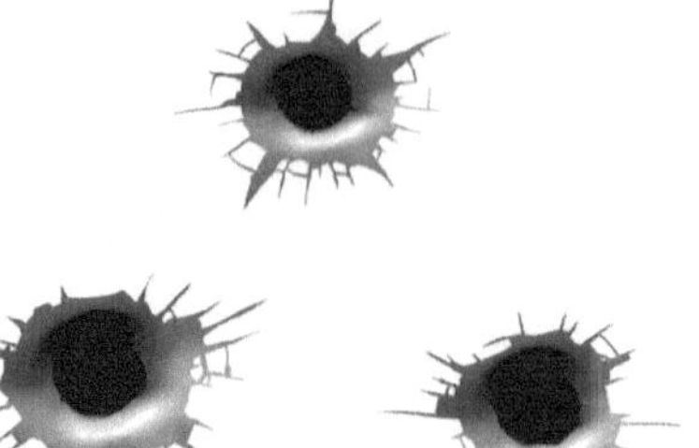

Chapter Thirty-Three

renetic is the best way to describe the pace at which President Brian Smith and his administration hit the ground running following inauguration. Immediately after becoming President-elect, Brian Smith put together a transition team of close advisors who met daily to discuss who would fill critical jobs in the new administration. With the United States Senate still firmly controlled by the Republican Party, President-elect Smith knew he would inevitably get all of his cabinet and other high-profile nominees confirmed, after tolerating the anticipated barbs sure to come from Democrats, still reeling from the bloodbath their party endured at the ballot box.

True to form, the sore losers took issue with a few of President Smith's nominees, but in the end, could do nothing more than whine. The Democrats' predictable charges of racism and bigotry against a few of the new President's cabinet nominees fell on deaf ears. Nothing could be done to deny the President his picks and they all knew it.

In addition to laying out for the country the names of the key people who would be running the new government, President Smith got right to work on rescinding a plethora of Executive Orders implemented by his predecessor, President Rob Ferrell. Crippling regulations on the oil and gas industry, as well as some adversely affecting the business community and the ability to create new jobs desperately needed to jumpstart the anemic economy, were quickly eliminated, fulfilling one of President Smith's campaign promises.

Following these acts, which he took unilaterally without the need for congressional approval, the President turned his focus to working with the Congress on tax reform and repeal of the controversial and job-killing National Healthcare Act. Most of what President Smith wanted to complete in his first hundred days in office he accomplished, resulting in immediate dividends for the country.

The economy seemed to be reacting favorably to the policies he supported, and the new President couldn't have asked for a better start. Within a year of taking office, President Smith had managed to relegate the legacy of Rob Ferrell to the ashbin of history, repudiating almost everything the uber-left President had stood for throughout his two terms in office. The open-border, pro-illegal immigrant tenor of the previous Democrat administration was also in total retreat. As part of President Smith's promise to take the threat of Islamic terrorism seriously, he did everything he could to plug up the porous border with Mexico and slow down, if not stop entirely, the relentless flow of illegals and contraband into the country. In spite of protestations by many Democrats, President Smith knew radical Islamic terrorists were more than happy to take advantage of unenforced borders to get their people into the U.S., where they could be positioned to wreak havoc on innocent Americans whom they regarded as infidels.

The FBI Director, appointed to his position by President Ferrell, had assured his new boss of his commitment to the President's desire to ramp up their effort at combating terrorism, ensuring his continuation as Director. It had been his idea to put together a special committee on domestic terrorism, a move enthusiastically endorsed by the new President.

The Director counted on his star agent Rich Michaels to land the first serious blow against radical Islamic terrorism, ensuring the nation of the Smith administration's seriousness about uncovering and thwarting plots by terrorists against the homeland.

President Smith held daily security briefings in the Oval Office each morning at precisely 7:00 a.m. with the FBI Director, the CIA Director, the Attorney General and the Homeland Security Secretary, as well as key members of his national security team. Having briefed the President on the FBI's investigation of Adnan Mustafa, the science professor at Morgan State University in Baltimore with ties to radical Islamists, the FBI Director informed the President about the upcoming raid on the Allah Haku Mosque in the Baltimore community of Highlandtown later that morning.

According to the Director, Mustafa, a prominent member of the Baltimore Islamic community, used the basement of the mosque to store electronic equipment the FBI believed would be used in an EMP attack, disrupting all electrical power in and around the Baltimore area. The information, according to the Director, originated with the CIA and the follow-up investigation and surveillance undertaken by FBI agents confirmed the validity of the intelligence. CIA Director J. Gordon Shirley, present at the briefing, nodded his consent to the President indicating the veracity of the FBI Director's comments.

"I hope everyone is aware of the potential mine field we're in by hitting a mosque," the President began. "How solid is your information?"

"We are aware of that, as well," replied the FBI Director. "Our terrorism committee met this past Friday to discuss the case. The agent leading the investigation gave us a thorough briefing and we feel we're on solid ground."

"In that case, do what you think needs to be done," said the President. "I'll have your back if there's any blow back on this. Let's hope to God your info is good."

"Thank you, Mr. President. I'll let you know as soon as I get briefed following the raid. I should know something by noon today."

Following the adjournment of the President's briefing, the Director returned to his office in the Hoover building and convened his domestic terrorism committee. He wanted everybody together when they received word from Rich Michaels about their raid on the mosque. They wouldn't have to wait long.

FBI Special Agent Michaels pulled into the parking lot adjacent to a strip mall, about a mile and a half from the Allah Haku mosque in Highlandtown. Two Baltimore City police cars and four other FBI agents assigned to Rich's domestic terrorism task force were waiting when he arrived. Spreading out a street map across the hood of his Crown Vic showing the location of the mosque, Rich pointed out to the raid team where he wanted them when they executed the search warrant. Donning his raid jacket with the large bold letters *FBI: POLICE,* Rich turned to address one of the uniformed officers beside him.

"You and I will go in the front door," he said, "and go straight to the Imam's office located inside on the right. You two (pointing to two of his agents) position yourselves on the northwest and southwest corners of the building. I want everyone else to go around back and take up positions outside the basement door. Once we're inside, we'll serve the warrant on the Imam, take the stairs down to the basement and open the door for you guys to come in. Any questions?"

There were none. Everyone got back in their cars and five minutes later pulled into the parking lot of the Allah Haku mosque, moving to their assigned positions. Agent Michaels exited his vehicle and along with a uniformed officer, walked into the mosque and straight to the small office on the right where he hoped to find the Imam. Standing in the open doorway of the Imam's office, Rich knocked on the doorframe announcing his presence and addressed the Imam seated behind his desk.

"Special Agent Rich Michaels, FBI," he said to the Imam, standing up from behind his desk. Stepping towards the Imam, Rich held out a folded piece of paper clutched between his fingers and handed it to the Imam.

"This is a federal search warrant signed by a federal magistrate, authorizing me to conduct a search of your premises," he continued. "The warrant authorizes me to search any and all areas of your mosque and seize anything we find of an evidentiary nature we believe may be associated to potential crimes against the United States."

Visibly shaken, the Imam grabbed the warrant from Agent Michaels and began to read it.

"This is outrageous," the Imam, replied, "this is a house of God, sir. We worship Allah here; we do not engage in crimes against this great country as you allege. I will call our attorney and see what he has to say about this."

"You are welcome to call your attorney or anyone else you like," Rich said. "But if you are considering impeding our search in any way, I suggest you talk to your attorney first. This warrant is valid and any attempt by you to interfere will expose you to legal jeopardy for interference in a federal investigation. I'll be happy to speak with your attorney when he arrives, but in the meantime the search will take place."

With that, Rich and the officer turned and walked out of the office and proceeded to the basement door.

Once downstairs, the officer opened the door leading outside, allowing the other team members to enter. Looking around the main room, Rich noticed several long tables and chairs, a big-screen television and some audio and visual equipment, but nothing unusual. Pointing to a pair of doors across the room, Rich instructed his agents to check them out. Those rooms contained more tables and chairs, but nothing out of the ordinary. A slight tinge of panic rushed through Rich's mind, as he had expected to find large, heavy electrical equipment he believed would be used in an EMP terrorist attack. The heavy equipment his surveillance agents had seen unloaded a few days prior.

"Some of you go upstairs and check out all the rooms up there," he ordered. "See if there's an attic or any other place they could've moved the equipment. As far as down here is concerned, let's start pulling some of this ceiling tile down and see if anything's up there."

What Rich had expected to find would not be found in the ceiling and he knew it. But right now, he didn't know what else to do. He had been sure what they were looking for would be found in the basement, but so far, he had hit a dry well.

What the hell is going on? It almost looks like they were expecting us, he thought.

An hour after arriving with search warrant in hand, the Imam he had served the warrant on and a man who introduced himself as the Allah Haku mosque's attorney approached Rich. Holding open the warrant to the section describing what agents would be searching for, the attorney addressed Agent Michaels.

"Your warrant says you are searching for *certain and specific* items you believe will be used in a terrorist attack on the United States," the attorney began. "Furthermore, it describes said items as being large, heavy electrical equipment which can be used in something your warrant refers to as an *electronic magnetic pulse* attack. Tell me Agent Michaels, have you found anything like that?"

Not lost on him, the cynicism from the attorney's tone seemed to drip from his lips as Rich replied, "not yet, but we've not completed our search."

Descending the stairs into the basement where Rich stood, one of his agents approached with a disappointed look on his face.

"We did a thorough sweep upstairs and came up empty," the agent said. "Also, there's no attic."

"Okay, thanks," replied Rich, who returned his attention to the Imam and the attorney. "I'm very sorry for the intrusion," Rich said, realizing he was in the middle of a monumental and embarrassing screw up. Turning to his raid team standing nearby and waiting for instructions, Rich announced they would be leaving.

"This is not the end of this," the attorney said to Rich as he and his team made their way to the door. "You have violated the sanctity of this house of God and we will sue the FBI for this intrusion."

As Rich departed, he recognized the exclamation from the mosque attorney as nothing more than an idle threat. He was on solid legal ground, in spite of whatever complaints might be lodged by the Imam and his attorney. His greater worry revolved around having to explain to his Director and the domestic terrorism committee how they got it so wrong. This wasn't the first search warrant Agent Michaels had served which failed to produce fruits of a crime, but it certainly would cause extreme embarrassment to the agency for which he worked.

"But what happened? What went wrong?" he kept muttering to himself.

Driving back to Washington, D.C., Rich phoned Deanna Mowery, his closest friend on the committee, to give her a heads up on what happened.

"Roger that, Rich," Deanna told him. "Just get here as soon as you can and we'll hash everything out when you get here. Don't beat yourself up, I'm sure there's a reasonable explanation."

"You may be right, Deanna," Rich replied. "But I can't figure out for the life of me what the explanation could be. I know the intel coming from the Agency was solid and I know what we saw when we had this guy under surveillance for the past month. We screwed up somehow, Deanna, and I've got to figure out why."

The FBI Director, immensely disappointed with the results of the search, was not anxious to relay the outcome to the President. Knowing it would create a firestorm with the President's political enemies and those predisposed to the supposition his administration was anti-Muslim; he picked up his phone and dialed the White House to convey the disappointing news to the President.

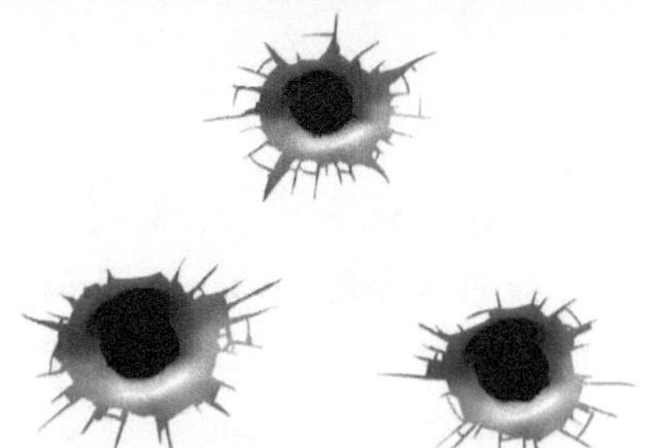

Chapter Thirty-Four

It had been more than two weeks since Casey Dean had seen the inside of the Washington Chronicle building near Logan Circle in D.C., her place of employment for two decades. Her tanned skin and effervescent smile were the result of spending the past fourteen days on a friend's boat anchored in the Bahamian waters near Cat Cay, a tiny spot in the Bahamas about forty miles east of Miami. A great deal of her vacation time had been spent diving for lobsters in the crystal-clear waters, gorging herself on conch fritters, red snapper and Jamaican rum, all the while enjoying a respite from her life as a hard-nosed reporter in a city replete with crime, intrigue and the occasional political scandal.

No one at the Chronicle begrudged her for wanting to get away and recharge her batteries; God knows she had earned it. At the height of the Presidential election season, which had brought Brian Smith to power, the relentless and tenacious manner she brought to her craft broke open the story that dominated every news cycle leading up to the election of Senator Brian Smith as President.

Beginning with the murder of liberal Supreme Court Justice Hayden Byers, it became apparent to Casey the subsequent murders of CeCe Diamond, Fred Stein and Democrat Senate leader Edmund Riley were tied together in some sort of elaborate conspiracy to rid the world of hard-left leaning liberals.

Ms. Diamond, an acolyte of famed socialist Saul Alinsky, ran an organization known as the Secular Progressive Alliance, a group dedicated to a progressive agenda many thought antithetical to American values. A community organizer with similar political leanings, Fred Stein had enjoyed a close personal relationship with Vice President Eric Hogue, at the time running to succeed the far-left ideology of the Ferrell administration. And Edmund Riley, the powerful leader of the senate Democrats, had vowed to use his power and influence to thwart the Presidential aspirations of Republican Senator Brian Smith.

In addition to these murders, an assassination attempt on the life of far-left T.V. host Mark Hayes failed when an undetonated bomb was found taped to the undercarriage of his car in the parking garage at NBC headquarters in New York City. Casey's reporting on this conspiracy, however, hit a brick wall after Steve Lick, identified as Justice Byers' killer, took his life by swallowing a cyanide pill shortly after setting off the explosion that killed Senator Riley.

FBI Special Agent Michaels and D.C. detective O'Rourke, now retired, used the conspiracy angle laid out by Casey Dean in her reporting to help frame their investigation. Unfortunately for them, the death of Lick seemed to bring their investigation to a screeching halt, unable to tie anyone else directly to Steve Lick and the conspiracy they still believe existed.

Jimmy O'Rourke, fully recovered from the stabbing he received from Lick after the Riley murder, retired and now lived in Front Royal, Virginia. His days were filled with tending his garden, working on his fledgling golf game and doing his best to complete the never-ending *honey-do* list his wife peppered him with on a regular basis. Agent Michaels had also moved on, now concentrating his efforts around his new role as lead agent for the FBI's domestic terrorism task force.

It had been much harder for Casey Dean to move on, believing as Rich Michaels and Jimmy O'Rourke did they had only scratched the surface of the murder conspiracy involving the untimely deaths of the aforementioned victims.

"Well, if it isn't our star reporter," said Casey's managing editor and boss as he approached her desk to welcome her back from vacation. "By the looks of your tan, I'd say your time away was beneficial."

"You have no idea," replied Casey. "I didn't know how much I needed a vacation and a little time away from this God-forsaken place," she added with a smile. "By the way, you don't happen know where I can find some conch fritters here in the District, do you?"

"I'm afraid not," her boss replied with a smile, as if he even knew what conch fritters were. "It's good to have you back, Casey. I didn't have a chance to tell you before you left, but our publisher wanted me to submit your reporting on the Byers murder conspiracy to the Pulitzer committee for consideration. You did a phenomenal job and he thinks it deserves to be recognized. I happen to agree. I have no idea of your chances of winning, but I wanted you to know how much your contributions around here are appreciated."

"Thanks, I really do appreciate that," Casey responded. "I wish I could say I thought the story was over, but you know me, I'm rarely satisfied. I just don't know where to go from here."

"Yeah, I know what you mean," the editor replied. "Byers' replacement has already been named by our new President and it's a lock he'll get through the Senate. For the time being, at least, we probably need to move on. President Smith is making a lot of noise about going after the terrorists and I'd like to see you concentrate on those kinds of stories. Your FBI friend is heading up their domestic terrorism task force, so it's probably a good idea to keep the channel open between you two."

"I know," Casey replied. "We're still in touch. We're planning on having lunch sometime in the next week or so. I'll try to find out what they're working on and see if I can make a story out of it. In the meantime, I need to sit down and start going through my emails. No doubt they're backed up having been gone for two weeks."

"Sounds good. Seriously, though, Casey, welcome back. You were missed."

"That's nice to hear," Casey replied. "Thanks."

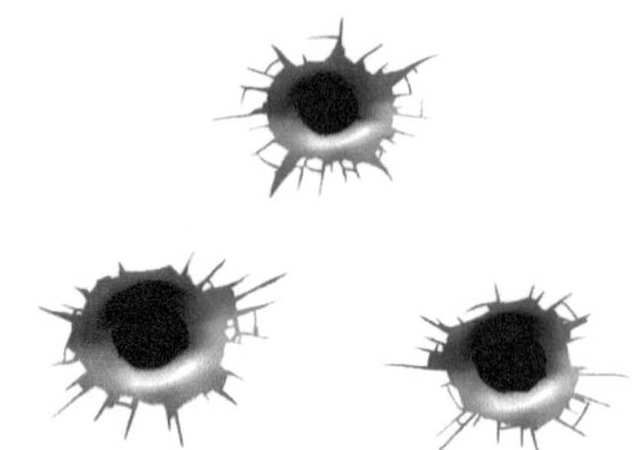

Chapter Thirty-Five

Dejected and somewhat embarrassed, Rich Michaels walked into the FBI conference room where he would be delivering a briefing to the higher-ups on what happened at the Allah Haku mosque when his team served their search warrant. Or more accurately, what went wrong. The committee knew, of course, the FBI investigation into domestic terrorism, which ultimately identified Adnan Mustafa as a possible terror suspect, had been aided by information relayed to Rich from the CIA. Nobody in the committee meeting would even think about asking for the name of his CIA counterpart or if there were any reasons to doubt the veracity of the information received. The specific name of the person Agent Michaels worked with at CIA was known to very few; the kind of information only shared on a need-to-know basis.

***

Months earlier, after being hand-picked as the lead agent on the domestic terrorism task force, Rich flew to Amsterdam for an initial meeting with CIA agent Chris Roth, who would be his eyes and ears inside the Agency pertaining to matters of terrorism. Besides Rich and Chris, the only other people privy to this meeting were the Directors of the FBI and the CIA. General Shirley had insisted on keeping the name of Chris Roth secret, even from those inside the FBI who would be working on terrorism issues. "The less who know, the better,"

Rich walked out of the lobby of his hotel in Hoofddorp, a small community west of Amsterdam's Schiphol Airport, and boarded the train bound for Amsterdam's main train station, Amsterdam Centraal. Pulling into the station, he couldn't help but notice the remnants of twisted steel tracks and charred concrete still visible, the result of an ISIS bomb attack in the station months prior claiming the lives of dozens of innocent victims.

Leaving the station, he walked twenty blocks and found the Café de Klos on Kerkstraat Street in the heart of downtown Amsterdam. Rich paused for a moment once inside the door of the small tavern so his eyes could adjust to the darkness. A very large rectangular shaped wooden bar, probably a hundred years old by his estimation, filled up the inside of the room. Alone at the far corner of the bar nursing a tall stein of draught beer sat the man he had come to meet. He waved at Rich and motioned for him to come join him.

"I could spot you from a mile away," Chris Roth said with a smile, as he motioned for the bartender to pour another beer.

"Let's not get too cocky," Rich replied, shaking hands with Chris. "You're a dead ringer for an Agency man if I ever saw one," he whispered with a grin as he pulled up a stool next to Chris. "Interesting place here, how'd you ever find this?"

"Oh man," said Chris, "they got the best smoked ribs on the planet. I never miss a chance to come here whenever I'm in Amsterdam. Make sure you get the baked potato with garlic butter, too. I'm telling you; it'll change your life."

"High praise, indeed," Rich said with a laugh.

The two men enjoyed their meals and beer, engaging in general small talk while they sat at the bar. Neither wanted to talk shop until they were outside on the street, away from anyone who might overhear what they had met to discuss.

"I couldn't help but notice some of the damage left behind by those bastards when I got off the train at Centraal," Rich began, as they walked along the banks of the Amstel River. "You guys making any headway on narrowing down the list of suspects for that one?"

"Yeah, we're close," Chris Roth, replied. "We've got something in the hopper right now we'll be moving on shortly, involving some of the bastards who did the bombing. We think they may be planning something else in the near future so we're looking there as well. Hopefully I'll have some good news to share with you soon on that front. One of the things I wanted to make clear to you was the need to keep our relationship on the QT. It's not that I don't trust a lot of government people or anything like that; it's just that I don't trust a lot of government people. So, I'll leave it to your discretion as to whom you mention my name. Obviously, the fewer the better as far as I'm concerned."

"Roger that," Rich replied. "Need-to-know only."

"I'll be honest with you," Chris continued, "this era we're in now with *you* and *us guys* sharing stuff back and forth is pretty new, not to mention a little awkward for some of us used to doing things the old way. I'm okay with it, mind you, especially with this guy we got in the White House now. This son-of-a-bitch is serious, and I mean serious. I'm liking his kick-ass and take names strategy."

"Yeah, I hear you man," Rich replied. "Both of our bosses seem to be totally on board with this new direction, so the least we can do is make it work."

A good first meeting, both men felt comfortable they could work with the other and both looked forward to marshaling their respective resources in the fight against radical terrorism.

Unfortunately, bumps in the road were inevitable and Rich now had to deal with a major one.

***

"I can promise you," Rich began, addressing the domestic terrorism committee members, "no one is more disappointed over coming up dry on this search than I am. I'm sure the information we have is solid and convinced the identification of Adnan Mustafa as a terror suspect is accurate. As I told you in our last briefing, we've had Mustafa under surveillance for a while now, ever since his name first surfaced. We saw him unload his van into the basement of the mosque, and based on how the van rode, we're positive he unloaded some very heavy equipment.

Somehow, in the matter of a couple of days, the equipment, whatever it was, disappeared and I'm at a loss for how it could've happened. Mustafa hasn't been back to the mosque since the day he unloaded his van. He's pretty much kept to his residence or the university, so right now it's a mystery. We'll stay on him and as soon as we see something worth reporting, I'll get back to you. In the meantime, I'm going to head back to my office and see if I can figure this out."

Rich thanked them for their time and excused himself from the meeting, heading straight to his office where he called one of his agents sitting outside Mustafa's home.

"Hey, this is Rich," he said into his phone to one of his agents on his task force, "is anything happening there? I just left my meeting where I had to swallow a pretty big bite out of a shit sandwich and I'm hoping you have something positive to report."

"Sorry Rich," the agent replied. "I got here at six o'clock this morning and the night shift guys told me he's been inside since early yesterday. His car is still in his parking spot outside his apartment building. I'll let you know the minute he moves."

"Thanks," Rich replied, hanging up his phone.

Rich and the rest of the team were unaware of what took place approximately eighteen hours previously.

Several times a day over the past few months, Adnan Mustafa would peek out the rear blinds of his second-floor apartment windows overlooking the parking lot of a strip mall, located about fifty yards behind his apartment complex. Situated in the middle of the parking lot rose a light pole, in direct line of sight from his apartment window. If Mustafa's contact wanted to get a message to him, there would be a tiny red ribbon tied around the light pole, indicating to Mustafa his contact needed to meet with him as soon as possible.

On the morning prior to the raid on the Allah Haku mosque, Mustafa picked up a pair of binoculars, looked out his back window and saw the ribbon tied around the light pole blowing in the breeze. Grabbing a small overnight bag he kept packed at all times, Mustafa stepped out onto his back balcony and lowered himself down to ground level. Walking a few yards away from his building, he scaled a wooden privacy fence erected on the property line between his apartment complex and the strip mall. Unseen by the FBI agents watching the front of his building, Mustafa made his way across the parking lot and two blocks later walked into a coffee shop where he met his contact.

"It's time for you to go," his contact told him. "You've done all you can do and it's time to get you out of the country. As we speak, we're moving everything out of the mosque to another location. As I'm sure you already know, the FBI is watching you so you can't go back home or to your office at the university."

The man slid a large manila envelope across the table to Mustafa who took it and placed it in his bag. Contained inside were thousands in Euros, British Pounds and Canadian dollars, along with a phony Canadian passport with Mustafa's photo and new name.

By the time Agent Michaels and his FBI raid team were concluding their search of the Allah Haku mosque the following day, Mustafa would be well on his way to Toronto where he would board a plane bound for London, eventually making his way to his home in Oman. Mustafa's contact, part of a cell of ISIS sympathizers actively planning on carrying out the terrorist attack feared by Agent Michaels, had been accurate about his assessment of Mustafa's contribution to the cause.

For the past six months, Professor Adnan Mustafa had been working with his science students at Morgan State University in Baltimore on the development of an electromagnetic survey system designed to conduct geological surveys through the use of a waveform pulse transmitter. When properly used, the device is designed to emit the transmission of electromagnetic pulses at a predetermined repetition rate, providing scientists with an accurate way of conducting the desired survey.

Mustafa, however, unbeknownst to the rest of his team, had altered the device in such a way that instead of emitting electrical pulses of limited power and duration, the device would act as an electrical bomb, producing one large burst of electromagnetic energy, generating an intense magnetic field capable of knocking out a large portion of a city's electrical supply, known as a wide area synchronous grid.

It was this altered device the agents observed being moved into the basement of the Allah Haku mosque and subsequently moved out when the terrorist group for which Mustafa worked got wind of the impending raid. Having instructed his fellow terrorists on how to detonate the EMP bomb he had created, Mustafa's services to the cause were no longer needed, necessitating his immediate departure from the U.S.

After three days of sitting outside Mustafa's apartment building with no sight of their suspect, Rich Michaels got worried that perhaps Mustafa had slipped away without being seen. They had come up empty on the search of Mustafa's mosque and he did not want to face his Director and the domestic terrorism committee and tell them they had somehow *lost* their suspect. Checking with his contact at Customs and Immigration Enforcement, Rich ran a passport check on Mustafa that came back negative, indicating he had not left the country. Unbeknownst to Rich, Mustafa had indeed left the country using his phony passport.

What the hell is going on? Rich thought. *What am I not seeing? What are they up to?*

It wouldn't take long for Agent Michaels and the rest of the country to know what Mustafa and his fellow terrorists were up to. At 5:00 p.m., four days after the search warrant at the mosque in Highlandtown came up empty, causing a public relations black eye to the FBI, a white panel van pulled to a stop outside the fence surrounding Baltimore's largest electrical power plant. Prior to exiting the van and getting into another vehicle beside him, the driver reached into the rear compartment of the van and flipped the switch on a timed detonator connected to Mustafa's EMP bomb. Five minutes later, as the car carrying the two ISIS cell members were miles away, the electrical bomb inside the van exploded, knocking out the power station and cutting off all electricity to a million and a half people.

In the midst of a discussion with the Speaker of the House and the Senate Majority Leader, summoned to the Oval Office by President Smith to discuss the President's legislative agenda, President Smith looked up at Bill Allen who had rushed through the door of the Oval Office and interrupted their meeting.

"What is it Bill," the President asked, noticing the look of concern on Bill Allen's face.

"We've been hit, Mr. President," the President's top counselor and aide said. "An EMP device detonated outside Baltimore's largest power plant. The grid is gone. Power is out for most of Baltimore and some surrounding areas."

"Get hold of the security team and get them over here now," the President responded, as he walked across the room and turned up the volume on the bank of televisions constantly tuned to all of the cable news channels.

News feeds were beginning to come in from Baltimore's downtown area, showing the power outages and commenting on the fact the sun would soon be down, causing total darkness throughout the city. None of the news anchors had yet tied the power outage to terrorism, but it would not be long for the connection to be made. By midnight, total chaos reigned throughout the city of Baltimore.

Cell towers, in need of electrical power to function, were out, disabling millions of cellphones. Store windows throughout the city were smashed as looters could be seen prancing around the streets carrying big-screen T.V.s and anything else they could grab. By the time the sun came up the following morning, over a hundred cars were left smoldering in the middle of the street, and twenty-two people were killed as a result of the bedlam.

In addition to the mayhem of lost lives and destroyed property, the stock market futures sold off during the night, portending a sharp sell-off as soon as the markets opened at 9:30 a.m. Everything the terrorists could have hoped for and more. Adnan Mustafa smiled as he looked at the Internet on his computer screen, safely tucked away inside his home, far away from all the chaos he had created.

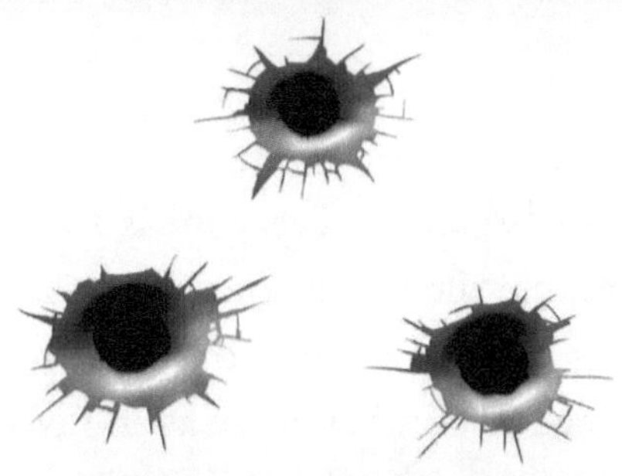

Chapter Thirty-Six

Members of the press corp who covered the White House, as well as others involved in reporting on issues of national security, were invited to the East Room of the White House for an early evening press conference. The White House press secretary had conducted his daily briefing with reporters earlier in the day and had been inundated with questions about the terrorist attack on Baltimore and what would be the administration's response. The press secretary deflected most of those questions, telling the reporters of the President's intention to hold a press conference later in the evening, where many of those questions could be asked and answered by the President himself.

Swept into office by the American people yearning for a leader with a steel spine who would take the fight to the terrorists, President Brian Smith would not cower in the face of the battle now before him. Unconstrained by the desire of many liberals to exhibit a certain degree of political correctness, the President had no hesitation in calling the attack in Baltimore what it really was: a terrorist attack on the United States by radical Islamic terrorists, bent on destroying the American way of life. A stark contrast, to be sure, from what the country had seen for eight years under the previous administration.

All of the T.V. networks, as well as the cable news outlets, had their cameras rolling as the President entered the room and approached the podium. Without delay, the President began the press conference with an opening statement before fielding questions.

"Good evening," he began. "As everyone is aware by now, the United States of America became the victim of a terrorist attack in Baltimore, Maryland, one of our nation's most prominent metropolitan cities. A very sophisticated electrical bomb, known as an EMP, or electromagnetic pulse device, detonated outside of Baltimore's largest electrical power plant, disabling the plant and wiping out power to the city and most of the surrounding area. Nearly a million and a half citizens lost power in the attack, and the ensuing chaos which followed resulted in the deaths of nearly two dozen people and an economic calamity, the likes of which we have never before seen."

"The Maryland Public Service Commission, along with representatives of Baltimore Gas and Electric, are working around the clock to see that power is restored as soon as possible," the President continued. "Everything that can possibly be done to repair the electrical grid damaged in the attack is being done. Experts have told me the repairs necessary to bring the power grid back on line should be completed in the next two to three days. While officials are working to fix the problem, we are continuing to see looting and other acts of violence resulting from the chaos this attack has caused. The Maryland State Police, Baltimore City Police and members of the National Guard are all on high alert, constantly patrolling the areas impacted by the outage. This will continue until the power has been fully restored."

"As of right now," the President continued, "the damage caused by the riots and looting that took place in the initial aftermath of the outage are estimated to be in the hundreds of millions of dollars. The loss of economic activity due to this calamity may approach a billion dollars and, in addition, a sell-off on Wall Street, directly attributable to the attack, has already wiped out close to a hundred billion dollars of wealth in the stock market. Needless to say, how we react to this attack will say a lot about who we are as a nation and what the terrorists can expect from us in the future if these attacks continue."

Pointing to a correspondent from NBC News seated in the front row, President Smith invited the opening question.

"Thank you, Mr. President," the reporter began. "You indicated you believe this attack is somehow related to Islamic terrorism. What do you base this assessment on and do we know the name or names of anyone involved?"

"I base it on the fact Islamic terrorism is real," the President answered, "and every indication we have so far points to radical Islamic terrorists as being the culprits in this attack. Our intelligence agencies, both domestic and abroad, have identified the man we believe is responsible for building the electrical bomb used in Baltimore. The suspect's name is Adnan Mustafa, and we have very strong evidence Mr. Mustafa was sympathetic to the cause of ISIS and indeed worked on their behalf. Mr. Mustafa entered our country on an H-1B visa and had been teaching science at Morgan State University in Baltimore. He is currently at large and being sought by the FBI in connection with this attack."

Casey Dean, among the reporters present for the press conference, jumped to her feet and started asking her question before anyone else could begin theirs.

"Mr. President," she began, "the FBI recently received criticism for executing a search warrant on a mosque in Baltimore. The search warrant produced no evidence of a crime, and many in the Muslim community were outraged at what they perceived was an effort by your administration to curtail their religious liberty rights. My question, sir, is this: is there any validity to their outrage and was the search warrant in question related to this attack?"

"First off, Ms. Dean," the President said with some consternation in his voice, "there is no validity to the claim by anyone which would imply this administration is engaged in, or ever will be engaged in, the subjugation of anyone's right to practice the religion of their choosing. Religious liberty is one of the hallmarks that have sustained this democracy for more than two centuries and it is something I revere. As far as it being related to this investigation, I am hesitant to talk specifically about an ongoing FBI investigation. I will leave it to the FBI Director when, and if, he wants to make specific comments regarding their investigation."

Not wanting to cede her opportunity to engage the President to another reporter waiting his turn, Casey went right into her follow up question as the President completed his answer to her opening question.

"You mentioned, sir, Mr. Mustafa is still at large," she began. "Is he the only suspect in this bombing at this time and do we know if he is still in the country or not?"

"We do not believe Mr. Mustafa acted alone," the President answered. "We also have no evidence to indicate he has left the country, so for now we are acting under the assumption he's still here, most likely hidden by other conspirators."

Part of the President's answer was truthful, and part was not. The President and the FBI clearly believed Mustafa did not act alone and other conspirators were involved. He did not, however, believe Mustafa to still be in the United States.

***

Days earlier, following the botched raid on the mosque and before the EMP attack occurred, Agent Michaels had been told by one of his team members there had been no sign of Mustafa at his apartment. Anticipating the possibility his agents had lost their target, and believing an attack imminent, Rich knew finding Mustafa became imperative.

Walking into a secure soundproof room down the hall from his office in the Hoover building, Rich lifted the handset of the Stu-III phone used exclusively by agents to place and receive *scrambled* calls which cannot be traced or intercepted. Chris Roth, relaxing on his boat moored at his dock on Lake Tiberius, reached for his flashing satellite phone, indicating an incoming call. Like the phone being used by Rich Michaels to place the call, Roth's phone also had the *scrambling* technology needed to place and receive calls in complete privacy, without the risk of having the call intercepted and listened to by others.

"We think we may have lost Mustafa," Rich said to Chris. "We haven't confirmed that yet, but my guys have been sitting on his apartment around the clock and haven't seen hide nor hair of him in quite some time. He's either collapsed inside his apartment and lying dead on the floor, which I seriously doubt, or he slipped out somehow without my people seeing him. If some kind of attack is imminent, and I think it is, it would make sense for him to disappear. If I had to make a guess, I'd bet he's heading your way."

"Roger that," replied Chris. "We tracked him to Dubai and Oman the last times he left the U.S., so I'm assuming those would be as good a place as any to start looking. I'll talk to my source over here and have him keep an ear out. If he hears anything he'll let me know. In the meantime, I'll take a couple of guys with me and we'll go check out Dubai and Oman. Maybe we'll get lucky."

Both Rich's and Chris' intuition proved accurate. Mustafa had, in fact, slipped out of his apartment, without being seen by the FBI agents, and as Rich had surmised, was able to get out of the country undetected. On the morning of the President's press conference regarding the terror attack, days following Rich and Chris' secure conversation, Chris Roth sat on a hillside overlooking a small residential community in Haima, Oman, and observed through his binoculars Adnan Mustafa walk out of his front door and get into his car. A woman and two small children, assumed by Chris to be Mustafa's family, stood on the front porch of their home and waved as Mustafa drove away.

Found you, you bastard, Chris thought.

Chris made two calls on his satellite phone, one to Rich Michaels and the other to Langley. The attack on Baltimore had taken place by this point and Chris knew his Director would want to be notified immediately about the whereabouts of Mustafa. What Chris would do about Mustafa, now that he had been located, would come later.

***

Always the skeptic, Casey Dean walked out of the White House following the President's press briefing regarding the Baltimore attack, convinced President Smith had held something back. She would reach out to Rich Michaels and try to get their lunch date on her calendar as soon as possible.

233

As the President's press conference drew to a close, CIA Director Shirley, summoned earlier in the day, sat in the Oval Office waiting on him to return.

"Good evening, Gordon," the President said as he walked into his office, extending his hand to the CIA Director. "What's the latest on Mustafa?"

"Hello, Mr. President," General Shirley responded, taking a seat in front of the President's desk. "As I mentioned to you this morning, we have him located at what we believe is his home in Haima, Oman. My man on the ground there has him under surveillance as we speak. His house is located at the end of a cul-de-sac in a relatively small community. Maybe fifty homes in all. It appears he lives there with his wife and two kids, at least that's all we've been able to see at this point. They're waiting on me for how next to proceed."

"Well," the President replied, "let's not have them wait any longer. I want you to handle this, Gordon, and I don't need to know the details. Let's just say I want a clear message sent the United States is no longer going to dick around with these bastards. The whole world is watching, including the ISIS leadership, as to what our response will be. I want maximum impact, Gordon. The message needs to be strong and it needs to be decisive. Just let me know when it's done."

"Understood, Mr. President," General Shirley replied.

The CIA Director left the Oval Office believing he knew exactly what kind of response the President wanted and it would be up to him to deliver it. The message General Shirley wanted to deliver to the terrorists on behalf of his Commander-in-Chief was simple: *Mustafa's fate is your fate if you screw with us!*

General Shirley went straight to his office and called Chris Roth. Having completed his conversation with his Director, Chris disconnected his call and placed his satellite phone on the ground beside him. The slight chill coursing through his veins accompanied the somber look on his face. His orders were clear, concise and unambiguous. Mustafa would pay the ultimate price for his deeds and it would now be the responsibility of Chris Roth to deliver retribution for his act of terror. Only in this case, the retribution would be nothing short of barbaric.

The chill felt by Chris Roth was the result of his Director's last statement: "Make sure his family is there," General Shirley told him. "I want the terrorists to know it's not only their lives they are putting at risk, but also their whole damn families as well."

It took Chris Roth about twenty-four hours to put all the pieces in place to carry out the task given to him. The exact latitude and longitude coordinates of Mustafa's house were programmed into the CIA drone flying thirty thousand feet above Chris' head. A little after six in the morning, he sat looking through his binoculars from his vantage point a couple hundred yards from the house as the sun began to peek out on the horizon.

Mustafa's car still sat in the driveway, and Chris had seen no one leave from the night before when he observed Mustafa, his wife and their two young children enter their home. Chris Roth thought long and hard about what he had been asked to do, figuring out long ago his job would sometimes require indecorous acts of brutality. In and of itself, this was nothing new to Chris. The deliberate targeting of innocents is what made this mission different.

But were they really innocent, he reasoned. *The kids may be innocent, perhaps, but probably not the wife. And who's to say his kids won't grow up to be just like their dad?*

As brutal and unseemly as it would appear to most, Chris concluded it wasn't his place to decide what is or is not appropriate when it comes to waging his country's war against terrorism. His job was to carry out the orders of those in charge with precision and alacrity and leave the moral judgments to others.

"We are in range," the drone operator said to Chris, as he continued peering through his binoculars, still trained on Mustafa's house. "Waiting on your command to initiate."

"Roger that," replied Chris. "Target is in place. Go when ready."

Lifting his binoculars skyward, Chris began scanning the heavens, now illuminated with the morning sun. Within moments he could see a vapor trail appear from the clouds above, produced by the AGM-114 Hellfire missile launched from the CIA drone and headed straight for Mustafa's home. Traveling at almost one thousand miles an hour and outfitted with a high explosive, metal-augmented blast fragmentation warhead, the missile struck Mustafa's home, penetrating the structure at the center of the roof. The devastating explosion instantly turned the home into a pile of rubble, engulfing the remnants of a once nice suburban middle-class home in fire. Chris Roth knew instantly no one inside had any chance of survival.

"Positive strike," Chris told the drone operator as he began his departure from where he had been sitting for the past eighteen hours. "Nicely done. Thanks for the assist."

"Roger that," came the reply. "We're bringing our bird home. Happy to help."

It wouldn't take very long for word to get back to the terrorists regarding the fate of one of their beloved soldiers, as well as the fate of his entire family. A clear message had been sent. Whether the message would make a difference or not would be determined at a later date.

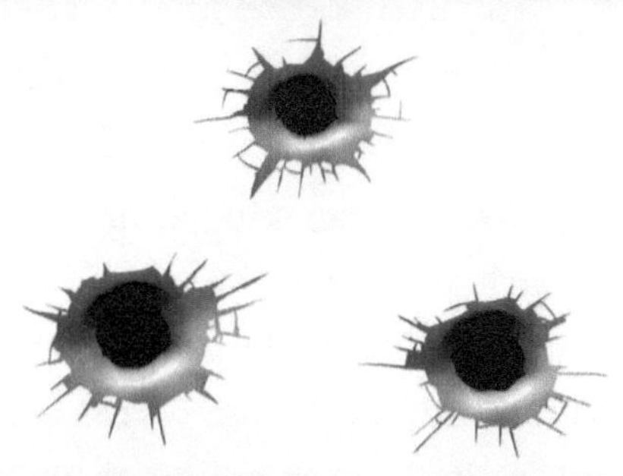

Chapter Thirty-Seven

Israel's largest fresh water lake, Lake Tiberius, is known as the Sea of Galilee and is fed by the Jordan River. Teeming with fish, it provides Chris Roth with the perfect *cover* as a small-time industrial fisherman plying his *trade* and giving legitimacy to his presence in the region. The tiny fishing town of Tiberius, where Chris keeps his boat docked, as well as the lake itself were named for the Roman Emperor Tiberius. With the ruins of the biblical town of Capernaum on the north shore, every time Chris launches on the lake he can't help but think of St. Peter and Jesus' other disciples fishing on this very lake some two thousand years prior.

A different time, perhaps, but nonetheless he considers his mission in life similar to those disciples as he, too, feels he is doing the Lord's work. Ridding the world of terrorists surely qualifies as such, or so he reasoned. Taking hold of the crank handle attached to a davit, Chris began reeling in the large fish net, which had been submerged in the waters next to his boat. When the net became completely suspended above the water, he swung it around into the boat so he could deposit his catch safely on board. Hundreds of musht (or tilapia) and biny (from the carp family) began flopping around on the deck of his trawler as a small fishing boat with a single outboard engine approached from Chris' aft.

The man piloting the boat, whose mere existence was known by only a select few people within the Agency, was Chris' source inside

ISIS. Code-named *Pegasus* after the winged horse in Greek mythology (for no other reason than Chris liked the name), his real name, known only to Chris, was Fareed Adib. Pulling back on his throttle control until he hit *neutral,* Adib idled up beside Chris' boat and tossed over a line, which Chris then secured to the railing of his boat.

"Come aboard my friend," Chris said to Fareed, who had already begun stepping across onto Chris' trawler.

"Thank you, Mr. Chris," Fareed replied, reaching both arms out to give Chris a hug. "It looks like you had a pretty good day on the lake this morning. You should get a very good price for your catch at the local market. If you are considering a change in careers, I think you may have found a profitable line of work," he said with a laugh.

"Not hardly, Fareed," Chris replied. "I can't stand the smell of these things."

"I am sure you did not call me out here to discuss fishing, Mr. Chris," Fareed said. "I think I know why I am here. May I assume it is to discuss what happened to Mr. Mustafa?"

"You may indeed," Chris responded. "What are you hearing?"

"Suffice to say, Mr. Chris," Fareed began, "the fate of Mr. Mustafa has gotten the attention of our leaders. I can tell you with absolute confidence they were shocked at what happened to him in his home. Not so much what happened to him, mind you, but the fact his family also died in the attack. As I'm sure you already know, we have been observing your government's responses over the past few years and this one seemed to deviate from what we would consider to be a normal response. What we are not sure of is whether or not this was an accident or if it signals a change in your tactics going forward. Can you tell me if the killing of Mustafa's family was accidental, or does it have something to do with the change in your President?"

"Fair question, Fareed," Chris replied. "I can tell you without hesitation it is directly tied to our change in leadership. We have a President now with steel balls and a steel spine. From what I can tell so far, he has no problem dealing with your leaders in a very vicious manner. Don't look for him to ease up, either. I think it's only going to get worse for you guys going forward."

"I think this is also the conclusion of my leadership," Fareed said. "I'm not sure how much it will change what they are trying to accomplish, though. To them, this is a *jihad*, a holy war if you will, and it's not likely they will retreat from it."

"I never thought they would," Chris said. "But make no mistake about it, Fareed, the shackles are off. We are coming after you with everything we have and we will not stop until your group is completely annihilated."

"I assumed as much, Mr. Chris," Fareed replied. "I wish I could tell you my people have learned a lesson and they will stop waging this senseless war against the West, but I'm afraid there's not much chance this will occur."

"Well, at least we have you, Fareed," Chris said, placing his hand on Fareed's shoulder. "I know how much you are risking and I want you to always know how much I appreciate it."

"Thank you, Mr. Chris," Fareed said as a sly smirk began to form on his face. "Just don't forget to wire the money to my bank account."

"Of course not," Chris replied with a laugh. "My government is more than happy to compensate you for your help. Now unless you are willing to help me gather up all this fish and put it on ice before heading back in, I suggest you get the hell out of here before I put you to work."

"Before I leave," Fareed began, as his tone became more serious, "there's something else I need to tell you."

"What is it, my friend?" Chris replied.

"At one of our recent meetings," Fareed began, "I overheard two of my superiors talking about Mr. Mustafa."

"What about him?" Chris asked.

"From what I could tell from their conversation, it was no accident Mr. Mustafa got out of your country before your problems occurred in Baltimore. The device he had been working on, the one that caused the power outage in Baltimore, had been in the works for months. At some point near the end, Mustafa received word your FBI had him under surveillance twenty-four hours a day. He got out when he did because we knew he was being watched. Someone in your government tipped us off. I have no idea who it was or how high up it goes, but you need to know we have someone on the inside."

Rocked backwards at what he heard, Chris Roth leaned against the console of his boat and raked his hand across his forehead as Fareed untied the line to his boat and prepared to depart.

Holy shit, he thought. *So that's why the search warrant got screwed up. But who the hell could it be? Who knew about it?*

Chris' mind continued to race as he began gathering up his catch and throwing the fish into the large ice bin on board before heading back to the dock. No one in the Agency, outside of himself, his station chief and Director Shirley knew anything about Mustafa. No chance, he figured, any of them had gone rogue. It had to be somewhere in the FBI, he concluded, but who? Chris had complete faith in Rich Michaels, so he didn't worry about him, but he didn't know any of the people who sat on the FBI's domestic terrorism committee. Rich had told him about briefing this committee on the case right before they went to DOJ for the search warrant. *Could it be one of them or maybe someone on Rich's team?*

Chris needed to let this bombshell from Fareed settle in before he said anything to anybody. He didn't know who he could completely trust so he would wait before saying anything. *If there's a mole,* Chris thought, *and apparently there is, we could be royally screwed.*

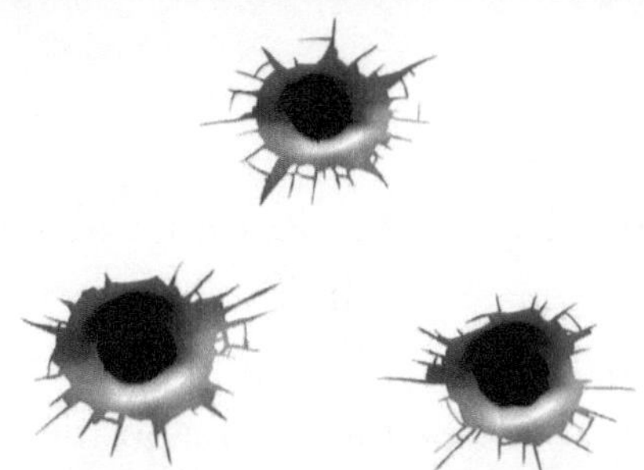

Chapter Thirty-Eight

As one would imagine, many fringe benefits come with being President of the United States, provided the person occupying the Oval Office can also deal with the overwhelming stress that comes with the job. One of the *pamperings* enjoyed by not only the President, but everyone else working on the White House staff, is daily access to the executive dining room where the White House chef and his staff prepare elaborate spreads for both lunch and dinner. President Smith encourages his staff to take advantage of the perk, believing they will be happier, and subsequently more productive, if they are well fed.

He, on the other hand, is more inclined to take his lunch break at his desk in the Oval Office, usually a sandwich and a salad. Almost always accompanied by his close friend Bill Allen, the President's *working lunches* provide an opportunity for him to speak frankly with his closest and most trusted advisor about issues of the day without the need to censor either the language or topic. President Smith knows he can bounce any idea off Bill Allen and he will get straight and unfiltered feedback.

After finishing his lunch and downing the last sip of sweet tea, Bill Allen removed a pouch of chewing tobacco from his breast pocket and inserted a tennis ball-size wad into his mouth as both men gazed at the bank of TVs across the room, always on and always muted. Bill grabbed the remote on the President's desk to turn the sound up on the CNN feed as the image of Senate Minority Leader Laura Reagan appeared.

Hailing from Seattle, Senator Reagan had represented the state of Washington in the senate for the past twelve years. Selected by her fellow Democrats to be deputy leader under the reign of Minority Leader Edmund Riley, her elevation to the position of leader was made possible following the untimely death of Senator Riley when his Capitol Hill apartment blew up with him inside.

Not quite the bombast as Senator Riley; Ms. Reagan was, nonetheless, a typical West Coast liberal. Since President Smith's ascension to power, Senator Reagan has been one of his most consistent and ardent critics. Her biggest beef with the President seemed to be the administration's stance on illegal immigration. A long-time proponent of sanctuary cities, Senator Reagan regularly asserted the President's efforts to curb the influx of illegals into the country, and his Executive Actions denying federal funds to cities that practice sanctuary policies, were evidence of his hatred towards Hispanics. Nonsense, of course, but Senator Reagan would not let truth and accuracy get in the way of a good narrative.

The President and Mr. Allen were watching the weekly press conference held by Senator Reagan. She believed doing so would provide her and her party the degree of relevance they desperately sought. In reality, however, the Democrat Party was in the midst of a power outage, not unlike what happened in Baltimore, the likes of which they have not seen in more than seventy years.

Relegated to minority status in both the Senate and the House of Representatives, the Democrat's political power and influence had been in free fall for years, not only at the federal level but also in state and city legislatures. Losing the presidency to the Republicans and Brian Smith wiped away the Democrats last vestige of power as the nation delivered a sharp rebuke to their philosophy of governance.

Senator Reagan's weekly presser, usually filled with invectives towards President Smith and his party's efforts to govern, were nothing more than political theater and devoid of any relevance. They did, however, make Senator Reagan feel good and much of the national press, wholeheartedly aligned with her way of thinking, was more than happy to give her airtime.

Senator Reagan's diatribe on this day included criticism of President Smith for *allowing* the terror attack in Baltimore to take place, when, according to her, it could have been avoided.

"The President and his administration," she commented, "has shown a level of incompetence that is, quite frankly, astonishing. They violated the religious rights and freedoms of Muslim Americans by raiding a mosque in Baltimore days before the attack, somehow believing the mosque had something to do with terrorism. Now, we find out the person they tell us committed the attack died along with his wife and children over in the Middle East, and the administration refuses to acknowledge they had anything to do with it."

That part of her press conference was actually true. When word of Mustafa's death reached the press, a reporter asked the President's press secretary what, if any, involvement the United States had in the killing of Mr. Mustafa. The always overly cautious press secretary would only say the President had been made aware of the death of Mr. Mustafa, after the fact, and he had given no order kill him; both statements completely true. When asked about possible involvement by the CIA in the assassination of Mustafa, the nimble press secretary commented it had always been the policy of the United States not to target anyone for assassination; also, a totally true statement. As it pertains to CIA involvement in this or any other endeavor, he added, the press would need to go out to Langley and ask them. They did, of course, and the CIA spokesman did what he always did; he refused to confirm or deny the CIA's involvement in anything.

As Senator Reagan's press conference ended, a sly look crossed the President's face as he hit the *mute* button on the remote while looking over at Bill Allen, depositing a mouthful of tobacco juice into a foam cup. "What a bitch," commented the President. "Do you think she knows how lucky she actually is, Bill?" he asked.

Knowing the President referred to an earlier time when they were involved with the *New Sons of Liberty*, Bill Allen smiled back at his boss, commenting, "I don't know, Mr. President, maybe we should put the band back together again."

With that statement, both men let out a loud laugh.

244

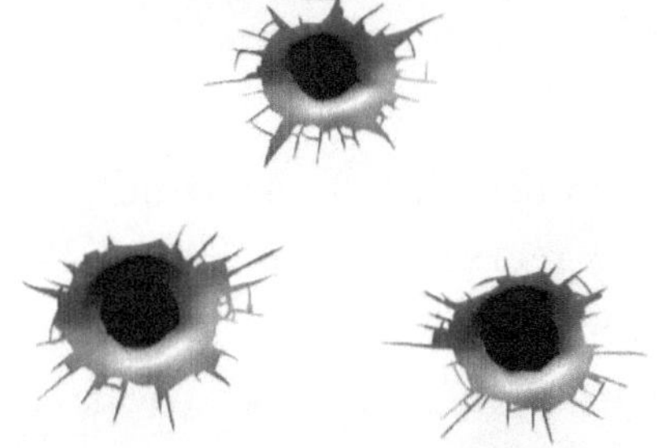

Chapter Thirty-Nine

From the moment President Smith assumed office, he had set out on a path to do something many past Presidents had failed to do or even attempt. Namely, do for the American people exactly what he said he would do when he campaigned for the office. One of the bedrock principles he had campaigned on was his promise to tackle the problem of illegal immigration. Democrats see illegal immigrants as a large pool of potential voters, provided they get them dependent on the government dole and convince them only the Democrats will keep the gravy train flowing. Big business, large contributors to the Republican Party, like some level of illegal immigration because it provides them with access to cheap labor.

Normally competing forces politically, these two factions for years have made it almost impossible to do anything substantive when it came to the problem of illegal immigration. President Smith knew going in it would not be easy taking on this issue, but true to his word he would try. President Smith had been openly critical of the Mexican government for their apparent willingness to look the other way when it came to taking on the Mexican drug cartels smuggling drugs into the U.S. Additionally, *coyotes,* responsible for smuggling illegal aliens into the U.S., enjoyed virtual free reign, unmolested by Mexican officials who had no desire to curb their activities.

U.S.-Mexican relations had suffered as a result of the friction between the Smith administration and the Mexican President. Although

Mexico had always been regarded as our friendly neighbors to the south and a major trading partner in this hemisphere, President Smith would not relinquish the strong posture he had taken against the Mexican government and what he deemed to be a weak effort on their part to work with the U.S. in curbing the border problems. As is the case with many things in life, the problem would get much worse before it got better, as evidenced by events about to unfold.

***

Nogales, Arizona, situated on the U.S.-Mexico border, is home to the nation's second largest Border Patrol station. Covering thirty-two linear miles of border between Mexico and the U.S., agents assigned to the office are responsible for enforcing immigration laws in an eleven hundred square mile area of land, much of it rough terrain, stretching north from the border. While many Border Patrol Agents man the various check points at the Nogales Station, allowing thousands of trucks a day to bring commerce to the United States from Mexico, other agents conduct continuous patrols east and west of the Nogales Station, looking for people and vehicles attempting to cross the border illegally, usually attempting to smuggle in drugs or illegal aliens.

Tom Chafey and Dave D'Amato were veteran agents of the Customs and Border Protection Agency, with more than thirty years of experience between them. Having spent their entire careers in Nogales, they knew every square inch of the desert-like rough terrain that made up most of the border area inside the Nogales district.

Working the midnight shift, as they usually did, Agents Chafey and D'Amato set out on patrol on a hot, humid night, not unlike most nights on the Mexican border. Fifteen miles east of Nogales, the two agents pulled their patrol vehicle to a stop along a stretch of road running adjacent to the border, less than a hundred yards from Mexico.

After killing their headlights, they opened the doors, stepped outside and hopped up on the hood of their vehicle, both men reclining against the windshield, making themselves comfortable for what they anticipated would be a long night of watching the border before them.

With night vision binoculars in hand, they began scanning the horizon in front of them, knowing the area where they sat to be a popular crossing spot for *coyotes* and smugglers. Two hours into their ritual, Agent Chafey spotted what appeared to be a van about a mile away moving north from the Mexican side of the border with its lights out. "I've got something," Tom said to Dave as he pointed in the general direction of the van.

"Yeah," replied Dave. "I see it. Let's go check it out."

Absent a real road to drive on, the van coming up from the south was only doing about ten miles an hour as it made its way over the terrain. Tom and Dave, driving an SUV with four-wheel drive and knobby tires, anticipated no problem intercepting the van. Their thoughts now turned to whether or not the van had drugs or people on board, a 50-50 proposition they presumed. As Tom put their vehicle in *drive* and pressed the accelerator, Dave picked up the mic to call it in.

"Sector, this is Bravo eleven, Nogales," he said into the mic, speaking to the radio command center located in El Paso, Texas. "We have a target spotted about fifteen miles east of the Nogales station. It appears to be a light-colored van, moving north towards the border, lights out. We are moving to intercept."

"Sector to Bravo eleven, Nogales," came the reply. "Copy that."

Intercepting a line of people making their way up from Mexico on foot, or in this case a vehicle with their lights out, occurred nightly for Border Patrol Agents along the border. As Agents Chafey and D'Amato proceeded towards their intended target, also with their lights out, they waited to hear confirmation from Sector an air unit from the Tucson Air Branch had been dispatched to assist. They didn't have to wait long. A Bell UH-60 helicopter pilot, monitoring the radio traffic inside the Tucson Air Branch office, grabbed the mic on his base station radio to notify Sector, and more importantly the two agents on the ground, he would be enroute to assist.

"Copy that," Sector replied.

Defining the exact location of the border between Mexico and the United States is easy for Border Patrol agents in populated areas along the border, or when using natural environs like the Rio Grande River. It's much more difficult in areas of vast expanse where no natural or man-made boundary lines exist, which is precisely where Tom and Dave were. As they continued moving in the direction of their target, they reasoned they were well inside the boundary of the U.S. when they decided to engage and make the intercept.

"Sector, Bravo eleven Nogales" Dave said into his mic, "we're approximately eighteen miles east of our station, moving in for intercept." Sector acknowledged the transmission and immediately radioed the air unit to make sure he copied, which he did.

"They haven't seen us yet," Dave commented as Tom continued driving their SUV, closing the gap on their target.

"That's about to change," replied Tom as he flipped on his headlights, illuminating the target van now thirty yards in front of them.

The driver of the van, a *coyote* who had thirty Mexican men wedged into the back of his van, stepped on the gas as soon as he noticed the set of headlights in his side view mirror. He knew right away he would never see the $5,000 he was set to make upon delivery of his *workers,* hoping now to get away and get back across the border where he could try again another night. Getting caught would result in a prison sentence in the United States, something he wanted to avoid at all cost.

Flooring his accelerator, the *coyote's* van began bouncing around as he attempted to make his escape to the south over the rough terrain, rendering the men in the back of his van helpless in avoiding injury as they ricocheted off each other and the inside walls of their vehicle.

As the chase continued, Agents Chafey and D'Amato had no way of knowing they had inadvertently crossed over the border and were actually now inside of Mexico, where they had no jurisdiction and no legal right to be. About a half mile inside of Mexico, as Tom and Dave continued their pursuit, a Mexican National Police vehicle raced toward them with blue lights flashing.

"Oh shit," Dave said, realizing immediately the mistake they had made. As the Tucson air unit hovered above, illuminating the Border Patrol vehicle with their spotlight, Tom brought their vehicle to a stop and watched as their target van successfully made their escape. Stopping beside Tom and Dave, four armed Mexican police officials jumped out of their vehicle and trained their weapons on the two U.S. agents. Without any other options, Tom and Dave raised their hands as they sat helplessly inside their vehicle. Thirty minutes later, U.S. Border Patrol agents Tom Chafey and Dave D'Amato found themselves seated on a rusty metal bench inside a jail cell in the tiny town of Nogales, Sonora, Mexico, stripped of their weapons, wallets and IDs.

Witness to their fellow Border Patrol agents being taken into custody by Mexican police officers from their vantage point in the sky above, the air unit informed Sector of what had transpired as they flew back to their base in Tucson. In a matter of minutes, the phone in the Oval Office rang, letting the President know of what had taken place on the border.

Karl Bostick, President Smith's choice to head up the Department of Homeland Security, the agency under which Border Patrol agents worked, arrived at the White House first thing the following morning to meet with the President. Mr. Bostick sat across from the President as President Smith picked up his phone and dialed the number to the U.S. Embassy in Mexico City. Asking his ambassador if a U.S. official had been dispatched to check on the agents' welfare, the President was informed the Consulate General in Nogales, Sonora had already made arrangements with the Mexican police to visit the two Border Patrol agents.

"Good," the President replied to his ambassador. "Get back to me as soon as you know something. I want to be sure they are not mistreated and I want this thing resolved quickly." Hanging up his phone, the President turned his attention to Mr. Bostick. "What do we know, Karl? How did this happen?"

"Apparently, our two agents were in pursuit of a van that had illegally crossed the border, somewhere east of the Nogales Station. We think it was a *coyote* bringing in illegals, but I guess it could have been loaded with drugs. Either way, they were on patrol when they spotted the van and moved in to make the intercept. A chase ensued and they ended up going back across the border, to the Mexico side, where the Mexican police stopped them. We had a chopper above to assist and they saw everything as it went down. According to them, the Mexican police drew down on our agents and pulled them out of their vehicle at gunpoint and placed them under arrest. They're being held at a jail a few miles south of our Nogales border station."

"Okay, Karl," the President began, "I want every one of our border stations beefed up to full capacity. Cancel leave, do whatever you have to do but I want everybody on board. Mexican President Suarez is no friend and I have a feeling he's going to want to use this to poke us in the eye. We'll try the diplomatic route first. Hopefully, our ambassador can convince Suarez to do the right thing, but I'm not real enthusiastic about his prospects. In the meantime, let him see that we're not going to take this lying down. Clamp down on the border. We can't look weak on this."

"Understood, Mr. President," Secretary Bostick replied. "I'll get that going immediately."

This was the kind of thing a lesser power like Mexico would love to use against a major power like the United States, and President Smith knew it. Yes, we were wrong, the President would acknowledge, but he would not roll over and let President Suarez embarrass him on the world stage. If his ambassador couldn't sweet talk Suarez into doing the right thing, then President Smith would have to act forcefully to bring them home. *Strength,* he thought, *is the only thing they will understand.*

Forty-eight hours after Tom Chafey and Dave D'Amato had been taken into custody for their unfortunate and unintentional trek into Mexico, negotiations to secure their release and safe return home were going nowhere. President Suarez had made several attempts to speak to President Smith regarding the imprisonment of the U.S. Border Patrol agents for violating his nation's sovereignty but had been told to deal directly with the U.S. ambassador. President Smith knew his Mexican counterpart wanted only to use the incident as a way to embarrass the U.S. and he would not assist him in such an endeavor. If President

Suarez did not want to deal favorably with the U.S. ambassador then President Smith would move on to a less *diplomatic* response.

Homeland Security Chief Karl Bostick, Counselor to the President Bill Allen, along with Chairman of the Joints Chiefs of Staff, gathered in the Oval Office at the President's request to address the issue now front and center in the eyes of the nation. The majority of opinion throughout the country was the two U.S. agents imprisoned in Mexico were basically being held hostage by our neighbors to the south, who were supposed to be our friends. It had been almost a week since they had been taken into custody and Americans were getting sick and tired of being taken for saps. They wanted something done and they wanted it done now. The President did not convene the meeting to get ideas and recommendations; he wanted to issue marching orders.

"General," the President said to his Joint Chiefs Chairman, "I want a full brigade moved into place from the Yuma Proving Grounds. Set them up right on the border in Nogales, right in front of them so they can't miss it. Once they're in place, we're going to make one final request to have them escort our two agents back to our side. If they refuse, we're going to go get them."

"Some might consider that an invasion of a sovereign country, Mr. President," the General responded somewhat apprehensively.

"I'm sure they will," President Smith replied. "But frankly, I don't care. We had eight years of us being the world's doormat with the last administration. Things are going to be different. Mexico is supposed to be our friend, but they're acting like they want to be our enemy. If that's going to be their posture then so be it, but I'll be damned if I'm going to let them walk all over us. We apologized for our mistake and we've used every bit of diplomacy to make things right, but Suarez isn't listening. We tried giving him the carrot, but apparently, he wants the stick instead. I'm going to give it to him."

"What do you want me to do, Mr. President?" asked Secretary Bostick.

"As soon as we have everything in place I want you to shut down the border. All the trucks, everything, turn them around until this gets resolved. The suspension of commerce between our two countries will hurt us some, but it'll hurt them a lot more. I want there to be no doubt in this bastard's mind I'm serious and he better get in line. Now make it happen."

Mexican President Suarez' *come to Jesus* moment came swiftly, as he began getting reports from the border of U.S. military assets being moved to the border in Nogales, all pointed south. With the U.S. ambassador seated in his office as these reports came in, the U.S. President's message to President Suarez came unfiltered and unambiguous: *release them or we're coming to get them.*

Used to getting his way with the previous U.S. administration, President Suarez found himself on unfamiliar ground. His bluff had been called and he knew it. He needed to fold his hand and get this matter behind him as quickly as possible. Within two hours, a black SUV pulled to a stop in front of the jail where Agents Chafey and D'Amato had been residing for the past several days. Stepping out of the vehicle as it came to a stop, the U.S. Consulate General for Nogales, Sonora, walked inside the jail with a big smile on his face as he approached the cell containing the two agents.

"Time to go home, boys," he said.

"Bout time," Tom Chafey said as he jumped up from his bunk.

Thirty minutes later the two Border Patrol agents were back on U.S. soil, safe and sound and no worse for the wear. The same could not be said for the Mexican President. He had been strong-armed by the U.S. President and put in his place and he knew it. Tom Chafey and Dave D'Amato were viewed as heroes in the press and the American people got an idea of what kind of balls their President had: big and brass.

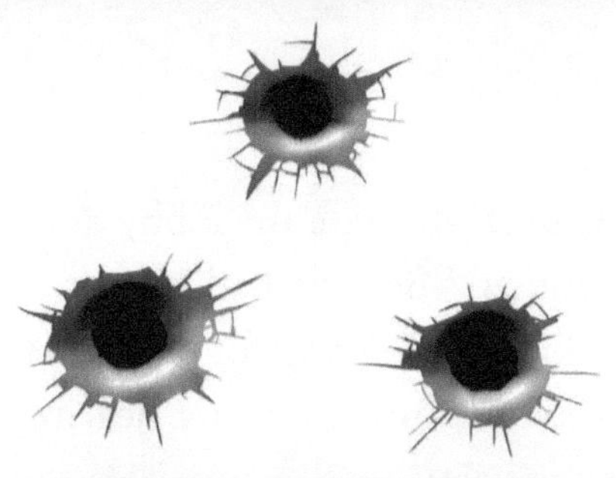

CHAPTER FORTY

Every four months or so Chris Roth traveled back to the States to meet with CIA Director Shirley. The boss preferred face-to-face updates on what's going on in the Middle East from his best agent, in addition to their weekly communications via secure phone lines. Roth looked forward to these trips, not only to appease his boss's desire for first-hand accounts of what he's doing, but primarily for the opportunity to satiate his palate with chicken fried steak and Southern barbeque, delicacies not available to him in his adopted home.

The trips also provided Chris with an opportunity to meet and strategize with FBI Agent Michaels and continue the fostering of their relationship, which had become vital to the success of their mutual efforts to combat Islamic terrorism. Having secured a room at the Best Western hotel in Woodbridge, Virginia for their meeting, Rich awaited the arrival of Chris and another man he had brought along whom Chris wanted Rich to meet. According to Chris, this colleague had been an integral part of their efforts in the Middle East and had already proven his worth by helping thwart the planned terrorist attack in Brussels.

"I'll park and meet you inside," David Kyle said to Chris as he pulled their car to a stop in front of the hotel.

"Sounds good," replied Chris as he opened his door to get out. "We'll be in room 110. See you inside."

Chris entered the hotel through the lobby door and headed straight to the room where Agent Michaels had been waiting, as David Kyle drove around the parking lot looking for a place to park.

"Come on in," Rich said to Chris after hearing the tap on his hotel room door. "Great to see you."

As Chris entered the room, Rich stuck his head out into the hall, looking in both directions for the second man he had been expecting.

"I thought you were bringing someone else?" Rich asked as he stepped back inside the room.

"He's parking the car," Chris replied. "He'll be here in a minute."

Pointing to a large Chick-fil-A bag on the coffee table in the middle of the room, Rich said, "I figured you guys might be hungry so I took the liberty of providing lunch."

"What, you couldn't find a good barbecue joint around here?" Chris said as he opened the bag and removed a piping hot chicken sandwich and some waffle fries.

"This is so much better than barbecue," Rich replied. "I promise, you can't get anything like this where you came from."

"You got a point there," Chris said with a laugh.

"Tell me about your friend," Rich said to Chris as he unwrapped his sandwich and took his first bite.

"I think you'll like this guy," Chris began. "He's ex-military, a no-nonsense type and he's very good with a rifle. He's working with us as a contract employee, which means we can pretty much do whatever we want with him. I don't think we could have pulled off the Brussels thing without him."

"Excellent," Rich replied, "I can't wait to meet him."

Hearing a knock at the door, Chris set down his sandwich to let his colleague in.

"David Kyle, meet FBI Agent Rich Michaels," Chris said by way of introduction as Kyle entered the hotel room, extending his hand to Agent Michaels.

"Good to meet you Rich," Kyle said as he shook hands with Michaels. "Chris has told me a lot about you, it's good to finally meet you in person."

Rich Michaels thought how fortunate not to have a bite of food in his mouth, knowing he probably would have choked on it, as he shook the hand and looked into the eyes of David Kyle. In an instant, Rich Michaels recalled the first time he saw this face and heard the name of David Kyle. His memory flashed back to the case file he put together, beginning with the assassination-style murder of Supreme Court Justice Hayden Byers and concluding with the murder of Democrat Senate Leader Edmund Riley by Steve Lick. While he never could tie anyone else directly to the conspiracy, Michaels knew David Kyle had served with Lick in the military and had become a suspect in his investigation before his case went cold.

"Nice to meet you, too," Michaels said, hoping the shock to his system at seeing Kyle did not show on his face. "Grab something to eat before it gets cold," he said, turning his gaze to the sack of sandwiches on the table and trying his best not to give away the turmoil going on inside of him.

"Thanks," Kyle said, removing a chicken sandwich from the bag and taking a seat. "I love these things. Best sandwich in the world."

Joining Kyle on the couch beside him, Chris Roth washed the last bite of his sandwich down with a diet soda and jumped right into why this meeting had been convened.

"Tell me about your warrant," Chris said to Agent Michaels. "We know you had the right guy. Obviously, Mustafa will never be a problem again, that's for damn sure. He got what was coming to him, but have you been able to figure out what went wrong?"

"Actually, no," Agent Michaels responded. "When we hit the mosque, it looked like it had been swept clean. We saw them unload what we think was the EMP device used in Baltimore, but it was almost as if they knew we were coming."

"I hate to be the bearer of bad news," Chris replied, "but they did. I met with my source a couple of weeks ago and he told me directly they had gotten a heads up before you guys went in with the warrant. Mustafa got out of there because he knew he would be arrested as soon as you guys found his device at the mosque."

"But how?" asked Agent Michaels. "I trust everybody on my team. There's no way one of them went rogue. I've been working with them too long."

"What about your committee?" asked Chris. "You briefed them beforehand, didn't you? It had to be one of them."

"You may be right, Chris," Michaels responded, "but it's still hard for me to wrap my mind around something like that. These are all career people, high-ranking officials who have been with the Bureau for years. I'll admit I don't know them very well, with the exception of one of the members, Deanna Mowery. She and I go way back and I have complete faith and trust in her, but somebody leaked it and I guess we have to consider everybody a potential suspect."

"Well, for now I would suggest keeping this to yourself," Chris said. "I'll keep working my source and see if he can come up with anything we can use to identify the mole. Right now, the only people who know about this are the people in this room and General Shirley, who will be briefing your Director later today."

"And one more," David Kyle interjected.

"Who's that?" Chris replied.

"The mole," Kyle said.

"The question we have to consider," Agent Michaels added, "is what to do about it when we figure out who it is."

"Good question," Chris replied. "Jail would be too good for this bastard. Whoever it is, he's putting all our lives in jeopardy and we need to prepare for an appropriate response."

"I'm not sure I'm comfortable with what you're saying," Agent Michaels said. "I agree I'd like to see him strung up in the middle of town, but I'm not sure we need to go down such a road. We all have careers to think about, you know."

"Who says we need to string him up?" David Kyle interjected. "There are ways to do it without leaving any fingerprints or jeopardizing anyone's career."

"Did you have something specifically in mind?" Michaels asked with a curious tone. "Assuming, of course, we find out for sure who the mole actually is."

"What if he ends up having a heart attack?" Kyle said with a mischievous tone. "He gets what's coming to him and everybody's career remains safe."

"What the hell did they teach you guys in the military," Chris said to Kyle. "How are you supposed to make a guy have a heart attack?"

"Have you ever heard of something called Adenosine?" Kyle asked.

"Adenosine?" Agent Michaels responded with a curious tone. "What the hell is adenosine?"

"It's a drug," David Kyle replied. "Introduce it into his system and he'll keel over like he's having a heart attack."

"Sounds like you have some experience with this," Chris said with a grin. "I'm afraid to ask how you know this."

"Let's just say I know it will work, and leave it at that," said Kyle.

The meeting lasted another thirty minutes before Roth and Kyle said goodbye to Agent Michaels.

"I told General Shirley we would head over to Langley to see him after we finished up here," Chris said as the two men prepared to leave Rich Michaels behind. "I'll give you a call sometime next week when I'm back overseas. In the meantime, be careful whom you talk to. You may be confiding in the mole, whoever it is."

"Roger that. I'll keep you posted if anything shakes loose on my side. Thanks for coming over," Michaels said as he shook hands with Chris and David as they left his hotel room, closing the door behind them. Not in a big hurry to get back to his office, Rich thought he'd stay behind a while longer and watch his alma mater Florida State battle it out with Duke in the ACC basketball tournament airing on ESPN. As he blankly stared at the game on T.V., his mind kept replaying the meeting in his room with Chris Roth and David Kyle, and the incredible encounter with a man he once suspected of being involved with one of his past investigations.

"What if he ends up having a heart attack? Adenosine." These were the words of David Kyle during their meeting, and they were nagging on Agent Michaels' mind. *It did sound like he knew what he was talking about,* Rich thought. Then, in a moment of epiphany, Rich Michaels jumped from the couch.

"Oh shit. Are you freaking kidding me?" he said out loud, reflecting back on his case involving Steve Lick, which pretty much consumed him for over a year.

He remembered his friend Casey Dean, the tenacious reporter for the Washington Chronicle, first introduced him to the idea of a conspiracy at play to assassinate far-left liberals, beginning with the death of Justice Byers. Although the case died with the death of Steve Lick, their primary suspect, he and Jimmy O'Rourke always believed the conspiracy involved others besides Lick.

In addition to Justice Byers, their investigation included the murders of CeCe Diamond, Fred Stein and Senator Riley as victims, all well-known proponents of liberal causes, as well as liberal T.V. host Mark Hayes, who narrowly escaped assassination when the bomb taped to the undercarriage of his car never detonated.

What their investigation did not include, now the source of his epiphany, involved the death of another far left liberal, which never made it into their case file. Namely, the death of Chris Dyess, a big-time donor to liberal causes who died of a heart attack after working out at his health club in New York City on the same day of Ms. Diamond's assassination.

Is it possible? he thought, considering the possibility Chris Dyess may also have been a victim of the conspiracy, based on the conversation in his hotel room with Chris Roth and David Kyle.

Driving back to his office in the Hoover Building in D.C., Rich considered his next move. He didn't want to reopen his conspiracy case based merely on a whim, especially since his primary focus now was on his assignment as head of the FBI's domestic terrorism task force.

Sitting down behind his desk, he began searching the Internet for anything he could find about the death of Chris Dyess. He found an obit article in a New York City newspaper following Dyess' untimely death, which talked about the funeral arrangements for the decedent and the memorial services in his honor. The article also mentioned the stated desire of Mr. Dyess to be cremated upon his death. Assuming the cremation took place, Rich wondered if it meant he had no chance of finding out whether or not Chris Dyess' death was anything other than a heart attack. He left his office and walked down the hall to the FBI lab to consult with the scientist in charge of the department.

"Obviously, cremation makes it much harder for us to do testing for trace amounts of drugs in one's system," Dr. Williams, head of the FBI lab, told Rich. "But not impossible. Usually, the cremated remains of a person will include small bits of bone fragments, which may contain traces of a foreign substance. The soft tissue in the body, where traces of what you are looking for are more readily available, become too charred during cremation to yield the results you are looking for, so we have to try and find them in the bone fragments. Like I said, difficult but not impossible."

Rich thanked Dr. Williams as he left his office, with a glimmer of hope he could determine whether Chris Dyess died naturally or should be added to the case file collecting dust in his desk drawer. Knowing he didn't have the time to pursue this lead, he pulled out his cell to call the one person he trusted to follow up and perhaps provide him with any new evidence he would need to reopen the investigation.

Jimmy O'Rourke was not surprised to see the name of *Rich Michaels* displayed on his phone as he reached to answer it. The two men had been in regular contact since Jimmy's retirement, getting together for an occasional round of golf at the Shenandoah Valley Golf Club in Front Royal, Virginia.

"You didn't take enough of my money the last time we played?" Jimmy said with a laugh after answering his phone. "Don't forget, I'm on a fixed income. I'm gonna need more strokes next time."

"More strokes my ass," Rich replied. "I know you've been practicing. I haven't even looked at my clubs since the last time we played over a month ago. But it's not golf I'm calling about."

"I'm not sure I like the sound of where this conversation is heading," Jimmy replied. "Don't tell me you need help again with a new case you're working on."

"Actually, no," said Rich. "It's an old one."

"I'm retired, Rich," Jimmy replied. "Have you already forgotten? I don't have any old cases. I plant flowers and tomatoes and occasionally hit the little white ball around. It's enough to keep me busy, and more importantly, it's exactly what I need to do to keep my wife happy. But, for the sake of discussion, what case are you talking about?"

"The Byers conspiracy case," Rich replied.

"What about it?" Jimmy asked. "I thought it died when the little prick that stabbed me chomped down on a cyanide pill."

"I did too," Rich replied. "But something new has come up. You'll never guess who I met earlier this afternoon."

"Who?" Jimmy asked.

"David Kyle," Rich said, anticipating a surprise reaction from Jimmy.

"You're shitting me," came the response. "The same David Kyle who served with Lick in the Special Forces?"

"The same."

"How the hell did you end up meeting this guy?" Jimmy asked.

"I can't really get into that right now," Rich hesitantly said, knowing Jimmy was not privy to the working relationship he had with Chris Roth and David Kyle.

"Sounds like a *need to-know* kind of a thing," Jimmy replied.

"Exactly," said Rich. "But something very interesting came out of our conversation. Something, which might actually have a direct impact on our case."

"Now I'm really interested," Jimmy said. "I know I'm going to regret asking this, but what did he say?"

"You remember the Diamond killing?" Rich asked. "The one out in San Francisco?"

"Of course, what about it?" Jimmy replied. "You're not saying he had something to do with it, are you?"

"No," Rich said. "At least as far as I know he didn't. It's not so much about her death as it is about someone else who died on the same day, in New York City. Ring any bells yet?"

"Not a clue, buddy," Jimmy said. "You're gonna have to give me more than that."

"Does the name *Chris Dyess* ring a bell?" Rich asked.

"Sure. Wasn't he some bigwig from New York who funded a bunch of liberal causes? He definitely would've been a good target for those guys, but if I remember right, didn't he die of a heart attack?"

"That's what the papers said anyways," replied Rich.

"Why do I get the feeling you think there's something else at play?" asked Jimmy. "I'm thinking your conversation with Kyle has something to do with it. Once again, I know I'm going to regret this, but what did he say?"

"Kyle made a comment to me about using a drug called *adenosine* to make it look like someone had a heart attack," Rich replied.

"*Adenosine?*" Jimmy said. "I've never heard of it."

"Yeah, me neither," Rich said. "I looked it up, and basically, it's a drug some doctors prescribe to help people with arrhythmia. If a patient has an accelerated heartbeat, the drug will help slow the heart rate down and bring it to normalcy. Too much of the stuff can cause the heart to stop. Without an autopsy, the drug would never be detected, making it look like the person died from a heart attack."

"And you think that's what happened to Dyess?" Jimmy asked.

"I think it's possible," Rich answered.

"You'll have to exhume his body to do a test," Jimmy said.

"I wish it were so easy," Rich replied, "but unfortunately they cremated his body."

"Now, granted I'm not nearly as smart as you are," Jimmy replied sarcastically, "but wouldn't that make it impossible to test?"

"For an *average* agent, yes, I would agree," Rich replied with a smirk.

"Oh brother, here we go," interjected Jimmy.

"But you're not dealing with an *average* agent," Rich replied. "Seriously, though, I talked to the guy who runs our lab. He told me there's a slight possibility the cremated remains of Dyess will contain tiny bone fragments, some of which may contain traces of the drug, if indeed they are present. We need to get a sample of his remains and take it to the lab."

"And how do you propose getting a sample of this guy's remains?" Jimmy asked with trepidation in his voice.

"I'm glad you asked," Rich replied. "That's where you come in."

"I was afraid you were going to say something like that."

"Look, here's what I have in mind," Rich began. "This may be a wild goose chase and frankly, I don't have the time to deal with it. I'm too busy with other things, namely keeping your ass safe. And to be honest with you, I don't really have anyone else I trust to treat this with the care it's going to need. I'm thinking I could bring you on in a temporary capacity, kind of like a contract agent. You'll get a badge and everything and report directly to me. You won't have to deal with anyone else in our agency, just me. I figure it's your way of paying me back for all I've done for you."

"All you've done for me?" Jimmy asked. "What the hell have you done for me other than deprive me of my retirement money every time we play golf together?"

"Well, for starters," Rich said, "let's not forget I pulled you out of a building after you managed to get a screwdriver shoved up your ass, we can begin there."

"You bastard," Jimmy said with a laugh. "You had to go there. And by the way, I'm pretty sure the screwdriver was sticking out of my chest, not my ass. Tell you what; I'll think about it and let you know in a day or so. I'm obviously going to have to run this by the boss. She has final veto authority on everything."

"As well she should," Rich replied. "Take your time and get back to me in a couple days or so. And thanks."

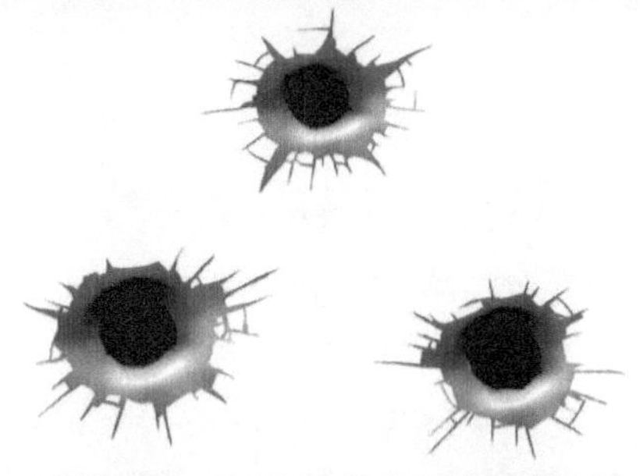

CHAPTER FORTY-ONE

Nearing the halfway point in President Smith's first term in office, the nation's political focus, as well as much of the media scrutiny, turned to the midterm elections where all four hundred and thirty-five congressional House seats and one-third of U.S. Senate seats would be contested. In addition to these federal congressional elections, thirty-six of the fifty states would be holding their gubernatorial contests as well. Historically speaking, midterm elections are usually regarded as a referendum on the sitting President's performance in office, and more often than not, result in the President's party losing seats in both the House and Senate, a trend President Smith wanted to buck. Washington Senator Laura Reagan, the self-appointed titular head of the Democrat Party, wasted no opportunity in her efforts to malign the Smith administration every chance she could. A willing mainstream media, for years in the pocket of the Democrat Party, were all too happy to provide her with the platform from where she could launch her attacks on President Smith and a Republican Party both she and most of the media believed had gone out of control.

The President's actions regarding the unlawful detainment of two Border Patrol agents by Mexican police officials was castigated by Senator Reagan as an example of the Smith administration's approach to foreign policy, declaring the President's actions were more reminiscent of a strong-arm dictator than of a U.S. President.

In spite of her protestations to the contrary, the majority of Americans did not agree with the Senator's assessment. Overwhelmingly, national

263

polls taken since the Mexican government had been *convinced* it was in their best interest to return the two wayward Border Patrol agents, showed the majority of Americans supported the President's tactics in gaining the freedom of Agents Chafey and D'Amato. Much to the chagrin of Senator Reagan, the Democrat Party and most of the liberal media, their criticism of President Smith had done nothing to change national sentiment. Americans in general had grown tired of being a doormat to the rest of the world and were excited to have someone in the Oval Office willing to stand up for them.

White House press briefings had become more contentious of late, as a White House press corp, full of liberals cheering for Democrat victories in the upcoming midterm elections, did their best to sully the reputation of the Smith administration in the eyes of the American electorate. What mainstream media types and most liberals failed to see, and what President Smith embraced, were the sentiments of most Americans who were sick and tired of being told showing strength on the world stage was somehow a vice.

Vetting refugees seeking sanctuary in the United States and actually enforcing existing immigration laws, something the Ferrell administration had been loath to do, were points of major contention with the present-day Democrat Party. Their PR battle against the Smith administration, led by Senator Reagan with help from the liberal media, was failing miserably and they knew it. Once a great party seen as being on the side of the *common man,* the Democrat Party had relegated itself to a bunch of whiners and complainers, decrying the desire by many of their fellow Americans to be exceptional in the world again, not a mediocre participant in the global community.

Riding high in the polls and seen as a competent and strong leader, President Smith's popularity helped the Republican Party gain seats in the House and Senate in the midterm elections, increasing their majorities in both bodies of Congress. Correctly reading the results of the election as approval of his job as President, Brian Smith became even more emboldened to continue on his path of reestablishing America's place in the world as the dominant superpower it once held, and no amount of caterwauling coming from the other side of the political aisle would deter him.

Congratulatory handshakes and laudatory praise for the midterm election results were heaped on President Brian Smith as he took his seat in the White House Situation Room, preparing to convene a meeting of his National Security Council (NSC).

A forum for considering national security and foreign policy matters with his senior national security advisors and cabinet officials, the NSC is chaired by the President and designed for the purpose of providing advice and assistance to the President on matters pertaining to foreign and domestic security concerns. Formally titled *Assistant to the President for National Security Affairs,* President Smith's top advisor on the council for national security matters is Kathie Collins, a long-time veteran of the State Department and the former head of *Center for Strategic and International Studies,* a Washington think tank created for *"finding ways to sustain American prominence and prosperity as a force for good in the world."*

Three cabinet Secretaries, along with the CIA Director, the Attorney General and the Joint Chiefs Chairman were seated around the conference table with the President when Ms. Collins walked to the front of the room to address the room. A large screen beside Ms. Collins began displaying video shots downloaded from a U.S. satellite earlier in the morning and delivered to her office in the West Wing.

"For the past three months," Ms. Collins began, "both the CIA and military intelligence have been compiling data on what we are certain are ISIS training facilities located throughout the Middle East; one in Syria, two in Afghanistan, and two more in Yemen. None of these camps, by the way, existed six months ago. We went back and looked at satellite photos of the same exact areas and nothing existed but desert and rocks. These have all been built and put into use within this time frame. As the threat and reach of ISIS continues to grow, so has their ability to train and equip new fighters. Virtually all of the monitoring up to this point has been via satellite, not wanting to unnecessarily risk exposure of our ground assets."

"Any idea how many personnel we are talking about?" asked the President.

"Yes sir, Mr. President," Ms. Collins replied. "Based on our best estimates there are anywhere from a hundred and fifty to two hundred ISIS fighters in training per camp at any one time. By looking at the large transport trucks going in and out of the camps, we believe they are rotating personnel about every two weeks."

"Are we able to determine if there is any down time?" asked the AG. "In other words, if one crew finishes their two-week training, does the camp go dead for a short time before the next group is hauled in, or is the transition to the new group immediate?"

"Excellent question," Ms. Collins responded. "Based on the images we've gotten over the past two months, we have seen no evidence of any down time at any of the camps. When one group finishes, the next group arrives to take their place. As best we can figure, the camps are operating around the clock, twenty-four seven."

"The question we have ladies and gentlemen," President Smith chimed in, looking in the direction of his CIA Director, "is what are we going to do about it."

"If you're asking me," General Shirley offered, "I say we napalm the shit out of them. They're fairly contained in each location and by the looks of the data Kathie has given us; we may be able to get about a thousand or so in one shot. Maybe more if we get 'em at shift change."

It was no accident President Smith looked in General Shirley's direction when he asked what should be done. He had a sneaking suspicion General Shirley's reaction would be exactly what he gave and the President wanted somebody else at the table to voice the same sentiments he felt. The CIA Director and retired four-star general did not disappoint.

Looking towards the Joint Chiefs Chairman, the President asked for his thoughts.

"No doubt it's doable, Mr. President," he observed. "Obviously, it needs to be a coordinated strike. We can't do it one at a time, or they'll shut the other camps down and get their people out of there as soon as the first one went up in flames. We would need to hit all five locations at once. I can get working on an action plan and have it to you in twenty-four hours."

"How many assets are we talking about?" President Smith asked.

"One squadron apiece, Mr. President. In fifteen minutes, we can turn each camp into a giant barbecue pit. They'll never know what hit 'em."

"Get working on the plan, General," the President ordered. "I want this executed as soon as possible. I told these bastards when I got into office I would come after them and apparently, they didn't get the message. It's time we start enlightening them to the truth. But I want to be clear about something at the outset. While I have no hesitation in using our military to make coordinated strikes against ISIS whenever and wherever we find them, we can have no allusions this strategy will ultimately end in the total demise of these terrorists. The reason they have been so successful in their recruitment of followers these past few years is tied directly to the fact they see themselves as victorious in the battle they are waging against Western democracies, in spite of their losses on the battlefield. Nut jobs in this country and throughout the world continue to be radicalized by their demented ideology and are inspired to join ISIS because the terrorist acts being carried out have not been responded to in an appropriate manner."

"My predecessor," President Smith continued, "did nothing more than try to coddle the terrorists. He said we should try and *understand* them and figure out why they hate us so much. This misguided and incompetent view of radical Islamic terrorism has only made the problem worse, and we are seeing evidence of this every day. The best way to *un*-inspire these deranged followers is for them to realize those engaged in a *jihad* against the West are on the endangered species list. I don't want to just kill these bastards. I want to massacre them publicly, center stage, and I want the entire world to see it. If we do that, I think it will go a long way in diminishing the desires of many who want to join this cause."

"General," the President said, turning his gaze in the direction of his Joint Chiefs Chairman, "make sure we get video from every fighter jet you send out. Let's splice it together into a one to two-minute video, showing these Islamic radicals being burned alive. After I declassify it, we'll get it to the press and have it run on every T.V. news station, as well as the Internet. After they see this, maybe some of them will give a second thought to whether they want to join up with this movement."

Seventy-two hours after Kathie Collins briefed the President and his NSC on the ISIS training camps operating throughout the Middle East, a hundred F-18 Hornets, with Mark-77 incendiary bombs attached under their wings, were gassed up and ready to go. The thousand or so Islamic terrorists at those camps, committed to a *jihad* against anyone who didn't think like them, were about to receive a personal introduction to the afterlife, courtesy of President Brian Smith and the U.S. military.

Too long they had been allowed to prosper because of the feckless leadership in America under the previous administration, as well as other nations too timid to take action against a cancer growing throughout the world. This would no longer be the case. Still concerned about the number of people in the world, including the United States, radicalized into supporting ISIS, President Smith believed the best way to reduce the rate of growth amongst those radicals would be to have them see the ISIS fighters they idolized destroyed on a grand scale. Here was the President's chance to do exactly that. The Admiral onboard the USS Harry Truman, floating in the Persian Gulf, as well as the commanders of two secret military bases in Egypt, all awaited orders from High Command to launch their Hornets, sending them on missions to wipe out five terrorist training camps in Syria, Afghanistan and Yemen. Having calculated within a minute the time it would take for each of the individual squadron of Hornets to reach their destination, the order came and the planes were launched.

Sitting in the Situation Room with Kathie Collins and the rest of his NSC staff, President Smith watched the screen as video feeds from each of the five squadrons were relayed back to him, showing the devastation being brought to bear on the ground as hundreds of

ISIS warriors were being burned alive. As bombs exploded on one side of a camp, the President could see groups of other men, perhaps in the dozens, running away on the other side of the camp, only to have another Mark-77 fire bomb explode in the middle of them.

As the Chairman predicted, it took less than fifteen minutes for the fighter jets to complete their missions once the bombing commenced. The after-action report, delivered to President Smith's desk the following morning, estimated the raids on the terrorist training camps killed eleven hundred ISIS fighters.

"Not bad," the President commented to his top General. "I'd say this was a pretty good day's work, wouldn't you?"

"Absolutely, Mr. President," the General replied, "I would indeed."

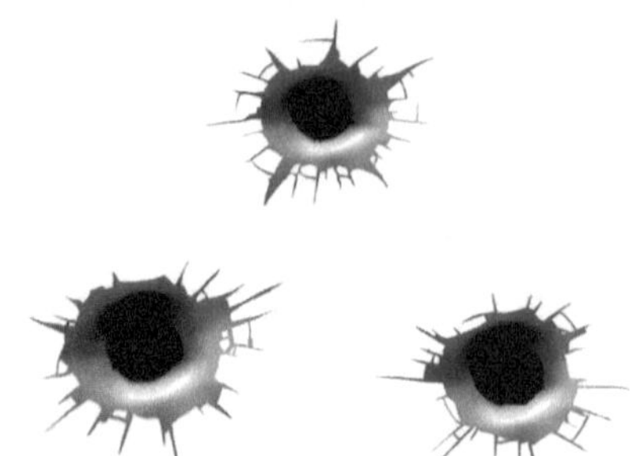

Chapter Forty-Two

Rich Michael's favorite lunch spot in D.C. was unquestionably the Old Ebbitt Grill on 15th Street, no more than a five-minute walk from the White House. Having arranged to meet Casey Dean there for lunch, he went ahead and ordered a plate of jumbo lump crab cakes as an appetizer as he waited for her to arrive. Finding Rich seated in one of the booths near the back of the restaurant, Casey approached his table as the waitress placed the plate of crab cakes down in front of them.

"Now that's what I call perfect timing," Casey said to Rich, greeting him with a hug and kiss on the cheek as he stood to greet her.

"You're timing has always been impeccable, Casey," Rich replied with a grin. "It's good to see you again. It's been too long."

"I agree," Casey said. "Since you're such an important person now, I wasn't sure if I would ever have the privilege of one-on-one time with you again."

"Oh, give me a break, Casey," Rich replied with a smile. "I'll always have time for my favorite reporter. You should know that by now. Have a seat. I invited an old friend of yours to join us, he should be here shortly."

As Rich and Casey got comfortable in their seats, their waitress came over to get drink orders as Jimmy O'Rourke walked through the door and approached their booth.

"Well, what do you know?" Jimmy said as he greeted Rich and Casey before sliding in behind the table. "Looks like the old crew is back together again."

Casey leaned over and kissed Jimmy on the side of his face. "I was hoping you were the one who would be joining us," she said. "It's good to see you, Jimmy. Looks like retirement life has been good to you."

"Who's retired?" he said with a touch of sarcasm, nodding in Rich's direction. "This bastard wouldn't leave me alone. It wasn't enough for him to drain my bank account on the golf course. Apparently, he couldn't do his job without my help, so he's talked me into coming back. On a part time basis, I might add."

"Really?" said Casey, sounding a bit surprised. "Now this is starting to get interesting. What could the FBI possibly want with a washed-up D.C. detective who doesn't have enough sense to stay retired?"

"I've been asking myself the same question," Jimmy replied with a laugh. "I guess you can only play so many rounds of golf. And my gardening skills suck. Everything I put in the ground ends up dying. I won't even mention the fact my wife is getting pretty sick and tired of me being around the house all the time. When I first told her about the job offer by our friend over here, her eyes lit up. I think she's looking forward to me getting out the house a little more."

"Somehow, I doubt that," Casey replied. "After what you went through, I'm sure she's grateful for every minute she gets to look at that ugly face of yours."

All three laughed as glasses of water were delivered to the table and the waitress reached into her apron to retrieve her pen and order pad. As she walked away after taking their orders, Rich turned a little more serious and let Jimmy and Casey in on why he had called them all together.

"Casey, let me catch you up to speed on something Jimmy and I have already been talking about."

"I knew there had to be more to this than a nice reunion and a free lunch," Casey said with a smile. "So, what's up?"

"First off," Rich replied with a sly smile, "nobody said anything about a free lunch. But seriously, there is something I want to bring you in on. Something I think you can help us with."

"I'm all ears," Casey replied. "You know I'll help any way I can."

"Obviously, you remember the Byers conspiracy case," Rich began.

"Of course," Casey responded. "What about it?"

"It concerns Jimmy's good buddy Steve Lick. You weren't aware of it at the time because we weren't exactly at liberty to share it with you, but during the investigation we identified some of the guys Steve Lick served with while on active duty. At the time, Jimmy and I felt Lick did not act alone, and we thought some of the guys he served with might be involved. We could never prove it, of course, primarily because the investigation came to a shrieking halt after Lick took his own life."

"A fitting end, I might add," Jimmy interjected.

"You got that right," said Casey.

"Yeah," Rich replied. "But I still would have liked the chance to have gotten him in an interrogation room and taken a crack at him. But no matter what's done is done. He definitely got what he deserved."

"How do I fit in all of this?" Casey asked.

"That's the part I'm getting to," Rich replied. "Now mind you, I have to be a bit guarded in what I tell you because of some active investigations going on. There's some stuff I can't even share with Jimmy, so you're both going to have to trust me on some of this."

"Of course," Jimmy said, as Casey nodded in agreement.

"One of the guys Jimmy and I identified as serving with Lick has reemerged. Jimmy knows who it is, but because he is involved with some ongoing stuff I'm working on I can't tell you his name. Actually, his name is not really relevant right now anyways. It's something I heard him say that is, and it's the reason I asked you and Jimmy to lunch today."

"Now I really am interested," Casey said. "What can you tell me?"

"You remember how you first came to me with your cockamamie theory about a conspiracy to assassinate left-wing liberals?" Rich asked Casey.

"You mean the theory that turned out to be true?" Casey replied with a grin.

"Yeah, that's the one," Rich replied. "It turns out there may have been another victim of the conspiracy we overlooked. At least that's my theory now."

"Another victim?" Casey asked. "Someone else who died under suspicious circumstances during the same time period?"

"Exactly," Rich replied. "Now I'll grant you, it's a bit of a long shot right now, but I think it's at least worth looking into."

"Whom are we talking about?" Casey asked.

"It happened the same day of Ms. Diamond's assassination in San Francisco," Rich answered. "A well-known bleeding-heart liberal passed away in New York City, and by all accounts there didn't seem to be any foul play involved."

"Wait a second," Casey said, sounding a little intrigued. "Are you talking about Chris Dyess, the liberal billionaire?"

"He's the one," Rich replied.

"Yeah, I remember him," Casey said. "He had some kind of massive heart attack after working out at his gym. How the hell does him keeling over from a heart attack tie into the conspiracy angle? Are you suggesting he didn't die from a heart attack?"

"I know it's a long shot at this point, but yes, that's what I am suggesting. My theory is one of the conspirators, perhaps even Jimmy's friend Steve Lick, introduced something into his system that killed him and made it look like he had a heart attack."

"Boy, now you're really reaching," Casey replied. "So how do you suppose we find out? He's been dead and buried for more than two years now."

"Actually, it's worse than that," Rich replied. "He was cremated."

"Well that pretty much ends that," Casey said. "With no body to exhume there's no way to do an autopsy to find out for sure. Or am I missing something?"

"For a lesser investigator, perhaps," Rich said with a smile. "Now I told you this would be a long shot, so bear with me, but there is one remote possibility I've been thinking about, and this is where both of you come in."

"Now I'm really intrigued," Casey said.

"You and me both," Jimmy added.

"I've already talked with the head of the FBI lab, Dr. Williams," Rich said. "And according to him there is a small possibility the cremated remains of Mr. Dyess might contain small traces of anything he may have ingested prior to his death. According to Dr. Williams, cremated remains usually contain bone fragments where tests can be run to look for foreign substances. Like I said, it's a long shot, but it's the theory I'm working on right now."

"I have one big question, though," Casey said, sounding quite skeptical.

"I know," replied Rich, already anticipating the question, "where are the remains and how do we get our hands on them."

"Exactly."

"I was thinking the same thing," Jimmy added.

"That's where you two come in," Rich answered. "I did a little research on Mr. Dyess, and he had one sole heir at the time of his death; a daughter by the name of Paula Eubanks. She lives on a sprawling estate on Manhasset Bay, a little northeast of New York City. Chances are she is in possession of the remains."

"What are you thinking, Rich?" Jimmy asked. "Get a search warrant for it? Correct me if I'm wrong, but that'll go over like a turd in a punch bowl."

"I agree," replied Rich. "I can only imagine what kind of response I would get if I asked for a warrant to seize the remains of a guy who died over two years ago. Especially when you consider I'm going on not much more than a hunch in the first place."

"But I'm sure you've come up with another idea," interjected Casey. "And something tells me it includes me."

"You always were the perceptive one," Rich said with a grin.

"Okay, let's hear it," Casey said.

"You're supposed to be this crack reporter, right Casey?" Rich began.

"Oh no, hear it comes," Casey replied. "It's starting to get deep in here."

"What I'm thinking," Rich continued, "is you could go up and visit Ms. Eubanks at her home, under the auspices of doing a feature piece on her late father. You know, something about shining a national spotlight on all the good work he did as a philanthropist, or some bullshit like that. Jimmy can go along as your assistant, of course, and once inside her house, while you've got her distracted with the interview, maybe he can poke around and hopefully find the urn containing the remains of the distinguished Mr. Dyess."

"Holy shit," replied Jimmy. "You weren't kidding when you said this would be a long shot. What if she doesn't have the urn? Or what if she spread his ashes in the bay? What do we do then?"

"All good questions," replied Rich. "Don't think I haven't thought of them as well. If it turns out she doesn't have the remains, then we'll go ahead with the fake interview and move on to plan B."

"I'm almost afraid to ask," said Casey, with more than a hint of skepticism, "but what exactly is your plan B?"

"I'm still working on it," replied Rich with a smile.

"Something tells me you haven't run any of this by your superiors," said Casey.

"Are you kidding me?" Rich replied. "Do I look stupid? I want to keep my job, you know. No, for right now I think it best we keep this between us. If we turn anything up I'll make a decision where we go from there, but for now this will be our secret."

"Understood," Jimmy said. "Probably a good idea."

***

It took a little over four hours to drive from D.C. to Paula Eubanks' home on Manhasset Bay, and Jimmy, never a fan of flying, had won the argument with Casey Dean on whether they should drive or fly.

"Come on," he told her, "it'll be a good chance for us to catch up. Anyhow, you can't see anything from thirty-five thousand feet. We can do some nice sightseeing on the way."

"I guess," replied Casey, relenting on an argument she knew she had no chance of winning. "But you're driving both ways."

"Deal," said Jimmy.

Pulling up to a fifteen-foot high cast iron security gate at the entrance to the Eubanks estate, Jimmy rang the buzzer on the keypad letting Paula Eubanks know they had arrived. Casey had been in touch with Ms. Eubanks, telling her how much she admired and respected her late father and how she wanted to do a feature piece on him, highlighting all the good things he had accomplished in his life. To make the ruse complete, she had prepared a notebook full of background information on Chris Dyess and several pages of questions to make her interview request appear legitimate.

"If this thing falls apart," Casey said to Jimmy as they slowly drove up the driveway to Ms. Eubanks' forty-thousand square-foot home, "I still might come out of here with a story I can print."

"And to think I came out of retirement to steal some dead guy's ashes," Jimmy said to Casey, who could only laugh.

Pulling to a stop in front of Ms. Eubanks' home, Jimmy leaned over Casey's lap so he could look out her window in utter amazement at the size of the house.

"How the hell do you keep something that big clean?"

"I'm pretty sure she has some help," Casey responded.

"You bet your ass she does," Jimmy replied. "A couple billion dollars in the bank can buy you a lot of help, that's for sure. I wonder if she even wipes her own ass."

"Now come on, Jimmy," Casey retorted, "let's not get down on her because she's rich."

"No, I'm sure you're right," said Jimmy. "She's probably a very nice person."

"Well, let's go in and find out, shall we?"

As Jimmy and Casey exited their car and made their way up the walkway leading to the front the house, the twenty-foot high front door, made from hand-carved mahogany and inlaid with stained glass, began to slowly open as they approached. Paula Eubanks, waiting to greet her guests upon their arrival, stood inside the front door in her foyer, whose floor and walls were encrusted with Italian marble.

"Welcome to my home Ms. Dean," said Ms. Eubanks as she extended her hand to her guests. "It's a pleasure to meet you."

"Please, Ms. Eubanks, call me Casey," she replied. "I'd like you to meet my associate, Jimmy Callahan, who's helping me on this project."

"It's a pleasure to meet you too," Paula Eubanks said as she shook Jimmy's hand. "And please call me Paula. Can I offer you something to drink?

"Perhaps a bit later if it's alright," replied Casey. "I must tell you, Paula, your home is absolutely breathtaking. I don't believe I've ever seen such beautiful furnishings as these," she said pointing to the décor adorning the foyer and keeping room near where they stood.

"Thank you so much," Paula replied. "Why don't I take you on a quick tour down here before we get started. Perhaps you'll be ready for some refreshments when we're done."

"Indeed," replied Casey.

The mini tour of Ms. Eubanks' ground floor took nearly forty-five minutes. The highlight of the tour, the part giving Paula the greatest pleasure, was showing Casey and Jimmy the large room she had converted into a home office. Her father's old desk, made from pink ivory wood imported from South Africa, anchored the room. The walls, covered with photos of her late father with various world leaders and dozens of plaques honoring him for his philanthropic endeavors, indicated to Casey and Jimmy how important and influential a man was the late Mr. Dyess.

"This room is gorgeous, Paula," Casey commented. "You must be so proud of your father."

"Thank you, Casey, I certainly am. My father was a great man and he did a lot of good in the world. I hope the article you write on him will reflect that."

Standing in front of the marble fireplace across the room from the desk, Jimmy noticed the interesting looking sculptured piece situated on top of the fireplace mantle. He had no idea he was looking at a one-hundred-fifteen-thousand-dollar Daum crystal grey Stanislas urn.

Jimmy turned to his host and asked, "Can you tell me about this piece?"

Smiling at the question, Paula happily told her guests it was the final resting place of her late father, Chris Dyess. Jimmy and Casey's eyes immediately met as both tried to hide the obvious glee both were feeling inside.

Jackpot, Jimmy thought. *Now I have to figure out how to get back in here and take a sample with me.*

Before arriving at the Eubanks home, Casey had told Jimmy her interview would last anywhere from an hour to two hours, depending on how open and accessible Paula Eubanks would be in talking about her father. As it turned out, it lasted almost three hours, taking place in the living room located on the other side of the house from Paula's office, where Chris Dyess' ashes were resting.

Halfway through the interview Jimmy excused himself to use the restroom, only to take a quick detour to Paula's office. While there, he quickly removed a small portion of ashes from the expensive urn on the fireplace mantle and dumped them in the plastic zip-lock bag he carried inside the breast pocket of his jacket. Returning to the living room where the interview was still underway, Jimmy winked at Casey as he returned to his seat, indicating to her the mission had been accomplished. After completing her list of questions for Ms. Eubanks, Casey rose from her seat at the conclusion of her interview and thanked Paula Eubanks for her openness and candor in reflecting on her father's life.

"I can't wait to get back and put this all together," Casey said to Paula as both she and Jimmy prepared to leave. "I'm sure this will make a great article. Your father was truly a remarkable man and we are both grateful to you for sharing this time with us."

"Absolutely, Paula," Jimmy chimed in. "Thank you so much for your time and for opening your home to us."

"My pleasure to be sure," Paula replied, as she walked her guests to the door. "Please call me again if there is anything you forgot or something else you might want to add. I look forward to reading your article when it comes out. Thanks again."

Jimmy guided his Nissan Pathfinder down the long driveway of the Eubanks estate and out the front gate, heading straight for the interstate. Casey pulled out her phone and dialed Rich Michaels with the news of their successful mission.

"Great," said Rich, "come straight to my office when you get back to town and I'll get the ashes over to our lab for analysis. Good job, you guys, and thanks, I owe you."

"You certainly do," Casey responded. "And I plan on collecting. See you in a few hours."

By the time they got back to D.C. it was after six in the evening, and Dr. Williams had already gone home for the night. Rich let him know via text he would see him first thing in the morning with a sample of something he needed analyzed. The following morning Rich sat outside the lab director's office when Dr. Williams arrived at work.

"This must be something important," Dr. Williams commented to Rich as he opened the door to his office, inviting Rich in.

"It kind of is, Doc," replied Rich. "Remember me asking you about whether or not it is possible to do an analysis of cremated remains, to see if trace evidence of a foreign substance is present?"

"Sure," replied Dr. Williams. "I think I told you it's sometimes possible to get it from bone fragments, which are almost always present in the remains of a deceased person. Do you have some ashes you want me to look at?"

"I do," responded Rich, removing the plastic zip-lock bag Jimmy had filled with the ashes he had stolen from Chris Dyess' urn. "How long do you think it will take for you to know if there's something here?"

"Not long, actually," Dr. Williams answered. "It's a small sample and I can get one of my guys on it within the hour. We should know something fairly quickly. Give me a couple of hours and I'll call you as soon as we're done."

"Thanks, Doc," Rich said as he got up to leave Dr. Williams' office and return to his own.

Three and a half hours later, as Rich prepared to leave for lunch, the phone on his desk rang. The caller ID indicated the call came from the FBI lab.

"Tell me you found something, Doc," Rich said after picking up his receiver.

"Adenosine," Dr. Williams replied. "Extremely small amounts but they're definitely present. My assistant is on the way to your office with the full report and what's left of your sample. Is this what you were looking for?"

"Well, let's just say I had a hunch," Rich replied.

His new dilemma was what to do with the information. For now, he would keep it under wraps. Even with the information, he had no way of tying it directly to David Kyle and he wasn't about to reopen the Byers case unless he could prove a nexus to Mr. Kyle, now on the government payroll.

No, he reasoned, *I need to keep this to myself.*

Leaning back in his chair, Rich looked at the lab report on his desk, delivered to him by Dr. Williams' assistant. Contemplating the possibilities of its implications, his mind began to race as he thought about David Kyle and his current position as a contract employee for the CIA. He worked for his friend Chris Roth; an agent Rich held in high esteem and whose character and loyalty to America was unassailable. Like a slap in the face, it suddenly hit him that Bill Allen, counselor to the President of the United States and Mr. Kyle's former military commander, had been behind getting David Kyle his job with the CIA in the first place.

Holy shit, he thought.

Rich Michaels' heart picked up a few beats as he wondered about the possibility of the man in closest proximity to the President somehow being involved in a conspiracy to murder a Supreme Court Justice and a handful of other political enemies. The ramifications of such a notion were mind numbing, and definitely not something he wanted to share with anyone, including Jimmy O'Rourke, and especially Casey Dean.

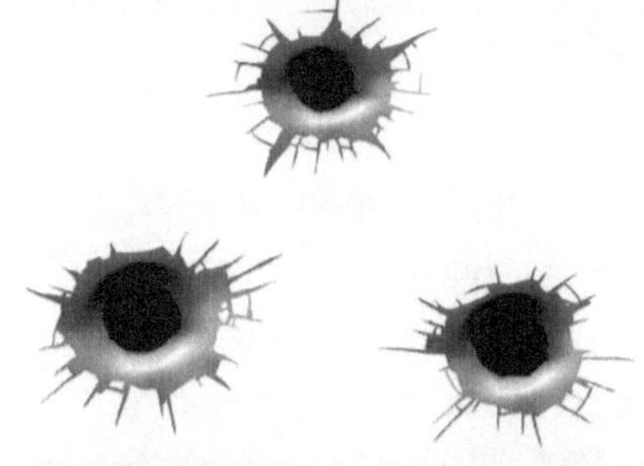

Chapter Forty-Three

Since the official establishment of the State of Israel in 1948, their continued existence has been due in large part to the foreign aid and military protection provided them by the United States. As the only democratically elected government in the region, Israel has benefited from their status as America's only true friend in the Middle East, despite the fact their relationship with the Rob Ferrell administration was at times strained. Instead of showing unequivocal and steadfast support for Israel, as had been the practice of previous U.S. American Presidents, President Ferrell too often displayed what some viewed as an affinity for the plight of Palestinians and their desire to form an independent state of their own within the borders of Israel.

Quick to criticize Israeli Prime Minister Aaron Glickman for the formation of Israeli settlements in areas populated by Palestinians, President Ferrell's critique of attacks against Israel by groups like Hamas and Hezbollah, seemed by many critics to be somewhat muted. In his last meeting with Prime Minister Glickman before leaving office, President Ferrell again reiterated his desire for PM Glickman to make more of an effort in accomplishing a two-state solution for peace by ceding land to the Palestinians and reverting Israel's borders to where they were prior to the Six-Day War in 1967. A war, incidentally, started by its Arab neighbors, won decisively by Israel, and which resulted in Israel gaining control of prime real estate such as the Gaza Strip, the West Bank and parts of the Golan Heights.

No foreign leader was happier to see the end of the Ferrell administration, as well as the rise to power of Brian Smith, than Israeli Prime Minister Aaron Glickman. After joining the Israeli Defense Force (IDF) upon his eighteenth birthday, as was required by all Jewish men reaching adulthood, PM Glickman saw his first military action in the Yom Kippur War of 1973. Israel was attacked by Egypt and Syria on Israel's holiest of days in an effort to reclaim territory lost to Israel in 1967. The IDF prevailed in the war, due in large part to the efforts of fighting men and women like Aaron Glickman. Upon completion of his military commitment, Glickman entered Israeli politics as a member of the Likud Party and served in the Knesset (the Israeli Parliament) until being elected Prime Minister half way through Rob Ferrell's first term as U.S. President.

Following President Smith's inauguration, the first official visit of a foreign leader to the White House was Prime Minister Glickman. Wanting to repair the damage to the U.S.-Israel relationship caused by the previous administration, President Smith wanted to adamantly show the Prime Minister the commitment and support he could expect from him and his administration. Over the following two and a half years, PM Glickman would make three more trips to Washington to meet with President Smith, the most recent visit to discuss the growing threat of Iran's influence in the region and their funding of the terrorist group Hezbollah.

"Our biggest problem, Mr. President," PM Glickman said to President Smith, seated in the Oval Office alongside Kathie Collins, the President's top national security advisor, "is not the random attacks coming from Hamas and Hezbollah over our borders. We have the assets in place to repel those and keep the damage to a minimum. Without a doubt, our biggest threat right now is Iran's ability to continue their development of a nuclear bomb and their willingness to use it on us. Our estimates, Mr. President, give them six months to a year before they will have nuclear capabilities."

"Are those numbers consistent with your estimates, Kathie?" the President asked his security chief.

"They are, Mr. President," she replied. "Their enrichment activities of uranium, which they will need in the production of nuclear war heads, has significantly increased over the past two years They have a delivery system already in place with the capability of launching missiles that can easily reach Jerusalem. The only question is will they have the balls to actually carry out such an attack, knowing what the potential consequences will be."

"Well, with all due respect, Kathie," PM Glickman responded, "let's not forget this is a regime who has stated over and over again their desire to wipe Israel off the face of the earth. We can't afford to sit around and wait to see if they will follow through on their threat. I choose to believe them when they say they want to wipe us out, and it is getting dangerously close to a point in time where our mere existence is in jeopardy."

"I happen to agree with you, Aaron," President Smith chimed in. "The sanctions they have been under have certainly hurt them, but it doesn't seem to be enough pain to stop their ambitious efforts in developing a bomb. A preemptive strike may be our only option, but I'm more than a little leery about getting U.S. forces directly involved in military action over there."

"You won't have to, Mr. President," Glickman replied. "Just take the shackles off that President Ferrell put on. Their primary enrichment facility is located about five miles outside of Tehran. According to our Mossad (the Israeli equivalent to the CIA), they have about two hundred military and civilian employees at the site. We could destroy it in about an hour, which we believe would set them back ten years. I simply need your consent before we take such a step."

"Well, one thing's for sure," the President said. "It will certainly set back any peace efforts for the region."

Turning his gaze in the direction of his top national security advisor, the President asked Kathie Collins for her thoughts.

"There's no doubt a preemptive strike against their nuclear facility will create a mess," she responded. "Obviously, the U.S. will be seen as complicit in the attack, regardless of whether or not any of our assets are used. As far as the peace process is concerned, at the very least it will take us back to square one. But, I'm in agreement with the Prime Minister, there's not much use in a peace process where one of the two sides no longer exist, and there's no question the goal of Iran is to eliminate the existence of Israel."

"I said when I ran for this office," President Smith commented, "and after I got into office, my commitment to Israel would be unwavering. I don't plan on going back on such a pledge, Aaron. You have my consent to take whatever action you deem necessary. I will instruct General Shirley to provide whatever assistance we can; under the radar, of course."

"Certainly, Mr. President," the Israeli PM replied.

"I also want a complete briefing before any action is taken," President Smith continued. "We need to know everything beforehand so we can plan for any contingencies surely to arise. We'll need to have every base in Europe and the Middle East on high alert when you hit them."

"Absolutely, Mr. President," PM Glickman replied as he stood to shake hands with President Smith and Kathie Collins. "And thank you, sir. We will never forget the courage you've shown today. You will go down in history as Israel's greatest friend."

"Let's hope we're making the right call," the President replied. "I don't mind being thought of as Israel's best friend, Aaron, I just don't want to be remembered as the guy who started World War III."

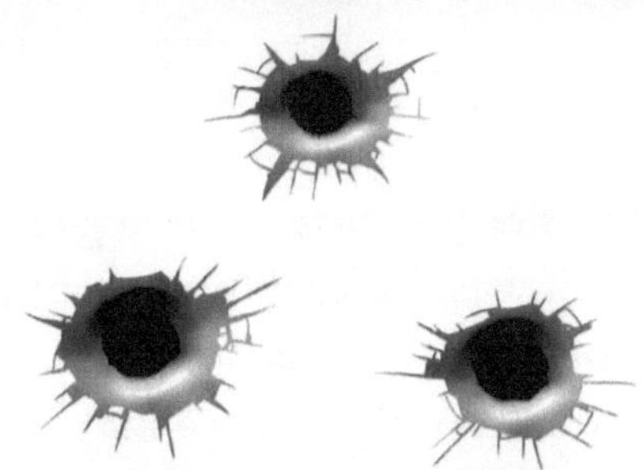

Chapter Forty-Four

Several large shopping bags hung from Deanna Mowery's arms as she waited for the elevator doors to open on the third floor of the Ritz Carlton Hotel. Deputy U.S. Attorney General Kevin Pearson, her secret paramour for the better part of a year, had no interest in traipsing up and down the various levels of the Fashion Center shopping plaza inside the Pentagon City Mall, conveniently connected to their hotel in Arlington, Virginia.

"I've got some emails to answer and a couple of phone calls to make," he told Deanna before she left on her shopping safari, "so go ahead without me. I'll hang back and wait while you shop. You'd probably enjoy it more without me anyways, since shopping is one of my least favorite activities, even when you're involved."

Deanna had been gone nearly three hours before returning to their room, content with her haul of clothing, some jewelry and a few other accessories. Although feeling somewhat guilty over the amount of money spent, she was especially fond of the four-hundred-dollar pair of Italian suede boots she found in Nordstrom's, her favorite store. Knowing Kevin would probably chastise her for spending so much on a pair of shoes, she felt quite confident he would approve once he saw them on, pulled up over her painted on, skin-tight jeans. Setting the bags down upon entering the room, Deanna could hear the shower running in the bathroom. As she began to get undressed, thinking Kevin might enjoy some company in the shower, she heard the sound of his cell phone ringing inside his briefcase, resting on top of the bedroom dresser. Assuming Kevin would probably not want to miss the call, she popped open the clasps on the briefcase to retrieve the phone and bring it to him while he showered. As she grabbed the phone, Deanna noticed the top portion of a piece of paper tucked away towards the back, with the words *Bank of The Maldives* printed across the top. Immediately consumed with an insatiable curiosity, she ignored her feeling of guilt for invading Kevin's privacy and retrieved what appeared to her to be some kind of bank statement from a foreign bank.

Quickly looking up at the bathroom door and hearing the shower still running, Deanna slid the document out so she could view it in its entirety. Indeed, a bank statement from the *Bank of The Maldives*, a tiny country located in the Indian Ocean southwest of India, indicated a series of electronic wire transfers into the account totaling more than a million dollars. Flushed with immediate concern when she saw Kevin Pearson's name as account holder, Deanna also noticed the deposits were made over the past five months. Hearing the sound of the shower being turned off in the bathroom, Deanna replaced the document before closing and refastening the briefcase. Trying to process what she had seen, and not wanting to ask Kevin about it for fear of retribution for invading his privacy, Deanna began unloading the shopping bags onto the bed as Kevin entered the room.

"Looks like you made a pretty good haul," Kevin said as he finished drying himself before retrieving his clothes and getting dressed.

"Spent too much as usual," Deanna replied, staring down at the bed so Kevin would not detect the obvious change in her countenance. "I probably better go," she continued, again averting her gaze directly away from Kevin, "I told my mom I would give her a call tonight before it got too late."

"I thought we were going to grab a late dinner?" Kevin replied.

"I know. I'm sorry. I totally forgot about calling Mom. Can we do a rain check on dinner?"

Deanna walked over to Kevin and gave him a short kiss on the lips before grabbing her shopping bags and exiting the room, trying her best not to let on how bothered she was about what she had seen. As the door to the room closed, Kevin stood motionless beside the bed processing Deanna's behavior, acutely aware of her sudden change in demeanor. With a look of confusion on his face, Kevin glanced around the room as he continued to dress, wondering what could have caused Deanna's change in attitude, obvious to him despite her attempt to conceal it. Walking over to the dresser where his briefcase sat, he opened it and noticed he had a missed call. Recognizing the number, Kevin picked up his phone to return the call.

Deanna Mowery aimlessly drove down the George Washington Memorial Parkway after leaving the hotel, trying to make sense of the bank statement she found in Kevin Pearson's briefcase.

Her mind raced. *Where the hell is the Maldives, anyway?*

She attempted to justify in her mind her boyfriend, the man she had fallen in love with, did not get himself involved in something untoward. Not able to make sense of what she had seen, Deanna pulled out her cell phone and called the one person she felt she could completely trust. She needed to talk to someone about what she had discovered in Kevin Pearson's briefcase, without jumping to conclusions or needlessly exposing its discovery.

"Rich," she said to Agent Michaels, unable to hide the concern in her voice, "we need to meet."

"Hey Deanna," Rich replied. "You sound serious. What's up?"

"I know it's getting late, but this can't wait. Can I meet you someplace? It's really important."

"It sounds like it," Rich answered. "Of course, we can meet. I'm working late so I'm still at the office. Can you come by here, or do you want me to meet you someplace else?"

"No," she replied. "Just stay put and I'll swing by. Should be there in about fifteen minutes. Thanks."

Hanging up her phone and returning it to her purse, Deanna turned her car around and headed for the Hoover building. Sitting behind his desk when Deanna walked in, Rich immediately noticed the concern on Deanna's face as she took a seat in front of his desk.

"Damn, Deanna, something is obviously bothering you; what happened?"

"I'm not sure, Rich," she answered. "Maybe nothing, but I saw something earlier this evening I'm concerned about, and I didn't know where else to turn. I had to talk to somebody about it, and you were the first person I thought of."

"Well, I'm certainly flattered," Rich replied. "You know I'll help any way I can. Just start from the beginning."

"First off," Deanna began, "I trust you completely and I know you'll keep this conversation confidential."

"Of course," he replied.

"Let me start with something you're not aware of. It's about someone I've been dating pretty much exclusively for about a year. It started out kinda casual, but lately it has gotten pretty serious."

"So, I'm a couple's counselor now?" he said with a smile, trying to breathe some levity in the situation. Not seeing his smile returned by Deanna, Rich quickly returned to a more serious tone. "Sorry, Deanna, go ahead. So, who's the lucky guy?"

"It's Kevin Pearson," she said.

"The Deputy AG?" he asked.

"The same."

"Wow," Rich responded, leaning back in his chair. "That's a bit of a shocker. I would have never guessed you and him."

"I know," said Deanna. "We thought it would be a good idea not to go public, so we've kept it under wraps. We both agreed our personal relationship, if made known, would screw things up for us professionally."

"Probably a good idea," Rich opined. "So, what's going on? How can I help?"

"Well again, I'm not sure there's anything to be alarmed about," Deanna replied. "It's something I saw in Kevin's briefcase, and I can't get it out of my mind. I'm worried there might be something to it."

"Well, it's obviously got you upset," Rich offered. "Why don't you tell me about it and you and I can figure out if there's reason to be alarmed?"

"We were staying over at the Ritz, next to Pentagon City Mall," she continued. "I had been shopping for a couple of hours while Kevin stayed in the room. He's not as fond of shopping as I am."

"So far, he sounds like a pretty reasonable guy," Rich said, the smile returning to his face.

"Why am I not surprised to hear you say that?" Deanna replied with a slight smile, beginning to feel a sense of ease as she began to unload on her friend. "Anyways," she continued, "when I got back to the room, I could hear him in the bathroom taking a shower. His cell phone began to ring inside his briefcase, so I thought I'd grab it and take it to him, in case the call was important."

"Makes sense," Rich replied. "Go on."

"When I opened up his briefcase to get his phone, I noticed a piece of paper stuck in the back and it got my immediate attention. It looked like a bank statement from a foreign bank located in the Maldives. I'll be honest with you, Rich, I don't even know where the Maldives is."

"It's a tiny island nation near India," Rich replied. "That much I do know."

"Well, anyways," Deanna continued, "I looked at the statement and saw there were several wire transfers into the account. Hundreds and hundreds of thousands of dollars, maybe as much as a million, I think. I'm not even sure how much to be honest. I only know it was a lot."

"Maybe it had something to do with a case DOJ is working," Rich suggested, trying to downplay the discovery.

"That's what I thought initially," Deanna said. "But the name of the account holder was Kevin Pearson. Maybe there's some reasonable explanation, but for the life of me I can't think of what it could be. Not that it's any of my business necessarily, but I certainly had no idea he had a personal overseas bank account. It's not only the existence of the account I'm concerned about, but the amount as well. Where the hell did he get so much money and why does he have it in a foreign bank?"

"Agreed," Rich said. "That is concerning, but like you said, there may be a reasonable explanation. What do you want to do with the information?"

"Why do you think I came to you?" Deanna asked, again managing a tiny smile. "I need you to tell me what I should do."

"Well, as you know, the *Office of Special Counsel* will need to be contacted if you think there's a possibility of corruption here."

"Yes, I do know that," Deanna replied. "I'm a little hesitant at going that route right now. What if there's nothing to it? What if there is a reasonable explanation we're not thinking of? If I go to the *Office of Special Counsel,* they're going to want to open up an investigation. If it turns out to be nothing, there goes our relationship. And I kinda like the guy, you know what I mean?"

"Yes, I do," Rich replied. "I think this is what we call a dilemma."

"Exactly," she replied. "So, what do I do?"

"First off, for the time being let's keep this between you and me. There's no reason anyone needs to know you saw the statement. I certainly will not admit this conversation ever took place, so you're safe there. We have some time to follow up and if we uncover anything else that looks like corruption, we can make the call then. In the meantime, snoop around a little more and see if you can find anything else that's alarming. Maybe get a picture of the statement you saw. If you're okay with it, I'll get Jimmy involved and have him put a tail on Kevin. I trust him completely to keep this discreet."

"I do too," Deanna replied. "That sounds like a pretty good idea. I'm a little uncomfortable about spying on my boyfriend, you know. I'm not sure how good I'll be at doing that. Don't forget, I'm a scientist, not an agent."

"You'll be fine," Rich said encouragingly. "Just don't let on you know anything. Try to act as normally as possible and everything will work out. Leave the detective work to Jimmy and me and maybe we can figure this out."

"Easier said than done," Deanna responded, as she got up to leave.

As the door to his office closed behind Deanna, Rich sat motionless behind his desk, thinking about what he had heard. *Kevin Pearson must be the high-ranking DOJ contact she told me about,* he thought. *Which means he knew everything about what our committee had been working on, including the search warrant at the mosque.* He was suddenly consumed by the thought of Kevin Pearson, the Deputy Attorney General of the United States, possibly being the *mole* who screwed up his investigation into Mustafa and the Highlandtown mosque.

"Son-of-a-bitch," he said out loud, as he reached for his jacket hanging on the coat rack in his office and prepared to go home.

Deanna left Rich's office feeling somewhat better, knowing she had a friend in whom she implicitly trusted who would do everything in his power to help her solve her dilemma. Reporting what she had found in Kevin Pearson's briefcase to the authorities would no doubt cast a cloud over him and destroy their relationship, something she was not yet ready to do. Driving home, Rich's words of advice to her echoed in her mind: *Act as normally as possible. Yeah, right,* she thought. *How the hell am I going to do that?*

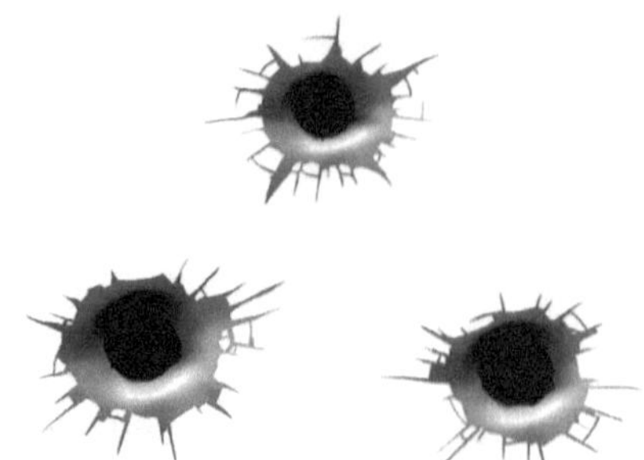

CHAPTER FORTY-FIVE

The FBI Director invited the D.C. press corp to the large conference room on the fourth floor of FBI Headquarters, to hold a press conference and answer questions about the progress being made to combat domestic terrorism. Prior to entering the conference room, he had met with Rich Michaels, his lead agent on the domestic terrorism task force; Deanna Mowery, representing his domestic terrorism committee; and Deputy Attorney General Kevin Pearson, representing the Department of Justice. All were there to assist the Director in putting out accurate information; as well as showing the public the scope and breadth of the FBI's efforts in combating terrorism. It would be the first ever face-to-face meeting between Agent Michaels and Deputy AG Pearson.

"Mr. Attorney General," Rich said, extending his hand to Mr. Pearson, "it's a pleasure to finally meet you."

"Thank you, Agent Michaels," Kevin replied, "the pleasure is mine. I've been hearing some very good things about you. Despite that little *hiccup* we had with your search warrant at the mosque, your efforts have not gone unnoticed over at DOJ. Believe me when I tell you, it's guys like you who make our job a whole lot easier."

"I appreciate that," Rich replied. "Hopefully we can avoid more *hiccups* in the future."

"We both do," replied Kevin.

Turning away from Kevin to greet Deanna who had entered the room, Rich could not help but think, *"Hiccup my ass."*

The FBI Director, the Deputy AG, Ms. Mowery and Agent Michaels walked into the conference room, ready to get the press conference underway. Before opening the floor for questions, the Director introduced the people on stage and gave brief descriptions of their individual roles in the country's anti-terrorism efforts. He then made a brief opening statement.

"The FBI, along with our partners in law enforcement, both at the federal, state and local levels are working non-stop to identify terrorist cells that exist in America and thwart any attacks on our homeland these groups have planned. Deputy AG Pearson, as well as the tremendous group of dedicated attorneys under his charge, have been instrumental in helping us with this effort. You will probably have questions for me I may be unable to answer, due to the sensitive nature of ongoing federal investigations. But let me be clear about something from the outset: our FBI field offices have current ongoing investigations into terrorist activities in all fifty states. Suffice to say, the threat of radical Islamic terrorism in the United States is real and it's not going away anytime soon. With that, I'll open the floor for questions."

Whenever Casey Dean was in the room, her indomitable demeanor usually overshadowed those around her, and this would be no exception. Leaping to her feet before anyone else, Casey got in the opening question.

"Mr. Director," she began, "since the terrorist attack at the Mall of America near the end of President Ferrell's last term in office, the United States has been primarily free from domestic terrorist attacks, with the glaring exception being the EMP attack on the Baltimore electrical grid. The loss of life in that instance was not directly tied to the attack itself but resulted from the looting and chaos that followed. So, while we have seen several murderous attacks take place in Europe and other places abroad, we have not seen similar attacks here since President Smith has been in office. To what do you credit this, and more specifically, do you think the election of President Smith is directly responsible?"

"There's not just one answer to that Casey," the Director said, "but a combination of things. Investigative agencies, not only the FBI but others as well, have taken a much more aggressive stance in going after these killers. And the President's posture on combating global terrorism and the threat of ISIS and other Islamic extremists has certainly, in my view, been a game-changer. We did not have this level of commitment from the previous administration, as you well know. All you have to do is look at some of President Smith's actions to see he is not one who is timid about confronting evil."

"Like his aggressive stance with Mexico," Casey blurted out, "when two of our Border Patrol agents were unlawfully detained?"

"Exactly. Some might say it had nothing to do with terrorism, per se, but we know ISIS fighters have been doing everything they can to get their people into the U.S., and the once porous border with Mexico was a great place for them to use. President Smith immediately began cracking down on the border, making it much more secure, and I think it ruffled some feathers down there. Mexico's actions were unacceptable and the President let them and the rest of the world know we will not be toyed with. I think the terrorists got the message as well."

"What about the military attack on the ISIS training camps?" asked another reporter, intent on not allowing Ms. Dean a monopoly on the questions. "Have you seen any kind of spike in terrorist activity as a result of the attack, either here or abroad? And additionally, Mr. Director, how has your ability to share intelligence with the CIA and other foreign intelligence agencies aided you in your efforts in combating terrorism."

"The FBI has been working very closely with our partners in the intelligence community," the Director replied, "particularly our friends at the CIA. Because of the manner in which intelligence can now be shared between our agencies, something fairly new, we are able to be more effective in protecting American lives. I speak with the CIA Director on a daily basis and working together like we have, there's no doubt we have been able to stop terrorist attacks in the works. As far as the attack on the ISIS training camps are concerned, we believe we dealt a major blow to their efforts in recruiting new fighters to their cause, so no, we have not seen a spike in activity as a result. We are always concerned about Americans over here being radicalized into joining ISIS, but when they see in living color what can happen to them if they join such a group of savages, I'm quite sure it gives them some pause."

"Can you comment on the FBI's case against Adnan Mustafa?" came the next question. "There are some reports suggesting he was assassinated along with his family after escaping from the U.S. and returning to his home in Oman after building the EMP device used in the Baltimore attack."

"Perhaps your question would be more appropriately answered by General Shirley and the CIA," the Director began his answer, "but clearly, assassinations are a direct contravention of U.S. law, so I reject the premise of your question. As far as the FBI is concerned, we took a lot of heat in the media regarding the search warrant we served on Mr. Mustafa's mosque, with some outlets going so far as to suggest we had violated their religious liberty rights. There's absolutely no factual basis for that, and as it turned out, we were right about Mr. Mustafa and his activities regarding terrorism."

"Then why did the search warrant fail to uncover any elements of a crime?" came the reporter's follow up question.

Without moving his head, Rich Michaels shifted his eyes to the left in the direction of Kevin Pearson, looking for any kind of reaction. He saw none.

"Not all warrants end in success," the Director responded. "The point is we had Mr. Mustafa in our crosshairs and we were right about him. Frankly, I would have preferred having him in custody so we could have interrogated him and perhaps uncovered the identities of some of his co-conspirators. Instead, Mr. Mustafa met a different fate. My own personal view is he got what he deserved, and any sympathy for him is misguided."

"What about his family?" the reporter continued. "Did they get what they deserved as well?"

"I think it's unfortunate when any innocent life is lost. But let's not kid ourselves. Mr. Mustafa is solely responsible for his demise as well as the demise of his entire family, and any opinion to the contrary is foolishness. The message to terrorists around the world, I think, is quite clear. If you engage in *jihad* against America, we will seek you out wherever you go and bring you to justice. There is no place on earth where you will find sanctuary and no place you will be able to hide."

With that last statement, the FBI Director thanked the press for coming and turned from his podium and left the room, followed by Mr. Pearson, Agent Michaels and Ms. Mowery. The American people had gotten a real taste of where their FBI Director stood with regards to his commitment to combating terrorism. Emboldened by the fact he now served a President not afraid to call Islamic terrorism for what it is, the FBI Director felt liberated to speak his mind on the topic, without worrying about the retribution he surely would have received from his previous boss. Watching the Director's press conference from his desk in the Oval Office, President Smith turned to his top advisor Bill Allen.

"What'd I tell you, Bill," the President commented. "I knew I was right about him. Keeping him in place was the right call."

"Agreed, Mr. President," Major Allen replied. "It certainly was."

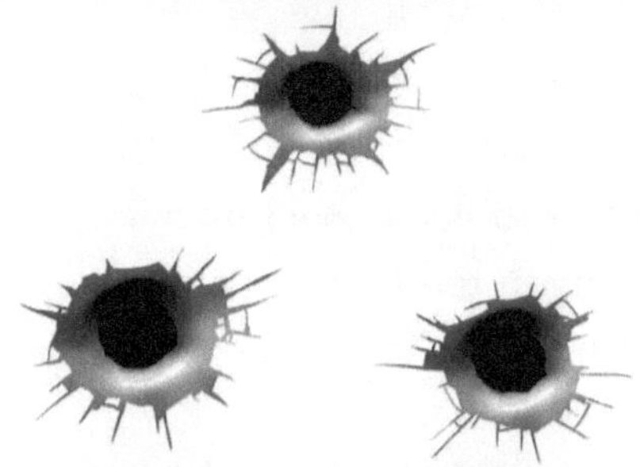

Chapter Forty-Six

The Chiefs of Staff for each military branch, along with their Chairman, gathered with President Smith and his top national security advisor Kathie Collins in the White House situation room. On an open line with Israeli Prime Minister Glickman, President Smith hit the *speaker* button on the phone so all in attendance could hear the call.

Adhering to the wishes of the President, made clear to PM Glickman in their Oval Office meeting two months prior, the Israeli prime minister had kept the President apprised of their impending attack on Iran's nuclear production facility. After receiving confirmation from his top generals that each U.S. military base throughout Europe and the Middle East was on high alert, President Smith gave PM Glickman the green light to initiate the military strike intended to cripple Iran's efforts in developing a nuclear bomb.

A Wideband Global SATCOM 5 satellite (WGS-5), orbiting nearly three hundred miles above the surface of the earth, began relaying live video to the large High-Def screen located on the front wall of the Situation Room. With its powerful camera lenses pointed in the direction of Tehran, the WGS-5 began capturing images of Iran's nuclear production facility as Israeli-launched Cruise Missiles rained down upon the site. Several explosions, occurring within seconds of each other, devastated the facility as large plumes of fire and smoke billowed in the sky above the plant. Within twenty minutes, the entire facility was reduced to rubble, an agglomeration of mangled steel and concrete left smoldering in the Iranian desert.

"Total devastation, Mr. President," commented Kathie Collins. "No chance of survivors."

"Exactly what we wanted," the President replied. "Now let's get ready for the aftermath."

Within hours of the attack, Iran's Supreme Leader and the head of their theocratic government filed an official protest with the U.N. and publicly called for all Arab nations to join them in denouncing what the Supreme Leader deemed was an *"unmitigated and unlawful attack on the sovereign nation of Iran."* Within days, an emergency session of the U.N. Security Council convened, for the express purpose of formally condemning Israel for their action. Known for their anti-Semitic views toward the State of Israel, the U.N. Security Council's action came as no surprise to the Smith administration.

With veto power over any resolution voted on in the U.N., President Smith had no hesitation in instructing America's U.N. Ambassador to veto the resolution, thus rendering the action by the Security Council moot. President Smith knew from the beginning the U.S. would be viewed by the world as either participating in or at the very least condoning the attack. The subsequent action taken in the U.N. would further strain U.S. relations with many of the member states of the U.N., but it was a calculated decision the U.S. President was willing to make. Of no concern to President Smith were the feelings of nations who hated the State of Israel to begin with, and as far as he was concerned they could all just go to hell. He would stand with Israel and that was all there was to it.

Predictable saber rattling by Iran and a few other Arab nations came as no surprise to the Smith administration. Some European leaders, whose socialistic views were generally antithetical to any show of strength, were anxious to express their dismay at Israel's actions, knowing full well the attack on Iran's nuclear production facility could never have taken place without the blessing of President Smith. Truth be known, Iran was in no position to wage war against a nuclearized Israeli state, which obviously had the unconditional backing of the world's most awesome super-power. Pretty much all they could do was liken Israel and America to Satan and further declare their desire to erase Israel from the face of the earth; a mantra of theirs since Israel's formation.

Anti-Semitic politicians are not limited to foreign governments alone. Senator Laura Reagan, leader of the Democrat caucus in the U.S. Senate, quickly condemned the attack and accused President Smith of being complicit in blowing up potential peace talks in the region. She even intimated the President might be guilty of potentially starting a third World War. As ridiculous as this accusation was, it conveyed the feelings of many Democrats and members of the mainstream media who were loath to comment favorably on any action taken by this President. Watching the statements being made by Senator Reagan on the television in the Oval Office while he and the President ate lunch, Bill Allen turned to the President with a smile on his face.

"Just give me the word," Major Allen said. "One phone call is all it will take and we won't have to listen to this bitch anymore."

"C'mon now Bill," President Smith replied, also smiling, "why would we want to stop her and the rest of the Democrats from making asses of themselves. Take a look at the polls. The people are with us on this one. We're showing leadership and strength, the exact opposite of what this country got from Ferrell. The Mullahs in Iran would never think about going to war with us. They know it would mean the end to their country and most certainly the end of them."

"Yeah, you're probably right, sir," Major Allen agreed. "But we better stay alert on the terrorism front. They might feel they need to make a strike somewhere to remain relevant."

"I don't plan on letting up with regards to terrorism, Bill," the President responded. "We're going to continue to hit 'em and hit 'em hard, wherever we find them. Give Karl Bostick a call and make sure he's doing everything in his power to vet these bastards before letting them in. I don't want us making a mistake on our own borders."

"Consider it done, sir," Bill replied. "And you're sure about Ms. Reagan? Really, sir, I don't mind."

President Smith could only laugh as his top advisor departed the room.

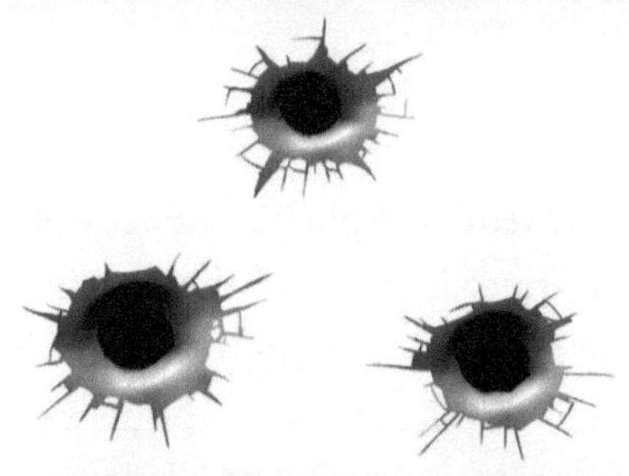

CHAPTER FORTY-SEVEN

Jimmy O'Rourke had been following Kevin Pearson for about three weeks and had seen nothing too much out of the ordinary. Keeping pretty much to his townhouse in Georgetown and his office at DOJ, Kevin led what Jimmy considered a pretty boring life. *What the hell does Deanna see in this guy?* Jimmy thought. *To each his own, I guess.*

Rich Michaels suggested Jimmy attach a *Bird Dog* tracking device on Kevin's bumper to track the movements of Kevin's car whether Jimmy was on his tail or not. The device enabled Jimmy to use his computer to pull up the track on his laptop, particularly helpful since he wasn't able to stay on his target around the clock.

As Kevin left his DOJ office one afternoon, Jimmy followed him to East Potomac Park, located alongside the Potomac River. Driving out to Haines Pointe, a secluded part of the park, Kevin parked his car, got out and walked over to a man standing near the water. Jimmy stopped about a hundred yards away, retrieved his camera from the back seat, equipped with a high-quality telephoto lens, and began taking pictures. The meeting between the two men lasted less than a minute and concluded after Kevin handed the man a manila envelope. The two quickly left and drove off in different directions.

Knowing the tracking device on Kevin's bumper would track Kevin as he drove away from this meeting, Jimmy decided to drop his tail on him and concentrate on the man with whom Kevin had just met. Making note of the suspect's tag number while they drove, the man led Jimmy to an apartment complex in Anacostia, Maryland. Finding a parking spot on the street in front of the apartment complex, Jimmy figured he'd sit on the guy for a few hours before calling it a night.

Kevin returned to his Georgetown residence where he showered and changed, scheduled to meet Deanna later in the evening at their *usual* get-away place at the Ritz. Kevin walked out of his townhouse and approached his car. Anticipating another sensual encounter with Deanna, he carried with him a bouquet of flowers and two large boxes filled with clothing items he had purchased for her, as well as his briefcase, a constant companion.

Stopping to place the items in his trunk, Kevin fumbled with his keys while trying not to lose his grip on the items in his hands. The keys slipped from his hand and fell to the ground as he tried to protect the flowers and gifts. After safely setting the items down, he dropped to one knee to retrieve the keys, now sitting on the ground under his rear bumper. As he reached for the keys, Kevin's peripheral vision picked up something strange, attached to the underneath portion of his bumper. After securing the keys, he grabbed the item and removed it from the bumper, secured in place by a magnet.

Having spent years as a government attorney in the Department of Justice, Kevin had approved many law enforcement affidavits from agents applying for a warrant to use tracking devices similar to the one he now held. He knew right away what it was. He also knew the *bird dog* tracking device was the type of device investigators used to catalogue the tracking of a vehicle over a long period of time, using one's computer to retrieve the data at a later date. Although alarmed by the discovery, he did not feel he was in immediate peril.

Kevin's mind raced. *How did this happen? How did they get onto me?* No answers were forthcoming. Driving to the Ritz, he remembered the last time he and Deanna had stayed there and how weird she acted after returning from her shopping trip. *"She had to leave to go call her mother,"* he recalled her telling him. *Why didn't she pick up her phone and call her from their room?* His mind continued to race as he approached the parking garage at the Ritz. As usual, Deanna had secured the room and texted the number to Kevin, eliminating the need for him to give his name at the front desk. The two had practiced this routine so both their names would not be associated to the same room, reducing the chance their *liaison* would be discovered. Reaching the room door, which Deanna had left ajar, Kevin realized he had forgotten the flowers and gifts. Of little concern to him now, he pushed open the door and entered, greeting Deanna with a hug and a kiss on the cheek.

"Howya doing, baby?" Deanna asked, as Kevin walked across the floor and placed his briefcase down on top of the dresser.

"Sorry I'm a little late. I got hung up at the office. I need to hit the head before we go out for dinner. I've been drinking bottled water all day, plus I need to freshen up a bit. I'll just be a minute."

"Sure thing," Deanna replied. "Take your time."

Kevin partially closed the bathroom door after waking in and immediately turned on the sink faucet. He had purposely left his briefcase unlatched, thinking if Deanna had something to do with the tracking device he found attached to his bumper, she might feel a need to go snooping in his briefcase. Thinking she had only a minute or two before Kevin finished in the bathroom, Deanna quickly walked over to where the briefcase sat and opened it up.

She looked for and found the same bank statement she had seen earlier with the name *Bank of The Maldives* printed across the top. Laying it flat on the dresser before her, Deanna took out her iPhone and snapped a picture of the document, hoping Rich would be able to make something out of it when she gave him a copy. Kevin stood inside the door of the bathroom, peering out the small crack he had left in the door. Realizing right then Deanna was responsible for the tracking device, he felt overcome by a sense of panic. He turned off the water, flushed the toilet and reentered the room where Deanna stood.

Kevin Pearson, who had felt for a long time he had met the love of his life, now considered whether or not his actual freedom could be at risk. *What did the FBI know? What could they prove?* The thoughts consumed him to the point he could no longer think straight.

"Okay, baby," Deanna said, noticing the strange look in Kevin's eyes. "Let's go. I'm starving."

As Deanna turned to walk out of the room, Kevin lunged at her from behind, grabbing her around the neck and throwing her on the bed. Before she could scream out and possibly have someone in the hallway hear her, Kevin grabbed a pillow from the bed and smashed it into her face. Using the weight of his two-hundred-pound frame to pin Deanna to the bed, Kevin continued to press the pillow harder into her face, cutting off her supply of oxygen. Deanna was no wallflower, as anyone who knew her would attest. She had been an athlete her entire life and had always maintained a strong and agile frame. But Kevin Pearson outweighed her by almost seventy pounds, and with the adrenaline now running through his system, Deanna had no chance of fending off this attack. As the amount of oxygen introduced into her lungs continued to diminish, Deanna began to lose consciousness and the flailing of her arms and legs began to subside. When she completely stopped moving, Kevin held the pillow in place for another minute or two, making sure she was indeed dead.

No coming back from this now, he thought. As he stood up from the bed, Kevin looked longingly into the face of the woman he had fallen in love with yet needed to kill in order to remain free. At this point, he couldn't care less about his career, knowing he had enough money in an offshore bank account to last him the rest of his life. He also knew the country of Maldives did not have an extradition treaty with the U.S. It was now time for him to initiate his escape plan, something he had long ago put together should it be needed. It now most certainly was.

Hidden behind the lining inside his briefcase, Kevin retrieved a phony passport and five thousand dollars in cash; items he would need to escape from the U.S. and reach the sanctuary of a foreign country. Leaving his car in the parking lot of Dulles International Airport, he bought a one-way ticket to London, England, from where he would continue his escape from justice, winding up at his small cabana overlooking the Indian Ocean in the Maldives. Before Deanna's body would even be discovered, Kevin surmised, he would be sipping margaritas on the balcony of his bungalow, watching the waves crash on the shore below. Although not the ending he sought, Kevin felt he did the only thing he could under the circumstances.

How did it ever get to this point? he pondered, as images of Deanna's face began flashing in his mind. For the duration of the long flight taking him to freedom, he constantly thought of his relationship with the woman he had murdered, content in the knowledge he did the only thing he could, necessary to save his own ass. Knowing he was out of the reach of U.S. law enforcement, he began to settle in on the notion he may never again step foot on U.S. soil. Arriving at the sanctity of his home on the Indian Ocean, Kevin looked out at the sights before him from the view on his balcony and concluded it did not seem to him to be an unfortunate plight.

An Arlington, Virginia patrol officer, called to respond to the Ritz-Carlton Hotel after a housemaid had discovered the lifeless body of Deanna Mowery, found Deanna's FBI ID in her purse and promptly called FBI Headquarters. The FBI Director was immediately notified by the switchboard operator after answering the call. He then called Rich Michaels and told him the news and to meet the Arlington Police detectives at the hotel who would be processing the murder scene.

"Keep a lid on this as long as possible, Rich," the Director instructed, "and make sure the Arlington PD does as well. At least until we have a better idea of what happened. Call me back as soon as you're on site and keep me posted."

"Will do," Rich replied, doing his best to repress the sense of sadness and angst he felt at hearing the news of his dear friend Deanna.

Driving over to the crime scene where Deanna's body lay, Rich could not help but wonder if he could've done something to prevent her murder. As far as putting together a list of suspects, his would begin and end with Kevin Pearson. To the best of Rich's knowledge, except for Deanna and Kevin, only he knew about their secret relationship and the frequent trysts they enjoyed at the Ritz-Carlton Hotel. Information he did not want to share, even with his Director, until he could figure things out.

Upon arriving at the hotel, Rich first stopped at the security office and asked for and received the previous day's surveillance tape of the hotel lobby. Seething with rage as he stood over Deanna's body while the Arlington PD crime scene technicians processed the room, Rich contemplated precisely what he would do, not if, but when he got ahold of Kevin Pearson.

Back at his office and viewing the hotel security tape of the Ritz-Carlton lobby, Rich was not surprised when he saw Kevin Pearson walk through the front doors of the hotel and disappear in the lobby elevators. He was equally unsurprised to find out the Deputy Attorney General had not shown up for work the past two days, with no one at his office having a clue as to his whereabouts. He then phoned Jimmy O'Rourke to tell him about Deanna, who did not take the news of her demise well.

"Was it Pearson?" he asked with total dismay. "I'm on my way," Jimmy added, indicating he would meet Rich at his office. "I'll be there in about fifteen minutes."

Rich had his face buried in his hands when Jimmy walked in. Looking up as Jimmy sat down in front of his desk, Rich made no attempt to conceal both his distraught and bewilderment over Deanna's murder.

"I pulled up the track on Pearson's *bird dog* earlier this morning," Jimmy said. "According to the GPS readout, his car hasn't left his townhouse the past two days."

What Jimmy didn't know, and would confirm later in the day, the *bird dog* tracking device Jimmy had secured to Kevin's bumper currently sat at the bottom of a Boxwood hedge growing along the street in front of Kevin's townhouse.

"My guess is he found the tracking device," Rich said. "Deanna told me she would try to get me a copy of his bank statement and anything else she thought would give us some idea of where all the money came from. I can't think of any other reason why he would snap like this. Adnan Mustafa, the guy who did the terrorist attack in Baltimore, got out of the country on a fake passport. I'm sure Pearson did the same."

"What's our next move?" asked Jimmy. "Do we get a warrant for him? If he got out of the country, he's probably sitting in a lounge chair on the beach somewhere. Maybe even in the Maldives. I'm sure he wants to be close to his money. Can't we go get him?"

"Would you believe there is no extradition treaty between the U.S. and the Maldives?" Rich replied.

"You're kidding me," Jimmy said.

"I wish I was," replied Rich. "I looked it up this morning. "You gotta hand it to this guy, Jimmy. He's smart. I think he planned this out from the beginning, including how he would get out of the country if things got too hot."

"Assuming he's definitely out of the country," Jimmy replied.

"I'd be shocked if he wasn't," said Rich. "Do me a favor, Jimmy."

"Sure, what is it?" he replied.

"Keep all of this to yourself. I need some time to think about where we go from here. I think I know who might be able to help us find this bastard, and for now, I want to keep everything off the grid, so to speak."

"No problem," replied Jimmy. "Hey, by the way," he added, changing the subject, "were you able to determine anything with the ashes I stole?"

"No," lied Rich, figuring it best to keep Jimmy in the dark for now about the possible culpability of David Kyle in the death of Chris Dyess. "That turned out to be a dead end."

With the murder of Deanna Mowery fresh on his mind, Rich Michaels no longer viewed David Kyle as a potential suspect to go after and prosecute, but a possible ally in hunting down Kevin Pearson and bringing him to justice. He wasn't thinking about the kind of justice found in an American courtroom, either. The only kind of justice befitting the piece of scum who murdered his friend would be barbaric, and David Kyle might be the one capable of delivering it. As Jimmy O'Rourke left Agent Michaels' office, Rich picked up his secure phone and dialed Chris Roth.

"I was going to call you later today," Chris said, seeing it was Rich on the other end. "I heard about what happened to your friend. I know you guys were close. I'm really sorry, Rich. Is there anything I can do?"

"That's precisely why I called," replied Rich. "Are you planning a trip back to the States anytime soon?"

"As a matter of fact, I'll be there by the end of the week," he replied. "I'll call you as soon as I'm in town and we can meet somewhere. What about services for Deanna? Anything planned yet?"

"We're doing something small here at headquarters," Rich answered. "Her parents are up from Florida and want to take her back down there with them. They really don't want anything big up here. Obviously, the Director wants to honor their wishes."

"Understood," Chris replied. "Again, Rich, I'm sorry for your loss. What do we know about who did this?"

"That's what I want to talk to you about," replied Rich. "I don't want to get into it over the phone. I've got some ideas I want to run by you, but it needs to stay between you and me."

"Absolutely," Chris said.

"And bring Kyle with you," Rich added. "I think he may be able to help."

"You got it," Chris replied. "See you in a few days."

Hanging up his phone, Rich could only stare across the room at the wall. The time he needed to properly grieve the loss of his dear friend would come later. Right now, he could only think about how and when to deliver the retribution warranted.

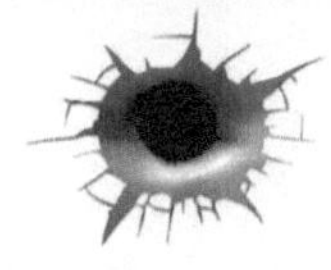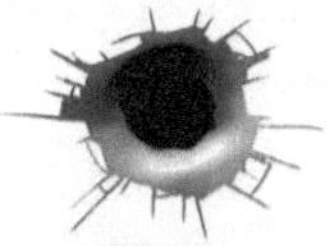

Chapter Forty-Eight

The murder of a high-ranking FBI official made headlines in the national news but was pretty much viewed as a local matter. The Arlington, Virginia police department would be conducting the investigation, but at present it had no viable leads into solving the murder of Deanna Mowery. Rich Michaels and Jimmy O'Rourke were the only two people with a good idea of who the guilty party was, and they were keeping it to themselves.

Jimmy had a sense Rich wanted to handle things his own way and would defer to his judgment. He, like Rich, considered Deanna a friend and thought jail too good for the bastard who killed her. Since no extradition treaty existed between the U.S. and the Maldives, Jimmy was doubtful Kevin Pearson would ever be brought to justice by legitimate means. Whatever Rich Michaels was thinking, Jimmy was okay with it, even if Rich did not want to share it all with him.

By now, the inexplicable disappearance of the Deputy Attorney General had not gone unnoticed, but no one had made the connection between it and the murder of Deanna Mowery. That is, except for Rich and Jimmy.

***

The worldwide tension caused by Israel's bombing of Iran's nuclear production facility began to subside. The saber rattling by Iran following the attack turned out to be nothing more than boisterous posturing on their part. Nobody, particularly Iran, would be willing to take on President Smith with anything more than verbal hostility. They weren't about to relegate their mere existence to the ashbin of history with open aggression against the most powerful superpower in the history of the planet, run by a man anything but timid in his approach to dealing with America's enemies. Their time would come, they surmised, perhaps with a different administration. Exacting their revenge on the Great Satan would have to wait.

The strength displayed by President Brian Smith in battling the forces of evil intent on harming America, and the ruthless manner in which he went after those enemies, began to show dividends. The United States was back on top, and the majority of Americans loved what they were seeing with this President, despite the incessant whining coming from Democrats in Congress.

The protestations of Senator Laura Reagan and other likeminded liberals seemed to be falling on deaf ears. As the country began to settle in for the President's campaign for reelection, nearly a year away, poll numbers indicated a potential landslide for President Smith, and a return for another term in the Oval Office. Try as they might to make themselves relevant, the Democrat Party had begun to look more like the permanent minority party, and right now they could do nothing to change their standing in the hearts and minds of the American electorate.

***

Rich Michaels secured a room at the Best Western hotel in Woodbridge, Virginia, the place where he had first met David Kyle. This time, his meeting with the two CIA operators would be quite different in tenor and would require a level of circumspection he had no doubt he would get from the two warriors.

"Thanks for coming, guys," Agent Michaels said as Roth and Kyle sat down on the couch in Rich's room. "Before we get started, I want to convey to both of you the need to keep this meeting between us. And I mean us alone. Nobody outside of this room can know about this."

"Of course, Rich," Chris Roth replied.

"Absolutely," David Kyle added.

"Good. I asked you here to discuss the murder of Deanna Mowery and the steps I think will be necessary to bring her killer to justice."

"So, you found out who the killer is?" asked Chris Roth.

"I've known all along," replied Michaels. "I didn't want to get into it with you on the phone the other day. I wanted to wait for us to be together before I let you guys in on what I know."

"Okay," replied Chris. "But why the secrecy? Why not take this to the guys running the investigation and let them handle it?"

"It's a good question," Rich Michaels answered. "After I tell you what I know I think it'll be clearer as to why I'm doing it this way."

"Alright then," replied Chris. "Lay it out."

"Deanna came to me several weeks ago and told me she found a document in the briefcase of a guy she was dating that she felt was problematic. It was a bank statement from a foreign bank in the Maldives showing several deposits totaling around a million dollars."

"Who's the guy?" asked David Kyle.

"That's where it gets interesting," answered Rich. "It's Kevin Pearson, the Deputy Attorney General for DOJ."

"Holy shit," exclaimed Chris.

"Exactly," responded Rich. "And on top of that, he was her high-ranking source within DOJ helping us with our domestic terrorism task force. The people under him were reviewing and approving our affidavits whenever we needed a search warrant."

"For Christ's sake, Rich," Chris exclaimed ever louder. "This bastard's the freaking mole."

"No doubt about it," replied Rich. "Deanna and this guy Pearson had apparently been carrying on a love affair for some time. She told me they wanted to keep it secret because it would probably jeopardize their working relationship and didn't want to deal with any hassles that could come up. I'm not sure if that's legitimate or not, but it was their call to make."

"I can see their concern," Kyle commented. "It probably made sense."

"Well, anyways," Rich continued, "Deanna was obviously concerned there might be something illegal, or at the very least, unethical going on with the bank statement she found so she came to me about it. If she had gone directly to the *Office of Special Counsel,* who handles stuff like this, she feared it would jeopardize their relationship and create a stink for Pearson, when maybe he hadn't done anything wrong."

"It definitely would have created a shit storm, that's for sure," interjected Kyle.

"Anyways, I told her to try and get a copy of the statement and anything else related so I could take a look at it. In the meantime, I had one of my guys put a tail on Pearson so we could track where he went and see if he met with any unsavory characters."

"Were you able to turn up anything?" Chris asked.

"My guy used a *bird dog* tracking device attached to his back bumper so we could catalogue his movement by pulling up the track on a laptop. We weren't on him very long before Deanna's murder, but my guy did see him meet with somebody out on Haines Pointe. He handed the guy an envelope and then left. The meeting lasted for less than a minute. The guy Pearson met lives in an apartment in Anacostia. We're trying to get more intel on him as we speak."

"Unfortunately, things went sideways after Pearson found the tracking device attached to his bumper. He dropped it in some bushes in front of his house before meeting Deanna at the Ritz where he killed her. Immediately after the murder, he went missing and nobody in his office has seen him since."

"Damn, Rich," Chris offered, "you're not blaming yourself for this, are you?"

"Let's say I'm dealing with it," Rich replied. "Right now, I want to concentrate on finding this bastard and making him pay for what he did."

"Now you're talking," David Kyle said. "I have my ideas on how to deal with this piece of shit, but what are you thinking?"

"I have a feeling we're probably on the same page," Rich responded, "which is why I want you guys involved."

"Absolutely," Chris added. "You better know we're in. The first thing we need to do is find him. If I had to venture a guess, I'd say he's in the

Maldives as we speak. I've been there. It's off the southern coast of India. You know we can't extradite from there, don't you?"

"I do know that," Rich replied. "I'm sure that's why he chose it for his offshore account. This guy is no dummy. He had everything planned out from the very beginning, including how to get out of the country when things went south, more than likely with a phony passport."

"Well, I can tell you one thing he didn't plan on," commented David Kyle.

"What's that?" asked Rich.

"Us," Chris answered. "Tell you what let's do," Chris continued. "I've got to be here for the next few days and handle some stuff for General Shirley. Let's send Kyle to the Maldives to snoop around and see if he can find Pearson. Trust me," Chris said, looking intently in Rich Michael's eyes, "if he finds him he'll know what to do."

"You bet your ass I will," David Kyle added.

"Just keep me posted," Rich said. "I want this son-of-a-bitch to get what's coming to him."

"Don't worry," responded Kyle. "If I find him, he will."

***

For the next two weeks, Agent Michaels' surveillance team put the suspect from Anacostia under a 24/7 watch. Subsequently identified as a Somali immigrant who had been in the country less than a year, he apparently had no job and no visible means of income. Despite this, he lived alone in a fifteen hundred dollar a month apartment, drove a thirty-thousand-dollar vehicle and ate out every night, usually at expensive restaurants. Agent Michaels thought the time had come to bring the guy in for an interrogation and instructed his team to go to his apartment and get him.

Unaware of Kevin Pearson's sudden disappearance, the Somali man had recently become nervous when Pearson no longer answered his calls. When Rich's agents arrived at the man's apartment, banging loudly on the door and announcing themselves as federal agents, he panicked and attempted to escape out the back. Climbing over the railing of his third-floor balcony, the Somali man reached for the limb of a large oak tree growing behind his apartment, intent on climbing down the tree and making his escape. Instead, his grip on the limb slipped, sending him crashing down on top of a wrought iron fence bordering the apartment complex property line, impaling himself on the fence's pointed metal tines. He died instantly. *An appropriate ending,* Rich thought when told about it. *If only Kevin Pearson would oblige us as well.*

***

David Kyle kept the photo of Kevin Pearson given to him by Agent Michaels in his pocket, spending the better part of fifteen days on a park bench located about fifty yards from the front door of the *Bank of The Maldives* main branch. Eventually, he assumed, Kevin Pearson would stop in to access his account, or at the very least check his balance. His patience paid off when he spotted his target enter the bank and leave after spending about fifteen minutes inside. Kyle followed Pearson from the bank back to his small cabana located half a mile away. After positively identifying the location of Pearson's home, Kyle went back to his hotel and called Rich Michaels.

"Just sit pat," Agent Michaels told Kyle. "I'm on my way."

At some point following his last meeting with David Kyle and Chris Roth at the Best Western Hotel, Rich Michaels had made the decision he wanted to be there when justice was delivered to Kevin Pearson. The rage he felt over the senseless murder of Deanna Mowery had not receded in the least.

The information he had uncovered indicating the potential involvement by David Kyle in the possible murder of Chris Dyess would remain with him and him alone. Under different circumstances, Agent Michaels would have pursued his case against David Kyle and got to the bottom of whether he had been part of the vast conspiracy case that had consumed him and Jimmy O'Rourke for over a year. But these were not normal circumstances. David Kyle had provided him immeasurable help in finding a man whom Rich Michaels detested with a level of passion he never knew he was capable of feeling. For this service, he would be forever indebted to David Kyle.

314

Kevin Pearson sat reclined in a lounge chair on his balcony, smoking a Cohiba Esplendido cigar, while sipping from a glass filled with Remy Martin Cognac. Gazing across the ocean as a cool tropical breeze pressed against his cheeks, Kevin heard the sound of his front door open and close.

"I'm out on the balcony," he hollered, assuming the person who had entered was a room service waiter bringing him his dinner order.

Hearing no reply, Kevin turned to look inside his living room, his view somewhat obstructed by the opaque sheers hanging in the balcony doorway, blowing in the breeze. Noticing a silhouette slowly walking in his direction, unaccompanied by a food cart, Kevin sat up in his chair with a look of confusion on his face.

"Who's there?" he asked. "Can I help you?"

Sweeping away the sheers obstructing his vision, Kevin stood up and stepped inside his living room, instantly aghast at the sight of Rich Michaels standing in front of him. Kevin's eyes quickly shifted to the semi-automatic handgun in Rich's right hand, silencer attached and hanging at his side. After a brief moment, Kevin could feel his heart begin to beat again as he addressed his surprise visitor.

"I'm sorry to break it to you Agent Michaels," Kevin proclaimed with an air of arrogance, "but you're definitely outside of your jurisdiction. You have no authority over here and I'm afraid to have to tell you this, but there's no extradition treaty here either. It seems like you've wasted a trip if you think you're going to arrest me and take me back home."

"I have no intention of arresting you," Rich replied, "and absolutely no intention of taking you back home."

Slowly raising his right hand, bringing the gun up to eye level and pointing it directly at Kevin's face, Rich continued. "I came here for one reason and one reason alone. To make amends for Deanna."

"Rich, wait, let me explain…" was all Kevin could get out. It would be the last words he spoke as the first shot struck him between his eyes. The second and third entered his chest cavity as he fell backwards, his head crashing through the glass balcony doors. Kevin Pearson was dead before hitting the floor. Turning to leave, Rich slipped out the front door and quickly descended the stairs. Waiting out front behind the wheel of a rental car, David Kyle reached over and put his hand on Rich Michael's arm as he got in and took his seat.

"You okay?" he asked.

"I will be," came the reply. "Let's go home."

The long trip home was welcomed. Time to sit, reflect and finally sleep; mourning Deanna's death would be a much longer process. Two days after returning, Rich was summoned to the White House for a late meeting. He hoped like hell the President was not about to ask for his resignation.

When he entered the Oval Office, President Smith stood at the fireplace, David Kyle and Bill Allen beside him. Agent Michaels, infinitely aware of the close relationship shared between David Kyle and Bill Allen, had no doubt the President had been made aware of what took place in the Maldives. He held his breath as his life quickly passed before him, considering the possibility he might even be arrested.

"Agent Michaels," the President said, walking towards Rich and extending his hand. "It's very nice to finally meet you."

"Yes sir. This is quite an honor for me," Michaels replied, looking over at David Kyle, who gave him a wink and a smile.

"Please join us in a drink," the President said. "You do like single malt, don't you?"

"Yes sir, always a good choice," Michaels replied, feeling a sense of relief coarse through his body. Short on words, he thought he might collapse at any moment.

Walking over and handing him his glass, David Kyle smiled broadly and slapped Rich Michaels on his back as the President offered a toast.

"A job very well done, gentlemen. You can all be proud of your service to our country. I know I am."

After taking a sip, Agent Michaels thought, *single malt never tasted so smooth.*

THE END

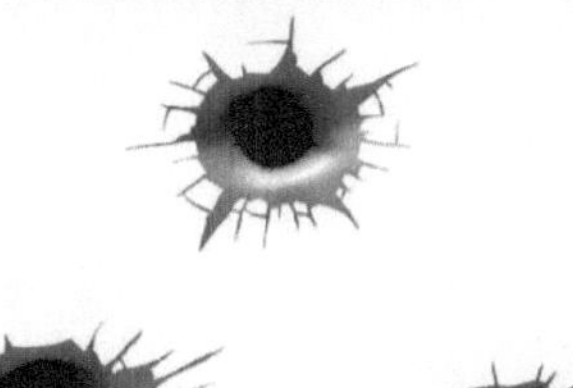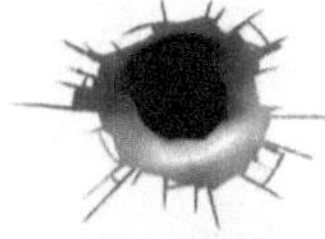

ABOUT THE AUTHOR

David Coppage was born and raised in Miami, Florida. He obtained his bachelor's and master's degree in criminal justice from Troy University in Troy, Alabama, in 1981 and 1985 respectively. He spent the next thirty-three years of his life pursuing his passion in law enforcement.

After five years as a police officer in Montgomery, AL, David became a Special Agent for the U.S. Customs Service. He began his federal career chasing drug smugglers off the southern coast of Florida, operating go-fast boats for Customs. He worked money laundering cases, as well as internal corruption cases as part of the Internal Affairs division.

After sixteen years with Customs, David transferred to the newly created U.S. Federal Air Marshal Service, formed after 9/11. After twelve years of flying domestic and international missions as an Air Marshal, he retired in 2014. His career is chronicled in his self-published memoir, *They Paid Me For This? Stories From Over Three Decades in Law Enforcement.* *Barbaric Justice* received "Top 5 Finalist" honors in the Next Generation Indie Book Awards. His novel *Sittin' In Amen Corner,* is a story of love and legacy, steeped in Southern pride, heritage and tradition. All of his books can be found online.

He resides in Senoia, GA with his wife Melissa and their dog Bentley. They enjoy spending time with their three grandkids; Luna, Thomas and Billie Jo.

DAVIDCOPPAGE1959@GMAIL.COM

www.ingramcontent.com/pod-product-compliance
Lightning Source LLC
Chambersburg PA
CBHW032336310726
48973CB00007B/1732